Books by Patricia Rice

SURRENDER
MOONLIGHT MISTRESS

Published by Zebra Books

MOONLIGHT MISTRESS

Patricia Rice

Zebra Books
Kensington Publishing Corp.

http://www.zebrabooks.com

ZEBRA BOOKS are published by

Kensington Publishing Corp.
850 Third Avenue
New York, NY 10022

First Printing: July, 1985
10 9 8 7 6 5 4 3 2

Printed in the United States of America

Dear Reader,

I grew up reading gothic horror tales and romance and, preferably, the two combined. I devoured the Brontës in elementary school, moved on to scavenging libraries for Mary Stewart, and gobbled up every historical romance that hit the shelves in the '70s. I considered every book a gift from heaven and devoted many hours to them.

In the early '80s, I sat down to write a story of my own. Plots and characters bubbled from the overflowing cauldrons of my brain. I didn't have any blueprints or guidelines other than the books I'd read over the years. I'd never taken a writing class, although if I had, in those days they would have frowned at the idea of writing romance. I just knew I loved a good love story, I wanted a hero more tormented than Rochester and sexier than Rhett, and a heroine who would fight like the devil to keep her man, whatever the circumstances. I think (she said smugly) I accomplished that.

What I didn't accomplish was a story that meets today's standards of political correctness. In the last fifteen years, romances have evolved from their more picaresque origins, but as a writer, I love all my fictional children, and Aelvina and Philippe—in all their rambunctiousness—are no exception.

To those of you who have been with me from the beginning, I think you'll enjoy this revised edition. To my newer readers, I issue a warning: The revision still deals with the outrageously passionate conflict of a fiery but very practical Anglo-Saxon maiden and her very Norman, very angry, and occasionally bewildered conqueror. I hope you'll enjoy the perils of Aelvina in the—very lively—spirit with which it was written.

Patricia Rice

Chapter One

Aelvina hung back within the shadows of the castle don-jon, attempting to find order within the chaos of the court-yard. The entourage of squires and servants, horses and pack animals, camp equipment and supplies spilled over into the stockade walls and stables and filled the yard with dust and clatter.

How, in all this melee of steel and men and animals, was she to find the one she sought? She had envisioned him riding in alone, all glittering armor and trailing colorful banners, astride a powerful white steed. The armor and banners and steeds were here in rich profusion. Where was the man who had set this motley caravan in motion?

Deciding that cowering in doorways provided no solu-tion, Aelvina fingered the dagger hidden in her kirtle and, setting her chin in determination, strode bravely into the courtyard. She could easily lose herself in this confusion and no one would be the wiser.

That was like assuming no one would notice should the moon cover the sun or the birds sing at night. Even though dressed in the humble earth-colored cloth of the peasants around her, Aelvina caused a minor stir and rumble through the crowd of men, and a path gradually opened before her. Blacksmiths laid down their hammers, fools set aside their caps, young pages gaped in longing as the slender, girlish figure with the cascade of unplaited silken silver hair strode questingly among them.

Covering her confusion at this sudden cessation of motion in her vicinity, Aelvina hurried on, seeking someone of authority. She found it in the monkish figure dressed in light Cistercian robes moving toward her, and she hastened to greet him.

"Father, a word with you, if you will," she said breathlessly, in a low voice of some urgency.

"Certainly, my child." Noticing her flushed cheeks and nervous glances, the monk led her toward the wall's shadows. His stout figure cut off any sight of her from the courtyard or castle keep behind.

"I have an urgent message for Sir Philippe. Where might I find him?" Aelvina hung her head, not daring to look the monk in the eye as she whispered these words. What would the holy father think of her real purpose? Not that she had been brought up under the strict precepts of the church. But like everyone else, she respected his position and beliefs, and knew beyond a shadow of a doubt that her mission was sinful.

The older man watched her through hooded eyes, expecting further enlightenment on the reason a young girl would be sent to speak with a seasoned knight. When the expected rush of childish chatter was not forthcoming, he studied her more thoughtfully.

Fine silver-blue eyes looked out at him from behind

long, dark-fringed lashes. High cheekbones and a steadfast gaze erased any further impression of immaturity. The mind of an intelligent female stared out at him from the eyes of a terrified child. She hid the terror with the proud tilt of her chin, but it lingered in the tremble of slender fingers clutching the gray mantle. The monk made a quick decision.

"Follow me." Striding through the shadows of the overhanging wall and its attendant shops and booths, the monk led a straight path through the courtyard to the stables in the rear. Aelvina followed close behind, keeping the monk's robes between herself and the blank windows of the keep above.

They halted in the shadow of the stable wall. In the heat of the June sun, the place stank from animals and dung, and the restless stamping of powerful steeds mixed with the cacophony of the myriad animals in the courtyard.

"He is in there." The monk nodded toward the dark stable door.

"In the stable!" Aelvina uttered with astonishment, gazing at the filthy horror of the hut. What was a grand and mighty Norman knight doing in the lowly confines of an animal shelter?

The monk's lips twitched with amusement at her stunned expression. "I will fetch him, if you wish."

She shook her head nervously. What she was contemplating was audacious enough. It was not fitting that the knight should come to her, or that a man of the cloth be the messenger. "I will find him."

She waited for the monk to depart. Instead, he gave her a quick, darting look, then stepped into the stable's doorway. "Philippe, you have a visitor." Satisfied that the man within had heard, the monk gestured for the girl to enter.

There was no retreat now, whatever she might have planned earlier. With the monk's steady gaze upon her, Aelvina had no choice but to enter that darkness and meet her fate.

The gloom enveloped her as she entered. At least here she was safe from prying eyes. She stood for a minute, adjusting to the darkness, enclosed by the girth of mighty draft horses.

The sudden apparition rising out of the gloom startled her. Stooped to examine a horse's hoof, the apparition now unfolded to its full height, hovering head and shoulders over her. Aelvina stared wide-eyed at a broad expanse of bronzed muscular chest, then slowly tilted her head back to meet startlingly emerald eyes in a dark face of rugged cut and hard jaw. A jagged scar along one prominent cheekbone emphasized the fierceness his other features formed—scarcely the charming, handsome visage she had envisioned from the descriptions given her. She gulped nervously before this savage giant.

"You seek me?" the giant prompted, eyes crinkling slightly at the corners as he realized his visitor was a mere wisp of a girl. Philippe St. Aubyn relaxed, resting his back against a sturdy beam and crossing his arms over his chest.

The knight's eyes raked assessingly over Aelvina's trim silhouette. Full, round curves placed her well within the realm of readiness, and his lips curled. His gaze returned to her fair, uptilted face, only to be met with a devastating scowl.

"Do you like what you see, sire?" she asked scathingly.

Aelvina's cheeks burned with embarrassment at this stranger's prolonged study, but she would not let him know of this. She met his amused gaze with defiance.

"Quite," he replied evenly, in the same Saxon dialect she had used.

Before she could respond with the pithy retort burning her tongue, the knight lazily rearranged his limbs to encompass her slight waist and draw her between his parted legs. Her thinly clad breasts pressed against his chest, and her lips parted in astonishment just within reach of his. Not waiting for her reaction to this maneuver, Philippe lowered his head to nibble at the corners of her mouth.

Aelvina pounded her palms against the iron-thewed muscles of the giant's chest and attempted to squirm from his hold. The thick, hard arm at her waist crushed her tighter, bringing her hips in daring conjunction with his. She battled the encroachment of his lips as they pressured hers, plying her mouth with kisses she could not avert. But when his arm lifted her against the rising hardness of his manhood, she understood his ultimate intent. Gasping with outrage, she reached for the slender knife at her waist.

She had learned to wield the blade well, and knew how best to prick a man to cool his ardor. Without his chained mail for protection, or the rough wool of his tunic, Sir Philippe was an easy target—too easy. The thin point pressed against the hardened toughness of his skin just above the place where his chausses stopped, the increasing pressure of his arm about her waist deepening the force of the blade against his skin.

In irritation and astonishment, the tall knight glanced between them at the ominous flickering of silver and the drop of blood drawn by its point, to the hand holding it. With narrowed eyes, he looked back to the icy gaze of the blade's holder, and then with a sharp laugh and the flick of a wrist, he knocked the blade into the filthy straw.

"Do not draw a knife on a man unless you mean to use it, little vixen." Without further acknowledgment of her murderous intent, he drew her closer, his mouth burning deeply against hers, his chest hot against her palms once more.

Furious more than fearful, Aelvina scraped her nails along his skin and kicked her feet at his shins. No man had ever been so insolent as to ignore the threat of her knife before; knowing she had come to him made the humiliation worse. But when Aelvina remembered her purpose in seeking this man, her furious thrashing died.

Bewildered, she attempted to sort out the sensations stirred by this overpowering male creature who now held her firmly in his grasp.

Almost timidly her lips parted at the knight's insistence, not understanding the meaning of his demand until his breath engulfed her and his tongue filled her, stealing the air from her lungs and leaving her senses reeling. Aelvina floated on the hungry demands of his kiss, drawn into the tide of his passion and drowning in its current. Clenched fists relaxed, and her hands crept up that broad, bare chest to the bobbed length of thick dark hair.

Haunting, dream-laden memories released a sudden fire of desire that swept through her with devastating effect. She dug her fingers into strong shoulders and responded to the giant's kiss with hunger, her body curving against his, welcoming the invasion of his marauding tongue and pressing needfully against his aroused maleness.

At this sudden switch from ice maiden to fiery temptress, Philippe gasped and jerked free, setting her from him. His eyes narrowed suspiciously as his gaze swept over her heaving breasts and disordered hair.

"Who in Hades art thou?" Philippe asked in his native tongue, not expecting any answer as he gathered his thoughts and forced his unruly body to coolness.

"Aelvina, daughter of Fairfax," she replied, clasping her hands before her and looking away as he adjusted his chausses. A flush heated her cheeks and her heart raced faster than humanly possible, but her mind was working again. This was the man fate had sent her. She still had time to escape, if she wished. His size and the frightening hardness of his angular features terrified her, but there had been no cruelty in his hungry kiss, and he had released her without rape. In these times, it was more than any woman could ask. She clenched her fists and held her ground.

"And what did you want with me, elf-friend?"

Her knowledge of the Norman language had apparently startled him, although it had been the language of the court for these past ninety years. Still, he returned her reply in the language of the serfs inhabiting this land. Her name represented the roots of Anglo-Saxon history. As Aelvina the Fair-Haired she could easily match the looks and spirit of her Viking ancestors. Her tattered clothing confirmed her status among the conquered.

At the Norman's use of her language, Aelvina studied his formidable visage cautiously. Not many of the court deigned to learn the language of her fathers or the mystical magic of the legends arising from the fogs of history. Her father had taught her the tales of the time when elves roamed the land like men, their powers and wisdom beyond the ken of mankind. Her name was a remnant of that history, but only the old remembered that now.

"I wished to know what kind of man you are, sire," she replied evenly, returning his emerald gaze with more coolness than she felt. Her body still burned at the points where he had touched it, and she forced her thoughts away from what would follow. When this scheme had been but words in the mouths of others, she had accepted it with logical decision. Confronted with the knight's masculine reality, she found herself suddenly uncertain of everything.

"And have you decided?" Philippe returned the girl's grave stare with equal solemnity, not regretting his earlier actions, but puzzled at the dilemma she represented. She carried herself with an air of breeding and spoke the language of the court as well as he, but dressed in the coarsest materials of the lowliest serf and spoke their language equally well. And then there was the matter of the change from outraged maiden to wanton. He waited.

"You are not a very chivalrous knight," she replied assessingly, looking him over much as he had done her earlier, "but you are not the beast I feared, either." Her gaze returned to his face. "Are you an honest man?"

"Honest enough to tell you I take my pleasure in war and not romantic folderol. Chivalry is for the weak-kneed and the fancies of idle women. Don't be too certain about the beast, either, just because I wasn't hungry enough to devour a meager morsel such as yourself."

Aelvina straightened her shoulders and glared. "I am sorry I am not to your taste. My lady will be disappointed."

He arched his eyebrows upward. "The Lady Ravenna? What has she to do with this?"

"There is no reason in my telling you now. I will tell her to find another." Aelvina swung around and stalked toward the door.

Philippe locked his hand in long silver tresses and stared down into the icy blue of her eyes. "Tell me," he ordered thunderously.

"I was to be your gift tonight, if my dancing pleased you," she replied brokenly.

"My gift!" Philippe could not control his surprise, and he loosened his grip on the girl to better observe her. Her kiss-swollen lips trembled beneath his glare, betraying her youth. Yet the soft swell of tender breasts beneath the coarse tunic stirred his loins in a manner not to be denied.

Aelvina withstood his inspection without anger this time. "She thought I might please you, sire. It makes things difficult that I do not, but it is better to know now than later. May I go now?"

Philippe did not release his grip on her wrist. Now that he had pulled his wits about him, he recognized a bribe when he saw one. King Henry had declared Dunstan Castle and the widowed Lady Ravenna's lands under royal guardianship until a suitable husband could be found for her. Philippe was here to inspect those lands and see what value could be had of them while the king went about the business of seeking an appropriate vassal on whom to bestow them. The Lady Ravenna evidently had ideas of her own and sought to curry favor. Philippe smiled grimly.

"No, you may not. I wish to hear more. If the lady wished to surprise me with such a gift as you tonight, why do you seek me out now?"

His piercing gaze brought color to Aelvina's cheeks again. She held up her chin defiantly.

"I wished to meet you before I gave myself to you. A woman has little choice in these matters, and I know fate would not let me escape much longer, but while I am allowed any alternative, I would choose for myself."

"So you came to see if I were beast or human."

Aelvina's head jerked upward at his chuckle. Emerald eyes glittered with amusement, and as she pulled away, his hand stroked her hair with gentle curiosity.

"Something of the sort, I suppose, sire," Aelvina whispered. His harsh features had relaxed into an easy smile, and except for the scar, he appeared almost handsome. What remarkable change had come over him?

"And what hast thou discovered? Do I meet the ideal of girlish dreams? And what didst thou hope to attain from this arrangement? Your freedom?"

Ignoring his first question, Aelvina haughtily answered the last. "I am already a free woman, sire. I am as free to come and go as thou art. I sought your protection for myself and an ailing companion. Since you do not desire me, I beg you to let me go."

"Whoa there, little vixen." Philippe held her firmly. "Who says I do not desire you? Let me understand you, first. After I take my pleasure of your lovely little body this evening, what is expected of me?"

A shiver rippled through Aelvina at his mocking mention of the topic uppermost in her thoughts, and the memory of his massive body pressed against hers further disturbed her composure. The fact that his hand now traveled from the relative safety of her cheek to the edge of her bodice did nothing to relieve her anxiety.

"I had hoped you would take Thyllda and me with you when you left, my lord. I cannot speak for the Lady Ravenna's plans."

"You are a virgin?" Philippe asked gently. At her silent nod, his fist knotted tighter in the strands of her hair. "And why would you choose me to introduce you to womanhood? Is that not a matter for a husband?"

"I have no dowry, no lands, no guardian," she replied matter-of-factly. "I travel from castle to castle with only Thyllda for protection, and now she is ailing. How much longer could I go without some man taking what little I have to give? The Lady Ravenna has agreed to look after Thyllda if I will do this for her. I have agreed, but I know if you leave me here, in the future she will offer me to every man she wishes to influence. I cannot live like that, sire, but I can give loyalty to one man, if you will have me. I will do my best to earn my keep. You are not a cruel man, I think. It is a better fate than many."

Philippe let out his breath in a slow whistle. He believed

the girl. The last years of civil strife had decimated the lives of many—the mighty and strong as well as the weak and poor. Only a miracle could have preserved the child this long—a miracle and the mysterious Thyllda, he ventured. He would like to meet that lady. He understood why the girl would trade her last treasure for the welfare of her benefactor. It was a cruel world, and he was part of it. She was right; if he did not take her now, somebody else would soon. What a pity to waste all that loveliness. But it was not those practical thoughts that made his decision. It was the searing response of her innocent kiss that left his loins aching and impatient to taste more.

"'Tis well said, little heathen, but I am not so certain thou dost understand for what you bargain. I have no taste for a night's frolic with a virgin child. If I should take you to my bed as you ask, it would be for so long as it pleases me. I would demand loyalty in exchange for my protection, the same faithfulness a wife gives a husband. If I should teach you how to ease my desires, I will not have you sharing your knowledge with other men. I have no use for whores," he stated harshly.

Aelvina raised her eyes to meet his, and the look she saw there tore her breath away. His eyes were like green fire, devouring her with their intensity, and her lips burned again with the memory of this knight's fierce kiss. He would consume her of a certainty, just as he had promised before, but her body began to throb and ache at the thought of his consumption. His touch had brought a frightening new knowledge of herself, and she had little time to study it. She nodded her head in acknowledgment of his warning.

"I will be as a wife to you, my lord, if that is what you desire. I will not look upon another man, nay, could not do so, while I shared your bed. Your protection will earn my loyalty, and if you can be kind to me, I will learn quickly. I am not ungrateful for what I am given."

His large hand brushed against her breast, cupping it carefully in his wide palm, and she trembled but did not back away. A flicker of some emotion bordering on sympathy crossed the knight's angular features, and with a sudden movement, he swooped to retrieve the silver dagger.

As he held out the dagger hilt to her, Aelvina glanced into the knight's dark face, but his eyes were shuttered and unsmiling.

"I swear by this knife, with God as my witness, that you shall have my protection for so long as you have need of it."

In wonderment, she watched Sir Philippe's face as he spoke these words, and as Aelvina realized his intent, she smiled in relief. With less fear than before, she wrapped her fingers about the dagger hilt, and with a bold gaze met his eyes.

"Upon my father's dagger, with God as my witness, I swear fealty to you, my lord, for so long as you have need of it." Claiming the dagger and slipping it back into her girdle, Aelvina dipped a curtsy from which she rose only at his insistence.

Their gazes clashed, and Philippe's dark face split in a broad grin. She was his vassal now. He was her lord. But something deep within those azure pools told him he might have some difficulty teaching her the difference. That fiercely independent Viking nature would not be tamed with those few simple words, but his warrior's blood raced at the challenge she presented.

"I see no reason why we cannot start your duties immediately. My quarters are in that tower directly across the courtyard. At the base of the tower there lies a door guarded by one of my men. It might be best if you slipped in there, unseen. Give me time to warn my men."

All color drained from Aelvina's face as she realized he had no intention of giving her time to prepare or to change her mind. She had sworn an oath to this man, as binding as any wedding vow, and she must abide by it. She had a sudden sense of her own vulnerability as he stared down at her impatiently, his great man's body nearly twice her own. What might he do to her when she lay beneath his heavy weight and submitted to the coupling she knew about only from observing animals? Yet it was no more than if she was truly his bride. The time must come in every woman's life that she find a mate, and at least she had been given some choice in the matter.

With a curt nod she gave her agreement, and without glancing back, Philippe strode out the door.

Chapter Two

Aelvina stayed hidden, giving Philippe sufficient time to warn his men of her approach. She had no idea what the Lady Ravenna would think of this premature meeting, but it would certainly not meet with her approval. Brushing away all thoughts of the mysterious dark lady who had dared suggest this immoral coupling, Aelvina concentrated on reaching the tower unnoticed.

There was still time to run, to escape the castle's stockade, and to enter the forest below, but it would mean leaving behind all she knew and loved: Thyllda, the cart she had called home these past years, the oxen that had pulled them from one nobleman's home to another. They were her livelihood, her family, her home. She could not, would not, desert them . . . not even for what lay ahead.

Casting her gaze toward the forbidding tower, Aelvina stifled the urge to shiver. Without Sir Philippe's compelling presence to quell her fears, the enormity of the act to which she had committed herself was overwhelming.

She had just coolly agreed to surrender her body and soul to a man she had never before met in her life. Her eyes widened at the innumerable possibilities that lay ahead. Love was preached and sung by troubadours and young gallants who wished to woo a way into a woman's arms, but reality remained another matter entirely.

Aelvina was too worldly wise to believe in the existence of so ephemeral an emotion as love, when she had seen for herself the cruelty of men toward their wives and daughters and mistresses. Women rated no higher than dogs— even lower, since they could not provide meat for the table. They were bartered like sheep for the wealth or power they might bring; love had no place in this world.

For Thyllda she would move heaven and earth. There were worse fates than Sir Philippe.

Remembering the laughing mockery of emerald eyes and the brawny strength of muscled shoulders, reckless excitement charged through her veins. She would soon know what it meant to lie in a man's arms and, at the same time, gain Thyllda's safety. It was well worth the effort.

Deciding the time had come, Aelvina darted out of the shadows and through the throng in the courtyard. Her gray mantle and undyed tunic blended well among the drab rags of the serfs around her. Only her silver-blond hair set her apart, but a veil would have been just as distinctive in this crowd. She hurried on, praying to escape the notice of Lady Ravenna and her evil cronies.

At a shout from behind, Aelvina hurried faster. The tower door lay just ahead. As she dashed toward it, a large, armored figure held the door open and cut off any sight of her from the courtyard. Before she could gasp her thanks, the door closed, and she was left alone in the darkness.

This tower was part of an ancient foundation originally used only as a lookout or guard post. The old walls had been incorporated into the newer structure with access to the castle keep at some interior point, but the ancient stone stairway still maintained its independent nature. Aelvina nervously glanced up the dark stairs, lit only by chinks in the outer wall, and braced herself for the climb from past to future.

It would not do to think about what fate awaited her at the top. It was midday and Sir Philippe had not yet had time to overindulge with ale, so she would not be taken with drunken brutality as she had feared would happen with Lady Ravenna's plan. Indeed, this knight did not appear the type to brutally ravish her at all. There seemed an air of refinement to him that presented a marked contrast to the brutes who had attempted to attack her before. Perhaps she would be lucky and he would be gentle this first time. It was the most that she dared to hope for.

Aelvina's teeth clenched in determination and her gait did not falter as she ascended the few remaining steps to the chamber door.

Sir Philippe gained his chambers from the castle keep entrance. Throwing aside his tunic, he stood towering in the center of the room, massive fists on narrow hips, glaring at the giggling girls who filled his bath with water carried from below. They ducked their heads with nervous laughter at the sight of his nearly naked torso, but made no move to depart.

Philippe frowned at this indication of their intent. The Lady Ravenna obviously sought to provide handmaidens to aid in his bathing. Damned thoughtful of her, but these two were not exactly what he had in mind. The promise of those intoxicating silver-blue eyes captivated him, and these simpering ninnies would not provide a substitute. He was well aware his quarry was nowhere in sight, but he did not hesitate. Curtly, he ordered the serving girls out. They stared at him incredulously, but when his glare grew blacker, they took heed and vanished, slamming the oaken door behind them.

Like a mighty stag on the scent of his mate, Philippe stood motionless, letting instinct sight the ancient cell's hiding places.

With a knowing glint, his gaze settled on a large chest half-hidden by a moth-eaten tapestry. In a few strides, he traversed the slight distance and flung the lid wide.

Aelvina gasped at the sudden intrusion of light into her dark enclosure; but then, recognizing the intruder, she smiled in relief.

"I feared the Lady Ravenna had discovered my plans," she admitted, taking his large hand for support as she untangled herself from the confines of the unlikely chamber. His palm was hard and rough and clasped her fingers with a firmness that spoke of both strength and gentleness. He did not release her when she stood beside him, half his breadth and scarcely reaching his shoulder.

"The lady is to be feared?" Philippe asked with curiosity.

"Only when displeased, and I fear not only spoiling her surprise, but leaving her custody will be displeasing. She would see me as her vassal, if she could."

Aelvina spoke in a low voice, not once taking her eyes from the fascination of his. They were like the promise of faraway places, glimmering like emerald isles in a dark unmoving sea, occasionally misting over so that she could not readily read them. Their warmth, she understood. The odd clouds that skittered across them, she would know more of.

"And you would choose me as your lord over her? Is that not an odd choice after the lady has so graciously taken you in and nursed your companion?"

Philippe's thumb traced a pattern against Aelvina's wrist. A flick of his arm and that hand would hang helplessly, yet she looked upon him without a trace of fear or shyness.

"I have earned my keep and now pay Thyllda's with all that I possess. I count that no mean payment," she replied defiantly, daring him to mock the price paid.

Instead, the hard line of Philippe's jaw softened, and a gentle finger traced the curve of her cheekbone. "Nay, if what you claim is true, you are paying too high a price. I am not in the habit of deflowering virgins, nor of taking advantage of the helpless. If you wish, I will release you from our vow and leave you untouched this night. The lady would be none the wiser."

Yet his fingers did not move from her cheek, and the provocative stroking had the effect of drawing her closer. The warm scent of horses and leather and sweat clung to him, filling Aelvina's nostrils with another fascination she could not resist. Her fingers itched to sample the wiry mat of hairs stretched across gleaming, powerful chest muscles, and a strange languor weakened her, melting her resistance the closer she drew to him. It was all she could do to concentrate on his words, but the matter was too vital to ignore. She shook her head solemnly.

"No, you promised. You said you would take me from here when you go. There is an evil here I can feel, and it will soon enthrall all within its reach." At the knight's skeptical look, she frowned and drew back. "Do not look at me so. I cannot tell you how I know this, but evil exists and it is here. You offer me protection and a place for

Thyllda. It is the best choice I have, and I will pay the price. I know I do not have the experience of some, but I learn quickly.''

The hand against her cheek moved to clasp her jaw with bruising strength. ''If you wish to learn the part of whore, I will teach you well, but you will be *my* whore and no other's. Know well the price you pay for my protection.'' He spoke with deliberate cruelty, forcing her to face the future she had chosen.

''I will be your whore, milord, but no man will be my master.''

The simplicity of her words, without a trace of tears or emotion to mar them, forced a measure of respect from the tall knight. This was no idle decision on her part, but rather a carefully thought-out plan of action. She wielded the weapons she possessed well, and he bowed his head in acknowledgment.

''Very well. I will not argue with your decision for it is entirely to my advantage. I have no pretty words to waste on ladies and no taste for the whores my men use. A maiden so rare and beautiful as yourself seldom comes by chance into a man's life. Do not expect your duties to be slight.''

The heated look he bestowed upon her as his hand traveled the length of her back left no doubt as to his meaning, and Aelvina stood mesmerized under his stare. It was as if her woolen tunic did not exist and she stood before him naked for his inspection. His hand stopped at her waist, propelling her closer, his emerald eyes glittering brightly as she made no resistance. She could feel the hard muscles of his thighs beneath the scant covering of his clothes, and she shivered at the massive strength holding her captive, but she felt no fear. He held her in the palm of his hand as she would a baby bird fallen from its nest—

gently, protectively, and with curiosity. That other urges lay just beneath these sensations was apparent in the hard stirring she felt against her abdomen.

With a nod of satisfaction as if she had passed some test, Philippe released her. "I would rid myself of horse sweat and filth first, and my bath grows cold. Since I have sent away the servants, you need take their place."

It was a command, and he didn't attempt to gauge her reaction as he moved abruptly toward the tub in the center of the room. Aelvina stood motionless and bewildered where he had left her. She had no training as a servant and no experience with naked men. Evidently there was more to this business than she had anticipated.

With widening eyes, she watched as the tall knight casually removed hose and chausses, displaying the powerful muscled legs beneath these garments. His rough covering of hair held her gaze until he turned to enter the bath, and then her eyes fastened with a mixture of awe and horror on his still partially erect manhood. He was built like a stallion. How could she possibly accommodate him?

Aelvina's cheeks burned as she raised her eyes to find emerald ones studying her carefully. Philippe climbed into the tub and submerged his more frightening aspects in the tepid water.

"You will be more successful in your duties if you come here." Philippe gestured impatiently to the side of the tub.

Wordlessly, Aelvina nodded and slipped to his side, kneeling where he indicated and taking the cloth in hand. This close, he seemed more immense than the massive destriers in the stable, but they responded well to gentling. How would this man act should she touch him?

It must come some time. He waited, watching her every move, and Aelvina suddenly realized how important it was to gain and hold this man's respect. It mattered more than anything else she had ever done in her life and, steeling herself, she reached out and applied the rag to his broad, sunburned back.

The effect was not so unpleasant once she was certain there would be no immediate repercussions. The taut, sinewy muscles relaxed beneath her massage, and rewarded by this discovery, Aelvina grew confident, spreading the soap farther along the length and breadth of his back.

When she had completed this surface to his satisfaction, Sir Philippe leaned back and rested his arms along the edge of the tub. It was then that Aelvina noticed the other scar blazoned along his ribs. With pain and compassion she touched her fingers to the old wound.

"You were lucky to survive such an injury, milord," she murmured.

"I serve the king in whatever way called upon and without question. It is a lesson you would do well to learn, though your duties will not be so treacherous," he reminded her.

"I will try, milord, but I am not accustomed to serving anyone," she replied mildly, beginning to soap the broad expanse of his chest. Under her ministrations, the small, dark nipples began to pucker, and with delight, she teased them further.

The growl deep in Philippe's throat gave fair warning. Aelvina jerked her head up, but not quickly enough to avert his action. His eyes glittered as he grabbed her shoulders, and his wetness dampened the front of her tunic.

"You will serve me, and sooner than you expect if you continue your present tactics. Behave yourself, wench."

With a suddenness that left her gasping, he closed the distance between them, plundering her mouth with a ruthlessness that told more than his words. The fierceness of his lips seared across the softness of her own, branding them forever. The rape of his tongue completed his mastery. Aelvina melted into his embrace, her hands clinging fiercely to his shoulders as she met his kiss with joyous reunion.

His wet hand fondled her roughly clad breast, shaping the curve of the unimpeded underside and coming to rest on the erect tip.

Aelvina cried out as ripples of pleasure pulsated across her skin and through her middle. Instinctively, she attempted to escape such a compelling hold.

Philippe held her firmly, his hand giving her breast one final caress before lifting her chin so she might meet his gaze. Aelvina trembled beneath the strength of his possessive hold.

"I do not take promises lightly. I am about to make you mine, in every sense of the word. I take care of what is mine, but I expect full service for my care. Do not try to run from me, for I will find you wherever you go."

In that instant, Aelvina well understood the enormity of the commitment she had made and did not regret it. She had grown up wild and independent of all reins, but this was a master she could learn to respect, or more.

"Do not use me cruelly, and you will have my loyalty for as long as you desire it, milord."

She did not retreat as strong fingers snapped the ties at her shoulders, allowing the tunic to fall down about her waist, releasing the full weight of her breasts from their encumbrance. Gleaming silver strands of hair tumbled across bare skin, scarcely concealing her nakedness.

His eyes commanded hers as his hand cupped what no man had touched before, but she could not control the tremor sweeping through her at the contact. His jaw set with satisfaction at this reaction, and he gently plied her nipple.

"At the moment, it is not your loyalty I most desire, elf-child. Shed those ugly garments and join me while the water is still enjoyable."

With his other hand, Philippe tugged at the belted girdle about her waist, and obligingly, Aelvina unwrapped it. In peasant style, she wore nothing beneath it, and the tunic fell to her hips as she knelt there, revealing the soft curve of a tiny waist and the sharp jutting of full hips.

Philippe caressed the curve of her hip, pushing the tunic farther down until it could go no lower. The touch of his rough hand against her bare buttocks sent a shiver of fear and delight through Aelvina. She knew he desired her to stand and let the garment fall free, to bare herself for his enjoyment, and with a sudden rush of pride, she desired it also. She wanted him to see what she had to offer, to see that he would be well paid for his protection. So proudly, she stood.

The tunic remained on the floor. Her breasts swayed as she shed the last of her garments. In the muted light of the castle tower, her skin glimmered, accented by the cascade of white-gold tresses and the darker triangle between her legs. She had only herself to give in trade for her life and Thyllda's; she would display her wares to their best advantage.

Philippe's gaze lingered long, heating her skin and heightening her coloring as he showed no sign of lessening his appreciation. He finally released her from his paralyzing stare, only to reach out and caress the soft triangle of hair between her legs. Aelvina shuddered and nearly collapsed at the unexpected intimacy of this electrifying contact.

Before she could crumple beneath his touch, Sir Philippe stood and encompassed her waist with one brawny arm. Emerald eyes gleamed as their bodies touched, but before such inviting contact could be further explored, he settled downward again, and the lapping bathwaters engulfed them.

Philippe grinned at her astonishment. "It is my custom to bathe regularly. I do not fancy vermin, and I expect my woman to comply accordingly."

Anger flashed briefly before she controlled it. "I am cleaner than yourself, milord. Since childhood I have been taught the value of cleanliness and bathe even in the coldest of winters."

The dark grin did not diminish as he wielded soap and rag and eyed the orbs bobbing above the waters. "Good. Come cold weather you will warm my bath better than any fire." Then, with a sudden sharp look, he asked, "What became of your parents?"

"They died of a fever within days of each other. You need not worry of risking their ire. I have nothing and no one, as I have said."

"Yet you were gently reared to be taught the niceties of bathing and to speak the language of the court so readily." Though his curiosity was obviously roused, more abiding hungers triumphed. With thoroughness, Philippe soaped her breasts.

Aelvina clung to the tub sides as his hands began their silken caress. He might have the experience to both talk and think at a time like this, but she did not. His every touch drove her to greater peaks of madness, searing her skin and stirring her insides into a turbulent storm that knew neither cause nor cure. She bit her lip to keep from crying out as exploratory fingers fondled a distended crest and breaking waves of excitement pounded through her blood.

At her silence, Sir Philippe ceased his motions and glanced at her quizzically. Enlightenment caused him to grin broadly.

"You have no fear of what I am about to do?" he asked, his fingers moving downward and brushing against her womanhood.

With her legs parted in the awkward position in which he had placed her, Aelvina was particularly vulnerable to the sensation of lapping waters and the closeness of his virility; the touch of his fingers at this sensitive juncture decimated all willpower. She slowly shook her head as his fingers repeated their urgent message.

Silver-gold hair cascaded past a slender throat arched backwards with pleasure, presenting a dizzying display of glistening breasts. Phillipe was not a stranger to lust, but this young siren stirred in him other desires alien to his nature; a desire to cherish and protect warred with his desire to plunder and possess.

The latter, being more adapted to his nature, won. Temptation was too near and his need too great. Wrapping her slender waist in his arm, Philippe lifted her bodily, positioning her in his lap so she could not fail to feel the extent of his desire.

Azure eyes widened at the hardness pressing against the gates of her maidenhood. Her hands flew to his shoulders to steady herself, as he held her poised in his arms, awaiting his desire.

The emerald mists of Phillipe's eyes dissipated, leaving a clear, sparkling green as his hand cupped the back of her head and brought her lips down to his. Aelvina shuddered at the electrifying contact of their mouths, then greedily claimed more, coming willingly into his arms as he gathered her close.

Time spun through darkness as their bodies met and

clung and joined together at their lips. The heated intrusion of his tongue bore promise of what was to come, and an ache built between Aelvina's thighs. Instinctively, she rubbed close to him, searching for that hardness that would satisfy her emptiness, and he groaned at this sign of her willingness.

With devastating force, Philippe crushed her lips beneath his, snatching away her breath and leaving her helpless in his arms. Then, with one mighty movement, he stood, carrying Aelvina with him.

Cool air swept over heated bodies, but neither noticed. The fur-covered bed lay but a step away, and it was to this that Philippe strode. Carefully placing her in the center, he stood back and with heated gaze admired what was now his to take as he would.

The desire in his eyes kindled strange yearnings in Aelvina's heart. For the first time, she felt a woman in fact, not just in body. A voluptuous desire to please inundated her limbs, and she lay easily under his gaze, one arm stretched above her head, heightening the full curves of her breasts.

She, in turn, admired the steely body of her chosen lover. He was a magnificent man of bronzed, hard contours. There was a firmness to lips and jaw that indicated an obstinate nature, but wide cheekbones and blazing emerald eyes told tales of a sensuality and passion to which Aelvina could easily respond. With daring, she allowed her gaze to drift downward, past the breadth of his shoulders and the rocklike muscles of his abdomen, to the root of his manhood.

A grin flitted across Philippe's lips at this bold inspection from his elfin treasure, but he could not be content with just looking. It had been too long since he had lost himself in the pleasures of a woman, and this one promised an extra excitement that heated his blood. Without warning, he bent over the recumbent figure on the bed, placing both hands like an iron prison on either side of his captive.

Aelvina cringed at the suddenness of his movement, then whimpered as his mouth enclosed a taut crest. With thorough enjoyment, he sampled both enticing ivory mounds before moving downward. She shuddered as his direction became evident.

Grabbing his hair, she entwined her fingers in it as she pleaded, "No, please, milord," but he paid no heed. With expert care, Philippe lifted her rounded bottom in his hands and gently kissed the place he soon meant to fill.

Aelvina writhed beneath the torment of his exploratory tongue, resisting his attempt to conquer her body. He knew she had no idea that his physical possession could be so complete, but she could no more resist the plundering of his tongue than prevent the sun from rising. Her hips arched convulsively at his persistent caress, until finally, her pace changed into one of demand instead of fear.

Sensing her surrender, Philippe lowered his full weight to the bed, covering her slight body with his larger one. Aelvina's arms reached eagerly to encompass him, and the fresh scent of her hair filled his nostrils as she tugged him down to meet her kiss. She was so slight beneath him that he feared crushing her, but the eagerness with which she pressed against him drove all thought of care from his mind.

Philippe's muscles rippling beneath her hands was an excitement in itself, but the awareness of hair-roughened skin rubbing against her own softness in so many unexpected places aroused Aelvina to further incredible peaks of desire. Whatever this was that flowed between them could not be bad; it was too beautiful to be sinful. As his large hands gently parted her thighs, tears sprang to Aelvina's eyes; she, who never cried, wept gladly.

Philippe scarcely noticed her tears as her body opened to give him entrance. Whispering senseless words of passion, he ran kisses from the corner of her lips to the lobe of a delicate ear, giving her time to adjust to his weight before seeking his release.

Aelvina clung to the reassuring strength of broad shoulders as his hardness probed deeper, stretching her to the breaking point. Her breasts brushed against his chest, the crests rising taut and aching as her nails dug into his back, and she whimpered at his fullness.

Then, with a whispered sigh, Philippe breached the barrier of her virginity, tearing away all childish notions and opening up the world of womanhood. The pain was minor compared to the onslaught of sensations produced by his overwhelming maleness, and Aelvina arched tentatively to meet his next thrust.

There was little time to marvel at her body's ability to encompass his hugeness. The rhythmic pounding of his thrusts should have torn her asunder, but instead she was swept mindlessly into his cadence, enduring all for the cresting waves of delight that each lunge brought.

Swept into this mindless maelstrom, Aelvina became part of his ecstasy, giving herself up so that she might become one with this mighty knight. It was a joy unimagined, this joining of their bodies into one complete creature, and when Philippe's seed exploded inside her, Aelvina exploded with it, in the inevitable culmination of such shuddering earthquakes as had possessed them.

They clung to each other as their bodies rocked together in the gentle aftermath. His fullness still claimed her, and for the first time, Aelvina became aware of how easily he could have punished her. But he had not. Her body tight-

ened rapturously at this realization, bringing a low moan
of satisfaction from Philippe's lips.

Aelvina met his gaze with shyness, but he stroked her
cheek reassuringly and fit his body more comfortably into
hers, and she relaxed. He had been more than gentle, and
this pleasure brought a desire for further delights. She
flushed even deeper at the realization.

Philippe chuckled. "It is past time for embarrassment.
You make love like a wild thing, without the inhibition of
many women. You pleasure me greatly, little vixen. Do not
grow shy now."

Aelvina radiated with pride and confidence as her fingers daringly explored the fascinations of his chest. "I
thank you for being kind, milord. I will try to pleasure you
always." Cocking her head to better observe the sharp
lines of his face, she asked, "Will it be like this always? I
have been taught to expect pain and unpleasantness. Had
I known it would be so good, I would have tried it much
sooner."

Giving a bark of laughter, Philippe cupped her bottom,
holding her tightly in place as he rolled over to release
her from his weight. Entangled in a waterfall of silver curls,
mesmerized by azure eyes, he could find no anger for her
ingenuousness.

"You would tease me out of the admission that there
has never been a woman who pleased me so much as you.
This coupling is merely a release for most. We have been
lucky. Do not tempt fate or my wrath by seeking elsewhere." His hand surrounded the swell of her breast, and
he noted how quickly the nipple tightened with excitement. His own body stiffened in expectation. He had spent
much time in satisfying her needs this first time; now there
was an overwhelming desire to take her fully, to make her

understand the completeness of his possession. He thrust deeply within her, warning her of his intentions.

Aelvina's eyes widened at the hardness pushing through to nearly rub against her belly. She searched his face, but only the pleasure of lovemaking blurred the chiseled lines. She relaxed as his hand pressed against her buttocks, and she settled hungrily onto the narrowness of his hips.

"I will have no need to seek elsewhere if you are always so lusty, milord," Aelvina replied to his rapturous groan. "Nay, I daresay it would be most difficult to seek elsewhere with you placed as you are."

"You are a bold wanton, but I shall soon break you to my saddle. I will ride you well before this day is out." So saying, Philippe rolled over, entrapping his daring vassal beneath his weight once more. "I should think, after what we have shared, you should be able to call me by name. My name is Philippe; I would hear it from your lips."

"Phil-ippe." She rolled the word on her tongue, liking its flavor. He was a Norman—that she understood well. His name had a foreign flavor, as did his shaven jaw and shoulder-cropped hair. But an Englishman had not sat the throne in many years, and she had no objection to his origins. With delight, she rolled the sound saucily from her lips once more. "Philippe, make me love you again."

Staring down into the azure innocence of her eyes, the sound of her accented Norman words striking his ears with a curious musicality, Philippe wondered if her phrasing were intentional or not. That he hardened further inside her at the thought did not register as more than a pleasing effect. She was a temptress, beyond a doubt, but he had weathered more experienced than she. He would possess her for as long as he had the need, keep her for as long as he wished, and set her aside when he grew tired. As calculating a wench as this one would understand that.

Still, she seemed an ephemeral wraith in his arms, and he had the disturbing notion that she could disappear at will if displeased. Such superstitious nonsense annoyed Philippe, and he thrust deeply inside her woman's body as if to impale her upon his manhood as one would a butterfly upon a pin. Grimly, the thought of holding her prisoner by planting his seed inside her passed briefly through his mind. It was a nonsensical notion, and he forced himself to relax and smile once more into her startled gaze.

"Milord, you are displeased?" Aelvina asked anxiously. His thrust had pained her, but not enough to douse the growing need just his look stirred. Her hands moved restlessly against his chest.

"Hold on, little vixen. I intend to claim you as you were meant to be claimed."

Holding her hips firmly with both hands, Philippe buried himself deeply, causing her to scream out with the joy and anguish of his thrust. The cry sated his need to disturb this wild creature as she did him, and with a throaty roar of his own, he plunged recklessly, taking her for his own.

Chapter Three

Afterward, Aelvina lay within the circle of Philippe's arms. Her body ached from the effect of his bruising hungers, but it was a sensual soreness healed easily by the languor overtaking her limbs. The feel of this knight's hand caressing her breast and the curve of her waist made all well, and she sighed contentedly.

A soft chuckle rumbled against her ear as Philippe wound his hand in her curls. "You purr like a gentle kitten to make me think you tamed, but I am not so easily fooled. You are a sorceress and I am your victim. Would you have turned me into a toad if I had not pleased?"

His fingers gripped her chin, tilting her head so her gaze met his. His words were jocular, but Aelvina sensed his seriousness, and her heart pounded faster at the possibility of having stirred more than his desire. He was a mighty warrior, one of the king's men, and a wealthy noble in his own right. She had no business thinking she could be more than a convenient vessel for his needs. But emerald fires warmed her heart.

"If you had not pleased, you would have been a toad instead of a man, without help from any sorceress. Men do not need magic to make them what they already are, only to make them what they are not."

Philippe grunted in agreement. "I have taken a philosopher to my bed. You will not only warm my nights, but exercise my wits. Who taught you, elf-child?"

Aelvina propped her elbows on his muscled chest and contemplated Philippe's bronzed visage. Despite his size, this knight was no brute beast. He carried himself with an air of refinement and spoke articulately in at least two languages. Why did the Lady Ravenna not choose to keep such a fair specimen for herself?

"My parents and Thyllda were my only teachers—they and all the others I have encountered in my travels," she amended. "The world teaches much to those thrown upon its tender mercies."

There was no bitterness in her speech, only practicality. Philippe stroked her cheek thoughtfully. "Have you no place you call home? No cottage somewhere, however humble?"

"My parents were my home. Since they died, the old cart we travel in and Thyllda have been both home and family. There are others worse off than I. I have known nothing but this life since I was born. My parents were the ones to suffer, for they were bred for better. These last twenty years of civil strife have destroyed the land and the people and all that could have been." She spoke sadly, her eyes no longer focused on the man beside her, but elsewhere, in another world painted by her father's words.

With the death of Henry I leaving no male heir, England had been torn between Henry's daughter Maud and his nephew Stephen, leaving the land ripe for takeover by unscrupulous barons. The coming of this new king, Henry II, son of Maud, meant little to her cynical mind.

"King Henry will be a good king, despite his youth," Philippe assured her. "The robber barons will rue his power. The Lady Ravenna knows that is why I am here today. This castle and all who dwell within its lands reverted to the king at the death of her husband. There has been no man to make that claim until now, and she has controlled things as she wished. You would do me a kindness by telling me what manner of woman she is, and what she hopes to gain by currying my favor."

Aelvina let her thoughts play back over these past few weeks. Thyllda had been her main concern. She had spent every possible minute at the elderly woman's side, but she also had to earn her keep. She had learned much and nothing. Nothing to which this sensible knight would listen, anyway.

Frowning, she again tried to remember the nights that had disappeared from her memory since her arrival at this castle, but each time she reached to grasp a fragile fragment a restive uneasiness flooded her, and she dropped the search.

"I can tell you little, milord. The lady is seldom seen by such as myself. She wears jewels but no colors, only black. She is very beautiful, but in a haunting way that makes one uneasy. When she sent for me and asked that I dance for you this evening, she gave no reasons, but made it clear I had little choice. She assured me you were a gentleman."

Aelvina blushed in remembrance of the lady's vivid descriptions of the visitor's pleasing manliness. The words had intoxicated her as much as the wine the lady had given her, stimulating an overactive imagination into desire for a man she had never seen. How does one describe such uncanny abilities as the lady possessed? The knight would have to see for himself.

"Why did the lady think I would prefer a serving girl for my bed when she knew I could take her if I had desired? Have I earned some reputation of which I do not know?"

Aelvina grinned and traced paths through the jungle of Philippe's chest. "I know nothing of your reputation, milord, but my lady assures me all men prefer young virgins and that my dancing enhances their desires to insatiable limits. You will have to judge for yourself this evening. If you still prefer ladies to servants, then you may bed the lady if you like, but I will hold you to your promise to take me with you when you leave."

Philippe flipped her against the bed and pinned her legs with his heavy, iron-thewed thighs.

"Do not think your duties will end so lightly, wench. You will bounce beneath me many more times in the future. I will make you pay for your prattling tongue. What manner of dance is this you do that drives men mad?"

Aelvina wriggled beneath his weight, each movement having the opposite effect of her intention. It would never do to raise this man's ire. He would be merciless.

"You will see tonight, milord," she gasped, as his caresses took her breath away. "My mother taught it to me. I have earned my way by entertaining others with it, but Thyllda usually acts as my chaperone and plays the lute. Tonight, I will dance alone."

"You do not look the part of gypsy. Where are the fiery dark looks and flashing black eyes?" Philippe teased. He nudged her legs wider apart with his knee.

"I am no gypsy. My parents were both fair as I. This coloring was the bane of my mother's life as well as mine," Aelvina babbled on, delaying the inevitable in revenge for his teasing. "As a child, my mother traveled to the Holy Land with her parents. They were Normans; that is why I speak your language well. But my mother's coloring caught the eye of a heathen prince, and she was stolen from her parents and placed in some sultan's harem. It was there she learned to dance to please men."

Philippe stopped his teasing, the wench's words striking him hard. Her parents must have been wealthy nobles or merchants to have traveled so extensively. But after a lifetime in a heathen harem, how could a woman be any more than the whore her daughter had become now? It was a poignant story of the downfall of the mighty, but he refused to be impressed.

Aelvina saw his scorn, not for herself but for her mother, and she attacked bitterly. "Think what you like, milord, but my father claimed she was still innocent when he found her. She was a delicate lady who would have died rather than be dishonored. Perhaps the heathens were not so heathen after all, nor so barbaric as the nobles of this great land. They gave her to my father when he did them some service, and she remained faithful to him to the end. When he died of the fever, she died too, though she had been on the way to recovery until then."

Scorn turned suspiciously near to tears, and even Philippe's hard heart felt the blow. Gently he kissed her eyelids, preventing the tears from falling. This wild creature retained her mother's delicacy of form, but he suspected her father's Viking nature warred within her soul. It was an enchanting combination that appealed to him in a way no other woman had ever done.

Philippe took her with more care this time, sensitive to the bruising he had given her earlier. Aelvina blossomed under his gentleness, learning more of those sensations his body could arouse in hers, and surrendering eagerly to the lesson.

Though he went slowly, the end came all too soon, and Aelvina sighed with a mixture of sadness and joy as his seed flooded her womb for the third time. The day grew late, and she knew she must leave soon. The thought of parting with him, even for a short time, seemed unbearable. She, who counted few possessions of her own, treasured these hours and would not part with them. She stroked the powerful length of his back and breathed his name softly, as if that might hold him.

"Good, you have learned my name at last," Philippe murmured against her ear. He, too, was reluctant to leave, though he knew there was much yet to be accomplished this day. It was unusual for him to linger when there was work to be done, but he feared he would not find this ephemeral nymph again once he let her go. His hands stroked the lovely body he had just so thoroughly possessed, proving her reality.

"It is time I returned to Thyllda. She will worry if I do not appear as usual." Aelvina wove her hand into his hair, her fingers lingering on the small scar on his cheek.

"What will you tell your guardian of us? She will surely have to know if you are to travel with my camp." Philippe delayed the inevitable for as long as he could, desiring to know more of this splendid creature who had fallen into his snare.

"I will tell her what is between us, of course. She is no fool. But I beg of you, do not tell her it happened because of her. I owe her more than my life, and this is small payment for services rendered." Blue eyes were beseeching.

"How soon will she be able to travel? I do not intend to linger here long."

"If you do not travel quickly, I think I can make her comfortable in the oxen cart. With your men to guard us, we need have no other fears, and it will not be difficult."

Philippe propped himself on one elbow above her. "You do understand you will be traveling at my side and not with the other women in the rear? I will have no one assuming you are available for all to use. One of the other women can tend to your Thyllda."

Pain crossed Aelvina's gaze, but she nodded obediently. "As you wish, milord." At his scowl, she hurriedly amended, "Philippe. Will I have permission to visit with her when you have no need of me?"

"Only under the protection of the monk, Chauvin. He has taken a vow of chastity—not so my men. They are loyal, but your beauty would test their loyalty sorely. An army camp is not always the best of places for young women."

Reluctantly, Aelvina rolled out from beneath him. "My mother spent a good part of her married life in one camp or another. I am not unacquainted with the disadvantages. I must go, sire."

Still propped on one arm, Philippe watched her move away, the long silver-gold tresses falling past her waist to brush against rounded buttocks. His body stirred in response, and with a grunt of exasperation, he stood and found his own clothes.

As Aelvina tugged the coarse brown cloth of her gunna over her head, he stopped her, rubbing the rough material between his fingers with distaste. "We will have to find you better than this. I will not have my woman dressed in rags."

Crystal blue eyes searched his face warily, but if she were to travel at his side and not in the caravan with the other prostitutes, he would have her wear something that would not shame him.

"I have others, milord," she replied softly. "You need not worry about spending your coins on my garments. It is more convenient and less dangerous for me to wear these when unprotected. I hope I shall not displease you." She tugged the tunic in place and tied the broken remnants of string that held it.

It was Philippe's turn to be astonished. Experience had taught him his mistresses expected to be well-clothed and bejeweled. Even the married ones expected his largesse to exceed their husbands'. It was a symbol of their trade, and they flaunted it flagrantly, often using his purse to attract another. But their cynicism had not yet touched this innocent. He would have to keep her far from court to protect such rare honesty—and dress her twice as well in recompense.

"We will see," was all he muttered as the long tunic once more covered her from neck to toe.

There was no parting kiss or words of love between them as Aelvina slipped from the room. Both knew such weakening would have only one result, and there were other duties to consider for the moment. Tonight, they would meet in the crowded great room as strangers, and it would not be the same again. Aelvina did not look back as she dashed down the dark corridor.

Chapter Four

Thyllda's faded eyes noted the flush of excitement on Aelvina's face, saw it was rubbed raw in places from a man's beard, and knew at once something momentous had happened to her young charge. Anxiously, she searched the crystalline honesty of blue eyes, and relaxed. Whatever it was, it had not marred the eagerness for life the child had always exhibited, even in the worst of times.

"Come in and tell me about it, child. You are brimming over with some news that cannot be contained long." She indicated a place on the bed.

Aelvina hid her sorrow at the emaciation of her loyal friend's once full body. Thick sorrel hair had long since whitened, but Thyllda still wore it proudly in a long waist-length plait. She had never been a beautiful woman, but her hair had always been her crowning glory. The lined face beneath it had lost none of its wisdom, though, and Aelvina gratefully clung to this harbor. She perched on the bed beside her friend and advisor, took the older woman's hand in her own, and searched for the words to begin. Thyllda had always been the one to make the decisions and lead the way, finding whatever was needed so they never went without. Her last decision had been to come to this place, refusing to stop elsewhere though the sickness drained her strength. Aelvina had not understood the older woman's desire to rest in this particular fortress, but she had respected it. Now it was time she made her own decisions. She only prayed her first had been the right one.

Thyllda eased the transition. "It is a man, is it not? I can see it in your eyes. Your mother looked thus when she looked upon your father. I hope he is worth your trust."

"He is, Thyllda. I know he is a good man. You have taught me much about the characters of men, so respect your own judgment."

"Tell me," the old woman demanded.

"He is a strong man, and a powerful one, but there is a kindness behind his eyes and a gentleness in his touch that I like well, Thyllda. He may be stubborn and harsh at times, but he will treat me well. I know this, Thyllda, with all my heart, so do not think badly of me when you know what I have done."

Thyllda had known the time must come. Unprotected as Aelvina was, she could not go innocent for long. Without dowry or guardian, she could hope for no better life than as the wife of some honest serf. Even the free men of town would not look upon her beauty as dowry enough for a wife. She was meant for a man's pleasure, but not to be the mother of his children. Thyllda sighed. It was a cruel world, and Aelvina had learned its lessons well.

"I cannot think badly of you, whatever you have done, Evelyn," she responded, using the girl's childhood name.

"Thank you, *ma mere*," Aelvina whispered, squeezing Thyllda's hand. "I knew you would understand. Philippe is a knight in the king's service. He has promised us his protection and will take us with him when he leaves. I think he means it, Thyllda. He would not lie."

Thyllda nodded tiredly. "They all mean it when they are hungry for what you have to offer. Do not lose your heart, little one. A knight is far beyond your ken, and he will set you aside for another soon enough. It is good that he has been kind to you this first time, so you will not learn to fear all others, but do not expect more than kindness."

"I understand, *ma mere*. It will be difficult not to love such a one as him just a little bit; you will agree when you meet him. But I know where I belong in his life. I will take care."

The old woman nodded again, more slowly this time. The girl's father had said that same thing when presented with his charming slave, and had married her soon after. The Fairfaxes never loved just a little; they loved as they lived, violently. Only, in this case, there was no chance for a happy ending. This time the Fairfax was a female and without choice in the matter. No marriage would come of this misalliance, only heartache.

Aelvina sensed the old woman's weariness, so she kissed her lined brow and slipped away. Tonight she would dance as her mother had danced for her father. She had always known of the dance's eroticism, but never before had she directed the movement toward one man. Her excitement rose as she understood the connection between what she had done this afternoon and what she would do this evening. She would sell her body all over again, and willingly, for just the price of the pleasure he would give her.

Giddiness enveloped her as she washed and prepared herself for the night to come. This time she would be bathed and scented and wearing the gauzy silks of the East, and he would know he had a woman he could show off proudly. Carefully, she added the heavy gold chain bearing her father's ring. Its glitter was all but concealed beneath the silk. With its addition, she carried memories of both her parents. Even the intrusion of Lady Ravenna's ancient companion could not dispel her mood of excitement.

The old crone entered without knocking and stood noiselessly in the doorway. Aelvina took notice of her and grimaced. Marta's robes were dark, as became her age; no jewels bedecked her throat or hands, as became her position. Still, Aelvina could not prevent the uneasy feeling caused by the old woman's dress. It seemed doubtful that this wizened, hunched figure had ever known youth. The others whispered behind her back and made signs against the evil eye after Marta passed, but Aelvina felt only distaste for the woman's stealthy habits and prying eyes.

"The Lady Ravenna desires your company before the performance. She has sent me to see that you are ready."

Aelvina presented herself for inspection. She had entwined her hair with silken ribbons and baubles that sparkled in the torch light, but only glimpses could be caught through the transparency of the veil covering eyes widened with a hint of kohl.

The rest of the costume did little more than cover her nakedness. Glimpses of milk-white breasts and thighs peered through the blue gauze with each movement, as the folds of silk swayed with the breeze. The supple belt molding hips and waist did little to disguise the free sway of her motions; in fact, it enhanced them.

Marta grinned toothlessly.

* * *

Below, Philippe waited impatiently for the meal's end. The Lady Ravenna presided at the head of the long trestle table on the dais, and he was seated at her right as an honored guest. She had made little conversation throughout the meal, which suited his mood quite nicely. He had only one thought on his mind at the moment, and his body stirred at the memory of sultry eyes.

Wine and mead flowed freely, and Philippe watched cynically as one by one, his men fell victim to overindulgence. They sang, they fought, they fell under the table. They fought hard and were expected to play hard. If this were their choice of pastimes, so be it.

He had more sympathy for those who held their liquor well but slipped away with one or more of the serving girls under their arms. The keep seemed well supplied with young women eager for a romp. It must have been a long time since any man had made himself known in these parts.

With that thought in mind, Philippe turned once more to his dinner companion. She was as Aelvina had declared, a curious creature. Widowed at an early age, he surmised, she was no older than he. Thick black plaits were well hidden behind cap and veil, all in black, as he had been told. She would have appeared almost nunlike, had it not been for the woven necklet of bloodred rubies and gold about her throat, and the dark flash of gems upon fingers and wrists.

She remained nearly motionless throughout the meal, dark eyes observing the antics of her guests passively. A mirthless smile crossed her pale lips as she offered her guest of honor a fresh goblet of wine.

"You do not drink with your men, Sir Philippe? But you must accept this cup in toast to what will hopefully be a long and pleasant relationship between this hall and our new king." Her words rustled like dry leaves in the wind and Philippe had to listen closely to catch them.

He raised the golden goblet as requested, and watched as the lady took her first drink of the evening before sipping of the nectar himself. The wine was potent and heady, and he developed a great thirst for it, swallowing large mouthfuls before returning the cup to the table. It had been a long, hard journey and he owed himself an evening's pleasure, but he fully intended to have his wits about him when presented with his sensuous sorceress.

The lights in the great hall seemed to grow dimmer, the pitch-dipped flares guttering low. The huge burning logs in the enormous fireplace at the head of the dais flamed higher, illuminating his hostess while casting the remainder of the room in shadow.

And then there she stood, a graceful silver-blue shadow hovering at his side, appearing from out of nowhere. Philippe shook the fumes of wine from his head, wondering how she had managed to creep up on him so noiselessly, without his sensing any trace of her presence. His first reaction was to reach out and see if this wraith was real, if she was the same flesh and blood he had so lustily sampled this afternoon; but the nervous sway of silken veils deterred that thought, and he reached for his goblet instead. For the wench's sake, he must show no recognition.

His hostess was whispering words at him again, indicating the frail shadow at her side. Philippe nodded obligingly, not caring what was said. The blood already raced heatedly through his loins, aroused just by the sensuality of that slight frame and the delicate fragrance assaulting his senses. He did not remember the scent from this afternoon, but was certain he would carry it with him from this day forward.

She faced him, azure eyes shot with silver flashing above the silken veil as she accepted the golden goblet offered by their hostess. Dark-rimmed lashes surrounded a well of promises as they held his gaze, and Philippe watched, fascinated, as she drained the drink to the dregs, her eyes never once leaving his.

The Lady Ravenna was lost to the shadows as Aelvina drifted from her side and took her place in front of the roaring flames. Her body swayed with a lilting music that came from nowhere and everywhere. The notes were an oddity to his ears and produced an exotic effect that emphasized the sexuality of her movements.

She began to dance, the natural ease of her motion swaying into a rhythm to match the music. Gripping his goblet tightly, Philippe stared at the ephemeral folds of silk enclosing the alabaster body he had known just a few short hours ago. He caught glimpses of silver skin and an occasional flash of gold as the silk swayed and the firelight danced, but just as he thought he glimpsed a honey-tipped breast or a rounded calf, the image would fade away and the blue silk would cover her once more. He stared harder, willing the shadows from his eyes, determined to see all there was to see.

The music grew faster, punctuated with the erotic beat of the shells fastened in slender hands as Aelvina dipped and swirled to a melody all her own. The firelight leaped higher as she whirled faster and faster, the silken veils flying into a misty cloud about a slender silver vortex, and the room and the music ceased to exist.

Trapped in the sensual spell she wove, Philippe could not look away from the slivers of silver tantalizing him beneath the silken cloth. As if she was aware of his fascination, Aelvina danced closer, her arms beckoning and teasing, her azure eyes taunting and dreamily unfocused as her body swayed.

At the suggestive swing of her hips, Philippe's loins tightened, and he knew the truth of her earlier statement. If this dance did not end soon, he would be driven to take her right here on the floor. He grabbed the golden goblet and drained the remainder.

The wine only added fuel to an already roaring flame. The blood pounded in his ears, drowning out all thought as Aelvina danced closer. Silver hair glimmered like priceless jewels in the flickering firelight, silver-blue eyes danced and leaped and called to him, and her slim white body played a sensuous siren's song for him alone. His gaze found the sway of firm young breasts at last. He followed her undulating movement to the taut, concave belly swinging enticingly between narrow, curved hips, and sought the dark triangle between shapely thighs.

When she slipped away at the last provocative moment, he drowned his curses in another drink of wine, the goblet having been mysteriously refilled, though he was in no state to notice. Raging lust focused on that elusive figure in the firelight and controlled all action and thought. Impatience bit deeply as his loins cried for the relief of being buried within that innocent vessel once again.

Aelvina was in no better state. The heady wine had loosened all inhibition, and the compelling figure filling her vision elicited shivering excitement. The fires of emerald eyes fed across her skin, evoking memories of sensuous touches and searing kisses, and her body responded to his call. The sexual tension of the dance grew more pronounced as her breasts begged to be plucked again and her hips made their need apparent. Her eyes focused on the whitening scar on Philippe's dark face, reading the hunger in the tension of his square jaw and giving herself up to it.

The room spun with the music and the liquor, and firelight danced crazily against the darkness, obliterating all other figures but the silver-spinning wraith and the towering dark knight. As the two closed together, a voice whispered through the blackness.

"Take her, my lord . . . She's yours to enjoy," came a sibilant hiss in the gloom.

Philippe needed no further goading. In one economical movement, he rose and snatched that slender waist into his grasp.

At this abrupt ending to her freedom, Aelvina gasped. Her head whirled curiously, her mind registering only the long, hard length of the male body pressed to hers. Then oblivion blotted out all further sensation.

As if in a trance, Philippe took no notice of the sudden limpness of the figure in his arms. A wraith had no weight, and he was most singularly possessed. Guided only by the searing lust in his loins and a whispering voice ordering, "Follow me," he obediently carried his prize into the darkness of shadowed castle walls.

Cold. After the heat of the roaring fire, she felt only cold. It stung along her skin, pressing like icicles on her spine, blowing across her breasts in a chilling breeze. She sought to cover herself, but was paralyzed, her wrists bound inexplicably to a place above her head. It was a strange dream she fought to shed, whipping her head back and forth in an attempt to wake, unable to even open her eyes against the heavy lethargy.

Silence, with only an ominous murmur in the distance to indicate the presence of life. Complete, unnerving

silence as she had never experienced, even in the nights
upon the road when the oxen's grunting snorts kept her
company. Her ears strained for the song of a bird, the
crackle of a fire, but found only that mysterious murmur
of sound like a silent river tumbling over the stones of a
deep cavern.

It must be a dream, and she strained to waken. Cold
ran like a stream across her skin, raping the warmth
between her parted thighs and raising her nipples to hardened points. She sought to curl her outspread legs together
for warmth and found they were also paralyzed with an
aching stiffness, her ankles attached firmly to unseen pin-
ions. Only then did she realize she wore no clothes, and
the night air blew across her nakedness.

Her screams split the stillness like an animal's shriek at
a predator's strike. The murmur grew with erotic excitement, and Aelvina screeched again, crying out to those
unseen presences she sensed in the darkness. She tore at
the ties binding her wrists together, and her hips rose
freely from the paralyzing coldness of her stone bed. But
neither her wrists nor her ankles escaped their manacles.
The murmur grew louder and more demanding, and took
on a chanting quality.

Her lashes suddenly flew open and Aelvina found herself
staring up into a starlit sky, the blackness complete except
for small dots of light and a strangely illuminated cloud
covering the moon. Whipping her head with terror, she
recognized the ancient stone monoliths that littered the
fields beyond Dunstan. The monstrous stones loomed
menacingly, casting their shadows across her body, piercing her soul as she lay bound to the stone pedestal in their
midst. As her screams grew hysterical, a wave of black
shadows drew closer from the base of the stones—hooded
forms of human shape. The chant grew more frantic and

more demanding, keeping time with the rise and fall of Aelvina's hips as she fought against her bindings.

A shadow stepped forward to caress her breasts, leaving a warm smear of oil across the tips as the fingers worked their way to the base of first one and then the other. Aelvina fought for recognition, but the fogs of her mind prevented thought and promoted only the sensation of warm fingers moving, massaging, caressing toward the apex of her being. Her screams died to moans, and her hips swayed with the erotic movement of the dance as a hypnotic trance overpowered her senses.

The sudden appearance of a massive shadow swaying above her in the space between her legs returned her terror. A dark shape blotted out the moon's light as this new menace formed over her. His arms pinned her head between their strength, his heavy weight pressed her inexorably down against the stone bed, the position unavoidably posing his male shaft at the vulnerable opening of her body. Aelvina's gaze flew upward and met emerald fires of lust burning against the night sky. His mouth crushing against hers cut off her screams as his tongue thrust between her teeth.

Aelvina gagged and fought, but he was like a man possessed, catching her hair in his fist while his lips and tongue and teeth raked across her skin and down her throat, and his other hand sought the softer purchases of her body. Horror held her still as his fingers plundered the opening he had violated only hours before.

Her thoughts whirled in hazy confusion, unable to escape the myriad of unpleasant sensations spearing her body. Eyes wide with terror, she gazed up into the blurred emerald fires hovering above her, unable to discover any reason or emotion beyond crazed lust in their depths. Her lips tried to form words of pleading, but no sound passed them. There was no recognition in Philippe's response as he shifted his weight to kneel between her thighs.

Coldness swept between them as he raised up on his hands. With fascinated terror, Aelvina's gaze traveled from the somber expressionless face above her to the massive shoulders and powerful chest of her dark knight poised to strike, and fixed upon the engorged weapon of his sex.

He was as naked as she, and every muscle bulged with the strain of resistance against a consuming desire. In that moment before he struck, Aelvina discovered the black shadow hovering behind him, and her gaze swung wildly about, facing the ring of robed observers surrounding the high stone pedestal on which she lay bound. Her throat opened in a primeval scream as the moon slipped from behind the clouds, illuminating the stone monoliths circling the sacrificial pedestal, casting its light on the virginal offering there.

Aelvina's screams drowned in the rising excitement of chanting voices, and as if waiting for that shaft of moonlight, Philippe plunged.

Aelvina's shouts changed pitch with that first battering assault. Her hips strove to avoid a second impalement, but her bonds only allowed an upward movement that took his thrust.

It was as if once losing her ability to choose, she also lost control of her body. It would not do as she commanded it. Her skin flamed with the need for Philippe's touch, and the increasing pitch of excitement of the chanting observers threw her hips into a frenzy of lust.

He lunged and plundered and battered her with all the weight and strength he had held in reserve earlier. Aelvina screamed and strained for freedom while her hips arched convulsively, over and over again, to meet his demand.

With this possession of her body, Aelvina's spirit slipped

away, hovering above the scene with disinterest. The moonlight grew more silver and dancing motes filtered down its beams, centering on the groaning, writhing figures on the pedestal.

As a star shot across the northern skies and torchlight flickered into flame, the dominant male roared and his seed spurted into the womb of the moon's mistress. The chant exploded into abandoned screams of ecstasy.

Mentally, Aelvina was only vaguely aware of a strange lethargy seeping along her limbs as Philippe's seed flowed hot and thick inside her. As his maleness grew hard again with lust her spirit drifted away, following a floating moonbeam into a cloud. The body she left below was no more than a slender etching on a cold stone bed raised high against the night. Idly, she watched as the rippling muscles of a broad, bronzed back bunched and surged and thrust again. Briefly, she remembered the explosive satisfaction she had known a century before; but the memory passed.

As the Greek god below released another silvery stream of seed into the fair body he possessed, Aelvina drifted away and was gone.

Chapter Five

The blackness was a comfort and she pulled it around her, covering herself with the lovely softness of clouds and resisting every effort of light to enter. At times, the blankness was so complete, she lost her grip and the clouds slipped away, but the sharp intrusion of memory woke her to the danger, and she sipped eagerly at the elixir of happiness and drifted away again.

She floated mindlessly, lost in the pleasures of darkness, only occasionally aware that somewhere below a body lay aching. As those moments of awareness became more lucid, she looked with sympathy upon the bruised and battered fairness in the foul bed below, and cried out for that liquid that would ease the body's pain and wounded spirit. Then she would drift into oblivion again, satisfied she had done all she could to relieve the body's suffering.

Only there came a time when awareness returned more frequently, bringing with it the torment of reality, and the elixir no longer produced oblivion. She raged against the loss of her clouds of pleasure and met no sympathy. She fought against the ties binding her to that hated body, but could not escape. With cries of protest, she became one with the body again and darkness swept through her soul.

Aelvina lay there emptily. The physical aches had disappeared, and the physical was all she noted. The straw pallet she lay upon was not clean. The air around her was damp and occasionally filled with the odors of cooking. Food was presented to her and she ate. Then she slept.

She slept away the days, eating and drinking when told, not questioning, only waiting for the blissfulness of sleep that followed. It was almost as good as the time of the clouds of pleasure. But the sleep, too, soon passed.

One day she woke to discover an old crone bent over a fireplace on the far side of the peculiar room in which she lay, and her gaze wandered over the room's interior. It was the first time she had noticed her surroundings and she was not reassured. The roughness of the stone walls resembled a cave, but an oaken door marked an entrance, and the stone hearth had a chimney to take away the smoke. Aelvina returned her gaze to the elderly woman bent over the fire's heat and searched her memory for names.

It didn't take long to discover that thoughts still evaded her and her mind roamed restlessly through a drugged haze. She gave into the foggy wafts of sleep, relieved not to have to ponder the problem.

The next time she woke, the woman brought her food, and Aelvina recognized the wizened features with a jolt. Marta! The name returned, but not the memory. An uneasiness invaded her mind, but she resisted its cause, accepting the food and eating silently.

More days wandered by in this manner, Aelvina's body

gaining in strength and her mind gradually clearing. She began to watch as Marta prepared the day's meal, often disappearing for hours at a time and returning with meat and herbs to mix in her simmering cauldron. Other times she returned and took down bottles of assorted oddments from the numerous shelves, pounding and mixing the ingredients to make a paste, potion, or powder that she carefully wrapped and carried out with her again.

These activities gradually roused Aelvina's curiosity and thence, her memory. Some memories remained shrouded in forgetfulness, but she remembered Dunstan Castle and the Lady Ravenna, that Marta belonged to them, and that Thyllda was in their care. The memory of Thyllda returned her speech.

As Marta approached with the evening meal, Aelvina caught the considering gaze in dark eyes and answered it. "Where is Thyllda?"

Wizened features nodded approvingly. "It is time you woke. Too long in the clouds of sleep and the body weakens and dies." She set the bowl next to the bed and began to move away.

With annoyance, Aelvina repeated, "Where is Thyllda?"

The old crone turned to study her again with a trace of irritation. "She is gone."

It was a flat statement, not meant to be questioned, but Aelvina could not accept it. "Gone where?" She did not allow herself to consider all the potential meanings of the words.

Marta's thin lips tightened. "She is no more." And with purposeful tread, she turned her back.

Stunned, Aelvina sat wordlessly, unable to accept the only possible meaning of Marta's phrase. Thyllda could not be dead, for that would mean she was all alone in the world, and she did not even know where she was or why.

That presented an easier train of thought and Aelvina followed it gladly. "Where am I?"

Marta threw up her hands in a gesture of disgust, left the boiling kettle, and returned to the bedside. The weeks of peace were ended. The time of trial had begun.

"In my home." Marta hoped this would satisfy the girl but knew it would not. She had known from the first that this silver creature was not the docile maiden her plans required. It was too late to turn back now.

Aelvina's fair brow puckered into a frown. "Why am I not at the castle? How did I get here?"

"You were ill and the others feared your illness would spread, so they brought you here."

That was sensible, and Aelvina relaxed. Illness spread, that she knew. It was how her parents had died. She could remember the great terror spreading through the army camp when victims of plague staggered from their dying towns in search of aid. People were terrified of the fever, and she could not blame them for sending her away. But then . . . if Thyllda was not here too, did that mean . . . ? It did not bear thinking. Wordlessly, she accepted the soup offered and ate. Afterward, she returned to her pleasant oblivion.

As the drug's effect gradually became less potent, the empty days opened with naught to fill them but questions. There was no urgency to them, only a wondering curiosity. A strange torpor shielded her from the nagging unease at the back of her mind.

Aelvina quiescently fell into the routine of Marta's day, helping gather the wood outside the cave hovel, stirring the boiling cauldron, feeding the fire, occasionally aiding in the kneading and mixing of herbs and potions at Marta's direction. Sometimes memories intruded upon this torpor. The painful ones she shoved aside for later, when she was stronger. But there were other ones: the laughing crinkle of emerald eyes, the pleasant scent of horses and male musk, the strength of warm arms holding her lovingly. They were strange memories, not linked to the past, and she eagerly sought them, reliving those few hours of joy in a man's arms.

She had learned not to question Marta too directly, but to slide her wonderings into the conversation and hope for some reaction. One day Aelvina casually mentioned the name associated with those emerald eyes and was rewarded by the suspicious stiffening of Marta's wrinkled visage.

"I do not know the man," was all the reply she received.

Aelvina tried again over the next days, attacking from every angle, but Marta would not admit a man of such name existed. The only satisfactory reply she received was Marta's admission that the memory could be part of a feverish dream. People had strange dreams when fevered.

Aelvina allowed the possibility to simmer in the back of her mind. If this man did not exist, if he was only some strange phantom of her fever, then the uneasy memories tugging at her were only parts of some nightmare, too.

As she worked, she cautiously explored those pain-ridden moments of horror, the chanting voices, the lustful battering, the terrible blankness of emerald eyes. They were excruciatingly real, but steeped in a heavy fog of darkness. It had to have been a nightmare.

But at the same time, she could not dismiss the face of Philippe St. Aubyn as a figment of her imagination. Those dark, scarred features and laughing eyes could not be the workings of a fevered brain. Now she clearly remembered the meeting in the stable and the promise he had made. Had he not said he was a man of honor and that he would keep his word? Had her illness frightened him away? Why had he not come back for her? If Thyllda was truly lost to her as Marta claimed, could she not go to Sir Philippe for protection?

With this thought, Aelvina rapidly regained her strength. She suspected the sleepiness that overcame her with each meal and left her lifeless the remainder of the day, so she insisted on preparing and serving her own meals. Marta grudgingly surrendered the task, and Aelvina's wakefulness increased.

Now, when she walked into the forest surrounding the hovel, it was with new purpose. She daringly trod farther down the animal paths she discovered. If she was gone too long, Marta found her and led her back, but she gradually learned the distance she could travel and despaired of ever finding the forest's edge. It would be easy to run from Marta's halting gait, but to where would she run? Marta was her only security. Why had Sir Philippe not come for her?

One humid afternoon, Aelvina almost imagined she heard the sounds of men and horses somewhere within the forest's reaches. She cried out, eager for some meeting with the outside world, and was rewarded with the sounds of advancing footsteps. With joy, she cried out again, and almost thought she heard her name repeated in reply. Before she could run in the direction of the sound, Marta appeared and tried to lead her away, muttering words of madness. Aelvina fought her off, desperate for contact with the tantalizing familiarity of that voice, but a sudden darkness filled her eyes and a suffocating odor filled her nostrils. The blackness of oblivion overcame her senses. When she awoke, she lay on the forest path and there was silence again.

At last, badgered by Aelvina's persistent questioning and increasing wandering, Marta agreed to show her the way to the castle gates. There were no paths or guides to follow, but the old woman unerringly wove her way through the forest's corridors. It took hours, and Aelvina felt her newly regained strength draining before they even reached sight of the towering stockade walls.

What she had hoped to gain by this journey, she did not know. The guards did not question them as they drifted through the open gate to the sleepy, dusty outer bailey. There were no prancing horses, no mounted knights or surly page boys, no portly monks, no tents, no army; only a few scrawny chickens and curious passersby could be seen.

Aelvina remembered none of the people she questioned. Nobody remembered her or Thyllda. At the mention of Sir Philippe, they eyed her askance, glanced questioningly at Marta, and drifted away. It did not matter. He was not here. Perhaps he did not exist.

With aching footsteps, Aelvina dragged herself home. Home—a filthy hovel of a cavern buried in a hillside of trees. There seemed nowhere else to turn. She had no stomach for asking after the Lady Ravenna and no desire to stay at Dunstan Castle. She had felt the evil of that place before, and the horror of it did not lessen with her nightmares. Marta's hovel seemed the only alternative.

Aelvina knew she still was not thinking clearly, but blamed it on the sleeping potion she had been fed for so long. With time, she would be back to normal and could think for herself. She still did not have the strength that had once carried her through miles and hours each day. Her body felt strangely heavy and languid, craving rest and food more frequently than in the past. It would be well to wait until she returned to normal before making plans to escape.

Summer became autumn almost overnight. One morn-

ing Aelvina woke to find her breath smoking the air and
the ground covered with the fine white crust of the first
frost. The amount of wood needed to tend the fire doubled.

By midday, the weather had warmed and her exertions
in tending the fire had caused perspiration to streak down
her face and dampen her hair. Marta had no tub for bathing and until now, Aelvina had satisfied her need for cleanliness by washing in a nearby stream. With the weather
cooling, this would not be practical, and she sought an
alternative.

With malicious satisfaction, she noted the size of the
heavy iron cauldron continually bubbling over the fire. It
was not of a size sufficient for bathing, but it would hold
a goodly amount of warm water. A warm bath on a cold
morning would be infinitely more pleasing than a cold
one, even if it was only a sponge bath.

Emptying the contents of the cauldron into every con-
ceivable container in the cave, Aelvina replaced it with
fresh water from the stream. When the water was sufficiently warm, she stripped to the skin, casting aside the
filthy rags that served her as clothing. She wondered what
had become of the exotic garments that had been her only
inheritance, but she had developed an aversion to the
dance that had once pleased her and did not let the
thoughts linger. Now, her only intention was to boil the
rags clean of vermin after she finished her ablutions.

Marta walked in just as Aelvina rinsed the goosefat soap
from her hair. Marta's hissing intake of breath caused
Aelvina to turn, emphasizing the silhouette of full breasts
and rounded belly.

Instead of expressing dismay, the wizened visage nodded
approvingly, and sharp dark eyes appraised the form so
outlined. "You are carrying low. A sure sign of a boy. That

is good." Without any seeming awareness of the astonishment rising up from the silent nude figure at the fire, Marta helped herself to a bowl of cooling stew and retired to a far corner.

Aelvina lowered her arms from the process of disentangling her hair, letting the heavy weight fall loosely about her shoulders as her fingers traced the outline of her breasts and abdomen. A new round fullness had replaced the childishly pert bosom of the spring, and her once concave belly was now distended and already burgeoning toward the pear-shaped figure of childbearing. Horror gripped her, and she could do no more than stare down at this reality of her nightmare. The unformed infant fluttered restlessly within her, as if confirming its existence.

A child! How could she be bearing the child of a nightmare? In fear, Aelvina explored the distended hardness of her belly, her fingers wandering down to the juncture of her thighs where Philippe's seed had flowed so warmly. She was well versed in the physical aspects of breeding, knew why a ram mounted a ewe and the result, and had no doubt of what had happened to her. At the time she had given herself, she had given little thought to possible consequences, knowing many women went childless for years and not suspecting the possibility of breeding in just one afternoon. But that was not where her fear lay.

Suddenly chilled, Aelvina grabbed the ancient coverlet of her bed, hiding her nakedness while automatically carrying out her original intention of boiling her clothes. The prosaic process of keeping clean was reassuring, and she gradually bent her mind to the task, shedding the unpleasant until she had time to herself, away from Marta's inquisitive gaze.

Aelvina continued to fight off the chill of her mind and body and soul as she listened to the old woman's heavy breathing in the still of the night. She no longer had any doubt that she was growing with child, but the fearfulness of her nightmare left her shaken. She remembered well the dark Norman who had bedded her so thoroughly, and if it was truly his seed growing within her, she had no cause for alarm. It was unexpected and undesired, but not unnatural. But the memory of that moonlit madness when her body had been possessed and battered to the chanting encouragement of unseen observers . . .

Aelvina shuddered. The man of that nightmare had possessed the form of a Norman knight but the soul of a devil. She had seen it in his eyes, and her thoughts grew sick with horror. What manner of beast could she be harboring within her womb?

As the autumn days grew colder and the first shock of disbelief wore off, Aelvina succumbed to a strange contentment with this new development. The child developed an identity of its own, at first fluttering in agreement with her thoughts, then kicking euphorically when she least expected it. The babe was hers—a part of her body—and she was no longer alone. She would soon have a family again, and her heart thrilled with the idea.

She gave no further thought to the child's father. Sir Philippe had promised his protection and reneged on the agreement. He had bedded her, drunk too much at dinner, woke with aching head the next morning, and departed without further thought to the servant who had provided his body with a moment's pleasure. She spared him no further thought—except at night, when her body woke, afire with the memory of his searing kisses.

Winter came, and brought with it an increasing clumsiness in her movements and a need to rest more frequently that kept her from straying far. Marta took over the task of wood gathering, and in return, Aelvina grew more proficient at the task of mixing potions and herbs.

In Marta's absence, she studied the ancient tomes, in runes and Latin, that rested upon one shelf. Her mother had taught her to read Latin verse, so she had a rudimentary understanding of the knowledge in the texts after the first perusals. They told of the medicinal properties of various herbs. The formula for the sleeping elixir was in there, along with the formulas to prevent or encourage childbirth, to summon or kill love, and many other remedies for all varieties of human ills.

The Latin passed the boredom of lonely hours, but the other tome, in ancient runes, presented a more intriguing and fearsome puzzle. Her father had taught her the meaning of the ancient runes on giant stones such as she had seen in her nightmare. Some of those same configurations were here, in this crumbling volume, and their conjunction made her shiver. Aelvina hastily placed this book on the shelf at the sound of Marta's return and began to look at her keeper through different eyes.

Until now Aelvina had not considered herself a prisoner or looked upon her ancient companion as a warden. It had always seemed escape would be easy but, with nowhere to go, not desirable. Now Aelvina began to realize her listlessness had been deliberately induced by herbs and potions in the foods she ate, and that the drugs were a more effective prison than any wall could make.

Not that this discovery availed her of much now. She was no longer drugged, but the advanced state of her pregnancy left her little strength for searching miles of forest for human habitation. January snows piled up outside the hovel's well-hidden door, making travel nigh on to impossible. She was well and thoroughly trapped for the moment, but once the child was born, it would be another matter.

With these thoughts to carry her through the misery of lonely winter days, Aelvina set about the task of learning all she could from her captor. It was now apparent that Marta was sought as physician and witch. How effective her remedies were could only be guessed, but Aelvina sought to gain this knowledge, which was greater than her own. It kept her mind occupied and away from the plight of her body.

As the winter snows began to melt, Aelvina's burden lowered and the tasks of sitting and standing became intolerable. The child kicked less frantically now, gathering strength for its emergence. Her dreams were haunted by mocking emerald eyes and a dark, scarred face, and prayers did little to drive the specter away.

March thaws left the forest paths muddy but traversable. Unable to bear the filthy interior of the cave any longer, Aelvina set out to explore the first signs of returning spring. As if life was returning to her for the first time in many months, she drank deeply of the healthy, ripening smells of vegetation. She dragged the old comforter around her shoulders and used it as protection as she waddled to a clearing where snow drops bloomed.

The startling sound of branches crackling beneath heavy feet woke her from her reverie. She glanced up, disconcerted by the sight of a monk's gray robes behind a hedge of tangled thorns. The figure apparently caught sight of her at the same time, and came to a standstill.

Embarrassment flooded her cheeks as Aelvina recognized the portly figure of the Cistercian monk, and from his startled reaction, she realized he recognized her. Here, then, was no dream. She turned to run, but the monk's sonorous tones halted her.

"Wait, my child. I mean you no harm."

She turned slowly, hugging the comforter to her swollen shape and fearfully watching this specter from the past.

The hedge of thorns prevented the monk from coming closer. "What art thou doing so far from the castle?"

Aelvina stared at him blankly, unable to piece together her scattered thoughts. "The castle? That is not my home. Why should I be there?"

With infinite patience at this witlessness, the monk tried again. "Do you live here in the woods then? How can you have survived the winter?"

"Marta brings me food." Her own fate had no importance at the moment. This link to the past would bring other news, and she searched for the questions she needed to ask. They were unladylike, but she had ceased to be a lady nearly nine months before. "Sir Philippe—has he returned to Normandy?"

The monk's eyes darkened, whether with sympathy or some other emotion, she could not tell. "He is in London, in the king's service. Henry has ordered the destruction of all unauthorized keeps, and Sir Philippe awaits his orders on which have defied the edict." Hooded eyes moved slowly to the obvious shape of her belly beneath the comforter. "The child—it is his?"

His words were more a statement than a question, and Aelvina looked away from his piercing stare. "The child is mine. I implore you, do not speak of this to him."

"He would want to know this. It is his duty to see to the child's care."

Anger rose in her at the thought of the Norman stranger interfering in her life once more. Let the arrogant knight go his own way as was his wont; she had no need of his charity.

"The child is mine. I need no man's help. I only asked

after him because of a promise he once made. He promised to look after a friend of mine, Thyllda. I had hoped to hear some word of her last days. Was she comfortable? Do you know?''

"There was an old woman in the keep he spoke with frequently. I was not aware of her death, nor was Sir Philippe, I am certain. If you would tell me how you can be found again, I will find out more of her, if you wish.''

Hope briefly flickered in Aelvina's heart, then disappeared. "I do not know how much longer I will be here. My time is almost due and I must leave as soon as I am able after the child's birth.''

"I am on my way to Sir Philippe now. He is expecting me, but I will return as quickly as I can. Tell me where you stay. The child will need baptizing and I can do that for you.''

Although she was suspicious of the monk's insistence on knowing her whereabouts, Aelvina acceded to his request to be present at the child's baptism. She had given little thought to such niceties, but this man knew her plight and would not question the child's lack of a father. It would also be good to know if Thyllda rested in peace. She relented, slightly.

"There is a hill not far from here. Behind a thorny shrub at the west side of this hill there is an oaken door. You will find me there. I do not think I will be able to travel far this next fortnight. But, I pray you, do not reveal me to Sir Philippe. I have no more need of broken promises.''

"Sir Philippe has other problems on his mind at the moment, but even so, he should know of his child's birth.''

"I would deny his fatherhood,'' Aelvina declared proudly, tilting her chin. "I have only one thing in this world to call my own and I will take no chance of losing it. Sir Philippe will not be pleased to hear of his bastard; you would do him no favor by declaring it.''

The monk sighed and accepted defeat on this point, but there was one other she had overlooked and he took care to avoid mentioning it. She had asked that the child and her hiding place not be revealed, but did not mention herself. He could not prevent Sir Philippe from following if he should be so inclined upon learning the girl truly existed. There had seemed some doubt on that point, but her existence could not be denied any longer. Moreover, there could scarcely be any question about fatherhood if he counted his days right, and he had reason to know he had.

''I shall try to return within the fortnight, then. Is there anything else I can do for you? You will be safe until then?''

Aelvina offered him the first hint of a shy smile. Nine months with no other human voice but Marta's—it was good to know the outside world had not entirely forgotten her.

''I will be safe. I need nothing, but would be grateful for your return to baptize the child. I only wish I had something to offer you for your trouble.''

''Your smile is sufficient, my child. In peace, then, until I return.''

And he was gone, leaving Aelvina with the reassurance that her child's soul would not be endangered, but stirring an uneasiness of another nature. The knowledge that Sir Philippe not only existed, but was still within this area, did not set easily upon her shoulders.

Aelvina shivered and hurried back to the cave, remembering the dark knight's fearsome gaze as he proclaimed her his vassal.

The contractions began in the late afternoon, several days later. Marta had kept close watch over her since Aelvina's meeting with the monk, and had given her no further opportunities to walk the forest paths. Aelvina couldn't conceal her spasm of pain now.

She took little notice as Marta disappeared out the door into the lowering light of late afternoon. The heavy weight pressing down upon her insides these last days had drained her strength, and this pain clutching at her belly seemed only the natural response to such a burden. She sat before the fire, staring into the flickering flames with an aching vacancy she could not name.

When the pains intensified, she finally understood what was happening to her. In awe, she stared down at the vast expanse of her contracting abdomen, and then in fear, she glanced around the room, searching for Marta.

The door blew open, flinging in the frail crone and her armload of wood and the first snowflakes of a March storm. Aelvina relaxed as the old woman efficiently began the familiar preparations for childbirth: stoking fires, heating water, and laying out linens. She was in the hands of an experienced midwife. She could ask for no more at a time like this, except for a husband whose hand she might grip for strength, but that thought was dismissed at once. Since the death of her parents she had known that she was not destined to have a husband. It was good that she could still have a child of her own to love.

At first, Aelvina refused the cups of liquid Marta offered to ease the pains. She wanted no more of the woman's witchcraft or medicinal herbs. The pains were price enough for the joy they would soon produce. She eased her aching position in the strange contrivance Marta had produced for her. The hard wood back held her partially upright and the wide arms gave her something to grip when the contractions rolled over her. The chair seat only gave room for her thighs to rest, but she understood its purpose. She groaned and strained to shove the babe from her body into the opening, where Marta's experienced hands waited to aid it into the world.

As the hours rolled by and the pains increased in violence without any results, Aelvina had no strength left to resist Marta's ministrations. At first she poured the warm liquid through her clenched teeth. Then, as the drug had its effect and her body relaxed, she swallowed obediently, slipping into that welcome oblivion of darkness that tolerated no pain. Her body continued to strain and heave below her, the pains very real but not touching that part of her which floated in a drug-induced haze.

The ripping, tearing pain of her opening body jerked Aelvina briefly back to reality. Her cries split the night air, punctuated by the leaping flames of the firelight in the cave's darkness before falling silent again beneath the drug's spell.

Into the silence crept the tiny wail of a new, living creature, and even in her drugged state, Aelvina's heart leapt with joy. She attempted to reach for the babe, but her arms would not move. With a greedy gaze, she watched as Marta lifted the child to the light, his tiny red fists clenched, his wide shoulders thrown back for a squall, and his thick thatch of silver-gold hair sparkling in the firelight. Her son.

As she drifted back toward the blackness that beckoned her, a sudden pounding at the oaken door jarred Aelvina into the room again. Marta did not seem the least bit startled by the sound, continuing to wrap the child in its swaddling clothes and drawing the length of an old mantle around it for warmth.

Without a further glance at the torn and bleeding figure in the birthing chair whose life's blood slowly drained into a pool on the dirt floor, Marta flung open the heavy door, the wailing babe in one arm. A gust of wind drove the mounting snow across the room, flinging a burst of flame to light the stone walls and chilling the half-naked form in the room's center.

As Aelvina watched, Marta threw a mantle about herself and the babe and stepped into the night. In drained horror, Aelvina screamed after the departing figures, screamed as the arctic wind blew the heavy door wide with its icy blade, and screamed again as the blackness encompassed her mind one final time.

And then there was silence. Only the low moaning of the wind as it sought the far corners of the cavern and teased at the dying fire could be discerned in the silence.

Chapter Six

Cold . . . cold reminding her of a night she lay strapped helplessly while her body was battered and abused, as it felt now. Her arms . . . Where were her arms?

Thundering, aching minutes later, she forced an arm into motion. It wasn't tied. Momentary relief swept through her, giving her strength to pull farther from the darkness.

The cold was worse—much, much worse than she had ever remembered. The darkness beckoned, but some tiny fragment of her mind screamed to ignore it, to wake, to get up from here. She obeyed, trusting the scream.

Her whole body ached when moved. Her limbs had no strength. The cold was punishing; the blackness so much easier. But a gust of icy wind swept a hole in the clouds of darkness, and she remembered.

Her son! They had stolen her son! Rage tore through her body, heating her veins, giving strength to frozen muscles. She must find her son! He was all she had. He was part of her body. She would move mountains if necessary.

Aelvina swayed as she rose from the chair. Her toes and fingers were numb. She didn't notice. Only one thought blazed across her brain, driving her on. She stumbled across the comforter blown from the bed in the gales of the storm. It would serve her now, and she gathered it around her shivering body, oblivious to the matted blood clinging to tunic and bare legs, or to the slow trickle reawakened by her movement.

The door lay open, revealing a world of pristine whiteness. The sun sent a crisscross pattern of shadows through the bare branches overhead. The woolen cloths wrapped about thin soles and ankles were quickly soaked in the wet snow. Aelvina didn't notice.

It was imperative to keep moving, but she had no direction. The snow lay unbroken except for animal tracks. She moved anyway. Somewhere out in that wide world an evil woman held her son and she must find him. She bore east, toward the rising sun, vaguely remembering the direction taken one day toward the castle.

Her legs refused to move through the thick snow for very long. The comforter grew wet and formed a heavy weight about her shoulders, dragging her down. She crawled, dragging herself along and disturbing the rabbits who nibbled at tender tree shoots. She forgot where she was going or why, but kept moving.

She must have help. If she could tell someone . . . Sir Philippe. A king's knight could do anything. He would save their son, even if he did not come for her.

She prayed, mumbling incoherent words as she grasped a twig and dragged herself another inch or two. Someone must come. Where was the monk? Thyllda . . . She prayed to Thyllda, who art in heaven . . .

Senseless sounds tore from her throat. Her body was a block of ice, frozen to the snow, no longer able to reach forward for the next twig or stone. A shudder shook her frame. And another. And then the scream dissipated and the cloud banks drifted in again.

Warmth woke her. Sweat poured down her face, drenching the heavy wool binding her. She struggled to disentangle herself, fighting off the heat that pressed her downward.

A fire crackled, as a shadow passed in front of it; Aelvina tried to scream objections, but only issued low moans. The shadow rested a cool hand against her fevered brow, and her weakened struggles ceased.

It wasn't an easy rest. She persistently fought against it. Sometimes her own screams woke her, and she would tear at the hands holding her, pleading for what was lost. She fought against the blankets that weighed her down. Strong hands held her still, and soothing words made promises that eased her screams until she rested again.

Aelvina woke, the ache in her chest gone, but the ache in her heart despairing. Nothing existed inside her any longer, and she had no strength with which to regain it.

She made no noise, but a slight figure wrapped her fingers in small, bony ones. Aelvina continued to weep, unable to control the black despair. The small woman at her bedside held her hand and let her cry.

At last, when the tears ran dry and her soul was too weary to care, Aelvina looked up and stared into familiar lines of wisdom and gentleness.

"Thyllda . . ." With wonderment, Aelvina gazed into that loved face for just one moment; then weary, her eyes closed and she slept.

When next she woke, Thyllda brought her a cup of strong broth and helped her hold it as she drank. Aelvina drank it, grateful for Thyllda's silence while she gathered her wits. How had she come here? Had it all been some dreadful dream?

The thatched hut was neither the dark cave she remembered nor the tent that had protected them on their journeys. There were no windows, only the wooden door that now swung open, letting in fresh, warm air. An unvented fire burned merrily in the center of the earthen floor, and a tripod with a kettle warmed over it. It was a crude cottage—the sort they had occasionally found shelter in from friendly villagers on the road.

Her gaze shifted back to the open door. The sunlight pouring in told her of warm spring days and, puzzled, she tried to remember the end of winter. All she could remember was the reality of her nightmare, and involuntarily, her hand covered her flat belly. She had not dreamed the child. She knew that as certainly as she knew the face beside her was Thyllda's, though Thyllda was supposed to be dead. Too tired to puzzle out this problem, she returned the empty cup to her companion.

"Thank you," she whispered, then turned her head and slept.

Nighttime returned her hunger and she woke once more. The broth she had supped on gave her strength to summon Thyllda. This time, Aelvina's mind was clear, and she cried out urgently, "My son? Have you found my babe?"

Thyllda halted, her lined face crumpling with anxiety, and she turned to the second figure in the room.

A shadow stepped from the far corner—a substantial shadow with broad shoulders and a thick chest and an almost rolling gait. In the fire's light, his short-cropped hair gleamed gold, and steady blue eyes crinkled with concern.

Aelvina appealed to them both, her voice a bare whisper over the fire's sputter. "Did you find my son?"

"Child, you are ill. You must not worry yourself so. We are looking. Gundulf knows the forests better than any man. Rest yourself, and let me bring you some broth."

Aelvina's gaze swept from the servant to the yeoman, for that was surely what he must be. His body seemed too great for the short tunic and heavy peasant leggings he wore, yet he moved gently as he knelt beside the low bed. His height was not much greater than average, but he was sturdily built.

"You are Gundulf?" At his nod, she whispered hoarsely, "Do you know where to seek my son?"

"I am sorry. I did not know to look until I brought you here. When the women told me you had recently borne a child, I went back, but the snows were already melting. I followed your path as best I could, but it came from nowhere. I could find no babe, though I have searched these past many weeks or more."

"The witch has him. Find Marta, and you will find my son."

From one so obviously frail and weak, the words were astonishingly firm. Two pairs of eyes met Aelvina's gaze before turning to each other at this mention of the Lady Ravenna's servant.

Thyllda stepped forward, offering a steaming cup of broth. "Marta has been within the castle keep throughout the winter. She has no child that we have heard of." Yet her gaze faltered and returned to Gundulf's even as she said the words.

Aelvina failed to notice. Her eyelids fluttered closed at this death knell for her hopes. What had Marta done with her son? The witch had pampered and protected her for some purpose; it was obvious the child was her interest, since she had left Aelvina to die. Surely she had not gone to such great lengths only to kill the child also? Aelvina's heart rebelled against such thoughts. The child lived—she knew it did. She must get well enough to find him herself.

She opened her eyes again and stretched out her hand. "Give me the cup, Thyllda."

Relief and joy lit the faces of the two people beside her, but only one consuming passion ruled Aelvina's thoughts. That she would not die might give pleasure to some, but it would surely wreak wrath and havoc among others. This she solemnly vowed.

It took longer than Aelvina expected to regain her strength. She had been snatched from the icy hands of Death, pried loose from its grip with love and devotion, but the devastation to her body was thorough. As she rested, Aelvina drew out the story of her rescue and Thyllda's miraculous return from the dead.

Thyllda's miracle was not so extraordinary as Aelvina's own. The older woman had been well on the way to recovery at the time of Aelvina's disappearance, and had grown so frantic with worry that she had risen from her bed within the week to search for her. Marta had lied about the sickness.

When she had learned that already no stone remained uncovered, Thyllda had left the keep on her own, selling the oxen and wagon for a price sufficient to find a place in the village while she awaited word of Aelvina's discovery. With winter's coming, she had given up all hope until the day Gundulf returned with his frozen burden.

At this point in the tale, Thyllda turned to the silent yeoman, and Aelvina had to plead with him for further enlightenment. After many tellings, Aelvina gradually learned how much she owed to the stalwart young man.

He had been out seeking firewood and checking his traps for catches to feed his mother's kettle. The lack of game had led him farther than usual into the castle's woods. His wanderings had taken him across a strangely marked path, as of a body being dragged, and the reddish stains in the snow had raised his suspicions. Another man might have sniffed danger and fled, but fear had never entered Gundulf's mind. His one thought was to help. His astonishment at discovering the bundle of rags at the path's end had been great.

Gundulf spoke lightly of his feat, but Aelvina knew it for the selflessness it was. But though Aelvina felt gratitude for his rescue, she had no room in her heart for more, and she met Gundulf's tender looks with only sisterly affection.

To Aelvina's surprise, Thyllda also kept a distance between her patient and the obviously devoted youth.

Aelvina noted this, but did not care. Each day she forced herself longer from the confines of bed. She needed the breath returned to her lungs and the strength to her legs if she was to find Marta's home and confront the witch with her misdeeds.

Her fingers curled around the slender knife safely hidden within her girdle. Thyllda had kept what clothes of Aelvina's she could find in the castle, and the knife had been among them. The silken blue dancing costume and the golden ring she had worn that night were assumed lost. It did not matter. She no longer needed blue silk or gold rings, but the finely wrought dagger was a man's weapon not easy to come by, and she clutched it carefully. Witchcraft could not hold out against cold steel.

Thyllda protested Aelvina's ventures into the outskirts of the forest separating village from Dunstan Castle. To Aelvina, the only thing of importance was to locate Marta's hovel and wait for her return. To Thyllda, it was pure madness.

"Child, you cannot go on like this. The babe is gone. You must think of yourself now. If Marta left you for dead once, she will most certainly kill you now if she learns you live. Evelyn, my own, hear me!"

Thyllda begged, but Aelvina refused to listen. She heard the words, and she knew Thyllda spoke wisely, as usual. Infants did not often survive harsh winters or the first year of life. An infant without his mother's milk to protect him, carried out into a raging storm before he scarcely took his first breath, had small chance of survival. But Aelvina refused to listen to common sense. The child lived.

She did give in to Thyllda's urgings to wait until Gundulf could accompany her on the forest walks. For Gundulf's sake, his family smilingly indulged Aelvina's fancies, even though they considered her determination a type of madness.

Eventually, Aelvina despaired as the days grew longer and their searches carried them deeper into the forest and the place forever eluded them. The hillside hovel was never where she remembered it. Gundulf, too, could not be certain if it was one particular oak under which he found her, or another, some miles distant. The forest changed disguises with the seasons, and nothing remained the same.

Each day that passed, Aelvina's thoughts turned more grimly to the monstrous keep looming over her life. Marta served the lady of that castle. It was in that cold fortress her child had been conceived. If she must, it was to Dunstan Castle she would go in search of the witch who had stolen her child and left her for dead. It was a foolhardy thing to do, and meant almost certain death if Marta was the first to see her, but all other hopes rapidly dwindled.

She grimly contemplated this future as she stirred the kettle one sunny morning, and scarcely noticed the crowd filling the street outside. Only Thyllda's greeting to Gundulf's mother awoke Aelvina from her reverie. As the two women chattered over some subject of no interest to Aelvina, she drifted to the open door to see what excitement stirred outside.

Women and children and the aged gathered along the dusty rutted road, waving hats and scarves and colorful rags in welcome to some riders still in the distance. With curiosity, Aelvina lounged against the doorway, wondering what noble personage deserved this reception. Her dun-colored tunic blended into the shadows, and her hair caught no sun beneath the darkened doorway. She was safe from sight and with impunity could watch the world go by.

That did not prevent her from gasping and retreating to the cottage's interior at first sight of the tall knight leading the procession. His mailed armor glittered in the sun's light, his wine-red tunic fell in graceful folds over broad shoulders and powerful chest, and the dark mantle slung royally over one shoulder proclaimed his rank. But his dark face was cold and tight and his emerald eyes glared straight ahead as he sat astride his massive destrier, looking neither left nor right.

The color drained from Aelvina's face, and her heart set up an erratic rhythm no amount of common sense could cure. Memories of those strong arms holding her close, of the feel of that muscular chest beneath her palms, of the sensations stirred by those green eyes as they looked upon her were best forgotten. Aelvina clutched the doorsill, feeling her knees weaken as his mount passed not three feet from where she stood.

Only after she tore her eyes from the back of Philippe's head did she notice the second figure in that procession, and the world swirled and grew still at the sight of the black-garbed, bejeweled woman on the black palfrey. The Lady Ravenna rode proudly second to Sir Philippe, her long black plaits entwined with silken ribbons and glittering with gems, her face covered lightly by a thin veil.

Thyllda threw a hasty glance to the cause of the commotion outside and bit her lips with frustration as Gundulf's mother helped Aelvina to a seat.

"She has been overworking herself again. I told Gundulf she was much too pale to be out in the fields, and now look at her. She will be back in bed again if she does not take care."

Gundulf's mother waddled back to the doorway to watch the end of the procession, keeping up a lively chatter as she did. "The Lady Ravenna certainly made a proud match in Sir Philippe, though what he sees in that skinny bitch besides her lands, I cannot imagine. They say her last husband was ready to cast her off for barrenness. Lucky for her that he died, or she'd not have caught so fine a man the second time. Not wed a year and churched already." She shook her head knowingly.

Thyllda muttered a few choice words beneath her breath at the other woman's ignorant ramblings, but Aelvina scarcely heard anything beyond the word "match." Sir Philippe married to Lady Ravenna! It was incredible. It made no sense. Surely he could have his choice of women. And why would the lady settle for a match she had worked so hard to avert?

Aelvina's head spun and she rested it on her arms, folding them on the table. The shock of seeing Philippe again—live and in flesh and blood—had set too many nerve endings atingle. She had not thought it possible to hate one man as much as she hated him. No wonder he had not come looking for her and had offered Thyllda no protection. He had been busy feathering his nest with ill-gotten lands. *May the curse of God be on his twice-damned head . . . and on that thing between his legs, also!*

She laughed sharply at her obscene thoughts and stood up abruptly. "I am going for a walk," she announced. Ignoring Thyllda's protests, Aelvina strode out the door.

It took a while to untangle her thoughts as she trod blindly down the cool forest paths. Somewhere, in the back of her mind, had been the hope that she could turn to Sir Philippe when all else failed. She had no desire to tell him of their son, but if it meant saving the child from Marta she would do it for the child's sake. Only now, the chance of Sir Philippe even listening to her was very remote, indeed. If Marta chose to hide the child, and the Lady Ravenna protected her, why should Sir Philippe side against his wife?

It was with Marta she must deal, then. The keep and its inhabitants were beyond her reach, but sooner or later, Marta must come out of hiding.

Aelvina shoved aside memories of laughing green eyes, a rumbling voice, and caressing hands. Images of those bronzed arms holding the skinny Lady Ravenna were too revolting to last long, but she used them to bolster her determination. He deserved his fate, but not his son.

While Aelvina pondered these uncomfortable thoughts, Gundulf was with Thyllda, and his thoughts were no less miserable.

"You are certain Sir Philippe is the father?" He had never questioned the child's parentage; it had not seemed his place to do so. Still, the thought that Aelvina had been looked upon by a nobleman had not occurred to him.

"If I had any doubts before, this morning removed them. Once given, the loyalty of a Fairfax is unalterable. They are doomed to love only once in a lifetime, and once chosen, never choose again. I fear Aelvina has chosen, whether she realizes it or not."

The mention of Aelvina's surname drained Gundulf's ruddy face to gray. The remainder of her words stiffened his shoulders. "Fairfax?" he questioned tightly, searching the old woman's face closely, uncertain if madness might not be contagious.

Thyllda nodded.

"Returned here?" It was too incredible to believe, and Gundulf strove to keep the awe from his voice.

They were still deep in talk when Aelvina returned, but she did not notice. They quickly ended the conversation and Gundulf departed, without the tender farewell he usually bestowed upon her. Aelvina felt the lack, but did not question it.

The next time they walked the forest paths, Gundulf kept his distance, treating her with deference but centering his attention on the game he meant to catch.

She stopped to gather a wild herb and add it to the growing collection in the pouch on her girdle. Marta and her books had taught her much, or the dream had. She had already tried some of the remedies and found them satisfactory. It gave her something to do while she wandered through this enchanted forest.

Gundulf stopped to examine an animal track, but Aelvina continued on, knowing his ability to locate her when he chose. This part of the forest seemed denser, less familiar. Perhaps they had just not intruded far enough before. Eagerly, she quickened her step. Over that next hill, perhaps . . .

A thrashing of leaves like a deer bolting caught her attention. She continued on more warily, for the stirring did not diminish. Instead, it seemed to be coming straight toward her.

Alarmed now, Aelvina stood still, searching for the direction of the noise, afraid she would run directly into the path of whatever animal was rampaging through the trees. The sound came from all around her at once, growing louder and more terrifying. The trampling of a thousand feet could not be more horrifying, and her voice caught in her throat.

The first furious snorts through the underbrush warned her too late. Before she could search for a tree to climb, the wild boar raged from the bushes, into the clearing where Aelvina stood with only the dagger in her girdle for protection. The huge, fiery-eyed boar snorted his fury as the blood poured from a wound above his ear.

Aelvina quit breathing, terrified any movement would draw the animal's notice. Her fingers wrapped about the dagger's handle, but what good would it do against a beast of such weight? She had come too close to death to wish to die now.

Her screams split the gloom of the forest as the animal charged. She ran, dodging behind a tree, briars snatching at her tunic while branches slapped her face and hands. She needed a low limb on which to pull herself up, but she could not look and keep her feet on the path at the same time. She screamed again, praying for help, praying the boar would find a more interesting victim, and knowing she could not possibly outrun the tremendous beast.

Her foot caught on a root and she went flying, all the

wind knocked from her lungs as she hit the hard ground. Dazed, she scrambled to pull her knees back under her.

The high-pitched squeal of the rampaging boar tore through the air as the forest floor thundered with mighty hoofs and coarse curses, diverting the wild pig from his prey. Aelvina pushed up from the ground, hoping to escape, but the ankle that had twisted under her gave a sharp twinge of pain, and she crumpled again. The boar gave one final squeal and fell silent.

Aelvina watched as a large knight dismounted and drew his lance from the boar's body not more than a few yards away. The smell of the dying animal's blood made her gag.

Fear was part of the nausea. Her ankle throbbed, and the rocks and twigs that had torn at her hands as she fell left jagged cuts rubbing in the dirt. These pains were of little moment, however, compared to the fear of discovery. Already, other mounted knights entered the clearing, and the one on foot advanced toward her.

With horror, Aelvina's gaze traveled over long, muscled legs, past the vast expanse of mailed chest and shoulders, to the unsmiling dark face with the scar jerking angrily over one prominent cheekbone. No compassion lit those gemlike eyes as they fastened upon her.

"So the sorceress of the forest has been brought down at last. Mayhap I should have waited a moment longer to see if witches bleed. Get up and face me, or will you use your powers to disappear again?"

Barely controlled fury shook his voice as he stood over her, refusing to lend a hand in aid.

"If I could do either, I would, milord," Aelvina replied, sarcasm masking her fear. She pulled herself to a sitting position, conscious of the jagged rent in her tunic, exposing the shabby chemise beneath, and of the leaves and twigs clinging to hair and clothes. Now that she had come face-to-face with the devil, she would not bow before him.

Philippe bent and, grabbing her beneath the arms, jerked her none too gently to her feet.

Aelvina winced and shifted her weight to one foot, not daring to meet his burning gaze, but scanning the small group of men behind him, hoping for a kindly face or some means of escape. The men returned her stare, some openly appraising, others guardedly blank. There was no escape there, and the tightening of leather-clad fingers at her sides told her there was little chance of escape.

"Thank you, milord." Her voice dripped sarcasm. "You have saved my life and I am not unappreciative, though it must have been the poor weaponry of one of your men that endangered me in the first place. If you will release me, I believe I can stand alone now."

"Release you!"

The words exploded from him, as if startled from some deep source, and unwillingly, Aelvina's gaze swept upward. Pain as well as fury marred his jaw, and she shivered at the inexplicable harshness of his voice.

"I'd sooner release Satan than let you go. You will pay for what you have done to me, and be lucky I do not tie you to the stake and have you flogged and burned for the witch thou art."

He caught her by the waist with one iron-thewed arm and was about to wrap the other about her knees when Aelvina screeched in fury and, catching him by surprise, shoved away. In a twinkling, the silver dagger glinted dangerously in her hand.

"I would rather die than have your hands on me again! Come catch me, brave knights. Drive your bloody lances through my heart! Am I not a worthy foe?"

She spat the words at them, inching painfully backward

while waving the dagger in Philippe's furious face. "Kill me, why don't you? You have made my life a misery; end it now, before I suffer the torments of the damned again!"

"Aelvina!"

The safe, sane, familiar voice of Gundulf drew her attention, and to her detriment, she turned at the sound. Philippe grabbed her from behind and wrenched the knife from her hand, throwing it beneath a tree.

Philippe's hold tightened as his gaze took in the newcomer. Aelvina kicked and tore at his imprisoning arm, but he took small notice of the hurts inflicted upon him as he studied the young yeoman with suspicion.

"Let her go." Gundulf's gaze steadily met his master's, his only weapon a stout staff.

"I will not. A disobedient vassal must be punished, and this one has escaped her fate too long." Philippe filled his hand with long silver plaits and jerked Aelvina's head up to face Gundulf. "Tell your paramour that you are ready to accept your punishment. Otherwise, he might find himself in the same position as you, though his punishment is more apt to be fatal than the one I have in mind for you."

The cold steadiness of Philippe's words chilled Aelvina's spine. She had no doubt he spoke the truth. She ceased struggling and met Gundulf's anguished gaze. She could not see him die for so unworthy a cause as herself.

"Take care of Thyllda for me, Gundulf." Tears sprang to her eyes as she read his face. The odds were overwhelming; he could not save her on his own.

Gundulf ignored her plea. "Let her go and punish me in her stead. Or give me a chance to defend her, one on one." He raised his stout limb in both hands, offering this challenge.

Aelvina groaned at this stupidity as she felt Philippe

tense with fury and take a step toward the upstart yeoman. She twisted in his grip, wrapping her fingers around the mail-clad arm imprisoning her. In frustration, she yelled at her defender.

"For mercy's sake, Gundulf! You have saved my life, but my virtue is beyond saving. Do not add your death to my burden also. Go! I entrust Thyllda to your care. You can at least do that much for me when others will not."

The barb hit its mark. Without another word, Philippe strode to his horse and, flinging his prisoner over the saddle like excess baggage, mounted behind her. With a gesture, he signaled his men to proceed, leaving the defenseless farmer to stand untouched in the clearing behind.

Having safely accomplished this one small duty, Aelvina fought the indignity of her position—cast across her captor's great horse like a sack of grain. She squirmed, seeking some footing that would either right her or free her.

Philippe's heavy hand caught in her girdle and dragged her upright, seating her between his thighs so that she was compelled to lean against his chest with her legs dangling over one side. Any attempt to struggle brought her intimately in contact with the hardness of his body. She fell still, holding herself as erect and free from his touch as humanly possible.

"You learn quickly," he muttered. "It will do you well to remember not to balk my power in the future. It will save you much grief."

His tone was ominous, but Aelvina was too furious to heed it. "I obeyed you before, and suffered enough grief to fill a lifetime. I am yours to command no longer."

Her bitterness scalded the ears. Philippe's fury mounted another notch. "I will not hear another word from you or I will throw you to my men now and teach you the wisdom of obedience even before I begin to exact my own punishment upon your tender hide.''

The meaning of his threat was clear, and the coldness of his tone told her that he meant what he said. Aelvina nervously eyed the half dozen or more well-built knights behind them and wisely kept silent. None looked directly at her, but she could well imagine the results should their leader offer her up for the taking. She did not think she could be so touched again. She prayed for death to strike her down now.

Death did not, but neither did Sir Philippe—not immediately, at least. As they marched westward into the setting sun, well past the hour of rest and refreshment, Aelvina succumbed to the need to close her eyes.

As she fell into exhausted slumber, a heavy, mail-clad arm held her in place against his steely chest, emerald eyes blazing in the darkness like green wildfire.

Chapter Seven

They stopped to rest once during the night. Sleepily, Aelvina took the wine flask offered and munched on a hunk of bread as the men watered their horses. Sir Philippe tended his own mount, but at no time was she left unguarded.

Aelvina understood only that the dark knight hated with an intensity to match her own, and thus she kept a wary eye on his movements. For the moment, his interest seemed only in his horses and men, and she relaxed slightly.

A short time later, he threw her rudely back in the saddle, and they raced down the road once more.

By morning, she was stiff and sore from the grueling ride, but Philippe seemed driven by some demon as they came in view of the camp.

The silken tents spread far and wide across a swath of land in full view of a vast keep, its wide moat separating

camp from castle. Dazedly, Aelvina looked at the morning
sun throwing its rosy hues across the billowing tents and
flapping flags, and thought how much like a fairy-tale world
it looked. Her father had inhabited such a world, and she
knew it to be a filthy, unwholesome life, but for just this
moment it was like coming home.

The horses raced among the awakening inhabitants,
throwing up clouds of dust and stirring vile curses as they
charged through the camp's center. As his men galloped
by, Philippe pulled his mount to a halt in front of a tent
larger than the others and bearing more banners. Its rear
backed against the forest they had just left, and its flap
opened to overlook the camp scattered down the hillside.
Its owner could see at a glance not only what went on
among his own men, but for as far as the castle keep.

Philippe dismounted, dragging Aelvina from the saddle
and carrying her like an unwieldy pack through the tent's
opening. He carelessly tossed her in the midst of the heaps
of pillows and furs that made his bed and stalked out again
without a word.

Too tired to protest, Aelvina lay where she had been
thrown and listened to the rumbling of low voices outside
the flap . . . posting a guard, she thought wearily. What
more could she expect? Exhaustion overcame any
remaining anger or fear, and curling into the luxurious
softness of the bed, she slept.

She woke again when Philippe dropped down beside
her, his heavy weight disturbing the pillows on which she
lay. Squeezing her eyes closed, she breathed evenly in a
pretense of sleep, and bit back a sigh of relief when Philippe did no more than roll over and make himself comfortable.

Not until his heavy breathing told her he slept did she
dare to open her lashes and study the man she had known

so briefly and so disastrously. The dark face seemed more haggard than she remembered, and thin lips set in a tight line even in sleep. With those blazing emerald eyes shut, long lashes softened his chiseled features, but that was his only redeeming softness.

The hard planes of his bare chest covered in its rough mat of black curls remained as massive as she remembered. Even in repose, the bulge of his biceps added to the image of uncompromising strength. Her gaze lowered with a flush, and she noted that he retained his chausses, for what reason she couldn't imagine, since she was certain it wasn't out of modesty. Perhaps it being daylight, he needed to be ready at a moment's notice.

Whatever his reasoning, he slept, and since she would need all the strength she could summon in the fight that would ensue, she drifted back to sleep with him.

The midday sun warmed the air inside the tent to stifling, and in her woolen tunic and chemise, Aelvina stirred uncomfortably. One long plait snagged beneath a heavy weight. Rousing from her exhausted torpor, she tugged to free it.

Opening her eyes to find her hair caught beneath a half-naked man, she remembered where she was, and bit back a flood of fury and frustration. She could not fall into his bed again.

Easing her hair from beneath his heavy shoulder, Aelvina sought some escape. Philippe lay between her and the tent opening. If she had a knife, she might sever one of the ropes pinning the tent to the ground and roll out from beneath. The only alternative was to crawl over him and pray no one guarded the entrance.

Aelvina decided any action was better than none and eased up from Philippe's side. Before she succeeded in inching farther than the length of his arm, a big hand pinned her to the pillows, and Philippe's dark form hovered over her.

"Where didst thou think thou wouldst go?"

No sleepiness blurred his eyes, and Aelvina gritted her teeth to keep from flinching beneath their baleful stare.

"As far from you as I can, my lord," she spat out. The pressure of his fingers against her shoulder hurt, and the dark, angry face above her looked capable of murder.

With two furious swipes of his great hand, Philippe stripped away her ragged tunic and chemise, leaving her nakedness exposed to the heated air. He did not look down upon her with pleasure, but with simmering anger.

"Then unless you desire to parade your nakedness before my men, you will get no farther than my tent."

The words were low and filled with loathing, finally impressing her with the peril of her position. Until now, she had relied on her memory of the man who had so expertly introduced her to womanhood, not the fiend who had raped her in front of an audience. The latter had been a nightmare in which she could not believe, but the cold eyes above her now were not the eyes of a lover. To parade in front of his men seemed almost preferable.

Meeting no further resistance, Philippe assessed his prisoner.

Aelvina froze as his gaze swept over her nakedness, then fought her rising panic as his hand followed the path of his gaze. She had known this was his intent, but now that the time had come, she did not think she could face it . . . not when he looked at her with such hatred.

She flinched as he fingered a sensitive nipple, her whole body drawing up in protest at this cold appraisal, and she attempted to roll away. Philippe forced her back against the pillows and trapped her legs beneath the weight of one of his.

"You swore to fill my bed until I grew tired of you. I intend to see that oath carried out." The scar on his cheek jumped angrily as he spoke. "I do not see the possibility of growing tired of such a comely wench as you too soon, so you may as well grow accustomed to your duties. Perhaps when my seed fills your belly and you grow bulky and ugly, I will send you back to your lover. He should be more than pleased to have a wench like you back in his bed again, and the extra addition of his lord's bastard will be gratifying when accompanied by a healthy purse. Spread your legs, whore, and ease my needs."

Philippe stripped off his garments as he spoke, but Aelvina scarce paid heed to his actions under the horror of his words. As the horror dispelled, fury took its place, and she struck at him with all the force she possessed.

Her palm stung with the impact of the collision with his rough jaw, but Philippe showed no pain. Calmly, he twisted her wrists in his powerful grip.

"Should you ever lift a hand to me again, you will regret it."

Aelvina's wrists ached where he held her, but she knew the giant knight withheld his full strength. Terror leaped briefly in her eyes, and Philippe watched its blaze with grim satisfaction.

"That's better. Fighting me is useless." He lowered his head to plunder her lips, and pinned her with his heavy weight.

Thighs the thickness of trees crushed against Aelvina's, and his maleness jutted against her belly, and his hands claimed her breasts. Aelvina tried to jerk her head away from his brutal kiss, but Philippe would have none of it. He caught her head and forced his lips upon her. She scratched and fought and twisted within his grasp, but his male strength was overpowering.

When Philippe at last removed his mouth from hers, Aelvina spat out all the curses she knew, in his language and her own. Fury filled his gaze as her words struck him, and with deliberate crudity, Philippe pried her legs apart with his knee. Harshly, he pinned her struggling arms to the bed and poised above her, waiting for her to recognize the inevitability of this unequal fight.

"I could kill you for what you have done to me, but I will not," he warned. "Not yet. Not until I have forced you to release this spell you have cast on me, sorceress."

His maleness lanced through her body, giving no chance of reply, and Aelvina screamed in anguish. Pinned soundly by Philippe's strength, she could not fight the force of his rhythmic fury, and her screams became hysterical as she relived that night of horror.

His fingers bit into her flesh, and through the haze of hysteria Aelvina gradually realized it was not lust or even anger blazing in his eyes as his body plowed hers. It was pure hatred.

A kindred emotion froze her body to ice and with shuddering control, she halted her screams. She was, after all, his promised whore.

At her silent passivity, Philippe unleashed his remaining control, repeatedly thrusting into her unresponsive body until he spilled his seed with a final lunge. Then, without a further word, he rolled from the bed, dressed, and strode out.

Numb, Aelvina lay within the tatters of her clothing, staring at the silk of the tent above her head. Her body remembered too well the pleasure of being held and loved and touched by warmth. Her insides ached, not with the physical damage of rape, but the poignant pangs of hunger. She could not lie to herself. She wanted Philippe as he had been before, and her body and soul cried out when it was not the same.

There were no tears. She was past the point where tears might heal. Revenge might assuage some of the hurt, but she doubted it would obtain her freedom. To kill Philippe would be a very pleasant thing to do at this moment, but would it return her babe?

Her mind could not dwell on that thought for long. Activity was the only salve to the injuries she had sustained, both physical and emotional. With reluctance, Aelvina dragged herself from the comforts of Philippe's bed and stared at the harshness of her situation.

Her clothing was beyond repair. Exploring, she discovered a chest with a wide assortment of overlarge men's garments. Since she was scarcely half Philippe's breadth and height, nothing was suitable, but she had little choice.

With maliciousness, she chose a fine white linen sherte and pulled it over her head. The sleeves dangled to the floor, but by using a sharp corner of the chest, she ripped a hole in the center of each sleeve and tore off the cuffs. With her hands free, she began on the hem, eventually ripping off a length that gave her some freedom of movement.

The width of the garment was still too great, but she solved the problem with the simple procedure of tying the castoff hem in a crude girdle about her waist. She accomplished this just in time, as the tent flap swung open and a sullen female entered bearing a tray of food. Another behind her carried a basin of water and some linen.

From the looks of the women he had chosen to serve her, they were little more than hardened prostitutes. Aelvina shivered, remembering a time in her father's camp when some lord had tired of his whore and thrown her out to join the others. The women had stripped the poor girl of her finery, and the men had taken turns at the body they had been denied for so long. It was a quick initiation and served its purpose. The girl had not been choosy over who came to her tent after that.

At least Philippe had said he would send her back to Gundulf when he grew tired of her. Not that she could trust him to keep his word, even if she could bear the thought of carrying another of his bastards. She knew ways to prevent conceiving if she could just obtain the right herbs, but that meant submitting to his rapes until another woman caught his eye. Neither alternative appealed. Death seemed the only answer. Perhaps if she antagonized Philippe enough, he would kill her in a fit of fury.

That would not save her child, though. It did not matter much if she should live or die, but she could not bear the thought of her son being reared by Marta. It was impossible to imagine what torment he might suffer at her hands.

Only one choice remained. Her life was worthless whatever happened, so she must expend it by freeing her son. Thyllda and Gundulf would see him safe, if she could just set him free. She must escape Philippe and find Marta, even if it meant entering Dunstan.

By the time darkness fell no plan had occurred to her. She had searched the tent for weapons and found none. A guard remained posted at the tent's entrance, and she did not have the strength to remove the pegs pinning the tent to the ground. She was forced to wait until an opportunity opened.

Philippe returned with a large wooden tub dragged and filled by a procession of servants, who left as silently as they came.

Philippe remained. He stripped off his garments as if Aelvina did not exist, shedding them carelessly on the earthen floor. Bronzed shoulders gleamed in the candle light as his sherte dropped to the ground. Muscles rippled across his broad back as he bent to untie his undergarments and add them to the other discarded clothes.

Aelvina could not tear her eyes from this unselfconscious disrobing. He was a magnificent man of no more than thirty years, straight and proud in his carriage, and powerfully built, with no fat to pad lean hips and narrow waist. He was a man in the prime of life, heavily tendoned legs straight and long, his manhood growing hard and strong under Aelvina's gaze.

He shot her a harsh look before entering the tub and sinking beneath the relaxing waters. "Have you forgotten your first lesson already? Bathe me." The abrupt command broke the silence.

"I am your vassal no longer. I will not." Aelvina spoke clearly in her defiance.

"I have not relieved you of your pledge. You will do as I say or be punished accordingly." Philippe did not raise his voice, but the threat was implicit.

"My pledge was given in exchange for your protection. You did not provide it and I consider the troth broken."

Fury lit his eyes, and Philippe began to rise from the tub. Regaining control, he sat down again.

"I did not break my word, but you have most certainly avoided keeping yours," he replied harshly. "Disobedient vassals can be flogged, or the tips of a few of your beautiful fingers can be removed, or I could provide you for the amusement of some of my men. I can try each method until I find what it takes to make you obey me."

She knew Philippe St. Aubyn was not a man to make empty threats. Aelvina had learned her body's limits; it could only take so much punishment before the life went out of it. She must live to escape. Whatever it cost her in pride, she must live.

Aelvina stepped from the shadows into the candlelight. There had been little point in rebraiding her hair after she brushed it out; the ribbons were in tatters. Her hair flowed in loose waves across her back and shoulders, doing no more to conceal her than the thin linen she wore.

Ignoring the narrowing of Philippe's eyes, she soaped the cloth and blanked out all thoughts of the tanned male torso rising from the tub. The desire to kill must not be too plainly seen, lest he decide to kill her first. Soaping broad shoulders, she gritted her teeth and checked the urge to plunge a dagger into his naked back.

Though Aelvina forced her expression to neutrality, and no hint of insubordination could be misconstrued in her touch, the dangerous glint of icy blue eyes gave her away. Philippe marveled at the passion hidden behind the snow-maiden composure, and if he weren't certain of the superiority of his strength, he would willingly admit his danger.

Since he had every confidence in his abilities, he relaxed and enjoyed the thorough massage of gentle hands. Though beneath the hardened exterior of a trained fighter lingered the remnants of a sensuous nature, he seldom enjoyed the merits of fine wine or soft clothing. With Aelvina for hand maiden, however, he could discover the delights of luxury. She owed him that much, and a great deal more.

Eventually, Philippe's gaze fell upon the white gauze she wore to cover herself. It scarcely concealed the pink crests beneath, and he frowned.

"Where did you find that?"

"In your chest, my lord." she answered coldly, following the path of his gaze. "I am not in the habit of standing naked before strange servants."

He snorted. "I do not doubt that you have stood naked before many a man before this and many more to come.

You had no right to help yourself to my things. That is stealing." He eyed the makeshift garment dubiously, "Though I find it hard to imagine my possessing such a rag."

"You have stripped me of my only possession. One sherte is small recompense."

Philippe frowned as he sensed that she spoke of more than the threadbare tunic in which he found her, but having already decided there was little pleasure to be had in rape, he held his tongue. He derived little satisfaction in forcing himself upon an unresponsive body. The punishment would be more fitting if he truly held her at his command, willingly and eagerly, mind and body. He smiled grimly at the thought and rose from the tub.

Aelvina offered the clean linen brought by the servants and he wrapped himself in it, gesturing toward the tub.

"The water is still warm. Wash."

She stood still, her blue gaze traveling from the tub to him. She had once expressed a preference for bathing, but apparently deciding she could not undress in front of him, she backed away, shaking her head.

"I said, *bathe.* I want my women clean. If you do not do it, I will do it for you, but there will be little left of that tunic or your skin when I finish."

Anger flared as she met his gaze, but trembling fingers unfastened the knot of her girdle. She wore only the thin sherte and this fell to the floor under Philippe's avid gaze.

"I thought perhaps my memory was afflicted by your spell, but I see you are more beautiful than I remember. Your body was made to give a man pleasure."

Aelvina sank below the water, hiding as much as possible from his sight. "I will bring you no pleasure, my lord," she warned.

"You are wrong, my little Viking. I intend to gain more

pleasure from you than any other woman I have known."
With a bitter smile, Philippe turned from her and strode
to the entrance, where he exchanged words with the man
on guard.

Aelvina was chilled more by his tone than the cooling
waters. She hurried her bath, cleansing the long hair she
had not washed in the small bowl she had been offered
earlier. While Philippe's back was still turned, she stepped
from the tub and reached for a dry cloth. A firm brown
hand halted her.

"There is time yet before food is prepared. I am more
hungry for you than for food. Will you lie down willingly,
or shall I carry you?"

The truth of his statement was evident. Aelvina kept her
gaze from straying to the proof of his desire, focusing
instead on the glittering hardness of his eyes.

"I will never come willingly to your bed. You bring dishonor on yourself more than me when you take me by
sheer force of strength. Your queen would find you most
unchivalrous if she learned of your propensity for rape."

"I told you once before, chivalry has nothing to do with
war and is not part of my nature. You owe me a debt and
I intend to collect it, if I must take it out of your hide. You
will find the giving much more pleasurable than the taking,
I assure you."

Moisture still clung to Aelvina's skin, and her hair trailed
in rivulets across her shoulders as Philippe raised his hand
to the peak of her breast. She flinched at his touch, but
his fingers teased the crest to readiness. Satisfied, he circled
her waist with his arm and lifted her hips to his.

Aelvina tensed at the probing thrust between her thighs,
but she met his gaze steadily. "I do not seek pleasure from
you. I seek nothing from a man I despise. Take what you
want; I have no strength to fight you, but I will never *give.*"

Mockery shadowed his eyes at this brave taunt. "The Valkyries would be proud of you, little Viking, but you will not receive their reward in this world."

He lifted her more fully against his chest so she was forced to cling to his shoulders for support. In a few strides, he carried her to the bed and dumped her there.

As swiftly as an eel, Aelvina slithered away, but Philippe grabbed her hair and jerked her back. Hot and hard, his mouth closed over hers. Aelvina fought its demands, shaking her head to force herself from his invasion.

Lips pressed together, Philippe reared back and glared down at her heaving breasts and icy gaze. With quick decision, he grabbed the fragment of linen she had used as a girdle and bound her wrists together. Aelvina stared back at him now with a mixture of revulsion and hatred.

She steeled herself as his lips crossed hers once more. Warm and persistent, they teased instead of demanded, and she remembered a time when she had welcomed them. How could she have trusted herself to this brute animal? A wealthy lord, with wife and title and lands, why could he not satisfy himself with what he had, instead of taking what was not his?

Philippe's hands rode exploringly across her body, sculpting the contours, molding to the fullness of her breasts, teasing pliant crests to hard, aching points. Involuntarily, she moaned at these long-denied caresses. His lips seared a path across her cheek and down her throat. Her breasts throbbed in expectation. As his teeth nipped them lightly, she writhed beneath him.

It was impossible that she give in so easily. It was impossible that this dark knight with his scarred face and brutal strength was so gentle. If she opened her eyes, she would learn the truth, but Aelvina could not open her eyes. She kept them firmly shut, surrendering to wave after wave of sensuous explosions across her skin.

When next his lips moved over hers, she met his kiss eagerly, parting her lips at his insistence and welcoming the warmth of his tongue. Philippe drank deeply of her surrender, then staked his claim.

As his hand covered the soft triangle between her legs, Aelvina whimpered, but he held her still, his fingers probing the moist opening, deliberately stroking the center of her excitement.

With lingering kisses, he returned to her lips. "Open your eyes, Aelvina. I want to free your hands, but you must open your eyes first."

He spoke coaxingly, and in wonderment, Aelvina opened her eyes and studied the darkly handsome face above her with suspicion. Triumph and grim satisfaction smoothed the lines of his mouth.

"I want to make certain that you know it is me possessing your body this time. I will not have you pretending it is some other." With these words, he unfastened the bonds confining her wrists.

Now that her hands were free, Aelvina did not know what to do with them. In various waves of emotion, she wished to slap the self-satisfied smirk from his face and to stroke the beard-stubbled skin tightening over his cheek.

Philippe guessed her confusion. "Do not make me force you again. I have every intention of taking you, one way or another. Let me do it gently this time."

His big body rolled over hers, and before she could voice a protest, he was inside her, thrusting swiftly. His hands curved around her buttocks, molding her into place as he filled her without the pain of before.

The sensation of being ridden so expertly was beyond the limits of her control. Aelvina's arms flew about his neck as the only steady hold in a rapidly disintegrating universe. She clung to him, not knowing how to respond to his demands, surrendering to his knowledge of their needs.

The lightninglike thrusts that exploded his body into shuddering tremors brought Aelvina only a hollow feeling as he pulled from her. In disappointment, she cursed him viciously for a "filthy pig son of a whore" and turned away.

The bed shook, and fearing another fit of rage, Aelvina inched away, but the sounds rumbling from deep within Philippe's wide chest had little to do with anger. His laughter erupted as violently as his rage. In astonishment at the unexpected sound, she turned to him, fearful he had gone quite mad.

His eyes were the misty emerald isles she remembered, as laugh lines crinkled his lips into a suggestion of a smile at her expression.

"You curse me more roundly when I take you gently than when I force you. You are a very difficult wench to please. Your tongue is sharper than a stablehand's. Where did you learn such phrases?"

He laughed at her! It was more than her rage could bear. Kidnapped, raped, forced into slavery, goaded into responding to his animalistic coupling, and then humiliated! Aelvina jerked the linen around her and rose from the bed, a number of more pithy phrases screaming for expression.

"No matter. So long as you are not chanting witch's spells, my ears are safe." Philippe rose, too, and caught her waist in the crook of his arm, twisting his hand in the drying silk of silver tresses. "Don't fight me next time and your pleasure will be equal to mine, sorceress. Have you not yet learned that from your other lovers?"

Aelvina shot him a look so full of venom, he shrugged and dropped his attempts at consolation. With total disregard to his nudity, he strode to the tent flap and demanded food.

Almost as soon as the request was made, trenchers of food and horns of drink were carried over the portal. Aelvina shrank into the darkness as the men unfolded the table and set down food.

After his men had departed, Philippe offered his hand. "Come, I am starving. Let us eat."

Aelvina scorned his hand and drew back, holding the sheets firmly about her. "I would rather starve," she stated coldly.

Puzzlement crossed his brow before dissolving in his usual Gallic shrug. "Suit yourself. I will wager you will not put up much of a fight when weak with hunger. Just remember the church frowns upon vassals who deliberately take their own lives, through starvation as well as any other means."

He calmly seated himself before Aelvina's screech of rage could reach a crescendo. "Who are you to speak of the church to me?" she demanded indignantly when rage calmed to some semblance of coherence. "I remember no commandment prohibiting starvation, but the one naming adultery was quite specific!"

Deadly silence permeated the tent from within and without as Philippe carefully laid down his knife and half rose from his seat, his hands resting on the table as if to prevent their rising elsewhere. The icy steadiness of his gaze and the cold tones of his voice sent an arctic chill through the air.

"You will make no further reference to my marriage if

you wish to leave this place in the same number of pieces in which you entered it.''

Aelvina retreated farther into the shadows, shocked more by the cold threat of his statement than anything else he had done. His leniency had flown with her outburst.

''I have changed my mind. I order you to sit at my table and share my meal.''

It was the same tone he had used when he commanded her to bathe him, and Aelvina had already learned the uselessness of disobeying. She stumbled forward, still clutching the linen sheet.

Philippe watched as she awkwardly sat while attempting to tuck the loose folds of material over her breasts. ''I will only divest you of those garments when we are done here,'' he warned. ''The time for modesty between us is long past.''

''The time for anything between us is long past, my lord. Why did you not leave me as I was?''

''Because I do not take a pledge lightly, and you owe me a debt far greater than you can ever hope to repay even should you lay down your life for me. To lay your body in my bed is small recompense.''

Anger coursed through her veins, but she was learning that to vent it cost more than it was worth. Aelvina wanted to ask how she owed him a life when he had nearly cost her more than her own, but that would reveal more than she cared to. To tell this man of his son would be a great folly. It would give him but one more hold, one more weakness to exploit. She bit her tongue and kept still. Taking her silence for acknowledgment of his right, Philippe returned to his meal.

When they finished eating, the men removed the remains of the meal and they were left alone again. Philippe placed his hands on her shoulders, his dark coloring contrasting vividly with her fair skin.

"Will you come willingly?"

"No, my lord," she whispered, head bent.

"So be it." He stripped the linen from her and carried her off to bed again.

Chapter Eight

He returned to their bed again in the early hours of morning. The fumes of wine still clung to him, but he held his drink well. He didn't touch her, but lay coldly apart, as if she were diseased and disgusting to him. Aelvina sighed with relief and returned to sleep.

Despite his late night, Philippe rose with the dawn. Aelvina made no pretense of sleep as he slid from the bed and donned his chausses. She lay curled within the small comfort his bed offered and watched as he paced the tent. It was like being confined in a cage with a wild stallion.

Philippe noticed her wakefulness and stopped his pacing, approaching the bed with narrowed eyes. In the rising heat of the day, she had not covered herself, and he glared at her nakedness as if she was the cause of his confinement.

"I am about to call my squire, madam. He is young and impressionable. I would suggest you cover yourself before he appears or I will get no further help of him this day."

Aelvina hastily complied. From experience, she knew the meaning of this early call, and she did not know if terror or hope tore at her heart.

"You are going to battle, my lord?"

He grimaced. "I do not call it battle. I wish it was. If it was mine to do, I would storm the keep and lay waste to the knaves without further ado. My sword arm aches to draw blood, but it is not likely to do so this day."

He strode away, speaking briefly with the guard at the opening before returning to see if his orders had been obeyed.

Aelvina wrapped herself carefully in the length of bed linen, draping the corners over shoulders and arms so no part of her could be seen. The furs and pillows were piled neatly about her, further hiding her from view. He nodded approval when he turned, but she scarcely noticed.

"If you are not to do battle, why do you call your squire?"

Philippe snorted. "I am not camped outside this keep for the joy of the open air. Henry has ordered it reduced to rubble and its owner is understandably reluctant to comply. He had no authority to build it and has claimed lands by force that rightfully belong to the king, so his fate is not likely to be a pleasant one. Henry will not tolerate these robber barons as Stephen did, but he prefers compromise and justice to war. So I am to persuade the keep to surrender willingly or destroy it with the least loss of men. Does that satisfy your curiosity?"

It did not, but the young squire had entered and Aelvina did not dare question further. Philippe's attention had already swung to the tedious process of donning leather padding and mailed hauberk and the other accoutrements of his trade.

As Aelvina watched those broad shoulders laced into their steel armor, she sighed. This was the knight she had hoped to see that day nearly a year ago: powerful, courageous, determined, and even handsome. But all these things that made him a fearless warrior made him too obstinate and arrogant to deal with on terms other than war, and so war it must ever be with him.

He did not acknowledge her presence as he strode out. No sentimental farewells or chivalrous promises from this knight. Aelvina wrinkled her nose with wry distaste, then rose and dressed in the makeshift tunic before the women brought her meal.

Though the elderly knight at the portal prevented her passing, Aelvina discovered she could stand in the entrance and easily observe the pageantry below. She easily located Philippe's standard at the head of the mounted horsemen; his broad figure towered head and shoulders above the others.

She watched as an equal force gathered in the battlements on the other side of the moat. Evidently neither side had presented all their strength; she could tell by the number of tents in Philippe's camp alone. This was just the talk before the action, the parleying for surrender. It could take all day or be brought to a swift end in a rain of arrows. The rain of arrows might suit her purposes; she could easily escape in the confusion of full-scale battle, but somehow, her heart was not in such an ending.

The heat of the day mounted and men and horses grew restless. A gust of wind occasionally blew the sound of voices to her ears, but she could not discern the words.

Her gray-haired guard developed a sympathy for her vigil and called for refreshments, allowing Aelvina to sit in the tent's shade with a full view of the field below as she ate. She shared her meal with him, but exchanged few words. All the camp knew she was an unwilling prisoner. Though they did not know her crime, they knew their

master well enough to expect there was one. Equal parts
of embarrassment and ignorance prevented conversation.

The day was well past prime as Philippe drew rein on
his steed and signaled his men to return to camp. He had
not been successful in obtaining surrender. Now the true
siege would begin. Already, the men readied the battering
rams, catapults, and machines of what use she could not
define. Swords and lances were cleaned and sharpened,
armor repaired. The air of war was not new to her, and
she retreated within the tent's emptiness.

Philippe did not return immediately, nor did she expect
him to. Since he had a war to wage, she could hope to see
little of him at all. In the heat of battle, she might escape.
She must set her mind to the best means.

But thoughts and schemes evaded her. The restless air
of tension permeating the entire camp was not strange to
her. Aelvina remembered well her mother's restless pacing
on days such as this, and forced herself to sit quietly. She
had no husband going off to fight, no man whose life or
death mattered in the least to her. She must wait for the
moment when she could slip into the forest and run in
the farthest possible direction from this camp.

She ate her evening meal alone, and when darkness fell,
retired to the comfort of an empty bed. Never before had
she such an abundance of pillows and fur to ease her weary
body. Their vermin-free cleanliness was a constant source
of delight after the straw-filled pallets of the past. Whatever
complaint she might make of this knight, he had seen to
her physical comfort. It was a pity the hatred between them
was so strong as to negate all the good.

As soon as he entered the tent's darkness, Aelvina knew
Philippe would not allow her to feign sleep this night. He
must have removed his hauberk earlier, for she did not

hear its clank as he shed his clothing. Still, there was no quietness in his purposeful movement.

Without a word, Philippe stretched his length upon the bed, turned on his side, and reached for her. He pulled her against his nakedness, not roughly nor gently, but demandingly. Aelvina did not resist as his lips covered hers, seeking solace from the frustration of the day. She willed her body not to respond—that was battle enough without the futile physical struggles she always lost.

He seemed content that she did not fight him. Wide hands slid over her body, bringing her closer, savoring the texture of softness. The rugged planes of his chest excited in a dimension she had never experienced. If he would just hold her like this, safe within the circle of his powerful arms, without demanding more . . .

Of course, he did not. Philippe laid her back against the pillows and once more sought a response from her cold lips; not receiving it, he returned to his own pleasures. He filled his hands with her breasts and suckled greedily, until Aelvina cried out with the pleasure-pain of his hunger. Then he parted her thighs and plied her with skillful fingers until her body was that of a stranger's, straining with inviting eagerness to welcome his invasion.

As his hardness became part of her, Aelvina wept and clung to the massive shoulders heaving above her. He took her without her consent and against her will, without caring how she felt, and—God help her—she did nothing to prevent it. She held him and let him use her and did no more than resist the temptation to give him more. The convulsive thrust of his release filled her with his seed, but she lay cold and empty within his arms.

Aelvina woke to the golden light of day still within the circle of his arms. Emerald eyes gleamed with amusement as this fact dawned on her, but Philippe didn't remove his arm from beneath her head. When she tried to roll away, his other hand held her in place, playing idly with her breasts and the thick silver-gold hair cascading about him.

"Have you not a battle to tend to, my lord?" Aelvina asked icily.

"Not today, enchantress, nor tomorrow, either. Does that foil your plans?" At her darkening frown, a smile played about his lips. "I canst see thou art overjoyed that I will not risk my life so soon."

His hand was doing things to her insides that she refused to admit. Her belly ached with a hunger that had nothing to do with food, and her blood rushed through her veins in a heated flood that colored her skin. In irritation, Aelvina attempted to slap him away. Philippe brushed aside the slap as if it were no more than the bite of an annoying gnat and continued his manipulations, his fingers caressing the upright curve of one breast before returning to the other.

"Nothing will sap my good humor this morn, not even your scowls and sharp words. Sieges are long, tedious things and generally not to my liking, but this time I have a beautiful wench to warm my bed and I am in no hurry to battle."

Philippe laughed at her expression, knowing he had accurately assessed her thoughts. Then he pulled her closer so that his need was more than clear. Aelvina lay cold against him as he nudged her, but still she did not fight. He counted it another victory.

"You intend to starve them out, rather than storming the ramparts and putting a swift end to their misery, just for the sake of a few tumbles in bed?" she asked scornfully.

"Marry, but the tyke displays an unfeminine interest in war! Do you see yourself as a spy for the other side? Or do you just wish to delay my attack with words?"

He laughed and moved over her. "Since my orders are known to all, I will satisfy your curiosity. I am to save my men by any means possible. Since those in the keep are more likely to starve before us, that seems the best method. I have other plans, too, but you must stay and see them for yourself." With that cryptic remark, he bent to ply her lips with kisses, and any further words were lost.

Once his needs were satisfied, Philippe climbed from the bed, leaving Aelvina to wallow in the humiliation of her almost total capitulation. He so arrogantly took her with ease, that she doubted her choice of passive resistance. Perhaps it would be better if he had to beat her senseless each time, but she wasn't certain that he might enjoy that, also. Nevertheless, Aelvina took advantage of his rare good humor and begged that she be sent a needle and some thread to occupy her time.

Philippe frowned as he halted before the door. "And what would you do with those?"

Aelvina glanced down at her ragged shift. "I would attempt to neaten the edges of this garment and perhaps repair the old one. With no chemise or kirtle, I am little more than naked when someone enters."

Philippe's lips quirked upward at this observation. Her nipples pushed at the linen, and a discerning eye could mark the place where slender legs met in a golden triangle. He nodded in agreement.

"I will send you some. Perhaps a docile activity will sweeten your temper." And with that parting remark, he was gone, leaving Aelvina to rant unheard.

Voices outside the tent later that morning warned of the approach of a stranger, and eager for any diversion, Aelvina slipped to the tent's entrance. Today's guard was not the elderly knight who had shown her kindness, but a muscular, heavyset man of two score years or more. Aelvi-

na's gaze slipped past his forbidding massiveness to the
slight figure whose voice had aroused her curiosity.

The woman carrying the small sewing box could not
be much more than Aelvina's seventeen years, but the
desperation in her eyes and the lines of her thin face gave
the appearance of one much older. No woman traveled
with the army of men unless it was for profit, and Aelvina
stared into the eyes of this whore with a shock of recognition.
This was what she would be in a few short years if
she did not soon make her escape. A tremor of despair
and anger swept through her at the memory of her body's
betrayal to the man who would turn her into this.

The flicker of sympathy in the whore's eyes at Aelvina's
obvious anguish passed away as the burly guard's demands
became clear. Not lust, but a knowing hardness lingered
in his eyes as he recognized her fear.

"Give me the box, Alice, and I will see it delivered. No
one else is to enter the tent." He held out his heavy palm
with its thick fingers.

Aelvina watched as the whore's gaze darted from herself
to the guard. A shiver of premonition made her turn warily
to this new guardian Philippe had set upon her. Nothing
in his manner indicated a need for fear, but she hastily
broke the ensuing silence.

"I am here. There is no need for anyone to enter. Let me
have the box." She held out her hand to the woman, who
started to step forward. The big knight's hand halted her.

"My orders are to allow no one to approach. The box
goes through me or not at all."

The two women exchanged glances; then with a shrug of
resignation, the young prostitute surrendered her package
and hurriedly departed before she felt the bite of the
guard's massive paw.

Aelvina remained in the doorway, in full view of the

entire camp, though she wore only the floor-length sherte to cover her nakedness. If she was in some danger from this man, she was safest here.

"May I have the box now?" she asked impatiently, increasingly uneasy as the guard continued to hold the tiny sewing box, making a pretense of searching it.

"Go back into the tent and I will bring it to you. I have something to say to you."

Aelvina studied the man's heavy jowls and narrowed eyes and felt the first knife edge of fear. He was not so tall as Philippe, but heavier, his bulk centering toward his middle and being more muscle than fat. She could not read the hard visage he presented to her, but she sensed no charity in it.

"I think not. If you have anything to say, you may say it here." Her cold tones brought a frown to his brow.

"I canst help thee escape, if thou wishes, but I will not do so in full view of the others," the man answered coldly. Then he handed her the box, turning his back and firmly blocking the tent s entrance.

Aelvina hurried back into the dimness of the tent's interior, quivering with indecision. She did not trust this burly knight, but she had been influenced by the other woman's evident fear of him. If this man could offer her freedom for whatever reason, had she the right to ignore it on the basis of a whore's fear? Perhaps the woman had some right to fear his scorn. Her son's life might rest on this opportunity—the only one she had been offered.

Fear was not an emotion with which Aelvina was comfortable. She restlessly paced in the center of the room, ignoring the sewing box she had requested. If the man meant her harm, she was now at his mercy. He did not need her permission to enter the tent at any time he chose. Did not his reluctance to do so indicate a desire to accept her decision?

Perhaps someone felt sympathy for her plight and sent this knight to her rescue. She could not afford to ignore the possibility, however slight it might be. Unable to tolerate a state of indecision, Aelvina stepped quietly to the tent's entrance.

"I am willing to hear what you have to say."

The knight glanced at the camp below, then swiftly entered the tent's protection. He stood just within the entrance, allowing his eyes to adjust to the dim interior.

"It is rumored in the camp that you are a sorceress and Philippe has stripped you of your powers. That is not all he has stripped you of, it seems."

Aelvina refused to back away as he approached. She had nowhere to run, and she would not show fear. The heat of his gaze scorched away the protection of her light covering, and her skin shriveled beneath his stare. Still, she returned his gaze with boldness.

"You said you might aid my escape, sir. I am a free woman, held here against my will. I have no jewels or coins to offer you in return for your aid, but I beg you take pity on my plight and let me go."

It was bravely stated, but already Aelvina realized the foolishness of her decision. The knight's large fingers closed around her shoulders, pulling her forward. His breath was hot upon her neck before she completed her speech.

"Your freedom is easily enough gained, wench. We have been too long from the comforts of court and home, and the whores below begin to pall. While Philippe is within short distance of his wife and can slide between her thighs whenever he wishes, he keeps the most luscious wench of all to himself. Let me sample what Philippe has enjoyed these past nights, and then I will see you to the forest's safety."

Even if every fiber of her being did not revolt at his lewd suggestion, Aelvina knew he lied. He would lay her and

leave her; she knew it instinctively. His hands took possession of her breasts as if she had already agreed, and she
hid her shudder of revulsion at their pawing. She had
learned the folly of fighting physical power. There must
be another escape.

"Take me to the forest first. It is not safe here." That
seemed a reasonable enough demand and gave her time
to think.

The guard chuckled and ran one meaty paw along the
curve of her hip, drawing her closer. "Philippe is in confer-
ence with the king's messenger and will not return soon.
I prefer the comforts of bed to the earth's dirt."

His hands bit cruelly into her buttocks as his mouth
crushed against hers, seeking a seal to their agreement.
Aelvina nearly cried out as he trapped her in his steel
embrace, and her unprotected breasts crushed against cold
mail. His mouth was like a live thing clinging to her lips,
and she turned her head in disgust.

"We have no agreement, sire. It is either in the freedom
of the forest or not at all. Release me, or I shall scream."

At this rejection, the guard's hands slid to her throat,
forcing her head backward with his thumb until she stared
up at him, wild-eyed with terror as her throat strained to
the snapping point.

"Scream, and I will break your neck. It will not be so
much fun, but when I tell them you tried to escape, it will
be easily explained."

At her silence, the knight relaxed his grip and slid his
hand beneath the wide neck of her sherte, groping the
softness of her breast. Aelvina shut her eyes in silent agony,
and then with swift determination, she threw them open
again. She stared over her captor's shoulder in horror,
and the single exclamation, "Philippe!" escaped her lips.

The guard's hand flew to his sword's hilt, and in that

instant Aelvina took to her heels, flitting around his broad
shape and out the door before his roar of fury could follow.

To bare feet, the dusty road scorched hot and painfully,
but Aelvina scarce cared. She traversed its path in panting
desperation, fleeing the horror behind and not giving
thought to the direction ahead. Escape was her only driving
force.

Her headlong flight halted abruptly as she collided with
a towering figure in her path and was swept into steely
arms. She groaned in relief as Philippe's strong arms closed
around her, but the relief was short-lived, shattered by his
harsh words.

"What is the meaning of this?" Philippe shook her
roughly before glaring at the lumbering figure following
her down the hill. "Raymond! How could you let such a
small wench escape you? Can I not trust you to this one
simple task?"

Anger rippled through Philippe's body as his fingers
dug into her shoulders, turning her around to face the
beast she sought to avoid. She shivered at the fury darkening the guard's eyes under the sting of his lord's sharp
words, but he hid the fury.

"She seduced me with soft words, sire. When I resisted
the spell she tried to weave, she spat at me and turned
into a black cat and dashed between my legs. I could not
stop her."

A malicious gleam flared in the knight's narrowed eyes
at Aelvina's irate intake of breath, but a sight behind her
hardened the gleam to a frown.

Aelvina twisted to watch the disappearance of a slight
figure over the shoulder of the hill and breathed a sigh
of gratitude. It was the young prostitute, Alice, who had
brought Sir Philippe to the rescue. Though he had no

mercy, she preferred his fate to the one the brutish Raymond had in mind.

Philippe's snort of disbelief returned her to her immediate danger.

"You let your lust guide you instead of your head, you dolt. I thought you too old for such foolishness, but it seems I must seek among the senile for those who are not open to her blandishments. Get you back to your tents, Raymond, before I regret my lenience and have you flayed for deserting your post."

Philippe seemed to have no awareness of the flash of hatred in his vassal's demeanor as he jerked Aelvina up the road past the chastened Raymond, but she sensed it and stored it away in her memory, as she did her gratitude to the young prostitute.

For the moment, Philippe's fury was all Aelvina could deal with. As he heaved her through the tent's entrance, it flashed across her mind that for one brief instant she had been free, and in that instant, her feet had turned to the safety of his arms rather than the freedom of the forest. She violently cursed herself for a fool as Philippe's harsh words lashed at her.

"The next time you attempt to use your wiles on one of my men, you will be the one flayed, not they. Much as I hate to mar that fair skin of thine, it is the only suitable punishment. Think hard on your worth after the whip stripes thy back with its scars. You will be known for the willful servant you are, and thy only employment will be beneath the weights of those who lust after you. If you find my attentions offensive, think what lies ahead if thou dost not obey me."

Not a soft line eased that uncompromising dark face, but the warning in his words was softer than she expected. Aelvina stared at him with curiosity. She sensed he regretted the need for punishment as much as she, yet he would do it. She shivered and looked away.

"I did not try to escape but ran to you for aid. If I sought to escape, I would not be so foolish as to run into your arms. I do not expect you to believe me, but I will have my side of the story heard for once."

Philippe's mouth twisted bitterly.

"I do not know where you were headed when you ran, but it was not to my arms. To my knowledge, you have not evidenced any willingness in that direction since I brought you here."

"Your anger blinds you to the truth and makes a fool of you, milord. You had best heed my words and not turn your back on Sir Raymond. I gain no advantage by being freed of one rapist to be taken by a murderer."

With those words, Aelvina turned her back on the distrust in his eyes and sat down to the task of mending her torn garments.

Philippe scowled and left her there. He had not yet replied to the king's message, and there were other things to do besides work himself into a rage over a serving wench. He dismissed the warning without further thought. Sir Raymond had fought at his back through many a campaign and served him well. It was true he was one of the king's hired mercenaries and not one of his own men, but they had fought enough battles together to trust each other's skill at warfare. That knowledge took precedence over his moonstruck madness for the silver witch.

He called up another man to guard his tent—an elderly one with granddaughters the age of Aelvina—and returned to work.

Chapter Nine

As Philippe rose from their bed, belted on his lightweight cotte, and left for the day, Aelvina sank deeper into the linens and pillows that still smelled of the musky odors of their last coupling. With uneasy wonder, she ran her fingers over breasts still bruised and raw from his kisses and felt the tightness of her swollen nipples. They hungered for his touch even when he was done with her. Was that normal?

Philippe no longer attempted to force a response from her, and for this she was grateful, because it took all her strength not to fall into his arms and give up pride and self for the tumultuous joining he had taught her once before.

In the future, she must summon images of her son in Marta's clutches to counteract the failings of her frail body. The need to find her son renewed her determination, releasing the reserves of strength she needed to combat Philippe's insidious poison. She would continue to fight him until he grew tired of the battle and threw her out in exchange for a more willing replacement. This thought strengthened her resolve, and Aelvina rose, wrapping herself in the bed linen so she might begin repairs on her ragged sherte.

The sun was high in the sky when Philippe returned, and Aelvina glanced up in surprise as his shadow darkened the doorway. "May I help you, milord?" she asked nervously as emerald eyes stared at her in hard contemplation.

"You had best come with me."

Aelvina's fingers dug into the material of the thin chemise she was repairing. What new torment had he decided to visit upon her? Had he already tired of her performance and decided to give her up to his men? The thought that he might be taking her down to the filthy squalor of the huddled tents at the camp's edge where the prostitutes dwelt made her eyes go wide with fear.

"Where are you taking me, my lord?" She remained seated, fearful of the direction in which her steps might take her.

"I need your help in this matter. Now get up from there and come with me or I will decide it for myself, and you may not be pleased with the results."

Philippe waited impatiently for her to rise, and nearly jerked her from her feet as he grabbed her arm to steer her toward the door.

Except for the day of her escape, Aelvina had not been outside the tent since he had brought her here, and she struggled against her presentation to the outside world. She had no wish to be paraded before the entire camp as his lordship's mistress. The humiliation was more than she could bear.

"My lord, I cannot go out in only this sherte. It does

not cover me properly," she protested, searching for some other means of delaying his proposal as she spoke.

Philippe gave the skimpy garment a considering glance and then, without a moment's hesitation, swept up the short Angevin mantle he used in the evenings and covered her shoulders. It neatly covered her to the knees and he nodded approval, before pulling her out into the blazing midday sun.

Curious glances followed their progress along the rutted road to the camp's edge. Encompassed in the voluminous folds of the heavy mantle, Aelvina scarcely reached Philippe's broad shoulders. She had difficulty keeping pace with his long strides, particularly since she wore nothing on her feet. She scrambled to keep up, curiosity melding her to his side.

The sight of the old oxen wagon sent Aelvina's feet racing down the pathway, her heart thumping with joy. A hard hand on her shoulder brought her to an abrupt halt and a realization of her plight, and the cry of joy died in her throat.

She walked stiffly beside Philippe as he approached the wagon. The vehicle's occupants remained in their seats, surrounded by well-armed guards, and Aelvina flinched as she recognized the sturdy figure beside Thyllda's short frame. She was grateful he could not see her near nakedness beneath the mantle, but Philippe's possessive arm around her shoulder spoke the tale well enough. She approached her friends as Philippe's chosen whore and an adulteress.

Thyllda's quiet gaze saved her. Aelvina drew strength from the love she found there and straightened her shoulders beneath the burden of shame.

"What do you here?" Philippe demanded, directing his words at the young man he recognized as his adversary.

"We have come to take Aelvina home," Gundulf stated simply.

"You, my vassal and sworn servant, dare take my cart and oxen"—Aelvina jerked nervously beneath his hand as he claimed ownership of animals and property once rightly hers, but Philippe ignored it—"and demand the return of a villein who has sworn her services to me? Under what right do you do this?"

"I swore thee an oath of loyalty when thou didst marry her ladyship and the king didst give thee baronial rights over my lands, but that oath doth not bind me to the criminal act of kidnapping and worse. Aelvina has no other challenger to stand in her protection, but give me sword and lance and I will fight thee for her return."

Philippe snorted in derision at Gundulf's speech. He turned to the wagon's other occupant. "And, thou, old woman, have thee come to challenge me, also?"

"I am no longer so young and foolish, but you know how I feel about the child. Let me speak with her."

A fleeting glance passed between the tall knight and the elderly but proud figure in the wagon, and Aelvina watched this display with puzzlement. What communication was there between these two who had never laid eyes on each other? Whatever it was, Thyllda lost. Her shoulders sagged slightly at his verbal reply.

"Speak then. There is no chain upon her tongue."

Aelvina grimaced and shot him a baleful look as she caught the sarcasm behind Philippe's words, but he continued to carefully watch her two champions. She returned her attention to Thyllda at her guardian's next words.

"Aelvina, have you told him?"

There was naught in the question for any to understand but the gray-haired servant and her quick-silver charge, and for them the communication was instantaneous. In response, Aelvina drew herself up, her narrow chin jutting stubbornly.

"There is naught to tell."

Philippe heard this exchange with suspicion, but when it seemed no more would come of it, he once more took command.

"If that is all there is to be said, choose how you would dispose of these presumptuous intruders. Shall I send them back from whence they came or hold them here?"

The question came as a surprise, and startled, Aelvina examined his stern features. No hint of his thoughts lay behind his implacable gaze. She sensed her choice in the matter was a small one and had much to do with the fact that he had once promised protection for Thyllda, also.

"It matters little what I say, milord. They have come here against my wishes, as you well know. I would prefer they return to the village, but they will not unless you release me to go with them. If you really wished to consult my preference, that is the course I would choose."

Though battered and a little worse for wear, Aelvina had lost none of her defiant hauteur, and Thyllda bit back a smile at the sight of the slight girl waspishly attacking the towering knight. Sir Philippe's expression was that reserved for an aggravating insect, but persistent needling occasionally had its results. Men have been known to die of spider bites.

Philippe growled at the waiting guards. "Take the man back to the barracks and keep him there. If the old woman wishes to stay, let her share Alice's tent and see Alice is recompensed for the use."

Philippe made as if to stride off, bearing Aelvina with him, but Aelvina dug in her heels and refused to budge. With exasperation, Philippe halted and awaited explanation.

"You would put Thyllda with one of your whores?"
Aelvina asked incredulously.

"There is no empty tent and young Alice will be grateful
for the coins. If she still wishes to practice her trade, she
must do it elsewhere. Trust me to have some understanding,
if you will."

Philippe's look was contemptuous and Aelvina bowed
before it, reluctantly turning her back on her friends and
following his footsteps. Aelvina knew the coins paid Alice
were in reality payment for her own services. She was Philippe's
paid whore in truth now, as agreed upon so long
ago. Why did she find the thought so much more humiliating
than she had then?

Once back within the tent's shade, Philippe let her go
and, hands on hips, stared down at her with a mixture of
suspicion and anger.

"What is it the old woman would have you tell me?" he
demanded.

"Ask her, if you care to believe an old woman's fancies.
I will tell you nothing." Aelvina strode across the tent, as
far as she could get from his overpowering presence. She
wished he would depart and leave her to her miseries.

"I will have the tale soon enough. Do not let your lover's
appearance give you foolish notions. You are mine to do
with as I will."

He turned as if to leave, but Aelvina halted his departure.
"What will you do with him, milord?"

Philippe gave her a venomous look. "See that his challenge
is answered, I suppose. A man enthralled with a
woman has little sense. He must be put out of his misery
before he causes someone hurt."

Aelvina's wail of fury and dismay left him untouched as
he strode from the enclosure.

Philippe did not return to his tent for the evening meal,

forcing Aelvina to anxiously pace the floor. How could he accept a challenge from a yeoman untrained in the arts of battle? Though Philippe scorned chivalry, such action would be outright murder.

The only comfort she found was that no tourney seemed in the making this day. Below her, the camp lay quiet.

Exhausted by overstrained emotions, Aelvina curled up in the softness of Philippe's bed and slept. She woke to find Philippe propped on one elbow, watching her in the golden glow of dawn. As her eyes met his, he grinned mockingly, then allowed his gaze to travel down to where her breasts pressed intimately against his chest. Only then did she realize the haven of warmth she had sought in the night was his embrace.

"Sharing a bed has some advantages, does it not?" he murmured wickedly.

His hand drew along the curve of her breast and hips, pressing her closer to the hard shaft of his manhood. Aelvina sighed and closed her eyes, turning her head from his mocking gaze as the now familiar wave of heat melted her insides.

No longer satisfied with Aelvina's frigid unresponsiveness, Philippe set his jaw at this turning away. He slid his hand from her hip to the entrance of her body, probing until she shivered and tensed. He glanced down at her pale face, her lovely eyes shuttered as she waited for the moment when he would put an end to her exquisite torture.

Instead, he pushed her from him, prying her fingers loose from his arm and pinning her against the pillows.

"Admit that you want me between your thighs as much as I want to be there."

Philippe's voice was gruff and Aelvina stared up at him with dismay and wonder. His chiseled features held only determination and she winced under the clarity of emerald eyes. It was as if he could see right through her, but admit it, she would not.

"Never, my lord. Take me if you will, but like it, I will not."

Instead of slapping her as she half feared, Philippe nibbled at the sensitive lobe of her ear, his breath tingling against her cheek and hair. His mouth moved downward, caressing the line of her jaw, teasing at the corners of her lips, pressing ardently against her throat, until he finally returned to her lips and she gladly met his kiss.

His mouth possessed her, and she begged for it. Her lips parted, welcoming him with uninhibited passion as his kisses took her lovingly, as they had once before. He released her hands and they flew about his shoulders, pressing him closer so she might feel all of him against her. His hardness stirred her more, and eagerly she sought to return his pleasures.

Again, Philippe pushed her away, his brown hand wrapped in the ivory tresses spilling across her shoulders. His eyes burned fiercely as they met her hesitation.

"Deny it now. Tell me your body does not hunger for my thrust."

With his hard body poised above hers, he waited for her to speak the words that would free them both. Aelvina felt the aching need between her legs, but pride and hate refused to bend. He had used her for a vessel of his contempt for too long. She would not surrender to his lust now.

"I deny it. I have no need to be your whore, my lord."

His eyes glittered, but still he did not hit her. His muscled body lingered just above her, held only by the bulging tendons of his arms. Slowly, he lowered his weight until his hips pressed against hers, his hard shaft probing at her weakness. Denied entrance, he dipped lower, until his mouth closed about sensitized nipples. Aelvina gasped with the fire of this contact.

Vainly she tried to shove away, but Philippe clung to her breasts while his hands played over her body. The pressures he applied decimated all control. Aelvina's fingers slid into Philippe's dark hair, pressing his head eagerly to her breast while her hips rose to the rhythm of his demands. The fires of desire swept through her veins, consuming all rational thought, destroying all reluctance.

"Philippe!" she repeated urgently, when he did not respond to her demand.

His tongue lapped around the hardened tip of her breast one more time before he raised up on one elbow, and waited silently, expectantly.

There was no pride in her as she raised her arms to his broad shoulders. "Please, Philippe, no more," she begged, unable to say the words he wanted, unable to resist the uncontrollable fires raging where he held her legs closed between his heavy thighs.

"Say it, Aelvina. Say it before I burst and we are both denied the pleasure we seek."

His tone was cold and flat, but the heat of his gaze spoke another story. The desire to rebel against one and surrender to the other warred within her soul. The gentle touch of his hand to her breast decided the battle, and with eyes closed she turned away to hide her shame.

"Please, Philippe. I need you inside me."

It was the surrender he wanted, but a twinge of disappointment flickered across his features at the manner in which it was given.

With a groan of mixed satisfaction and frustration, he lifted her hips and plunged deep.

Aelvina cried out her relief. The need was so great she

responded instantly, carrying her far past the point of control into the valley of passion. When he exploded within her, she shuddered beneath a ripple of exquisite pain that told her how close she had come to succumbing entirely.

Philippe's hand brushed a tangle of hair back from her flushed cheeks. "You still fight me, little Viking. There is no sense in it," he murmured, pulling his hands through a length of silver-gold.

"I cannot do elsewise, my lord," she whispered, almost as disappointed as he. Her body ached with the need for release, but she rebelled against coercion. She must give herself willingly, or not at all.

"You will, sorceress, you will."

He kissed her then, a long, lingering kiss of promise that told her the siege had just begun. Aelvina wrapped her arms about his wide shoulders and savored this momentary tenderness, certain it would be a long while before she tasted it again.

They rose and dressed in silence. They had reached a stalemate with which neither was satisfied.

After eating, Philippe surprised her by handing over the mantle he had used to cover her on the previous day's excursion. "I have something I wish to show you," he offered in explanation to her questioning gaze.

With trembling fingers, Aelvina fastened the clasp. She instinctively knew that Gundulf again occasioned this outing. "He is but a farmer, milord," she stated tentatively as they passed through the tent's entrance.

Philippe halted and stared at her. "I have not yet told you our destination. What makes you think it concerns your arrogant yeoman?"

Aelvina shrugged away the question. "He is a good man

and serves you well in the fields. His land produces twice as much as any other. He has a way with plants and animals that no other has. If you spent more time listening to your people and less time at war, you would know he is harmless."

Philippe's face darkened and he turned her in the direction of the barracks. "Do you speak as sorceress or lover? Does he have a way with women, too, that makes them seek his bed and no other?"

The bitterness in his voice was surprising, the more so because she could find no reason for it. What had happened to him this past year to turn him into this bitter, unreasonable man? Had marriage been such a disappointment? His bride's price had gained him much land and the service of many knights. And the Lady Ravenna was still young and beautiful enough to provide him with many sons. How could such a marriage be a disappointment?

Though she longed to answer his anger in the manner it deserved, a rash reply would not save Gundulf from his fate. "I would not know, milord," she replied in answer to his question.

They were in the center of camp and Philippe did not stop to argue the question, but gave her a disbelieving look that hurt her.

A space had been cleared amid the tents of the army's lower echelons, and already a crowd had formed around its perimeter. Aelvina clutched at Philippe's arm as they entered the crowd and halted at the clearing's edge.

Worriedly she scanned the open space. She saw no sign of a whipping post, but that could leave only one alternative. Since Philippe wore no armor, he had chosen one of his men to accept Gundulf's challenge. Without lance or armor, Gundulf had no chance of escaping unscathed.

Philippe's command would determine whether he lived or died.

Vaguely nauseous at the thought, Aelvina turned her head away, but Philippe's grip tightened on her shoulder, forcing her to face the ring.

John, Philippe's young squire, entered the ring's center, bowing low before Philippe. He wore no armor and carried only a lengthy oaken staff. Philippe accepted his homage and signaled for the second contestant to enter.

Aelvina breathed a sigh of relief and relaxed. Gundulf entered, his short-cropped hair burnished bright in the sunlight, his blue eyes instantly seeking and finding Aelvina in the crowd. He, too, bore a stout staff and made his obeisance perfunctorily to his lord. It was to be an equal fight—one in which Gundulf had a fair chance.

Philippe caught the relief and surprise in her expression and smiled grimly. "I am not given to cold-blooded murder, my dear. He will have his chance to defend himself."

"And if he wins?" Aelvina could not keep from asking, eyes wide with wonder but little hope.

The dark mask of his face nodded as he read her thoughts. "He will be given a choice of fates, but you are not among them."

She had not imagined she would be. Philippe's hold over her was too strong and not easily broken by so simple a thing as a vassal's challenge. She only dared pray Gundulf's life would be spared.

The clash of strong staffs brought Aelvina's attention back to the ring. John was a youth of much the same age as Gundulf, but slighter and swifter. Trained in all the forms of battle, he handled his weapon with skill, but Gundulf's greater strength had an advantage.

Held at either end in powerful fists, the staffs crashed together, their wielders straining to catch their opponent off balance. Sweat poured from their faces, soaking their tunics as each fought for the upper hand and the clashes became more furious with frustration.

Aelvina's fingers bit into Philippe's arm with each mighty blow, flinching at the teeth-shattering force of the strikes. That they fought for her gave her no pride. Aelvina closed her eyes and prayed harder as she thought of the younger brothers and sisters waiting for Gundulf's return.

Philippe glanced down at her closed face but said nothing. Well aware of the slender hands clutching his arm and jolting at every blow, he lost his taste for the show and waited for its end. The girl's Viking ancestry might flow strongly in her veins, but it was a defensive spirit she held. Blood sport evidently held no appeal for its own sake, and he was sorry he had brought her to it. Honor had prevented his ignoring the challenge but did not require her presence.

Another mighty blow sent the squire stumbling backward, but his staff swung out in defense, catching Gundulf hard upon the shoulder. The yeoman scarcely noticed; the scent of victory in his nostrils, he leapt upon his fallen adversary.

John swung again, more wildly this time as he hit the ground. The crowd roared as the staff cracked along the blond giant's ribs and he did not falter. He held his staff like a club, knocked John's weapon from his hands, and pinned his fallen opponent with his weight. One flick of his wrist and the squire's neck would snap.

Aelvina heard the crowd's uproarious cries and opened her eyes in time to catch Philippe's nod of approval. Gundulf rose to his feet, leaving the young squire to his comrades. She felt relief but nothing more at this meaningless victory, and released Philippe's arm as if it were hot coals.

At Philippe's gesture, Gundulf approached. His broad

torso was soaked in sweat and a bruised swelling rose along the line of his jaw, but his gaze was fixed on Philippe.

"You have won fairly and well. As victor, you are entitled to some reward. I offer you two choices: You may return to your home and family with a purse of coins, or you may enter my service and be trained in the use of arms. How choose you?"

Aelvina clenched her fists, praying he would take the first and knowing he would not. She heard Gundulf make the choice and wept silently at such foolishness, but his request caught her by surprise.

"My lord, I ask a moment's word with your lady, if you would. I will not take her from your sight, but I need speak in private."

At the words "your lady," Aelvina flinched. Gundulf was being polite, but he had already assigned her ownership to the Norman. Was this how her people had been conquered . . . by honor and politeness? She'd sooner take a knife to the lot of them.

Philippe noted her frosty gaze and smothered a chuckle. If he guessed rightly, the lad was not about to hear any encouraging words of love from this vixen. With a distant nod, he indicated his acceptance of the request, and allowed Aelvina to follow her champion farther down the hill and out of his hearing.

With care, Gundulf maneuvered her into a position where his actions could not be seen. Before Aelvina could say a word, he produced a familiar dagger from the folds of his tunic and guarded her well as her hand closed about its hilt and swiftly hid it in her own garments.

"Know you have but one chance to use it. Choose your moment well," he warned, his eyes scanning her features anxiously.

Aelvina smiled as her fingers caressed the familiar carv-

ings of the weapon. She should not have judged Gundulf
so hastily.

"I know not how to thank you," she whispered.

"By using it wisely. Only you can be the judge of that."

Sorrow etched his eyes. Thyllda had awakened Gundulf
to much he wished he had not known. Aelvina's eyes shone
with an intensity that had not been there before, and the
brittle shell she had been a week ago now brimmed with
life and vigor. Hatred did not cause such changes.

Philippe, too, watched the change in Aelvina's expression. How did the young dolt succeed in turning the icy
fury of the sorceress to beaming pleasure with just a few
words? She had never turned such a smile on him, though
she must know such a smile would produce her every wish
but one. How then had this untrained lad elicited it?

Aelvina was silent on their return walk. Philippe glanced
down on her upon occasion, but could not discern anything from her composed features. He refrained from
touching her, but matched her stride so no chance of
escape opened.

Once he had escorted her to the tent, he turned to
leave, but Aelvina's hand rested lightly on his arm.

"Milord, a boon, if you would?"

Philippe glanced at her questioningly.

"I thank you for sparing Gundulf's life. He has made
his choice and will remain loyal to you now, without question. But I would talk to my servant, Thyllda, if you please.
She is old, and I care for her comfort."

Philippe drew his brows down in a frown as he contemplated the innocence of her expression. She might well
speak the truth, but he had no intention of allowing her
to wander the camp unsupervised.

"When I have time, I will see her sent to you. On no
account are you to go down into the camp after her."

Aelvina's lips set in a thin line, but she nodded her understanding.

Only when he had gone did she finger the shaft of the knife of freedom.

Chapter Ten

Restlessness itched at her fingers and toes. She had been cooped up in this tent for over a week and the morning's excitement had whetted Aelvina's appetite for adventure. Waiting for Philippe to return each day and drive her body to the brink of disaster was sheer physical torture. The thought of her son drawing ever farther away from her was a mental and emotional anguish she could not tolerate for long. Something had to be done, and the time could not come too soon.

It exploded with the realization that Philippe had forgotten her request to see Thyllda. The noon meal passed with no sign of her, and Aelvina longed desperately for the words of wisdom only Thyllda could offer. One more broken promise added to the list, and Aelvina's lips set in rebellion.

Noting the guard's near napping position in the warm afternoon sun, Aelvina slipped to the shadows of the forest side of the tent. It would take swiftness to accomplish her intention and madness to reach her goal, but she would not stay within this silken prison another moment.

Aelvina shoved the heavy chest to one side, produced the silver dagger, and sawed at the heavy rope binding the tent sides to the ground. In minutes she had an opening large enough to squeeze under.

With care, she checked to see that no one watched, then slid into the freedom of the outside world. To hide her route, she dragged the chest back in place and hid the cut rope under it, protecting her escape route should she be returned to this prison again.

Free at last, Aelvina darted into the forest's shadow. From here, she could observe the camp below and remain unseen. She already knew the general location of the prostitutes' encampment, and her eyes sought some clue of the occupants.

While she watched for sign of Alice or Thyllda, she also noted the changes in the countryside that Philippe had made. Evidently, he did not intend to rely solely on starvation for the keep's surrender.

He'd already positioned the big war machines at the moat's edge, out of reach of arrows from the battlements. Wooden shields and battering rams and catapults lay strategically placed about the castle's walls and the keep entrance. But the machines mining the moat walls, draining its protective waters in one place and damming them in another, gave best evidence of Philippe's strategy. Once the moat emptied, they could begin mining beneath the castle walls, until the toss of a torch would decimate the tunnel structure and with it, the solid stone walls above. Once the outer walls were breached, the keep would be the last defense. Philippe did not intend to waste his time lying abed until they all starved as he threatened.

It mattered little to her. She intended to be far from this place before it fell, holding her son in her arms if it be God's will.

Aelvina finally spied the figure of the young prostitute who had aided her, marked the position of the tent from which she had departed, and hastened to work her way around to the forest closest to it. Once there, it was a matter of darting from the forest's safety into the nearly deserted streets of the lower encampment, praying no one would notice her.

Thyllda gasped with surprise at the suddenness of her entrance, but showed no shock at Aelvina's freedom. She gestured to the tent's other pallet.

"Have a seat and speak quickly. You will be missed shortly and this is the first place Sir Philippe will seek."

Aelvina grinned wryly. "The second. He will tear down the barracks with his bare hands looking for Gundulf first."

Thyllda accepted this knowledge complacently. "Sit, and tell me why you have not told his lordship of the child," she commanded.

Thyllda had been a loyal maid to the Lady Fairfax, a nurse to Aelvina, and a servant in the Fairfax family for all her years, but she still had the power to order her young charge about. Aelvina sat, but her chin jutted defiantly.

"I will not give the man that power over me. He has used me as his whore and given nothing in return. The child is mine alone . . . fair payment for his broken promises."

"He broke no promises to you," Thyllda stated sternly. "His protection may have been lax, but he had no reason to suspect he would be drugged. He suffered as much from his folly as you."

Aelvina fought a tumult of emotions at this sensational statement. She wanted to believe it. She wanted to believe

Philippe had come after her, scoured the woods in search of her. And she wanted to believe he had suffered the torments of the damned as she had, but knew he had not. He had acquired land and wealth and power while she had been stripped of her one possession, denied her freedom, and had her child stolen from her. He would pay for his broken promises one day, she vowed.

"I did not come here to listen to placating foolishness. I am leaving this hell. Do you wish to come with me or rely on his lordship's dubious protection?" she demanded scornfully.

"I will stay here and so will you. It is your only chance of finding your child. How do you think I lived this past year? Did you really think that poor old wagon and worn-out oxen provided shelter and food for so long a time?"

"You drove them here. I recognized them. You said you sold them," Aelvina stated accusingly. Thyllda had no compunctions about lying when it served her purpose; she had known that for a long time and occasionally used it for her own designs. But Thyllda's goal had ever been Aelvina's happiness and she could see no reason for this lie.

"I did, but the buyer insisted they be left available for my use. He had some notion I might consider them home and family as my foolish young charge did."

Aelvina gaped at Thyllda's calm repetition of her words. Only one person would know of her attachment to those foolish relics. "Philippe bought them! Why?"

"Because he had made a promise and intended to keep what portion of it he could. He agreed to leaving me in the village to search for you instead of accommodating me in the camp as planned, but other than that, he has been true to his word and seen to my care, though you did not warm his bed as expected. Your virginity had some value, it seems.''

Aelvina's lips twisted into a grimace of distaste. ''I am glad my virginity had that much price, but a guilty conscience probably doubled its value. There is no excuse for his deserting me to the witch's clutches. I will never forgive him for that.''

Thyllda sighed. Aelvina had ever been a stubborn brat. It would take the powers of a master storyteller to paint the tale in all its colored facets so she might see what was there, right before her nose.

''He did not desert you, gapeseed. That is what I am telling you. The Lady Ravenna claimed you never existed, that he had drunk too much and hallucinated, but Philippe tore the keep apart until he found me. Marta didn't expect him to know of me and had not attempted to hide my whereabouts. I reassured him that you were quite real, and from there he was like a man demented. I think he would have tied the lady to the rack if he could have done it without risking reprisal. I take the blame for not letting him go so far. If I had known then what I know now, I wouldn't have been so squeamish.''

Aelvina clasped her hand to her stomach where it seemed a thousand wild butterflies had been set free. How much of this tale had Thyllda made up to get her own way? It coincided too well with all the hopes and dreams that had been shattered so long ago. It could not be true.

''I don't believe you,'' Aelvina answered dully, not daring to look the old woman in the eye. ''He had an army at his disposal. I was not so far that Marta could not walk to the keep every day. How could he not find me if he truly searched?''

''You could not find it and you knew what to look for,'' Thyllda pointed out. ''He searched. His men scoured the woods for weeks. One day, he brought me this, covered with mud. That was when I gave up hope of finding you alive.''

Thyllda reached inside her tunic and removed a gold object attached to a chain which she pulled over her head, handing it to her suspicious charge. "I thought only death would part you from it."

Aelvina's fingers curled around her father's ring, tears springing to her eyes at the homely feel of the familiar object. "Why did you not tell me earlier?" she whispered, afraid to admit the truth of Thyllda's words, even to herself.

"I saw no point in stirring hopes and dreams that could not come true. Philippe married and was beyond your reach. Things have changed since then. Tell him of the child and he will listen. He is your only hope, Evelyn."

Aelvina sat vacantly staring out the tent flap, clutching the ring in her fist. It would be simple to prove the truth of Thyllda's words; she had only to ask Philippe. But his accusations still rang in her ears, their meaning clearer now, and she scarce needed to ask. She still did not understand his hatred, but he most certainly thought she had broken her part of the agreement, while he had attempted to keep his. The ring nearly proved it.

His guilt may have driven him to act out a show for Thyllda, but she doubted it. If Philippe had committed rape deliberately, he would have felt no guilt. No, he had been as drugged as she. Marta evidently counted on his retaining no memory the day after, though why was beyond Aelvina's reasoning.

A commotion stirred the dusty street outside, but Aelvina ignored it, her thoughts churning to assimilate all this information. Thyllda rose and watched from the tent's entrance. She turned back and prodded Aelvina gently.

"They are searching the camp for you. He will be furious.

Go back and tell him of the child. It is the only way, I promise you."

"He will not believe me," Aelvina said. Her thoughts had led her thus far.

"That is possible, but you must take the chance. Go; they will find you momentarily."

Aelvina rose and handed the ring back to Thyllda. "Keep this for me. He will not allow me to have it. He fears I will escape should I possess any means of doing so." She gave a wry smile at this admission that she intended to return to her prison.

Thyllda smiled. "He will help you, even against his will. Go to him now."

She hid her tears until Aelvina slid as quietly from the tent as she had come. She was sending the child out into the world on her own now, pushing her from the nest and praying her wings were strong enough to fly, and that the hawk would be gentle with her. Thyllda clasped the ring in her fist much as Aelvina had done, and prayed for forgiveness from the ring's previous owner.

Aelvina hovered on the forest's edge, making certain no one waited in the tent. When all was clear, she darted across the grass, pushed the chest aside, and rolled under the tent wall, reappearing in the tent's shadows a moment later. She buried the knife in the earthen floor beneath the chest, cleaned herself in the washing bowl, replaited her hair, and waited to be discovered.

It did not take long. John, the squire, entered in search of some object his master had requested, and forgot all else at the sight of her seated at the bed's edge, sewing her rent tunic. Philippe was systematically turning the camp upside down in search of this gremlin who now sat exactly where she was supposed to be.

"I hope you were not too seriously bruised in this morning's bout, John," she murmured conscientiously.

He stammered, dumbstruck, made a hasty bow, remembered himself, returned the cap to his head, and backed toward the entrance. "No . . . No, thank you. I am fine. . . . I . . . His lordship wishes to see you . . . Stay right there. . . ." And he dashed off.

Aelvina bit back a smile at his precipitous departure. Philippe would be in a black enough mood; it would not do for him to find her smiling.

She was not far wrong. Philippe's towering form passed through the tent flap like some ominous thundercloud rumbling and spitting lightning. He glared at her with eyes of wildfire, his dark face grim and scowling.

"I have half my men scouring the woods for you. Where in the devil's own hell have you been?"

"Hell is where you find it, milord. Mine has been here and in worse places. If you continue glowering at me like that, I'll regret my decision to return."

Her taste of freedom had returned her courage, and Aelvina faced him coolly. She watched as he fought the desire to smack her for her insolence and swallowed his fury, only to turn to the door and vent it on his men. After chastising the guard's laxity and ranting orders to end the search, Philippe returned to face her with a look of suspicion replacing his earlier fury.

"How did you leave here?" he demanded.

"Do you think me fool enough to tell you?"

His great fists clenched in anger, warning she trod dangerously near the edge of his patience. Aelvina hastened to divert the topic.

"Why did you not tell me you searched for me when I disappeared?"

Philippe's expression swept from fury to astonishment

to wariness. That she had returned after making good her escape had set him off balance. He steadied himself and called loudly for a drink before answering her.

"You desire that I make a total fool of myself for your amusement?" he asked hollowly. She sat there looking so damned pure and innocent, Philippe felt a strong urge to wring her pretty neck—to disturb her as she did him.

"And that is also your reason for not telling me you kept your promise to care for Thyllda, too, I suppose?" Aelvina continued.

"How did I know the old woman chose not to tell you?" Philippe asked irritably. "What difference does it make that I was fool enough to believe you had been spirited away against your will? Are you sufficiently amused by the admission? My stupidity is over. I know better than to believe your deceitful eyes now."

Aelvina's hand rose involuntarily to her eyes. "My eyes?" she asked in wonder.

"That innocent azure you use to melt men's minds and those flashing silvered promises to heat their loins," Philippe answered disdainfully. "They lie. There is no innocence and you keep no promises, just like any other whore, more fool I." He grimaced in disgust at himself.

Could it be possible? Had this towering Norman knight truly stooped to notice so small a thing as the color of his vassal's eyes? Despite the irascibility of Philippe's words, color flushed Aelvina's cheeks, and her hand trembled as she set aside her sewing.

Rising, she dared his angry proximity for the sake of reading the truth in his face. "Did you look for me later, much later? Call my name out loud?" She prayed the hope in her voice stayed hidden.

"I looked for you a thousand times, if only to beat you into senselessness for what you had done to me." Philippe fell silent as a servant entered with a flagon of wine. He drank deeply before completing his answer. "And once, yes, I even called your name. So obsessed had I become, I actually thought I heard you calling me ... taunting, more than likely. The very trees laughed at me."

"It was I, milord, not taunting but begging."

The quiet statement fell into a lengthy silence. Philippe examined her face and words for all that was not said.

"Explain yourself."

Aelvina sighed, wishing for some easy way to make him see. Distrust and hatred ran too deep, and he would not believe her. But Thyllda had assured her this knight would help, that some remnant of honor still clung to him. She must try it, for her son's sake.

"You will not believe me, milord. You have already made up your mind." She sighed.

"Tell me, anyway. The day is gone and I enjoy a good tale as well as any." Philippe threw himself down on the pillows and drew another long drink before setting aside the flask and proceeding to remove his tunic.

To his surprise, Aelvina came to his aid, folding the material before untying his footgear and leggings. "I was drugged as you were that night," she spoke as she worked. "I was carried into the forest, to some cave Marta had fashioned for her uses. I believe I was kept drugged for a long time. My injuries were healed by the time I regained my senses."

He flinched at this mention of the results of that night's work, but he said nothing.

"By the time I realized I was with child, winter was almost upon us, and I had no place to go. You were gone; I was told Thyllda was dead. I had nothing but the child in my womb, and his protection was more important than my freedom."

She heard his slow intake of breath as she removed the last legging. He swung his legs away abruptly to pace the room, wearing only his chausses and a loose sherte.

"You are right. I do not believe you. Where is this child that kept you from my bed?"

Aelvina watched Philippe's furious pacing in the darkening light. His broad shoulders filled the small space of the tent, and she despaired of ever reaching him again. Too much had gone between them and all was lost. She clenched her fists to fight back tears.

"He was stolen from me at birth, milord. I was left to die and would have, had it not been for Gundulf. I have only just recuperated from my illness or I would have sought him much sooner. As it is, you dragged me away from my search."

Philippe caught at this reprieve. "You are telling me you have had no other lovers since that night? This Gundulf did no more than rescue you from your sorry plight? And you expect me to believe that!"

"I told you I did not expect you to believe me, milord." Aelvina rose bravely, her head scarce reaching his shoulder. "I only told you so you might understand why I cannot uphold my part of the agreement. I must find my son before Marta destroys him. Thyllda said you would understand, but she was wrong. You will never understand, and you will never hold me here, elsewise."

It was a farewell of sorts, and Philippe's thoughts churned rapidly. He did not believe in witchcraft, but she had already found some means of escaping him. One thought rose above all others: She was offering him a means of keeping her here. Suspiciously, he turned her tale over in his mind, testing it for weak places, his stomach tightening with sickness at the possibility of its truth.

"Do not be so hasty, little Viking," he murmured as his

thoughts twisted and leapt to incredible conclusions. He would keep her here; he had that power. Maybe, in time, he could drive out this obsession that made his loins hunger for her alone. At the same time, he would revenge her lies by reducing her to the same hungering obsession she had produced in him . . . if she lied.

Aelvina waited silently as he paced like a restless stallion stalking his stall.

"You tell me you have borne my child? A son?"

"Yes, milord." She heard the incredulity in his voice but felt no bitterness. She had not believed it herself, at first. "I think I would remember had there been another that night," she added sardonically.

Philippe swung to face her again. "You have some proof? Or do you wish me to swallow the tale whole?"

Aelvina's lips quirked without humor. "I have no wish to prove the child yours. I only seek to have him returned to me. If you will not help, I shall look on my own."

Philippe caught her by the shoulder and jerked her up against him. "Do not play with me. Tell me everything or I will shake you until your teeth rattle."

Caught against the hard breadth of his muscular chest, Aelvina had no desire to do other than he asked. She wanted to make him believe, prayed he would believe.

"I did not tell you because I hated you for what had been done to me. Now I see I was wrong and you were not entirely at fault. Ask the monk, Chauvin."

"Chauvin?" Of course. The monk had showed him the place where he had found the girl, and they had searched the place diligently, Philippe's rage and hatred growing ever stronger at this new treachery. The monk had said nothing of a child.

Ignoring Aelvina's explanations, Philippe strode to the door and demanded the monk's presence. He would swear this monk was honest. They had been together long: Philippe, in Henry's conquering armies; Chauvin, bringing enlightenment to the conquered.

The monk appeared, his robe in disarray, his hands wiping sleep from his eyes, and Philippe discovered with astonishment that the evening was well advanced. This tale had driven all thought of sleep or food from his mind.

"You wished to see me, sire?" The monk's cautious gaze swept from the fever of Philippe's dark visage to the paleness of Aelvina's.

"When you spoke to me of finding the wench in the forest, did you keep something from me that I ought to know?"

The monk turned from Philippe's anxious expression to Aelvina. Her eyes were slightly accusing that he had revealed her, but she nodded acquiescence.

The monk directed his answer to Aelvina. "I returned for the baptism as you requested, my child, but you were nowhere to be found."

"It is no matter, Father . . ." she began, but Philippe's roar intruded.

"Baptism! You two-faced, mutton-headed son of a . . ."

"Philippe!" Aelvina shouted, shocked into outrage, but the monk waved her to silence and faced the noble's rage with equanimity.

"You wished your child baptized, did you not, sire?" he asked as Philippe's tirade dwindled to a mutter.

"My child! You have some proof that it was my child, if child there be at all?" Philippe asked nastily, returning to his pacing.

"I may be celibate, but I am not blind. I know a woman heavy with child when I see one and I can count as well as any other, particularly since I had every reason to know the days. . . ."

"Enough!" Philippe roared, stopping the flow of ridicule. "Why on God's earth did you not tell me of this then?"

"Taking the Lord's name in vain is a sin, sire," the monk declared stoutly, ignoring Philippe's mule-headed rage. "I did not tell you because the girl requested it. I had full confidence you would see for yourself without need of breaking my word."

Philippe's furious gaze swung from one stubborn face to another, and he swore under his breath. The girl spoke one truth, then. A child had existed at one time. It was enough to act on.

"Wait outside, Chauvin. I have a way you may atone for not telling me sooner, but first I must speak with the obstinate wench in private."

The monk turned worriedly to the girl, who seemed defenseless against the noble's rage. But Aelvina nodded her agreement and held Philippe's gaze in a desperate battle of wills. Uncertain as to the victor, Chauvin slipped from the tent.

"How do you know the child lives?" Philippe demanded.

"I do not. I only know Marta went to much trouble to obtain him. It seems reasonable she would go to equal trouble to keep him."

Philippe nodded, though he was not at all certain her reasoning applied. "If the child lives, you wish me to find him? Is that your purpose in returning here this afternoon?"

"Milord, I would give anything for his return. . . ." Aelvina's voice broke at this unexpected answer. "Please, milord, he would be with Marta. It would be so easy for you . . ."

Philippe waved away her pleas. She had given the answer he sought before he even asked. "Marta has no child or

I would have heard of it. It will take care and patience to find a child someone wishes hidden, and you cannot do it. Marta would kill you on sight if what you tell me is true."

"It does not matter," Aelvina replied fiercely. "I would rather die than have my son raised by that witch. I *will* find him. I *will!*" she screamed, pounding her fists against the earthen floor.

Instead of responding with rage at her insolence, Philippe raised her from the ground. He stroked silken plaits as he watched azure eyes slip to silver-blue. He could almost believe her wild tale true—all the more reason for doing what he must now do.

"No, little Viking. Let me try first. As you say, it would be much easier for me."

Aelvina's palms flattened against his chest. Her heart thudded against her ribs. No tenderness marked his chiseled features, and she held her silence.

"There is a condition attached."

The words rumbled from deep within his chest, and Aelvina steeled herself for what was to come. She had said she would do anything for her son's return. How far had she meant that promise to go?

She took a step away, but Philippe's hands closed around her wrists. Emerald eyes hardened.

"If your tale is true, it would be dangerous to the child should either of us ask questions. I will send the monk to search the fief, but you must stay with me and keep your part of our agreement."

There was nothing of menace in his tone; the threat was implicit. She had little choice. Aelvina's fingers curled to fists, and she bit back words of rage. She must do what was best for the child. Her thoughts probed for other possibilities, but he was right. Only her pride rebelled at the price.

"You are asking me to commit adultery, milord," she pointed out, with a trace of bitterness.

Philippe's expression tightened. "That is not a much greater sin than the one of prostitution, which you so readily agreed to the first time."

His words cut more sharply than a knife and Aelvina looked away. "But then the only person harmed was myself. Adultery is different." She could not bring herself to think of the Lady Ravenna lying in Philippe's arms.

"If that is your only consideration, I will relieve your mind on the matter. The lady knows better than to ask anything of me, including fidelity. She cares not if I take one mistress or a dozen."

Aelvina could not bear to hear more. She abruptly changed the subject. "How do I know you will keep your promise this time?" she asked, deliberately omitting any titles of respect.

A tight smile bent Philippe's thin lips. "If you are willing, you may hear me give Chauvin the orders and give any of your own. Once he knows of your plight, he will scour the land with his bare hands if need be to return your son. You need not fear I will countermand the orders once they are given. Chauvin takes his orders only from God. He will only accept the ones from my mouth that fit his godly notions."

There was irony in his tone, and Aelvina could well imagine the monk telling Sir Philippe what he could do with his commands. The monk would do what he thought right, not what man or woman told him. She had already seen evidence of that. If he agreed to search for her son, she could trust he would do the task thoroughly, even against Philippe's orders.

At her prolonged hesitation, Philippe released her wrists and walked away. "I will give you time to think of it if you wish. The monk can come back when you are ready."

"No!" Aelvina halted his progress. "Do not send him away. Every day we waste could bring disaster. I will agree to anything. *Just find my son!*"

It was a cry from the heart, and even Philippe heard the pain and anguish that had torn the words from her. The child really did exist, then. He almost felt remorse for his harsh words and actions, but the memory of her duplicity prevented any weakening emotion. He turned back to pin her with his gaze.

"You understand what I am asking? I am tired of holding a frozen statue in my arms. I want you willing and eager to please."

Aelvina bowed her head. "I will do my best, milord. It is . . . difficult, sometimes, for me. After that night . . ." She shuddered at the memory.

Sudden understanding blazed through Philippe's mind. His memories of that night were few, but he feared her young, newly opened body could not have taken the full force of his without suffering greatly. The other conditions would have been devastating if she had not been prepared for them. His thoughts stopped there. It did not seem reasonable that she did not know what would happen. She was as much a witch as the rest.

He kept the thought to himself, however, and returned to the tent flap to call the monk.

Chauvin entered, his gaze immediately fleeing to Aelvina. Her ivory hair fell in waist-length plaits over the front of her thin linen sherte, and her silvered eyes glittered defiantly. It did not take clairvoyance to know she had committed herself to a sin. His gaze turned accusingly to Sir Philippe.

Lost in his own thoughts, Philippe ignored the monk's air of condemnation. Briskly, he explained what needed to be done and why, until Chauvin's nearly apoplectic features finally caught his eye.

"You object to this task?" Philippe asked, genuinely puzzled. He had thought the monk would be eager to perform such a charitable act.

"You know very well to what I object." Chauvin's gaze swept to Aelvina, who had lost heart in the giving of orders and wandered to the entrance.

Philippe, too, gazed upon that slender form, but hunger, not compassion, leapt to his heart. "I will have her whether you carry out the task or not," he warned.

"It is madness," Chauvin responded.

"It may be sorcery, for all I care. The girl is mine. I paid the church's price for the other. I will pay the devil's for this. It could not be much worse."

The bitterness ran so deep beneath these words, Chauvin feared he had lost this soul for certain. For the girl's sake, then, he must take on the task.

"You wish me to look for a child? Of what age?"

Philippe's snort of exasperation returned Aelvina to the conversation. Her son's fate lay in the hands of these men, and they were glaring at each other like two little boys tossing taunts.

"The child is mine, Father," she stated, gliding between them.

"Yours? I thought . . ." The monk's expression showed he had assumed the child had died, a common enough occurrence under the circumstances.

"What do you think I have been telling you, you unripe gapeseed? She claims the child has been stolen. . . ."

Aelvina understood the antagonism between these two had more to do with a conflict of interest than dislike, but it slowed the proceedings considerably. Impatiently, she interrupted Philippe's tirade.

"The witch Marta stole him from me at birth. Please, I need your help to find him. . . ."

"Him?" Gray eyes narrowed and Aelvina found herself the one ignored as the monk stared accusingly at Philippe.

Philippe's gaze remained blank. "She claims he is my son. I want the fief searched for a boy child of nearly two months. Do you understand?" This last was stated with threatening emphasis. Philippe cut off further reply by turning to Aelvina. "Can you remember any identifying features?"

Aelvina summoned that pain-filled night, the one moment clearly imprinted on her memory if all else was lost, and she smiled forlornly at the image. "He was a strong, lusty boy, with wide shoulders and long legs, just like his father's, but his hair," her voice fell to a whisper, "his hair was that of a Fairfax."

"Fairfax?" the monk asked, bewildered at this switch to the native tongue. The oddity of her Norman speech had not struck him until she changed to the Saxon dialect.

"She means he has hair like hers," Philippe explained, touching his hand to the silver-gold plait on her shoulder. The warning was still in his eyes, but the anger had fled.

Chauvin nodded in slow comprehension.

"Philippe, by all that is holy, you must know as well as I . . ."

"I have never looked upon the brat," Philippe cut him off, "and there may be others. Search everywhere. I would know of every child anywhere near that age, be he black, brown, red, or mauve. I would know for *certain* . . ."

Aelvina glanced up at the violent emphasis on the last word, not quite understanding the gist of his command.

Perhaps he thought the witch would try to disguise the babe. That was a possibility she had not considered.

Chauvin glanced at her skeptically. "She does not know?"

Philippe waved his hand in dismissal. "Find him, and we all will know. I will catch up to you in a moment."

Aelvina scarce heard this exchange in the sudden awareness that she was to be left alone with the man to whom she had promised herself. She was repeating her foolishness, exchanging her body for his protection. What price would she pay for her sin this time?

With the monk's departure, Philippe twisted her silken braid in his palm. "I must see to the horse and supplies for the monk's use. I have your promise you will be waiting when I return?"

His presence dominated her senses, destroying all rational thought. She feared him, feared his strength, feared his ability to turn her body into a vessel for his use. Yet she had agreed to lay herself open for his punishment. It was a slow means of dying, but it was as near to heaven as she would ever come.

Aelvina nodded. "I will be waiting. Hurry back."

As Philippe hurried after the monk, Aelvina stood in the center of the tent, wondering what she was expected to do. She now knew he expected more of her than lying on his bed, waiting for him to slake his passions. She had done that this past week, and he had made it quite clear that was not sufficient. What now?

There must be something she could do to keep him content, keep him from destroying her before he found her son.

If she had a fine gown, she would don it for him, but the loose sherte was too ugly for her purposes. She stripped off, hoping her nakedness would entice him as much as a gown.

Aelvina marveled at the anticipation stirring in her that she would please a man who had treated her cruelly. Yet she held no grudge against him. He had taken what he had considered his and would have done so gently had she been willing. It was not in his nature to question vassals, as it was not theirs to question him. That was the order of things, and she must learn to accept it.

Aelvina sprawled among the furs and pillows and tried to check her mounting excitement at the thought of Philippe's hard hands riding her with tenderness. Mayhap she was a born wanton, for her fingers strayed to the golden triangle between her legs and her hips arched at the touch.

A low growl from the doorway startled Aelvina, and she rolled beneath the covers before looking up to find Philippe standing over her with undisguised lust.

"Philippe! You startled me." He gave her no further time to speak.

"You're a born whore," he muttered, lifting her by her hair to meet his kiss.

Aelvina's natural reaction was to beat off this crude performance and shout her outrage, but she stopped her struggles just in time. If this was the way he wanted it, she must let him have his way, but disappointment licked at her insides that there would be no gentleness, no affection, even now.

Her arms wrapped about his sturdy neck, crushing her breasts against the muscles of his chest. Philippe's mouth rekindled the excitement his entrance had dampened, and Aelvina responded uncertainly.

Philippe breathed raggedly as he laid her against the bed, forcing her into the pillows with his heavy weight. "Whore," he muttered again, before burying his lips between her breasts while his hands crushed their pliant softness.

Aelvina nearly screamed at this ruthless mauling, wanting to rip the sherte from his back and repeat the favor. With a flash of maliciousness, she grabbed the fine cloth of his sherte. Squirming beneath him, she filled both hands with the cloth and tugged upward until she bared his legs. As Philippe's teeth closed about her nipple, Aelvina heaved upward, jerking the remaining cloth with her.

With arms propped on either side of her, Philippe glowered at her. "If that is the way you want it, do not stop there, little bitch; take it all off."

He sat up, dragging her with him. The problem of undressing a man twice her size might have terrified her once, but fury and excitement drove away all inhibition. Her fists wound in the cloth separating them as she ripped it away until flesh rubbed flesh.

"Come to me, vixen. Don't stop now," he murmured hoarsely against her hair.

His hand separated her knees, opening her to him as she kneeled above him. Aelvina blushed but the fire inside her belly demanded fuel, and there was no mistaking her position astride his lap.

His arm held her poised at the point of no return while his mouth suckled her breasts into a frenzy of desire. Aelvina writhed in his embrace, seeking ease for her needs, until his grip loosen, giving her freedom to do as she would.

Aelvina cried out with the mindless joy of surrender, all tension dissolving as they merged and his body was hers, one and inseparable. With the freedom of his body, he gifted her with the pleasure they both had missed.

Eons later, they stirred, Philippe lifting his heavy weight

to ease her burden. She murmured warm words of non-sense, not wanting the parting that was sure to come.

"Philippe, love, please," she whispered protestingly, as he moved from her.

Propped on one arm, he teased the puckered tip of her breast. "Did I not tell you it was better not to fight me?"

"Then why did you make me fight you now?" she asked with curiosity. "I would have come willingly."

"You feared me, and there is no pleasure in fear. This way, you have fought me and won. Perhaps you will fear me less next time."

Amazement warmed her. She had known his intelligence but had not expected understanding from this bulk of a man. Men, particularly those of Philippe's rank, were quite accustomed to taking what they wanted and caring little how the people below them felt. Yet he had understood her fears and sought to ease them in the only way he knew, with anger.

She smiled and ran her fingers across his scarred face, feeling the tenseness melt beneath her caress. They had much to learn of each other. Perhaps there was time to find a little happiness; it might not be too late. She was no more than a nobleman's whore, but where was it written that she could not enjoy those few pleasures the position brought her?

Chapter Eleven

It was not all sunshine and roses, but it was good—better than she had dared hope. This was what would have been had Marta not interfered, Aelvina thought, as Philippe held her in his arms for one last lingering good-bye. The excitement never failed to rise in her veins every time he held her like this, every time he so much as walked into the tent. She was drawn to him like a moth to a flame and would surely singe her wings soon enough, but not yet.

Philippe loosed his grip and set her down, striding out the door before Aelvina could gain her breath. She knew he grew impatient to end this siege, but he could only act on the king's orders, and they did not bid him attack. The forty-day service Philippe's men owed him was up, and he had released some of them to return to their lands. The more valuable warriors he paid to stay on, and the king's hired mercenaries stayed where they were told. The moat was drained, the mining almost complete, but still they

waited. Aelvina glanced over the encampment that had
been her home this past month and allowed a smile to
flicker across her face . . . just like old times.

Aelvina retreated within the tent's shadow, stroking the
fine rose silk of her new bliaut. She and Thyllda and Alice
had spent many hours stitching the new gown from the bolt
Philippe had brought her, just one of the many surprises he
laid at her feet these past weeks. The long train of the
gown rustled seductively as she straightened clothes strewn
from the previous night's lovemaking.

Philippe liked to see her in pretty things, and Aelvina
smiled in memory of the night he returned the blue silk
dancing costume to her hands.

Aelvina leaned dreamily against the pole, remembering
that night and the others that followed. The costume and
the ring had been all of Aelvina that Philippe had discovered, and those had been well hidden. The ring he had
returned to Thyllda for its value, but the costume he had
kept, as proof of an elusive memory. She had proved her
reality often enough since then, but sometimes she still
caught that look of distrust and disbelief in his eyes, as if
he feared she would dissolve in midair if he peered too
closely, or that she would stab him in the back when he
was most vulnerable. That thought brought a spasm of
pain, and Aelvina hurried from the tent, eager for some
distraction.

Philippe had gradually given her the freedom of the
camp with only the requirement that she take an assigned
guard with her. It seemed a silly stipulation now that the
entire camp knew Philippe would wreak a terrible judgment on any harming her. When she saw no one about,
she strode out on her own.

She saw Thyllda every day and Alice frequently, She had
seen little of Gundulf in her excursions from the tent. He

stayed busy with the hard labor of the other foot soldiers, mining the walls and forging the weapons of battle. It was a waste, but he had chosen his fate as she had chosen hers, and it could not be undone. The few times she had seen him, he did not approach her, but he had watched her until she was out of sight.

She would not let these thoughts darken her day. Philippe had presented her with a clean bolt of linen with the request that she make herself a new chemise, but Aelvina had other ideas. Thyllda and Alice were in sore need of new linen, and Philippe could use a new sherte. It was better that she set her mind to work and not the dark thoughts cluttering the hidden crannies of her soul.

The paths to the prostitute's end of camp were generally deserted in the early morning, and Aelvina hurried through them without a second thought, giving care only to where she stepped to avoid dirtying her new slippers in the open sewage. The day would be a warm one, but thunderclouds hovered on the horizon. She would prefer company in a rainstorm.

A large figure stepped through the flap of one of the more derelict tents. Without hauberk or supertunic, he could be any of the soldiers just leaving an early morning tumble with one of the whores, but Aelvina recognized the wide girth and swerved to avoid him. It was a useless attempt. Raymond stuck out his massive hand and caught her arm, dragging her close enough to smell the stink of stale wine on his breath.

"Fortune shines on me today. Has your noble master finally sent you to join the other whores, or are you on your way to meet a more profitable lover?"

Aelvina struggled to loose his grip, kicking at his shins with fury. "Philippe will have your fool's pate on a platter for this. Let me go!"

The kicks of her feet were little more than a thorn scratch
to Raymond's thick-thewed legs, and effortlessly, he swung
her into the tent.

"There. Let that one tell you how useless it is to argue.
Get up, whore. I have found one better to take your place."

He shoved Aelvina to the tent's interior, where she might
have a better view of the last poor creature who had resisted
his efforts. The woman lay in a crumpled heap upon a
filthy pallet, her dark hair tangled in knots about bruised
shoulders, her large breasts uncovered by the torn gunna
at her waist. It took a moment before Aelvina recognized
the woman's battered face.

"Alice! My God !"

Aelvina flew to the girl's side, smoothing the dark hair
back from torn cheeks. Alice struggled, protesting.

"Go! Run from here!" she whispered hoarsely. The
panic and fear in her eyes were unmistakable, warning
Aelvina of her danger.

Aelvina jumped to her feet and swung around with a
screech of fury. "You fiend! You revolting, hoofed devil
of a many-tailed . . ."

Raymond clamped a hand over her mouth, snatching
her by the waist and holding her against him so she could
not flee. "You will keep your voice down, bitch, and this
will be over in a minute. What's your price? Another fancy
gown like this one? A shiny jewel for your pretty neck?
What does it cost to get you to spread your legs quietly?"

Her struggles only aroused the knight's lusts to greater
heights. Aelvina's foot cracked against his shin as his hand
slid beneath her bliaut to cup her breast.

She was too furious to be scared and swore at herself
for not carrying the silver dagger she had buried in the
tent. To sink it to the shaft between this dolt's shoulder

blades was a sin she would gladly commit. As Raymond's heavy fingers bit into her tender breast, she cried out.

"You doddering jackanapes! There is no treasure in the world that will buy my silence. I will scream until the entire camp knows your perfidy and do not try that threat of broken necks on me again. I would rather die than give myself to a filthy ass like you, and Philippe will not believe your story of escape this time. He will slice off your testicles and shove them into that bloated mouth of yours to stifle your screams when he slits your intestines and dips you in a vat of boiling oil . . ."

She gasped for breath, her fury stiffening her body into an icicle of sharpness. Raymond slowly lowered her to the ground, his dark eyes clouded with horror and anger at the spitting witch whose curses rang uncomfortably possible in his ears.

"Go! Get out of here before I scream just for spite! Run before I change my mind!"

Aelvina's voice rose to a threatening crescendo, and Raymond heeded the warning. He turned and strode for the entrance, but before departing, he threw back the last word.

"Just wait, bitch. When your nobleman tires of you, it will be my turn. You will pay for this yet." And he was gone.

Shattered by the intensity of her own fury, Aelvina collapsed in a puddle, drained of all further emotion. A stirring in the far corner returned her senses, and gathering the shreds of her wit, she crawled to Alice's side.

"Why?" was all she could utter wearily as she helped Alice cover herself with the torn gunna.

"He could find no one else and there was no one to stop him. I have lived through it before. Do not worry yourself. Where are your guards?'' Alice tried to sit, but Aelvina held her back.

"Rest here. I will see if Thyllda has some salves. If Philippe would only let me . . .'' She shook her head, remembering the arguments they had had over Aelvina's wish to gather the herbs she needed.

As if she sensed the path of her drifting thoughts, Alice whispered, "When he is angry at you, I have heard Sir Philippe call you a Valkyrie. What is that?''

Aelvina smiled at the girl's wanderings and felt her head to be certain it was not from fever. "A Viking goddess of war, I believe. Why do you ask?''

"After what I have just seen, I believe he is more right than the others.'' Pained amusement twitched Alice's lips. "The men say you are a sorceress or a druid who can disappear into the trees at will, but only a goddess of war could so terrify Sir Raymond.''

It was not the first time Aelvina had been called a sorceress. Philippe accused her often enough in jest. But the men had taken it more seriously, particularly after she had used the few dried herbs in her pouch to soothe some fevered rashes and bring sleep to a man whose hand had been crushed in an accident with one of the machines. The herbs were almost gone now, and though she had access to verdigris and quicksilver and other more basic medicines provided by the camp's leeches, they would not ease Alice's suffering. It would be convenient if she truly were a sorceress.

"A goddess of war or a sorceress should come better provided with weapons than I. After what Raymond has done to you, I should like to see him hung by the thumbs and castrated.''

"Aelvina!'' Alice whispered, horrified at Aelvina's crudity. "Sir Raymond has done no more than others before him. It shocks no one but you. If you are here without guards, you had best not mention this at all. Sir Philippe would look on it with suspicion."

Aelvina's lips set tight with anger. It was true. She had best remove herself from here quickly before Raymond returned or Philippe found her. With a sigh, she rose to her feet.

"I do not like to leave you, but Thyllda will come and tend you as soon as I fetch her. Lie quiet; I will be back."

When Philippe returned to the tent that evening, he was met by an angry wraith in the ragged linen tunic he had bade her dispose of weeks ago. His square jaw tightened.

"What is the meaning of this? Where are the clothes I brought for you?"

Aelvina ignored the ominous warning in his voice, her own temper having already boiled to a constant roll earlier. "I no longer have any desire to profit by our arrangement, milord."

The sarcastic term of respect added an angry twitch to Philippe's jaw muscle. "Take that damned thing off and put on something decent!"

The knight's commands were not meant to be disobeyed, but Aelvina refused to budge. "What will you do to me should I refuse? Beat me as your men do their whores?"

"Do not tempt me, wench!" With a growl, Philippe caught his hand in the neck of the thin sherte and ripped it from her. "Now, don your clothes before John or one of the others enters."

"They have seen naked whores before. Why should I be any different? At least the others may roam where they will and leave camp if they choose, but my finery scarce covers the loss of my freedom."

Aelvina backed away from him, keeping an arm's length from his stalking fury until she hit the tent pole. Philippe placed himself in front of her, his arms crossed over his massive chest as he contemplated her with a growing frown.

"What are you asking? You want jewels to match the gowns? Or do you want to join the other whores and enjoy the arms of other men? Stop speaking in riddles."

Philippe's dark face glowered from above the dark maroon of his form-fitting surcoat, his broad figure dwarfing her as they stood nearly toe to toe. Yet Aelvina felt no fear even at the implied threat of his words.

"Alice has been beaten by one of your men. I want the freedom of the forest to obtain the herbs to salve her wounds and ease her suffering."

The tension slid from Philippe's jaw, and the suspicion always hovering beneath the surface of his eyes temporarily vanished. He picked up the bed linen and threw it at her. "Put it around you before someone enters. I have no desire to fight my own men."

He waited while she wrapped the linen over her nakedness. Aelvina knew him as a man whose passions seldom lingered far below the surface. He made love as he made war—with heart, soul, and mind. If he was angry, the whole camp knew of it; if he was glad, the camp rang with laughter. But now his expression was unreadable, and all the more frightening. When she had covered herself, he nodded approval.

"I am sorry to hear about Alice. I had hoped she would not need to practice her profession. . . ." Philippe waved away Aelvina's protest. "It does not matter, I tell you. I have not guards enough to protect you in the forest under normal circumstances. But now there is word of an approaching army, and I can take no chances."

Aelvina's eyes grew wide with worry. "An army? I thought

this was just one baron who defied the king. Who else must you fight?''

At this quick end to the argument, Philippe smiled. There was as much tactical maneuvering to handling a woman as there was to a battle, particularly with this temperamental sprite.

"The baron's son, a few of his vassals, and very probably some hired mercenaries. Not a large band, but dangerous enough for such as you.''

"All the more reason why I should go out now. There will be injured and they will need tending.''

Philippe gave a roar of exasperation and caught her in a rib-crushing hug. "Over my dead body!'' he growled, before burying his mouth against the base of her throat and putting an end to further argument.

Much later, when the darkness was complete and the camp settled to silence, Aelvina lay staring at the blackness of the billowing tent, and Philippe leaned over and smoothed the hair from her face.

"You do not sleep.''

Aelvina stroked his rough cheek and he gathered her into his arms, holding her slight weight against his chest.

"You worry about the child.'' Philippe did not need the nod of her head to know the answer. "I had word from Chauvin today.'' She tensed and he wondered that she did not question eagerly, but then he realized she feared the answers. Briefly, he debated telling her all, but discarded the thought. He would not make a further fool of himself if she already knew, and if she didn't—well, there was no reason in raising her hopes, either.

"He is still looking. From what I hear, scarcely a child under the age of a year in the entire fief has escaped baptism by now, but so far, none fit the description. All have been well accounted for by doting parents and neighbors. He still looks, elf-child."

She nodded again, and a teardrop fell upon his chest. He tightened his grip, and she slept, rocked in the cradle of his arms. Philippe lay awake long after.

No more was spoken of the needed herbs the next day, but Philippe had Alice and Thyllda's tent moved closer to the top of the hill where Aelvina could visit unmolested. Salves and bandages appeared at her disposal, and Aelvina sighed and surrendered the battle, for the moment.

She sat with Thyllda at Alice's side when a messenger came from Philippe, requiring her return to his tent. Puzzled by this unusual demand—Philippe scarcely had time for her during the day—Aelvina hurried up the hill to the gaudy silk tent she called home.

Inside, she found Philippe and a stranger: a knight with unfamiliar heraldry on his shield, an easy smile on his sculpted face, and a pained expression in his eyes as he bowed his blond head in greeting.

"You are wounded, milord!" Aelvina cried, her gaze quickly darting to the place on the stranger's shoulder where his mail hauberk had parted. She gave Philippe a scathing look and immediately turned to the messenger at the door with a list of commands.

As she turned back to the interior, both men rose to their feet, and the stranger attempted a more courtly salute. The need to clasp his hand to his shoulder somewhat weakened the effect, but Aelvina scarcely noticed. His flashing white teeth and unruly locks had no impact as she turned her attention to the wound.

"My lady, I have heard of your beauty, but none said . . ."

"Sit down before you start the bleeding again," Aelvina interrupted sharply.

In the shadows, Philippe smothered a laugh but watched carefully.

The stranger did as he was told. Aelvina removed the tight chain mail without disturbing the open wound, but her concentration on this act did not prevent her hearing Philippe's words.

"He is a king's messenger, he tells me, so treat him gently." Laughter hid beneath the low rumble of his voice.

"Philippe, you always had strange humors, but this is a fine time to jest," the stranger complained. "I do not know how the Lady Ravenna tolerates . . ."

The sudden jerk of Aelvina's nervous fingers and the instant tension in the airless room warned the knight he had committed some faux pas. The black scowl on Philippe's features as the hauberk was at last pulled from him only underlined the magnitude of his mistake. Of course, they said at court that the lady Philippe had taken to wife was as dark as he. By all the saints in heaven, he had done it this time.

"I am sorry. I only assumed . . ." The king's messenger watched as the lovely figure in trailing robes of silk turned away, the fresh color gone from her cheeks as she set aside the hauberk and accepted the warm water a guard carried in. His gaze turned back to Philippe's scowling visage.

"I should have made the introduction clear." Philippe spoke curtly. "Aelvina"—deliberately giving her precedence, he waited until she had set the bowl on a low stool before completing the introduction—"this is Sir Geoffrey de Harcourt, an old friend of mine."

Aelvina made a low and graceful curtsy before returning to the more prosaic task of sponging the torn fabric of Sir Geoffrey's tunic from his wound.

"The Lady Ravenna is at Dunstan where she belongs," Philippe growled.

The knight's gaze rested speculatively on Aelvina's graceful form as she bent over him, her ivory hair caught back in a chaplet of silver. It did not take imagination to guess her position here. "Saxon?" he whispered.

"If it relieves your mind," Aelvina replied calmly, wringing out the rag.

Philippe's dark gaze followed this exchange but made no addition. "You brought a message, I believe?" He prodded the visitor abruptly.

"At no small cost and just in time, it seems." Sir Geoffrey winced as Aelvina tore away the sherte and tunic over his shoulder. "Bohun's damned men must be everywhere." He nodded at the leather bag attached to his jeweled girdle. "It is in my pouch, there."

Aelvina untied the pouch and wordlessly handed it to Philippe. Azure eyes remained shuttered and cool as they met emerald ones; then she returned to her task.

"I heard Henry tell it to the scribe and can tell you what it says," Geoffrey offered as Philippe unrolled the parchment.

"No matter. I can read even the clerk's befuddled Latin," Philippe announced calmly.

That a Norman man of war would admit to such bookish learning was not unknown, though uncommon. De Harcourt knew of his friend's talent but had thought to save him the trouble; however there were other ears present and he took the hint. He returned his attention to the enchantress dressing his wound.

"A lady such as yourself would do well at court. Would you not like to see London?" De Harcourt's words were low, so as not to disturb the knight engrossed in the intricacies of the king's message.

"I have heard King Henry has great plans. I would enjoy

a visit to see how the court fares under his hand," Aelvina answered easily. "Though I would not like to stay there."

From his seat in the corner, Philippe could hear all, but he did not raise his eyes from the parchment he studied.

"Westminster is much grander than an army camp," Geoffrey pursued, without a qualm. His friend was a married man, and a battlefield was no place for a girl as beautiful as this one.

"That may be, but I have seen grander, and they have held nothing for me."

That effectively silenced the blond knight, and a suspicion of a twitch worked at Philippe's lips as he continued his reading. Aelvina's reference to grander halls than the king's put a different perspective on the lady's standing. Though Philippe guessed it to be a ruse, he knew it gave Geoffrey food for thought.

The reference to grander halls had not silenced Geoffrey, but the girl's loyalty to Philippe had. He thought it strange that Philippe allowed her presence here. Though the ladies gave the dark knight more than his share of encouragement, Philippe had never been known as much of a wencher. Now it seemed he had accumulated both wife and mistress within a year's time.

Perhaps he had mistaken the lady's answer. Not many women ignored Geoffrey's charm or gave up a chance to visit the court, particularly one who could be bought. As Aelvina smoothed the bandage in place, de Harcourt caught her fingers and kissed them.

"Such hands as these were made for better things, my beauty. Let me take you back with me and show you the splendors that can be had for the asking."

The knuckles on the parchment page turned white and a dark jaw twitched violently, but Aelvina's back was toward him. Philippe could see nothing of her expression.

"You mistake me, sire," Aelvina replied calmly, disengaging her hand and stepping away. "I have all that I need here for the asking, I need no more." She picked up the washbasin and walked out.

De Harcourt watched her go, then turned to find Philippe's thoughtful gaze following her graceful sway as it disappeared down the road.

"You lucky bastard," the younger man stated without rancor.

But Philippe's familiar wolfish grin of agreement did not appear.

Chapter Twelve

Aelvina did not need to hear the king's message to know it finally gave Philippe permission to attack. His lovemaking after Geoffrey rode off later that night spoke more than words could ever tell.

He seemed driven by a hunger and fury beyond his control. His lips attacked hers greedily, as if he would drain her of all she had to give; yet she kept on giving. His hands dug into her flesh with a frenzied need to possess, and no portion of her lay untouched by the time he mounted her, sealing his ownership.

They both lay awake as the first sound of running feet disturbed the camp's before-dawn stillness. Aelvina ran her fingers deep into the rough thickness of Philippe's dark hair, kissing his unshaven cheek as many times as possible before the inevitable interruption.

As he held her small white body against his own, Philippe faced his own mortality for the first time, and disliked the

feel of it. Death had been ever present in his life, and he
had paid it no heed. Now, its shadow swept around the
fragile form he had taken into his care, and he rebelled
against the separation. There had not been time enough
to rid himself of this obsession; there might never be time
enough, he realized, and he grieved at the injustice of fate.

"Aelvina." He brushed away her kisses, laying her gently
against the pillows. "If anything should happen to me, you
could be in grave danger. These mercenaries know no
other leader and will do as they want. If I should fall in
battle, do not linger. Take the coins and papers in my
pouch, gather what of my men you can trust, and hasten
to St. Aubyn. I will leave Sir Alec with you—he knows the
way—and my castle will keep you until you send the papers
to the king. Chauvin will continue looking for the child
with or without me, so you need not hesitate. Will you do
as I say?"

"It will be a small battle, you said, so there is nothing
for me to fear. You will come back to me tonight and yell
at me for not mending your tunic, and then I will show
you there are better ways to get what you want than yell-
ing." She pulled his head down to meet her lips.

Philippe's thoughts strayed ahead, knowing the coming
battle would be greater than he had said, and he did not
realize she made no promises. The arrival of his squire
with the sentry ended all else, and he rose from the bed,
covering Aelvina's nakedness with the furs.

Aelvina watched from the hidden depths of the bed as
Philippe listened to the sentry's report and sent him to
waken the others. Refusing to lie quietly, Aelvina wrapped
the linen about her. She would not leave John be the last
to touch him before he went to battle.

Silently, she and John helped him don sherte and tunic,
leather padding, and the heavy mail. The young squire

sensed Aelvina's wish, made some excuse, and left her to complete the lacing by herself. She did it carefully, weaving her prayers into Philippe's protection.

When done, he stood before her, the indestructible knight of her dreams: armor burnished and gleaming, sword and dagger at his waist, holding the shield with the St. Aubyn arms emblazoned on it, but not yet the Dunstan insignia. His chiseled features were dark and remote, almost that of a stranger as they looked down upon her. Yet Aelvina knew her dreams of indestructibility were but a fable, and the man beneath the armor, all too human.

She did not wish to think of Philippe's failings now. She wished she had colors to tie to his arm, but she had none, nor the right to do so; that belonged to his wife. He was impatient to be off and had no thought of such romantic nonsense, anyway. With a sad smile, she gave him a kiss, and he was gone.

The sun was not yet up, and the rainstorm that had passed them by had left cooler weather in its wake. From the river beyond, a dark miasma of fog rose, casting its eerie shadows across the landscape. The slight stirrings of the camp were muffled in its thickness, and Philippe's dark figure soon lost in its confusion.

Sir Alec, the elderly knight who had once before sat with her, appeared again. If he resented being lowered to the position of guarding his lordship's mistress, he gave no sign of it. Concern was the only emotion his lined face expressed.

"Ye'd best cover yourself, lass, and be ready to move if it becomes necessary."

Aelvina looked at him blankly for a moment, then, remembering something of Philippe's earlier words, disappeared into the tent to don a simple tunic and chemise. Philippe had said his pouch contained coins and papers, and her hands brushed lightly over it, locating it in the darkness if some need arose. He must trust much to leave her these means of escape. As an afterthought, she retrieved her dagger from its hiding place and tucked it in her girdle. It was a symbol of nobility to which she had no right, but it had been her father's and she proudly wore it now.

Sunrise tinged the darkness as she returned to the entrance. The fog smothered the landscape too heavily to discern much that was happening on the field below the castle walls, but dark shadows moved purposefully through the camp, and the sound of snorting horses caught her ears. They were mounting, preparing to ride at first sign of the enemy.

Thyllda joined them, and Aelvina made room for her silently, not turning her eyes from the shadows gathering in the mist below. Standards appeared, Philippe's taller than the rest and farther down the hill, at the head of the formation. Their banners lay limp and lifeless in the still air.

The call to charge blared through the early morning quiet, startling Aelvina with its abruptness. She had not been prepared for the suddenness of the attack and had heard no sounds of an approaching army, but the huge destriers raced down the hill, shattering the earth with their hooves.

Aelvina was never to remember that day without shuddering in horror. As Philippe's army crashed down the hillside toward the seemingly empty field, an army of mounted knights swarmed from the forest, dashing over the grass in an attempt to reach the castle walls before the attackers. A hail of arrows poured from the battlements above, falling short of the mark as Philippe reined his men into position beyond the dry moat bed.

In the heavy fog, one dark shape was no different from another, and Aelvina paced nervously from the tent to see more clearly before Thyllda dragged her back to safety. The horrifying clangor of steel hitting steel rang through the valley below, the only sound above the horses' hooves, at first. She could not sit still, knowing Philippe was in the center of the melee.

Then the screams rose ... war cries, Aelvina thought, remembering her father's bloodcurdling yells as he rode off to battle. Her mother had never let her near the field of battle. This was the first time Aelvina had ever been within hearing distance of the actual fighting, and her nerves stood on end as the screams continued. The ones ending in shrieks were no war cries, she soon learned.

The sun burned off enough haze to reveal the path of the battle. Evidently the forest band had intended to reach the safety of the walls first, before Philippe's swift maneuver had cut them off. Now, they fought wildly to gain their original destination, backing the king's men into the empty moat and the line of fire from the battlements. Given time, Philippe's much larger forces could destroy the attackers, but in the fog, too many lost their bearings and fell victim to their eagerness. The screams of horses and riders falling off the broken cliffs grew stronger.

Aelvina wished for the monk, Chauvin. A prayer was needed, and she feared hers were worthless. Instead, she sent Thyllda to locate linens for bandages and warm vats of water. The wounded would be many this day.

Philippe's standard still waved high as he gathered his mounted forces together in an attempt to avoid the moat cliffs. With the fog lifting, his archers had better targets, and the actual attack on the walls began. The men on the battlements now had more to deal with than the band of mounted knights. The archers were hidden in all the crevasses of the dry moat bed, and their aim improved with the rising of the sun.

The grassy field became a bowl of dust, and the smoke from the fired mines mixed with the dust and fog to create a thick choking haze that obliterated the sunlight over the camp. Anguished cries rang out from within the walls as the castle occupants began to fully realize the extent of their danger.

As the first of the mines under the castle walls collapsed in a rumble and roar of shuddering stone, the remainder of Bohun's knights dashed into the shallow edge of the moat and over, aiming for the castle's postern gate in a last attempt at safety. Philippe's standard flew high behind them, his massive destrier shredding the turf, leading his men to victory. Whether the gates opened or not, the besieged were sure to die before the day closed.

And then it happened. There was no explanation for it, no rhyme or reason. One moment Philippe's flag flew high, his squire rode at his back where he belonged, his men rode hard behind him, the enemy in front; in the next, the flag tumbled, and Philippe's figure flew over the head of his fallen horse, in front of the charging band of mounted knights.

Aelvina screamed, but her screams mixed with the roars of battle and went unheard. The path of Sir Alec's gaze had been the same as hers, and he grabbed her arm before she could run.

"Where is John? Why was he not behind him? What happened? Oh, Lord, let me go." Frantically, Aelvina fought the hand holding her, but despite his years Sir Alec was strong.

A figure leapt from the dry crevasse, not John's but a larger one, straddling his fallen leader as the charge swept on around them. Other figures—foot soldiers—ran through the filthy haze, dragging the fallen rider into the safety of the moat's walls.

Thyllda materialized at their side, and Sir Alec grunted with relief as the older woman took hold of Aelvina's struggling figure and calmed her. "There are horses in the woods. Get what ye need from the tent and we will be on the way," the knight ordered.

Thyllda turned to Aelvina instead of following orders. "Get quiet and tell me what to take."

The calm order worked better than a slap, and Aelvina's mind snapped back to the two people beside her and away from the hellish figures painted across her vision. "Take?" she asked dazedly, the pain at her insides scratching and clawing like some wild thing.

"Sir Alec has orders to take us from here and wants you to fetch your things. Is there anything you wish to take with you?"

Aelvina's eyes grew wide with horror and fury. "No!" The morning's words returned clearly now . . . Philippe's warnings. He had known, then, that this would not be a simple battle. He wanted her away from here, but she could not go now.

Sir Alec suppressed an irritated frown. "Sir Philippe's orders. I'm to take ye to St. Aubyn as quickly as possible. We have not the time to dally. The men are already within the castle walls."

Aelvina's gaze swung back to the scene below. A pile of bodies lay stacked outside the unopened postern gate; battering rams worked at the drawbridge, but already soldiers poured across the crumbled outer walls. The battlements were empty. All survivors had withdrawn into the keep. Philippe's plans continued without him, carried out by loyal vassals such as Sir Alec. But once the soldiers claimed all the easy booty within, disorder would reign, and Philippe would not be there to halt it with new commands.

"I will not go. I must know if he lives." Aelvina stared at the older man, her jaw lifted in defiance.

Thyllda sighed and shook her head as the grizzled knight turned to her for aid. "I knew it. She is a fool, but we have no choice. She is like quicksilver and would slip from our hands the instant we carried her off. We must find out at once if Sir Philippe lives."

Sir Alec did not like this delay but could understand the justification for it. He, too, wanted to know if his lord survived. The thought of St. Aubyn lands in the hands of the witch of Dunstan caused him to shiver.

"I cannot leave her unprotected. We must find someone to send . . ."

"No. He comes now," Aelvina stated calmly.

Both graying heads turned to the dust and haze below them, searching for what loving eyes must see, but seeing nothing. They turned back to the wisp of a girl between them, silver eyes shining with a light that must pierce the darkness of hell itself, and shook their heads.

"Where, child? We see nothing," Sir Alec asked, uncertain whether she or he were crazed.

"There, coming over the hill. Gundulf is with him, and John. I think John is wounded too. Sir Alec, you must go to them. Thyllda, bring the bandages and medicines here. We will have need of them."

"He lives then?" Joy lit tired eyes as Sir Alec took her words for truth without proof.

"Yes, but I cannot see how badly he is wounded."

"It is enough to know he lives. Now, we must leave before he sees us. My back is too old to take the stripes he will lay upon it if he discovers I have disobeyed orders."

With serene curiosity, Aelvina turned her gaze to the worried knight. "Go? I just told you, he lives. I cannot go."

Alec groaned and Thyllda bit back a smile of sympathy. She had lived with the girl's perversity long enough to have predicted this result, but Sir Alec had not yet had the experience. Without a word, Thyllda turned to follow Aelvina's commands. The knight would learn soon enough who was in charge here.

"He will not blame you for my disobedience. Go to him, or I must," Aelvina repeated with an inner authority that brooked no argument.

Without recognizing the change in leadership, Sir Alec replied to it. "But I still do not see them."

Aelvina pointed to a place amid the haze. "They are there."

Sir Alec's eyes widened as he followed her finger. Just where she had indicated, three dark figures stumbled from the gloom, impossible to see moments before, but emerging from the smoke just as the sun burned away the fog. With a cry of recognition, he ran to add his shoulder to the mission.

Philippe was conscious, and his curses blistered the ears as Sir Alec and a bedraggled Gundulf hauled him across the tent portal to meet Aelvina's defiant gaze.

"Get her out of here! Is there not a man among you who can make a woman mind? Must I do everything myself?" Philippe's tirade erupted into incoherent curses as they lowered him against the pillows.

John and Sir Alec looked at each other, and then to Aelvina. She paid them no heed, but hastened to Philippe's side, where Gundulf cut the laces of his hauberk.

When no one responded to his orders, Philippe bellowed in rage and attempted to lunge to his feet. "If you cannot carry her out of here, I will!"

"My lord, you are going nowhere but straight to hell unless you lie still and allow me to stop the bleeding. There is no priest at hand and your sins mount with each passing minute."

With Aelvina's quiet words, Sir Alec waved dismissal to the young squire. "Go have your wounds tended. My neck is already on the block for the lady." So saying, he joined Gundulf in holding the large and furious knight to the bed.

At this betrayal of his loyal retainer, Philippe fell silent, his eyes roaming accusingly over the three figures at his side.

With wily determination, Philippe turned his gaze to the young yeoman removing his torn leather jerkin. "I cannot protect her any longer. If you can carry her from this place, she is yours."

Aelvina's lips tightened, but she said nothing as she took her dagger to Philippe's sherte and sliced it from his wound. Her gaze, as it met Gundulf's, was icy.

Gundulf shrugged and shook his shaggy blond head. "What would I do with her, sire? She would slit my throat and feed me to the wolves before nightfall. You are the only one who can tame her."

Philippe grunted as Aelvina lifted his torn shoulder to examine the extent of the wound, but whether in pain or in response to Gundulf, she could not tell. The mists were closing over the emerald isles of his gaze as it drifted back to her.

"I could not keep you before; now you will not leave. Must you ever defy me?"

Aelvina's gaze softened as she saw the pain deepening the lines of his handsome visage. "It seems so, milord. I told you once I recognize no man as master."

Philippe's eyes closed and his words came as if from a distance. "Yet you serve me well, wench."

His big body fell forward limply as they rolled him over to dress the large tear through shoulder and back. The power of such a blow could have broken his neck. Aelvina stared at the enormous wound with horror, then lifted her eyes to meet Gundulf's and Sir Alec's, to see if they understood what she had seen. They met her gaze with mutual horror.

"He has been struck from behind." Sir Alec looked as if he wished to swallow his words once they were out.

"It is not I who needs protection, then," Aelvina pointed out. "Only his men should have been at his back."

Wary about casting blame on his comrades, Sir Alec sidestepped the issue. "There is no certainty. Strange things happen in battle. He went down; anything could have caused it."

"But you will guard him?"

Aelvina returned her attention to Philippe, leaving Sir Alec and Gundulf to determine how to carry out her orders. She washed the wound with wine and cursed the lack of eggs and herbs that might seal the gash from evil humors. She bit her lower lip, glancing about the tent until she located the small sewing box; then her eyes lit with another memory.

Her mother had learned something of the art of healing from her Eastern captors, and Aelvina remembered the time she had used needle and thread to close a gash such as this one. She must take every precaution to make the muscle heal as it should so Philippe might swing his sword again. Under Sir Alec's doubtful gaze, she threaded the needle and neatly stitched the skin in place. The patient stirred and cursed restlessly in his sleep but did not return to consciousness.

Gundulf watched Aelvina's devoted attentions to this Norman knight with saddened eyes, knowing he had lost all chances—given them up deliberately, as well he should. She was not meant for the likes of him. After a word with Sir Alec he left the tent.

Aelvina never noticed his absence.

Drunken carousing echoed throughout the camp and inside the battered castle walls that night, but the men kept a respectful distance from the tent on the hill. The ring of Philippe's loyal knights camped outside had much to do with it; fear and respect for the valiant knight who had delivered the stronghold also held sway. Wariness for the sorceress whose silvered gaze was reputed to turn men to stone completed his protection. This same sorceress treated the injured with a skill and gentleness surpassing all others and provided an additional deterrent; so for the nonce, the rioting remained in the valley.

Philippe woke during the night and tried to turn over, but Aelvina was instantly there, soothing his restlessness and holding his head so he might drink from a dipper. He relaxed with his head in her lap, his fingers sliding beneath the folds of her kirtle to stroke her bare leg.

"Why do you stay?" Philippe murmured. "The monk will find the child, not I."

Aelvina slid her hands through his hair, testing for signs of fever. He was slightly warm, but the loss of blood had been great. Not a danger signal yet. Still, his murmurings left her uneasy. Why did she stay? It was not an easy question.

"I am loyal, if not obedient, milord. I stay until you tire of me, as promised. Are you tired of me?"

She thought she detected a chuckle, and his hand tightened about her leg. "Not dead, yet, *ma chérie.*" His hand loosened and fell still, and Aelvina knew he slept; but she continued to sit there, smoothing his hair.

She had little time for contemplating anything in the next days. Thyllda and Alice tended to the less seriously injured in the other tents, but others besides Philippe needed Aelvina's attentions, and her days filled past overflowing.

When the living sobered, they buried the dead. None of the forest party had survived, including the baron's son, who had died attempting to enter the castle walls. The baron and his household were presumably still alive within the keep, but there was no one in authority to negotiate with them.

The men systematically destroyed the castle walls, one of the few orders Philippe made before the fever took command of his senses and left the army leaderless again. Sir Alec and the other loyal knights continued the pretense of his recovery to control the mercenary troops, but the game could not go on forever.

Sir Alec watched as Aelvina forced water between Philippe's parched lips, with little success. The dark bruises and cuts of his fall healed slowly, but the enormous gash from the battle-ax festered, shooting ominous threads of evil red across his broad, bronzed back.

"We've had no reply from our message to the king. I do not trust these hirelings; they disappear and I do not know if the message goes through at all or how it comes out when it arrives. I would go myself, but there are too few of us left," Sir Alec muttered.

Aelvina knew what the old man meant. The men grew restless, and not a night went by without a brawl outside, sometimes daringly close to the tent on the hill. She had heard the taunts, though Philippe's loyal knights silenced them as quickly as they could. She dared not roam far from Philippe now, and the situation grew dangerous. If someone sought to kill Philippe, it would be easy to do through her. Raping a whore and causing a brawl were common enough practices.

She would not dwell on the reasons why someone would wish Philippe dead. He never spoke of his life, so her imagination had free rein. It was a senseless endeavor. Instead, she sought some solution to Sir Alec's immediate problem.

"Would it help if the message were written? Would the men think it from Philippe's hand and be more careful of delivery?" she asked cautiously. Sir Alec already looked upon her with suspicion. The knowledge that she could also put quill to parchment might unsettle him entirely.

"It would help, 'twere it possible, but I fear his lordship is in no condition to make a mark." She heard no suspicion in his tone, only anxiety, and Aelvina breathed a little easier.

"I have some knowledge of letters. If you would tell me what to write, I should try to make it convincing. I am certain there is no man among them who can read."

Sir Alec looked skeptical. "Where would a lass like ye learn to make letters?"

Aelvina mentally crossed herself and prayed for forgiveness before she answered. "In a convent, sire. I learned to copy passages from the holy word."

The old man started at this unexpected revelation, but Aelvina's meekly bent head eased his suspicion. "How came a good lass like ye to be a . . ." He gestured helplessly, unable to complete the phrase.

"It is no matter now, is it?" she asked quietly, diverting the opportunity to weave a more elaborate tale. "Do you wish me to fetch the materials?'' Relieved of the embarrassment of learning more, Sir Alec agreed.

The message went out that night, with more of Aelvina's words than Sir Alec's, if he had but known; yet she knew its reply would never be read by the man in the bed. Philippe's fever soared and the infection spread. If he still lived by the time the reply arrived, he would not be conscious enough to read or understand it.

Only one other choice remained. As she had deliberately defied his orders already, Aelvina saw no reason she could not do it again. It was time to put the witch's tricks to good use and recover some value from that year of evil. With the last of her precious herbs, Aelvina mixed a weak concoction of the sleeping draft and poured as much of it between Philippe's lips as she could. It would not do if he cried out and someone discovered her absence.

Assured Philippe slept soundly, she sought Gundulf. He was never far away these days, as neither were Sir Alec and John, but she trusted Gundulf's loyalty the most. When the young yeoman entered, she explained her plans.

"I am going into the woods to fetch what I need for medicines. Sir Philippe sleeps and will not cry out, but I want no one to know I have gone. See that all stay from this tent and none will be the wiser.''

Gundulf's eyes clouded with the darkness of a sudden storm. "The forest is more dangerous than before. The woods crawl with mischief makers, and the men care not what they hunt. Send me.''

"You cannot know what I seek and I will find it more quickly.'' When she noted Gundulf's unusual resistance, Aelvina smiled sadly and touched his sleeve. "It is not for you to do, Gundulf; you have a family to protect. Philippe is the father of my child, and if he dies, my life is worthless. It is best this way. Do as I ask, please.''

The sorrow in his eyes brought regret that things could not be elsewise, but with determination, Aelvina saw him gone. She heard his voice with Sir Alec's, gathered up her herb pouch and knife, checked on Philippe's even breathing one more time, and slid beneath the tent posts as she had before.

As she wandered through the forest's cool shadows, her thoughts were mixed and hopped uneasily from one subject to the next. Philippe's words still rang with disturbing clarity in her ears. Why did she stay?

He had given her every means and opportunity to leave. Every day that she remained with him saw another sin heaped upon her soul. If she left, she could aid the monk's search and perhaps earn forgiveness and God's blessing once more.

Still, her feet carried her into the dark reaches of the forest with an instinct stronger than morals or reasoning. Her eyes sought the colors and foliage of the herbs she needed to pluck. Her pouch filled, and with her knife she dug roots and cuttings of plants to bring back. It was foolishness—all foolishness. She could not make a home of an army camp. And the man she worked to save could never be more than lord and master. Was that what she wanted?

The picture of Philippe with the Lady Ravenna on his arm and children at his feet revolted her beyond any mere physical pain she had known. She knew she could never bear another man's child or feel another man's hands on her, not even the honest Gundulf's. Her body rebelled at the very thought of another man possessing her as Philippe had.

She was bound for a hell of her own making, but she trod the path to its doors willingly. To leave Philippe before he cast her aside had become unthinkable. Aelvina knew she had committed herself to a folly of unfathomable dimensions; nevertheless she turned her feet toward the camp and the Norman knight who had captured her soul as well as her body.

As she rolled beneath the flapping tent silk, she knew at once that something had changed. She lay still, her gaze sweeping the tent, observing nothing unusual. As she stood, her gaze traveled to the bed, and she caught her breath at the sight. Philippe's emerald eyes glittered with fury.

"So that is how you do it? No sorcery, then. Where did you find the knife? Your lover brought it to you, I suppose? Why does he allow you to stay? Does he wait for the gold you will bring him when I let you go?"

Aelvina held her breath. She had not expected this attack. The sleeping draft must have strange effects to bring back his senses so strongly.

At the sound of Philippe's angry voice, Gundulf appeared in the entrance, his gaze finding Aelvina with short-lived relief. Philippe's roar of rage shook the tent. "Get out of here, you whoremongering, traitorous son of a she-wolf! I'll kill her before I let you have her."

Gundulf stared in amazement at the dark knight struggling to right himself in the bed's soft confines. "He is mad!"

Aelvina advanced into the tent, shaking off her horror. "Mayhaps, but it is with a madness that has eaten at his insides far longer than the fever. He has no trust in me. You had best go."

Philippe staggered to his feet, his bronzed body still menacing despite its suffering. Before he could lunge after the intruder, Aelvina flew to his side, wrapping her arms around his broad chest so his weight fell on her.

Philippe's vivid curses rang out, bringing John and Sir

Alec running. Between them, they managed to fight the struggling patient into bed, but Philippe's cries and curses continued to rent the air. For the first time since he had fallen, Aelvina was visibly shaken.

"It is the fever, my lady," Sir Alec offered. "We had best summon the leeches so he will rest."

This restored Aelvina's senses to a degree, and she shook her head vehemently. "No! He has lost too much blood as it is. See how his body weakens so even an old man and a boy can hold him. Could you do that were he well?" she asked scornfully, knowing she must regain command or they would take it from her. That Sir Alec referred to her as "lady" was of little note.

Aelvina touched her fingers to the wound Philippe had torn open again. Philippe shuddered beneath her touch. Hungrily, his eyes sought hers, then closed once more.

"It is my fault. If I had been at his back when I should, I would have taken the blow." John's mournful eyes looked at Aelvina. "What may I do? There must be something . . ." he pleaded.

Aelvina studied this stripling lad. She guessed him to be several years older than herself, about Gundulf's age or a little younger. He had not Gundulf's size, but was light and wiry, his broad shoulders indicating he had not gained his full weight as yet. She read honest sorrow in his gaze, and loyalty as strong as family ties, but Aelvina frowned.

"Why were you not at his back when you should?" she demanded. It was a question that had long clamored for answering.

Sir Alec interrupted. "The lad is guilty of nothing but carelessness. I have already inquired, and he suffers enough."

Aelvina turned to the older man for explanations, with the same look as a wolf protecting her young.

"The lad was where he belonged, but thinking only our own men behind them, he relaxed his caution in the eargerness of the chase. A lance caught him in the side, and he near lost his seat. That was when Sir Philippe was attacked."

"How could one of the enemy be among our own soldiers? They ran. I saw them."

There was no other answer. It had to have been one of their own men's lances that had shoved John aside. An accident in the heat of the chase, perhaps, had it any other result. Philippe's wound spoke otherwise.

"We are doing all we can, my lady. It will be up to Sir Philippe to find the traitor."

Aelvina's gaze swept over the loyal trio. She knew they would give their lives for Philippe's protection and she could not ask more. Aware of Sir Alec's respectful tone, she turned to him questioningly.

"Sir Philippe is lucky to have so loyal a vassal as you, Sir Alec, but surely this loyalty does not extend to such as I. Why do you not call me by name?"

The grizzled knight looked embarrassed and tugged at the worn threads of his shabby surcoat. "It don't seem right, somehow. Ye're not like them others, and coming from a convent and all . . . it just don't seem right," he ended stubbornly.

Gundulf gave Aelvina a startled look at the mention of a convent but held his tongue. Even Gundulf's limited imagination dared not linger long on the thought of Aelvina's temper and tongue in a convent. The nuns would be deaf with horror by now.

Aelvina felt a twinge of guilt at her deception, but the rumor would strengthen her position, and she needed what support she could obtain. "Thank you, sir. I will do all that is within my power to see that your loyalty is justified.''

It was a regal dismissal and all three men recognized it. While the others departed, John lingered nervously. "Please, my lady, is there anything I might do?"

The anxiety and pleading in his eyes touched Aelvina, and she searched for some simple task to relieve the youth's guilt. The only chore her thoughts lingered on was abhorrent to her nature. The Lady Ravenna had not yet been told of her husband's injury. Why did she have the feeling that the lady already knew and did not care? It was superstitious nonsense.

"What needs to be done cannot be done now, I fear. Your loyalty and presence is needed here for the nonce. I can treat my lord's wounds, but I cannot guard his life. That must be your task."

John nodded sadly and left her alone. If the herbs she had gathered did not work better than the sleeping draft, she would be more alone than she had ever been in her life. The thought shook her, and she hastily returned to work.

Chapter Thirteen

Aelvina lost track of the number of days she pounded and mixed and rubbed the results into the festering flesh of Philippe's shoulder. She lost contact with the outside world, and cared nothing that the knight sent by King Henry had arrived and was incompetently handling both mercenaries and negotiations. Nothing mattered but that the spreading streaks of poisoned flesh halted and slowly began to retreat.

Philippe's fever abated, leaving him with occasional bouts of consciousness when his wandering gaze would fall on Aelvina. He did not repeat the last angry incident, much to Aelvina's relief. She feared the distrust that ate at him but, not knowing its cause, could do nothing to dispel it. She was only grateful he submitted to her ministrations.

At night, she curled up by Philippe's side, so that when he woke he could reach for her. Some nights, she lay awake praying for those moments when his hand would twist in her hair, or touch her breast. She would hold his fevered body next to hers and listen to his hoarse voice whispering her name. Other nights, she waited in vain.

The day finally arrived when she woke to find smoldering green eyes open and watching her with clear comprehension, and her heart leapt with joy.

A dark beard shadowed his jaw, but there was no mistaking the light in Philippe's eyes as they raked over her. Teasingly, Aelvina stretched, allowing him to look his fill. It had been a long time since he had pleasured her body, and it responded eargerly to just his glance.

Noting how the crests of her breasts puckered beneath his gaze, Philippe's lips twisted in a sardonic grin. "I'm starved, wench. Wouldst thou lie there all day?"

Aelvina sat up, but Philippe's uninjured arm snaked around her waist and pulled her down on top of him. She sprawled along his naked length, feeling the muscles of his hard body tense beneath hers.

"My lord?" she asked, not certain whether she was to be met with an angry tirade or a playful tweak. She was not certain of anything anymore.

"I thought you to look as hungry as I. Was I wrong?" Philippe taunted.

His hand traveled over the curves of her breast and waist and came to rest on the flare of her hip. She felt the hardening of his desire between her legs, and comprehension dawned. Aelvina raise herself slightly so she did not rest on his wounded shoulder and stared down into the boiling depths of his eyes. Her fingers dug into the rough fur of his chest, resisting a wild surge of hope.

"You are not wrong, milord, but fasting will not hurt us half so much as feasting will. Your wound has not yet begun to knit well."

"My shoulder is not the part of me that hungers, sorceress. If you wish me well, you will tend to all my needs."

There was an air of defiance to Philippe's words, daring her to refuse, and though she feared disturbing the wound, refusing was the last thing she wanted to.

"You will lie still?" she asked doubtfully. Eager as she was to obey his command, she could not risk weeks of work.

Philippe grinned, the wolfish grin she remembered well from their first encounter. "Serve me well and I will. Do not, and I will warm your enchanting bottom for you."

"I can see nothing ails your humor, my lord," Aelvina replied haughtily, but the glimmer of her eyes belied her tone. With care, she raised herself as he had taught her once before, savoring the power of withholding their pleasure by teasing at his heated flesh. Such play could not last long with a man as hungry as Philippe, and impatiently, he caught her waist and pulled her down over him.

Aelvina gave a piercing cry of joy as he surged into her. To be joined with him once more was a pleasure she had feared never to know again.

She moved slowly at first, fearing to harm him, but from the impatient rocking of his hips, she knew it would be better to be quick. Sunbursts of fiery white light exploded in her head as Philippe responded to her rhythm. Philippe's shuddering release brought hers, and she groaned softly, not wanting the moment to end as their bodies clung together as one.

Philippe cupped her breast, then slid downward to where they joined.

"So small a wench to bring such pleasure. Do I hurt you when I do this?"

Aelvina gave a muffled laugh and kissed his wiry jaw. "You hurt me when you do not. It has been too long."

"How so? There is an army of men out there eager to oblige you. Why suffer when you need not?"

"Fie on you, milord. If you are so witless as to think that . . ."

Aelvina tried to disentangle her legs from his, but Philippe held her in place. Fever might have weakened him, but he still had strength enough to hold her.

"Tell me about it then," Philippe demanded roughly. "Tell me why you linger at my bedside when you could be romping through the court with de Harcourt or rolling in the hay with your eager young yeoman. Tell me, elf-child. I would hear the words."

Aelvina was terrified by the ferocity and tenderness of his demand, unwilling to admit even to herself what he asked. She glanced up with relief as a voice from outside the tent intruded upon the growing silence.

"My lady, didst thou call?"

She smiled at young John's voice. He must have been their guardian for the night, and she could well imagine his puzzlement at the sounds from within the tent.

Philippe watched her closely. " 'My lady,' is it now? Have you captured my squire in your snare, too?"

"Yes, and all the king's men," she whispered mischievously. With a swing of her hips, she was free and darting for the protection of the screen at the tent's rear.

"Go fetch my meal, John, and a whip for the lady's hide," Philippe roared, but laughter twitched at his lips.

It did not take long for word of his recovery to race through camp. Aelvina was at wit's end to keep all and sundry from breaking his rest with their boons and complaints. When awake, Philippe watched with amusement as she strictly parceled out his time. The little lass in her silken braids had donned a robe of dignity Philippe did not recognize, but it was obvious the others respected it. Even his mighty knights bowed before her commands.

Their days were suddenly full, but at night Philippe taught Aelvina the gentleness of lovemaking; the means of satisfying their needs without using their bodies to fight each other as they had so often in the past. The tenderness she had lavished upon him these past weeks, he returned in an amazing variety of ways.

Aelvina had known the fearless Norman knight possessed a core of kindness, but she had not imagined the tenderness he could bestow upon her when he chose. To lie in his arms like this was much more than she had ever dared ask, and she feared some divine retribution would shatter this haven of shelter she had found.

It was wrong. Aelvina knew what they were doing was wrong. She must find her child and Philippe must return to his wife. There was no happy ending to this story. He had lands needing his care, heirs to breed, and she could have no place in that life. Already, his job here was almost done, hampered only by his wound. Soon, there would not even be that excuse.

As she lay restlessly turning in his arms one night, Philippe's grip caught her. "What is wrong, Aelvina? You pace like a nervous cat during the day and prowl the floors at night. What is on your mind?"

Aelvina picked at the hairs on his chest, drawing her fingers through the tight curls and unwinding them. "There has been no word from Chauvin?"

"You know there has not. Do you wish me to send for him?"

"I wish to go to him, to help him search. I know I could find my son; I know it, Philippe."

His arm tightened about her waist and she sensed the deepening frown on his face. "If your witch's powers tell you that much, they must tell you also that you would die before you found him. Do you think Marta has not heard of your presence in this camp?''

Aelvina fell silent. It was a foregone conclusion that the inhabitants of Dunstan Castle must know by now, that Sir Philippe had installed a mistress in his bed. This did not sit easy with her. Had Lady Ravenna been anyone else, Aelvina would never have tarried so long, fearing harm to a new bride. But she held no sympathy for that hated lady. The thought of them knowing her name and whispering it between them was not something she had considered, though, and it gave her a peculiar, uneasy feeling.

"She thinks me dead. Surely Marta cannot know it is I," she whispered, half to herself.

"The camp is full of spies, you foolish creature. My wife's vassals are required to serve me as well as my own. They are not many—there are few men left on Dunstan lands— but there are enough. It is a certain thing they know you live. It is one of the reasons I wished you safely in my home at St. Aubyn. I fear you may be in danger even here."

Aelvina had recognized her danger here, felt it all around her, but she had assumed it was Philippe's death they sought through her. His version was nothing less than astonishing.

"It is you they cleaved with a battle-ax, not I. How can I harm anyone?"

Philippe lay silent, drawing his hand through the silken length of her hair. There was no doubt in his mind that this feckless sprite had saved his life. He had once vowed to bring her willingly to his arms, to see that she was as obsessed as he. Only now, when he had every reason to assume his success, he could not carry out his final revenge. He did not know her part in his downfall, but he could not see her as more than the innocent she seemed. He sighed. For her own protection, it was time she learned some things he had told few.

"I think you might explain that question better than I, *ma chérie*. You are the cause of this tangle I am in. Is it not time to tell me truly what happened that night we met?"

Aelvina started up in horror, the weary distance of Philippe's words tearing at her heart and shaking her complacency. What was he asking?

"I have told you all I know. I was drugged and you raped me. It was outside and I must have been tied to one of those giant stones. There were others there, but I could not see their faces, only yours. You hurt me and I lost consciousness, and that was all I knew for a very long time. I thought it to be a nightmare, but the child proved otherwise." Aelvina's voice choked on a sob at the memory. She tried to tear from his grip, but Philippe held her tightly.

"The child could just as easily have been a result of our afternoon together, but I do not think we both had the same nightmare." He held her shaking body next to his, fitting the pieces of the puzzle together and discovering a chilling picture emerging.

"I think it was intended that we remember it as a nightmare—at least I was," he continued. "You, they intended to kill after your usefulnesss was over. If you had not come to me that day, I would never have known of your existence. You are a danger to whoever planned this."

"What are you saying, milord?"

"Aelvina, *ma chérie,* you must know as much as I. It is you who baited the trap; you must have known what would happen. Perhaps then it mattered little to you if the price was right, but surely now you can tell me what you know. I will pay you more than they can ever summon if you will give me proof enough to have this marriage annulled."

"What?" Aelvina sat up abruptly, wishing she could better see the face of this man she had never really known.

Philippe's voice was harsh and almost cruel as he raised himself from the pillows. "Just tell the king how they used you to bait the trap to put me in Lady Ravenna's bed. I want nothing more than to get out of this devil-borne marriage!"

"I know nothing of what you speak," she stated flatly, drawing away. It was as if he had deliberately set out to kill what was between them. Though some part of her heart fluttered at the news of his desire to be rid of his wife, she shut off its clamor, willing herself to face this calmly.

"Know nothing! How can you expect me to believe that? It was you who deliberately filled my thoughts and loins until I could do no more than follow where you led; you who filled me with such an inhuman madness I would take you anywhere, under any conditions, just to rid the lust that burned my soul; you who led me to your lady's bed and whatever folly I committed there in my obsession. It is you who, whether willingly or not, provided the child that ensured my lady's claim and forced me into this misery in which I am bound!" Philippe cried with explosive passion.

"You are mad. You are quite mad!" Aelvina edged away, refusing to hear what he was saying. He could not mean this. The fever must be returning.

"You are right! I am quite mad, crazed with a madness that infects my soul like some insidious poison, and *you* planted it there. Now tell me, for God's sake, why?"

It was a tormented scream and Aelvina turned to run, but Philippe grabbed her wrist and flung her against the pillows. "You are not going anywhere until you tell me why. This affects you as much as me; it is in your own interest to tell me all, at once."

Philippe's tone was more rational, but the grip on her wrist was harsh and accusing. Aelvina lay as one stunned. She strove to find an answer that would please him, that would make him release her, but his words ran like madness through her ears.

"I know nothing of that night, Philippe! Nothing! I was bound and drugged and unable to lead you anywhere. Please, I know nothing of what you speak!"

"Then why is it I bedded *you* and woke up with the lady and a roomful of witnesses to swear of my scandalous behavior? And you were gone! I tore the place apart looking for you to swear to my innocence, and you disappeared as if the walls had swallowed you! And you tell me you know nothing? Speak, Aelvina, before I strangle you with my own hands."

"It was your own hide you sought to protect and not mine, then! You did not seek me, but release from the follies of your lust. I should have known, you bastard. And you accuse me!"

Furious, Aelvina fought the hands binding her to the bed, hands she had loved, hands she had thought belonged to a man she could trust. Anger and despairing fury warred within her, and she fought like a crazed lioness.

But Philippe was not done with her. His strong hand closed about her throat as he held her pinned with his weight. "The lady bothered me not that day; it was you I sought. My obsession was not eased, and I cared not what happened to the lady. That came later, when the lady told the king she was with child and demanded retribution. She got it. She got my name and no more. When the child was born, I called it mine, but I remembered none of its making. I have a wife and child I do not want and you to blame."

A child! He had a child by that witch and had said none of it! She would kill him. How dared he use her like this, pretend his affection, when all he wanted was a means to rid himself of wife and child? By all the saints, how could she have been so blind and foolish?

"Kill me and be done with it, then," she spat from beneath his imprisoning fingers. "What is a dead whore to anyone? But if you do not kill me, you will ever have to look to your back. I'll not allow you to get away with this."

Philippe's fingers tightened around her throat and his rage was such that he could easily have followed through had it been anyone else but this vixen. He had wrung no admission from her and had accomplished nothing but to disturb a great aching throb in the vicinity of his shoulder. He released her throat but kept her beneath him.

"If you kill me, you will never live to see your child," he said wearily, all anger suddenly fled. Everything was in ashes again; he had advanced no farther than that day a year ago when she had eluded him.

Aelvina grew still. "What do you mean?"

"I do not know yet whether your child lives, but a child bearing my name lives. If they are one and the same, as I assume, he is Lady Ravenna's insurance of holding Dunstan. If I should die, the child is her only hold. She would kill you before you even set foot on Dunstan lands. I am your only hope to retrieve the child."

With that, Philippe rolled over and covered his eyes with his arm. The whole scheme had become so blatantly clear, only Aelvina's part in it was hazy. He was too weary to rehash again what he had already gone over in his mind so many times.

Aelvina rose, wrapping the linen around her before padding the floor in search of her clothes. She would not stay here another minute. He had known her child could be in a cradle in Dunstan Castle and had said nothing. She could kill him for that reason alone.

"Where do you think you are going?" The voice was still weary, that of a man bordering on the brink of exhaustion.

"I am not staying here—that is for certain." She had not thought beyond fleeing from this man who had ruined her life not once, but twice.

"Yes, you are. I am your only protection, your only chance of ever seeing your child. You will stay here as agreed, until I grow tired of you." The simple command held no anger. She had no choice and he used the fact brutally.

Aelvina stopped, recognizing the words for what they were—a threat. If the child in the castle was hers, he had the power to keep her from it. She had abased herself this far for the sake of the child; why stop now? Her life was worthless. What right had she to pride? But someday, she swore, she would kill him.

Chapter Fourteen

The estrangement between the lovers was obvious to the men close to them, but they were at a loss for explanations. Aelvina continued in her place as before, tending Philippe's wounds and sleeping in his bed at night, but she had returned to the icy-eyed prisoner of earlier days. Philippe was little better, snarling when approached, barking if interrupted. The men shrugged and avoided speaking to either of them.

Thyllda noticed the change at once, and approached her charge cautiously, but Aelvina remained cold and impassive. It was obvious even Thyllda had known of the child in the castle and had not told her. She feared she had no friends, not even the monk, Chauvin, and her heart weighed heavily within her.

Could the child be hers? The thought was with her day and night, even while Philippe slaked his lust with her body. She could no longer remain unresponsive to his touch; too much had gone between them for that. She still cried out with joyous reunion when he planted himself deep inside her, but it wasn't the same. The infant she had seen for that brief instant of birth wailed before her eyes, even as his father moved within her.

While Philippe mended and called military conferences in their tent every day, Aelvina wandered farther afield. Her little herb garden had taken root, but she had lost interest in it. The walls of the castle keep loomed large above the valley, and she wondered about the inhabitants imprisoned inside. Did they feel the same hopeless desperation as she, locked in a prison from which there was no escape but death?

On the ground overlooking the banks of the river, Aelvina watched as the camp women washed their clothes. It was strange, but she never remembered washing her own clothes as these women did. Of course, even when she had returned to England with her parents and they spent their days traveling in the old wagon, Thyllda had been with them, and the faithful servant had taken care of these chores. However, after her parents had died, she had no coins to pay for Thyllda's services, yet Thyllda still did the menial jobs. It was strange what things one took for granted.

A movement among the women caught her eye and diverted her attention. One of the women was dressed all in black, an odd sight since she knew of only whores in this camp, and black was not among their favorite colors. Philippe's warnings returned, and with suspicion, Aelvina started down to the riverbank. The black figure broke from the group and hurried into the woods.

Aelvina questioned the others, without success. Even if they had known anything, they would not have told the nobleman's whore.

She wondered if she should mention the incident to Philippe. It could have been any of the villagers up to trade with the women of the camp, but Aelvina had an uneasy suspicion it was not. What would Marta want here, though?

Aelvina lifted her skirts and climbed back up the river-bank, her thoughts drifting from one question to the next. At the top, a figure emerged from the shadow of the woods, and Aelvina stepped backward, startled with the unexpectedness of this appearance. Her surprise changed to annoyance. Raymond grinned unpleasantly at her expression.

"Thought I had forgotten, did you not? I bide my time. I hear your nobleman has not been too pleased with you lately. How much longer do you think I will have to wait?" he asked, his heavy-lidded gaze raking over her bosom beneath the tight bodice of her girded tunic.

Aelvina's skin crawled at the coarse grating of Raymond's voice. She had not seen him in camp and thought perhaps he was one of the many deserters, but luck evidently was not with her.

"Until hell freezeth over, my lord," she replied through clenched teeth, and with a twitch of her skirts, she hurried off, half surprised that he did not halt her.

She was in no humor now to endure Philippe's black moods, so she sought solace in Thyllda's company until it grew dark and she could delay no longer. Then, reluctantly, she turned her feet toward "home."

Her entrance evidently served as a signal for the evening meal. The bustle of activity prevented any exchange of words. After the room cleared, they sat in silence, Aelvina picking at her food and Philippe pretending not to notice. At last, unable to tolerate the listlessness of her usually animated features, he sought a topic to interest, if not to please her.

"If, perchance, the child is found, how do you intend

to keep him?'' It was one of many topics eating at his thoughts, making it nigh on to impossible to concentrate on what he must.

Aelvina looked up with surprise. ''I would like to find a cottage somewhere, with a small yard for a garden. I could grow my herbs and sell them, and perhaps earn a little with my salves. We could raise our own food, and mayhap, if we find work, we could have a cow. The child would be happy with such a life, I think.''

A dreamy expression had replaced the listlessness, and her eyes glowed a soft azure as she contemplated this impossible future. Philippe knew it to be absurd and punched small holes in her bubble.

''Without a father? Who will teach him to hunt and to ride and to be a man?''

Aelvina frowned. ''He will learn, if I must teach him myself.''

''You think I have no rights in the matter? He is my son, too, and I would not see him raised by a houseful of women.''

Aelvina's eyebrows shot up as she met Philippe's stare. ''You are willing to admit the child is yours!''

''It does not look as if I have much choice. From what you and the monk have told me, your child was born at nearly the same time as the Lady Ravenna's, and since I presumably lay with you the same day . . .'' He shrugged expressively. ''The lady may have been bearing another man's seed, but unless you found a lover shortly after you left my arms, I know you were not.''

Aelvina did not trust the light in his eyes. Was he saying he believed her, that he knew she had waited for him? Philippe did not always speak what he thought, and it remained to her to read behind the words. She was too eager to believe the best to judge wisely. She shook her head and shut her hopes away in her heart.

"There was no other. Who should know better than you? But it matters little. I will not make demands of you in the child's name. My only wish is for the child's return."

"And I have said I will not allow my son to be raised by women. Whether he be heir or bastard, he is my own, and he will be raised fitting to his breeding." Philippe spoke softly but firmly.

"His mother is a whore, sir. In what manner do you raise a son bred of a whore?"

Philippe's large fist crashed against the small wooden table, jarring the flask of wine and the goblets. "His mother is a pigheaded ass, but she is only a whore if she makes herself one. And then I will personally throttle her and there will be no argument."

Aelvina did not know whether to laugh or cry. They were arguing over a child that might or might not exist and whether she be ass or whore. It was entirely nonsensical, and her trembling hand reached for the wine rather than seek a sensible answer. Philippe did the same, seeing she did not intend to reply.

Aelvina's nose wrinkled in distaste as she raised the goblet to her lips, and then her eyes widened in horror. Flinging the cup aside, she threw herself across the table and slapped Philippe's goblet from his lips.

"What is this, then? Am I not to drink because the wine is not to your taste?" Philippe asked scornfully.

"My lord, you have drunk none of it?" she asked anxiously, wrapping her hand firmly about the base so he could not raise it again.

"Nor will I if you do not let it loose." Philippe frowned, suddenly realizing this was not part of their ongoing argument. "What is it?" he demanded.

"Is there some animal in the stable you wish to dispose of gently?" she asked, still staring in horror at the liquid that could so easily have passed his lips.

With quick understanding, Philippe summoned the guard at the tent entrance. Young John appeared, and Philippe grimly handed him the goblet. "Feed this to that ass whose leg will not heal. Do not taste it yourself or you may meet the same end we planned for the animal."

John's eyes grew wide with horror, knowing they had just spoken of destroying the animal, and he gingerly took the cup.

Silence descended between them again as John disappeared into the night. The food on their trenchers began to congeal and Philippe ordered it carried out and buried away from the dogs. Whatever appetite he'd had now dissipated. John's return came almost as a welcome respite.

"Well?" Philippe asked irritably.

"It died instantly," John answered in awe-filled horror. His hand shook as it returned the goblet to the table.

Philippe stared at the cup with disgust. "Take it away and bring me some ale from the men's larder. Then find out who filled this flask and brought our food."

As John departed again, Philippe gazed at Aelvina's bent head, remembering how close she had been to swallowing the liquid. Evil gripped at his intestines and fear seized his soul. Fear was not an emotion with which he had much familiarity. To ride into battle against a known enemy brought a thrill of excitement, but this . . .

Philippe digested the bitter knowledge that he did not know how to fight this kind of battle, nor did he know his enemy. And it was not his life alone that was endangered.

"It seems we are both expendable, *ma chérie*." He had not called her that since the night he had told her of his child, but Aelvina scarcely noticed.

"It is the witch, Marta. I thought I saw her at the river today but was not sure. The potion is one of hers; I recognized it."

The words were soft, without emotion, and Philippe thought of the months she must have spent in the hands of that evil bitch who served his wife. His fingers tightened against the table, imagining Aelvina's fair delicacy at the mercy of unspeakable horrors. He was not given to flights of fancy, but a dire dread now gripped him.

He sent for more men to search the area but knew it was useless. Marta would know at once her plan had failed and would disappear like the witch she was until she had formed a new and better one.

If only he had finished his work here. . . . He was tired of this cat-and-mouse game. He was a man of action, and there was no action in sitting here waiting to be casually slaughtered.

"Why would they harm you, milord?" Aelvina asked. "With you dead, the king could claim guardianship of both the lady and your heir, could he not?"

Philippe grimaced and played idly with the dirk at his side. "Henry is not the thief the others were. The lands belong to my heir and there would be little profit in marrying off a lady with no lands of her own. She has accomplished what she had intended, evidently. As long as I do not interfere with her affairs, she cares not what I do, but she must be growing nervous of your presence. To kill us both would lay any question to the child's origins."

Aelvina gasped. "Then I had best leave, milord. She would leave you unharmed if she did not fear me."

Philippe uttered a short bark of laughter. "Unless you think Marta rode behind me, swinging a battle-ax, it is not so simple as that. There is something here I do not like. It falls too easily. . . ." He paced off again, frowning.

They could do nothing. Aelvina could see that clearly, but she watched his pacing in silence. Philippe would never sit quietly; it was not in his nature, and she would not have it any other way. He was destroying her, piece by little piece, and she could not help letting him. Even now, she sat here wondering if his words meant he finally believed her; if at long last he trusted her, when she should be walking out the door.

As if he read her thoughts, Philippe swung around. "You could have let me drink that wine and none been the wiser. You have wished to kill me for some time now. I have seen it in your eyes. Why did you not?"

"I can hate you easily, Philippe, but if I choose to kill you, it will be by my hand and not another's evil. Besides, as you have said, you are my only hope to ever see my child again."

He caught her shoulders and lifted her from the small stool, his features shrouded in darkness but his eyes glittering. "Then until the child is found, it is in our best interest to stay together, I think. Can you deny that you enjoy our bed play as well as I, whatever else our differences?"

Caught in the spell of his gaze, Aelvina could deny nothing. Beneath his hands, her whole body yearned for his closeness. It was not just his lovemaking she desired, though she ached for that with every fiber of her being; she wanted more of him than she dared express and than he was willing to give.

In understanding, Aelvina unwrapped her girdle an let it fall to the floor.

"I think you are the most beautiful woman I have ever seen." Philippe's words were almost a mutter as he lifted her hair from her shoulder and traced the curve of her breast to the point where it rose against the thin linen. "You could grace the bed of kings. Even Queen Eleanor cannot match your loveliness, though her beauty is sung throughout the continent." His hand cupped her breast and caressed it. "It gives me pleasure to know your beauty is mine alone to enjoy. Take off the garment, Aelvina."

His words had as hypnotic an effect as his stare, and Aelvina complied. He had never spoken to her thus and she knew not how to react elsewise.

As her chemise fluttered to the floor, Philippe carried her to the bed.

Chapter Fifteen

Though the nights were sweet, the constant vigil against their unknown enemy did not improve the mood of their days. Aelvina spent the hours watching for Chauvin's arrival with word of her child. Philippe, in turn, began a feverish pace of activity to destroy the keep so that he could report his duty complete and turn to his own business instead of the king's. That the king had not yet authorized the end of negotiations did not improve his humor.

Sweat poured down Philippe's face from under the hood of his hauberk as he inspected the preparations he had ordered beneath the cliff walls of the drained moat. The dark shadows of the keep loomed over their work, and upon occasion an arrow flew from its slitted windows, but Philippe ignored all in his impatience to end this siege.

His shoulder was not entirely mended, and it ached beneath the weight of mail and leather as he strode the path back to camp. Before he had reached the tent, he hollered for Aelvina to help him with the cursed hauberk so he could shed its heat. She hurried from Thyllda's tent, following him into the shade of their own silk, her nimble fingers quickly unknotting soaked laces. John joined her, and together they tugged off the heavy armor. John remained to aid with the leather padding while Aelvina sought a flask of wine or ale that would not be tainted.

On her return up the hill, she saw a puff of dust coming from the woods, and she stopped to follow its path, as she had watched every visitor these last weeks This time, her vigilance was rewarded. The portly figure of the monk astride a young donkey emerged from the cloud of dust, and her feet fairly flew up the remaining path.

"He's here! Chauvin has come! Hurry, Philippe. I go to meet him."

Philippe had already stripped to a short tunic over leggings, but the relief of removing one weight was quickly replaced by this new burden. He took the flask offered and caught Aelvina's shoulder before she could spirit herself out of sight again.

"Together . . . we will go together. There is no hurry. We have waited this long; another few moments will not harm us." He took a deep drink of the liquor, wiped his mouth and, holding Aelvina firmly in hand, proceeded out to meet the monk.

For the last steps, Aelvina broke free of Philippe's hold and raced to catch at the monk's robe. Chauvin's heart went out to her anxious gaze, and he prayed for the words that would restore happiness to the dark cloud behind it.

"Did you find him? Please, Father, I must know. Is he well? Is he strong? Is he cared for?" The words tumbled out in an eager, musical chain, and the monk raised his hand to halt the flow.

"I think this is something that must wait until we are in

private." His gaze traveled over the girl's head to meet those of the dark knight. Philippe's features stiffened at the message he read too easily.

"Well, Chauvin?" Philippe's deep voice rumbled over Aelvina's head as they reached the tent.

The monk had prepared his speech well on the return journey, but Aelvina's heartbreaking gaze nearly destroyed all thought. Chauvin tried to fix his eyes on the large man at her back.

"I have been over the entire fief, my lord. No child has been fostered anywhere in the villages; there is none even remotely resembling the description. In fact, there are few children in Dunstan lands at all. The men of your wife's lands have been destroyed by the previous baron's war, and what ones survived escaped for better surroundings when the lady became a widow."

Chauvin watched Philippe questioningly, and he nodded. "I have told her. What have you discovered in Dunstan keep?"

Chauvin breathed in relief. "First, I must tell you, it has been rumored for years that the Lady Ravenna is barren. Her late husband threatened to have the marriage set aside if she did not produce an heir."

"That is meaningless." Philippe spoke impatiently. "The man himself could be at fault; you know that well."

"That is so, but there are those who claimed the baron had bastards but no heirs. Whatever the truth, the Lady Ravenna sent for the witch Marta, who is known among the villagers as a source of miracle potions. It is superstitious nonsense, but with enough truth to give her powers credence."

"Enough of you intellectual ramblings, Chauvin. You are saying the lady sent for a witch to cure her barrenness." Philippe prodded the monk.

"There are worse rumors than that, my lord, rumors of the return of ancient rites and worse. It is not a happy land. They say the last baron died mysteriously after he set out for London to ask the king's permission to set aside his wife."

Chauvin watched Aelvina's suddenly pale face. He knew there was more to the story of the child's birth and conception than he had been told, and guessed Marta's witchcraft or mischief-making as the chief source of pain in the girl's eyes. He wished for some way to console her, but the circumstances were too complex for easy comfort.

"You are saying my lady wife is barren and a murderess. That is very reassuring, Chauvin. And my son? What tales dost thou carry of him?" Philippe's tone was scornful, but it hid a well of pain and hatred.

"The child is fair-haired and well-built. A nurse has been with him since birth, but Marta alone assisted in the birthing. The lady stayed confined to her chambers in the last months of her term and no one saw her outside of bed until the child was delivered. From what I have been able to observe, the boy is healthy, has eyes like his father, and the wet nurse treats him with kindness."

He directed this last at Aelvina, who seemed on the verge of collapse. He had deliberately refrained from stating his conclusions. Two people as dark as the Norman knight and the Lady Ravenna could not possibly have produced a child as fair as that one, if any had but bothered to look.

"He has been baptized, Father?" Aelvina spoke the words, without conscious thought. The time of decision was upon them, the moment when her trust of Philippe lived or died.

To Aelvina's surprise, Philippe answered, his voice low and sad. "He was baptized Charles Philippe, after my father. It seemed fitting my only legal heir should bear his name."

Charles Philippe—her son had a name. Joy flickered dangerously at the edges of her heart. Her child lived! She tried to summon images of the fair-haired boy child with emerald eyes, and a smile lit her face. With eagerness and hope, she swung to seek Philippe's face. What she saw plunged her joy to the very depths of her being. His chiseled face was hard and dark, and no joy transformed those emerald eyes as they met hers. Still, she could not let him defeat her without a battle. She withdrew from his hold and spoke formally.

"The child is mine. Surely you must see that now?"

"It would seem the child is ours, yes." He emphasized the word *ours*.

Aelvina took a deep breath and demanded, "When will he be returned to me?"

She heard the monk's small exhalation of breath and ignored it. Philippe's rigid features clouded her thought.

"He is my son and legitimate heir to Dunstan and St. Aubyn. He is where he belongs, at the moment."

Aelvina trembled with a rage so great it seemed her small frame could not contain it. *"He is my son and he belongs to me!"*

Without waiting for a reply to this declaration, Aelvina stalked from the tent, her feet carrying her hurriedly toward the livestock. A swift pony would be best; he owed her that much. She had waited long enough. The time had come to take matters in her own hands.

A powerful arm gripped her waist, halting her flight. Aelvina's hand flew to the dagger in her girdle. "Let me go, Philippe! Our agreement is ended. I am going to my child!"

"You will do as I tell you, vixen."

Philippe swung her around, his dark face contorted with rage, but his eyes flew wide with surprise at the silver arc flashing before them. He had no time to avert the blow, and the dagger plunged into a place just short of his nearly mended wound. Philippe's roar of rage was mixed with pain as his grip closed tighter on the struggling wildcat in his arms.

The street filled with curious faces and pounding feet. Philippe's roars brought his men running and they ripped Aelvina from Philippe's familiar hold. Unseen fists gripped her as her hands were caught and tied behind her back, and the silver dagger torn from her fingers. Rage and sorrow and fear fueled her struggles.

Shouting and commotion surrounded her, but the last thing Aelvina heard clearly was Philippe's order. "Take her to St. Aubyn!" Then the blackness of her swirling world closed in and she knew no more.

A hand about her throat returned a moment's wakefulness, but it was only Thyllda. She placed the gold chain about Aelvina's neck and whispered, "Sir Philippe is sending me to be the babe's nurse. He will be safe."

Soon that moment was also gone, and she surrendered to the enveloping blackness once more.

The merciful darkness did not last long enough. Glaring sunlight beat against her closed eyelids, adding to the throbbing in her head, and Aelvina lay still, praying for the return of unconsciousness. Sharp straw dug into her arms where her wrists were bared and bound together, and the rough jolting of her body told her she rode in the back of some wagon.

Voices above her warned Aelvina of the wisdom in lying still. She strained to hear their words and then drew a breath of horror as she recognized the smug tones of Sir Raymond.

"I get the first turn at her; the bitch owes me that much."

Another voice, one Aelvina did not recognize, replied in a whine, "He ain't said nothing about that. Said take her prisoner. I don't want to feel the blunt of that one's fist if he finds out we have taken turns at her."

"She's a whore, you gapeseed. What else do you do with a whore? Giving her to us was the next best thing to saying, 'Have at her, boys.' "

"But he didn't . . ."

"Shut up, fool. Here comes the old man."

Metal jingled as another horse rode up alongside the wagon, and conversation died. Aelvina lay quietly, her stomach roiling at the thought of being placed in the safekeeping of Sir Raymond and his sycophantic comrade. Sir Raymond had been right about one thing: Philippe's placing her in their charge was a certain sign he had washed his hands of her.

"There is a spot ahead where we may stop for the night. We cannot make St. Aubyn this day."

Sir Alec! Her other guard was Sir Alec. She was not entirely unprotected, then. But remembering Raymond's words, Aelvina quivered in fear. Some harm could come to the old man if he put up a fight in her defense—if he put up a fight at all. She had tried to kill Sir Philippe. Such an action would not sit well with the loyal man.

Aelvina shuddered as she remembered the sickening feel of that knife slicing through Philippe's flesh. The anger was gone now, replaced by a strange remorse. How had it come to this? For a while, it had been so good—like some impossible dream, shattered now by her violence and his brutality. How could he deny her her own child? The cry wrenched at her heart, destroying everything she had come to trust in him.

The wagon halted, and she was left in her uncomfortable

bed while the men made camp. They fed and watered the horses and tethered them for the night. Darkness enclosed the wagon and small, whining insects flew about Aelvina's face, but she was helpless to swat at them. Her hands and feet seemed to have lost all feeling, and misery ate at her heart. It was over, all over. If she was lucky, she would die this night.

"Sir Philippe's said ye are to be treated as any other prisoner, and so I must." Sir Alec strode to the wagon with sorrow cutting deep in the lines of his face. "But I would see you treated gently." He cut her bonds and helped her to the fire.

She couldn't find relief within her as Gundulf appeared, holding out a flask and some bread and cheese.

He spoke quietly, for her ears alone. "I have no weapon but the one you left in the master's back. I do not think I will return it to you this time. You do not choose your times or your aim wisely."

"I have made very few wise choices lately I fear, Gundulf. Is he punishing you, too, by sending you with these pigs?"

Gundulf frowned. "I do not know his intent, but if anyone lays a hand on you again, I will see this blade between his shoulders. If Sir Philippe wished to see Sir Raymond dead, he chose wisely."

"Then perhaps you had best give me the knife after all, for your only reward for such an action would be the hangman's noose. My life is worthless, but your is not. Take care, Gundulf."

"I must, since you do not." He stood abruptly, and returned to the wagon before the others could grow suspicious.

While she ate, Aelvina surreptitiously kept an eye on her foes. Sir Raymond was the beast she most feared, for his strength was great and his hate and lust greater. The younger knight at his side was not small, but she judged his character to be weak. She had no physical strength with which to combat any of them, but this young knight in his drooping mustache and pointed beard could be easily influenced. Unfortunately, Sir Raymond was more in a position to do the swaying.

Why would Philippe send these mercenaries to guard her instead of his own men? Had all that happened between them meant nothing, then? She knew she was no more than a mistress for catering to his needs, but men cared more for dogs than to give them up to brutal masters.

The question rang in her heart unanswered as Raymond quaffed his ale and lumbered to his feet. His beady eyes had not once left her, and they shone with evil glee as he approached.

She would not see Gundulf killed and Sir Alec shamed for the likes of her. The forest held fewer terrors than this clearing, and Aelvina's jaw set firmly.

"Sir Alec!" She kept her voice light and unafraid, as if she did not see the hulking knight advancing upon her.

Sir Alec looked up from his grim contemplation of his cup. "Yes, lass?"

No longer, "my lady," but still comforting. Aelvina held herself erect, ignoring the knight hesitating on the far side of the campfire. "I must wash and"—she made an embarrassed gesture—"tend to my personal needs. Is there a stream nearby?" She knew there was; she could hear it gurgling behind her. If she could only get out of sight for a moment. . . .

Sir Alec looked uncomfortable, his gaze falling on Sir Raymond's massive form before returning to Aelvina. "The forest is not safe, lass. There are wolves about, and thieves. Ye may use the stream, but do not harbor foolish ideas. Ye are safer in my protection than out there."

He was warning her, telling her running away would be more dangerous than staying, but Aelvina knew otherwise. Sir Raymond would slaughter them all to obtain what he wanted, and she would not allow that to happen. Better she died alone.

With a nod indicating her understanding, she slipped into the bushes. Behind her, Sir William asked eagerly if he should follow, but she did not wait for the reply. As quickly as a hare with a fox at its tail, she darted between trees and bushes, putting as much distance between herself and the camp as she could before her escape was discovered.

She did not even consider the direction she took and ignored the possibility of wolves or other predators. She had only one goal in mind—disappearing into the trees like the druid men claimed her to be.

A cry of alarm rang out. She had made little progress in the tangled undergrowth. Aelvina ran harder, glancing upwards. She could not possibly hope to outrun them; they had horses and she did not. Desperation called for desperate solutions.

Pounding feet behind her told her they were on the trail. Someone yelled out, calling them to separate and beat the bushes. Aelvina kept running. They were disorganized yet; there was still time. The forest was large and the arc of their searches must grow ever wider.

A sudden thought brought a grim smile to Aelvina's face. She circled about, gauging the direction of the campfire from the location of the voices. They would be going farther afield, and she would find her hiding place close by. With luck . . .

The tree she sought came into view. Low-hanging limbs were a necessity, and a heavy shield of leaves a plus. With the litheness of some forest animal, she scrambled onto the first branch, hiking her skirts up so she might climb safely.

Vivid curses and angry commands rang below her. They had not ranged far in their search. Aelvina prayed they would continue to scour the woods long enough for her to carry out her plan. With a horse, she had a chance of escape; without one, her only hope would be that she fall asleep in her lofty perch and break her neck.

The air grew chill, and Aelvina ached in all the places the day's battering had produced. She jerked alert at a sound in the shrubs. One of the searchers came this way. She held her breath, fearful any sound would cause them to look up.

To her surprise, the searcher stopped. She heard no additional noise close by, though she could still hear calls ranging farther into the distance. Had she been mistaken? Perhaps it had only been some animal lurking in the bushes. She must reach the horses, but she feared what awaited below.

Heart pounding erratically, Aelvina pushed aside the branches and strained to see through the blackness. With a gasp, she recognized Gundulf's brawny figure lounging against the base of the tree where she sat. What to do now?

As if in answer to her thoughts, Gundulf spoke seemingly to the empty bushes. "They are almost far enough. You may start coming down if you are quiet."

Aelvina practically fell from her perch, but caught herself, and slowly descended. She did not think Gundulf would reveal her, but she had no wish to involve him in her plans, either. Perching just above his head, she whispered, "How did you know I was here?"

"When your trail disappeared into nowhere, I figured you either vanished into the ground or the air. I place little faith in witches, so I assumed a more natural conclusion than yon daft knights are swearing." He stood and glanced about; then, satisfied no one was near, he held up his arms. "Hurry."

Aelvina fell gratefully into their safety, not even protesting when they held her tightly to his chest for a brief moment. Abruptly Gundulf set her down and indicated the direction of the horses.

"They are saddled. Your guards were not enthusiastic about my joining the search. We must be quick."

Two of the horses were not only saddled, but the reins to the oxen wagon and the others were cut, a judicious use of their one weapon. Aelvina gave her rescuer a brief smile and said nothing when Gundulf tucked the silver dagger into his sash.

The sound of horses galloping down the road brought yells from the men in the forest, but the two gave their massive steeds their heads and allowed the horses to lead the way.

The mad gallop far outdistanced their pursuers and still they raced. The night was fraught with danger. The woods held both four-footed and two-footed predators, and they could not stop to rest. Without weapons, their only protection was speed.

After a time, Aelvina's arms grew numb, but her mind raced as quickly as the horses. Now they fled pursuit, but soon they must find a direction. Which way should the path of her life take?

Chapter Sixteen

They left the woods behind just as the sun shot its first rays over the horizon. The road before them stretched in a narrow ribbon threading between two hills and into the distance. Pastures and fields spread out as far as the eye could see, and on the horizon, smoke rose from the breakfast fires of a small village.

Aelvina's stomach grumbled, but she was too tired to search the saddle pouches for food. The pain in her head nearly matched the aches of the rest of her body, and she leaned, exhausted, against the horse's neck. It had been a long ride, not just in terms of distance. The past lay in shattered, broken shards somewhere behind her. The future was what she must make of it now.

She took the flask offered by Gundulf and drank thirstily, the warm liquid flowing in her veins and reviving some semblance of courage. When Gundulf's eyes rested on her questioningly, she was prepared.

"To Dunstan Castle?" he asked.

Aelvina's shoulders straightened and her chin went up with firm decision. "To St. Aubyn."

Gundulf's jaw nearly dropped to his chest before he thought to close it. "Have you lost your senses?"

"Mayhap," Aelvina replied absently, her gaze traveling far beyond the horizon, seeking that which could not be seen.

"Why?" Gundulf cried, returning her to the present.

"I have had all this night in which to think. That is where Sir Philippe wishes me to be, for whatever reason, so that is where I must go."

Gundulf nodded glumly and looked away. "You love him that much, then?" he asked quietly.

Aelvina's lips turned up. "Yes, I suppose I must. Do not think unkindly of me, Gundulf, for I cannot help myself." She touched his sleeve, drawing his gaze back to her. "Return to Dunstan, if you wish. I can find my way from here."

Gundulf sighed and picked up his reins. "I was fairly warned. There is no reason for me to turn back. I will be at your service for so long as you need me, and it seems that might be a while yet. Tell me, what makes you think Sir Philippe has any desire to see you again after you put a dagger in his back?"

Aelvina smiled without reason. "Oh, he will want to see me, if only to thrash me to within an inch of my life. I have no doubt of that. What puzzles me is why he chose Sir Raymond to send as my guard. It is not like him to allow others to deal out the punishment he has chosen."

"I am not so certain that Sir Raymond did not choose himself as guard. I heard Sir Philippe say naught of such an order. Let us be on our way. I would rather be within the protection of St. Aubyn when that one reappears."

They traveled more slowly now, eating the food in their pouches as they rode, resting and watering the horses, fighting fatigue. It seemed easier than their backbreaking pace of earlier.

Aelvina doubted that Sir Philippe would have any interest in keeping her as mistress now, but she could not help feeling he would continue to act in her best interests. Perhaps love muddled her thinking, but sending Thyllda to care for their son was the next best thing to going herself, and it relieved her anxieties in that direction. Philippe had known that; it did not seem the act of a cruel man.

She had the vague notion that Philippe had deliberately staged the previous day's disaster. He had goaded her into exploding, choosing the most effective method and waiting until they were in a public place to set it off. He had wanted her openly disgraced and shipped safely off to St. Aubyn while he took the risk of dealing with Marta. He had intentionally set her aside from the time he had told her of the child.

She approached the forbidding gates of St. Aubyn with trepidation. Named for the home of Philippe's Norman ancestors, the castle rose from the top of a natural hill, not a man-made *motte* as the older wooden keeps had used. Fortified entirely in stone, it had no moat. The flat cleared land extending far beyond the castle walls prevented anyone approaching without notice.

Still, they rode into the bailey without disturbing more than a flock of chickens. Gundulf glanced around uneasily, Aelvina with interest. The walls were strong and thick, the donjon guarding the entrance was impressive, and the keep itself appeared a new addition, with all the amenities a stone fortress could provide. Yet no life stirred within the safety of this mighty hold.

They dismounted and tethered the animals in a deserted

stable. Entering the great oaken doors of the keep, they gazed up at the smoke-darkened walls of the hall, empty of all but a few moth-eaten tapestries. The rushes beneath their feet had moldered and stunk for months, judging by the state of their decay, and Aelvina turned up her nose in disgust at the pig sty of her prison.

Gundulf's call brought the lunging clatter of a half-dozen massive hounds, their baying howls of welcome presenting less than a frightening aspect. They leapt upon the newcomers with joy, tongues lapping their greeting, and it was all but impossible to pet all the heads at once.

The rocking gait of an old woman followed the dogs. Her heavy weight and bowed legs prevented any attempt at speed. Her round face beamed with joy beneath a dark kerchief as she waddled to greet the visitors.

"There have been none to stop here in many a day. What brings ye here?"

Wishing she had taken the time to make herself a little more presentable, Aelvina stepped forward.

"Sir Philippe has sent us. His men will follow shortly. Might we be given some water and a place to rest until they arrive?"

"Sir Philippe, now!" Good-humored eyes narrowed thoughtfully, taking in the rich rose silk of Aelvina's tattered kirtle, her pale face and soft hands, and the delicacy of her features. A smile lit her cherubic face. "Ye must be the one they talk of, the lord's lady. A faerie, some say, but a cruelly used one if that be so. My name be Girta; I'll show ye to your chambers."

Girta hastened to show Aelvina the massive stairway to the upper chambers. Built with some pretensions of comfort, it possessed wide windows overlooking the inner bailey, and rare tapestries to keep the chill from the walls.

Beds graced several of the chambers, and it was to one of these that Girta led Aelvina.

"I'll bring ye water for a bath. The master was always one for a bath, he was. Be he returnin' soon, then?" The woman wrapped her hands in the coarse homespun of her gunna, watching with hopeful gaze as Aelvina stroked the moldering tapestries.

"Not soon, I fear," Aelvina said sadly. "There is much on his mind and the king's work to be done. How long has it been since he has been here?" The state of the household answered her question, but she wished to hear more of Philippe from this woman who must have known him long.

"Many a year, my lady. When Henry came, Sir Philippe rode with him and they stopped. We were in sorry shape, then, and he has done naught but order repairs. As ye say, he is a busy man, and the land has long lain fallow. His father had much hope of this place when it was built, but the troubles have kept Sir Philippe in his mother's lands. He and his father did not agree on many things, they did not."

Aelvina read behind the woman's words with the knowledge borne of her own experience. Sir Philippe's father must have been one of the barons supporting the first Henry's nephew Stephen, instead of his daughter Maud, a dispute that had torn the land to tatters for twenty long years. If his mother had lands in Normandy, Philippe had probably been knighted in Maud's court and remained loyal to her cause, while his father supported the king annointed in England.

His father's loyalty must have saved the St. Aubyn lands. She would have liked to have heard the whole story, but already Girta hurried off to bring the promised bath. There would be time in the days ahead to learn more, if she survived them. She had hoped to find more protection from Philippe's loyal retainers here . . . foolish thought!

The bath restored her spirits. A little rest and she would take on the devil himself. She had chosen to take her stand here and hold this keep she would, against any and all comers. Aelvina's chin set determinedly as Girta combed the snarls from her hair.

Aelvina gratefully sank into the comforts of the massive canopied bed. Philippe had learned his appreciation for the finer things from his father, it seemed. With a sigh of relief, she closed her eyes and slept.

When she woke, she ran down the stairway to search out the knowledgeable Girta. The chance to learn more of Philippe and his home was all that filled her head as she made her way through the great hall and into the corridors beyond.

The kitchen was an immense room of dark shadows and cold stones. The cavernous fireplace filled a large portion of one wall with iron tripods and cookware scattered over its surface. Girta bent over a large kettle, humming a tuneless song as she stirred and sparingly added a few precious herbs. Gundulf sat on a low stool, skinning a hare for the pot. They both looked up at Aelvina's entrance.

"There ye are, milady. Ye look well rested. Did ye find the gunnas in the wardrobe? No, I see ye have not. They be old, but they may suit ye until your things come. Sir Philippe would not wish ye dressed that way."

Aelvina sat on a stool and accepted the mug of mulled cider the woman offered. "Have you no help here? Surely Sir Philippe cannot expect you to keep up with all this. . . ." She threw her hand out in a gesture to indicate her immense surroundings.

Girta shrugged and continued stirring. "There be none here to wait on. Sir Philippe did find me an overseer to look a'ter things, but he be more interested in the taking than the looking. 'Tis been myself alone these many months.''

"Does Sir Philippe know of this?" Aelvina asked incredulously, not believing wealth so great could allow such rich lands to lie fallow and untended.

"Sum'mat must tell'e, not me. How would I tell a lord o' such a thing?''

Aelvina waxed indignant but held her tongue. She was scarcely in a position to tell the lord anything, either.

It was almost pleasant sitting before the warming fire, eating the meal Girta provided and allowing her hurts to dissolve beneath this feeling of well-being. Gundulf's stalwart presence gave her a sense of security, and the walls of Philippe's home stirred feelings and memories not entirely offensive. She wanted to belong here, among Philippe's possessions, and Aelvina took the first tentative steps in that direction.

"Do you think there would be others willing to help set this place aright? If Sir Philippe were to come, he would not like finding his home a sty.''

Girta threw her a shrewd look and answered carefully. "There were others prepared to work when Sir Philippe brought home his new bride, but it seems the lady has no wish to see her husband's home.''

Aelvina gazed out a window over the kitchen's neglected gardens. "I think it more a case that the husband does not wish the lady in his home. But his heir must come here sometime.''

Gundulf's gaze hardened at these words, but Girta's eyes lit expectantly. " 'Tis a pity nobles cannot marry where they will, but where they must. Dunstan lands lie close to these, and Sir Philippe must have thought to protect them. He has done his duty as he should. If his lady wife cannot give him all else he desires. he is entitled to search for it elsewhere. The old man, his father should have done so when his wife returned to her lands, taking their son with her. It made 'e a bitter man.''

The words were meant for solace, and Aelvina turned a grateful smile on the old woman. If only she could be certain she could provide what Philippe desired, her mind would rest easier. Instead, she seemed only to bring him hatred and rage. Still, there were imperative reasons why she must try to reconcile with him.

"We will see what can be done, then," Aelvina replied. Only Gundulf understood that she referred to more than the cleaning of the keep.

The peaceful moments were banished with the howling of the dogs at the front entrance, and Girta hobbled to welcome the knights Sir Philippe had sent to protect his lady. Aelvina and Gundulf remained in the kitchen, exchanging worried glances. The protection they had sought in this place was nil; their time of trial had begun.

They could not hope to hide their presence, even if Girta's chatter could be silenced. The destriers in the stables gave them away even before the men entered the keep. Sir Raymond's mighty roar echoed through the empty rooms with the first opening of the great doors.

"Where is she? Where is that devil-ridden whore of a . . .''

Girta fell backward uncertainly before his tirade. Sir Raymond paid her small note as he strode to the center of the great hall and stared around him, as if expecting Aelvina to crawl from beneath the rushes. Despite his mediocre stature, his mighty girth seemed to dwarf the room. His crimson surcoat and heavy armor created a terrifying figure as he glared into the far reaches of the hall.

Sir Alec's entrance was a much milder one, and he

unfastened the hood of his hauberk almost apologetically before the housekeeper's uncertain gaze.

"Is the lass safe, then?" he asked, ignoring the baleful glare of the younger man.

Girta executed a clumsy curtsy before the knight she recognized as a loyal vassal to St. Aubyn. "Safe if such be said of one who looks sore tattered and bruised, my lord."

"We are starved, old woman! Bring us drink and food and send the wench out to us," Sir William demanded impatiently. Girta sent the young knight a look of distaste, took Sir Alec's nod of agreement as an order, and stalked past Sir Raymond without a word.

Aelvina had heard the bellowed orders and quietly filled trenchers of bread with the meal Girta had prepared. She could not spend her days hiding or running away. She must find some way of standing up to these crude men and making them see the folly of their demands—either that, or kill them.

She met Girta in the dark corridor between hall and kitchen, and the older woman glanced at her nervously. "It is not meet that the lord's lady serve the likes of them. Let me take those." She tried to take the trenchers from Aelvina's hand but Aelvina held firmly to her purpose.

"His lordship sent me here as his prisoner, not his lady. If this be my punishment, I will take it. You cannot be expected to run back and forth to wait on these pigs and cook, too. Sir Alec will look to my care."

Girta did not look convinced, but the news Aelvina was a prisoner here was so startling, she let her slip by.

Aelvina's appearance in the great hall hushed the angry voices. Against the towering walls, her rose silk might appear almost ephemeral, she supposed, but there was nothing mystical about the way she strode into the room and slapped the trenchers on the table.

"Your meal, my lords," she snapped.

She left before any of the astonished men could speak.

By the time she returned with horns of liquor, they had recovered from their astonishment. Raymond grabbed his horn and while quaffing the drink greedily, caught Aelvina by the waist. Wiping his mouth on his sleeve, he set the horn aside and wrapped his hand in her hair, jerking her head backward.

"Witch! Did you think I would give up so easily? You will pay for making me ride these miles in that beastly contraption."

"Leave the girl alone," Sir Alec warned, his hand going to his sword hilt.

William grimaced painfully as he sat down to his meal. "Forsooth, I do not fancy chasing her across the countryside again so soon. Let us at least eat."

Raymond growled and let loose his hold, sneering as Aelvina stumbled and almost fell at his abrupt release. "Let her serve us at the table now and in our beds later, then. It seems a fitting use, since it is for her benefit that we are stranded in this empty outpost."

Icily, Aelvina stood before the table until she had claimed their attention. "I will serve you at this table by my choice. I have already proved my ability to escape you at any time I choose. If any here attempts to molest me in any way, I will disappear again, and next time I will not return. It is your choice whether you would wish to slake your lusts now and meet Philippe's wrath later." With that announcement, she slipped into the shadows again, her movement so swift it left her listeners temporarily disconcerted.

Having obtained this brief respite and accomplished part of her purpose, Aelvina did not wait to discover the results. She located the back stairs and hastened up them to her chamber, throwing the bolt home as soon as the door closed behind her.

The men would either drink themselves into a stupor or attempt to batter the door down in the next hours, but Aelvina's confidence in her own powers grew steadily. She would use their superstitious natures against them, and pray Philippe arrived soon.

Restless, she explored the room that must once have belonged to Philippe's mother. The wardrobe of moth-eaten kirtles spoke of once well-dressed luxury. Aelvina fingered the soft materials and wondered why a wife would leave a husband who cared enough about her to dress her so finely. Not all men were so generous.

Philippe must have been raised by his mother, probably in the "house full of women" he had so openly scorned for his own son. Perhaps he had to fight to be the man his nature meant him to be, and now that he was free of all feminine influence, continued to fight from habit. A man like that would consider any softening emotion a weakness, and would rebel against it all the harder.

A tear crept from Aelvina's eye at the thought of those moments when Philippe had held her tenderly and touched her with reverence. They had been all too few, and he had thrown them away rashly and violently. Still, she could not give up hope. No one could dictate to so fiercely an independent nature as his, but it might be possible to appeal to the kindness buried within him.

Deciding the kirtles could be taken in and mended to hide the moth holes, Aelvina removed her torn gown and returned to the bed in her chemise. The bed was large and empty without Philippe's protective presence, but she smiled sleepily at thoughts of her son—Charles Philippe.

Chapter Seventeen

Aelvina was not foolish enough to believe her threats would permanently deter Sir Raymond, but her brief success gave her courage. She arose early to discover all three mighty warriors snoring amid the dogs and rushes in the great hall, and tiptoed past them into the kitchen to join Gundulf and Girta.

Girta watched her more warily than the day before, and Aelvina wondered what the old woman had heard to dim her friendly spirit, but she did not make a point of it. Gundulf sliced some meat and bread for her and they ate at the kitchen fire, neither speaking a word.

Sir Alec joined them, his faded eyes blurred from worry and lack of rest. He took the cup offered and sat down heavily.

"Lass, I am grateful ye found your way here on your own, but I am not so certain it was the wisest thing to do. I am an old man. I can bear Sir Philippe's wrath for letting ye escape, but I do not know if I can bear my own conscience should anything happen to ye while ye're under my care." He sighed deeply and drank from his cup with the air of a man sorely tried.

"Tell me only this, did Sir Philippe choose those two as my guards? Answer that for me, and I will relieve you of all responsibility for what happens from here on."

Alec grunted and gave her a strange look. "Sorceress they say ye be, but even ye cannot do that. Sir Philippe placed ye in my care, said your life be in my hands. He made no mention of yon great oafs."

"That does not ease my mind. If I knew Sir Philippe had chosen them, I would be gone this day. As it is, I must stay and bide my time. You must do as you think wisest, my lord."

Aelvina saw the scowl on Gundulf's brow. He thought she was a fool and so she must be. Sir Raymond and his foppish friend would make her life hell, but there was nowhere else to go other than Dunstan, and she might endanger her son's life should she risk that. The stakes were too high to give up without a fight.

"There is work to be done. Sir Alec, did Philippe say anything about hiring help? I would tackle the filth of this place while I am here." Aelvina stood, defying any to argue.

"He said to close the gates against all but himself and those I know to be trusted. I know of none hereabouts that I can trust, lass. Ye'd best spend your time behind stout oak doors."

Aelvina gave him a look designed to wither the hardiest nature. "No man holds me against my will and I will not be a prisoner of fear. We will begin with the hall. Those tapestries must come down and the filth of those rushes be cleared."

It was a command, and to Girta's astonishment, the two

men followed meekly at Aelvina's heels. If the lady were not royalty, she must indeed be a sorceress. She should have known that a girl who dared put a knife in the back of Sir Philippe and lived to speak of it was someone to be respected.

Raymond and his cohort stayed out of the way as the hall was stripped and scoured during the day, but their appearance for the evening meal did not begin auspiciously. After the first broad pinch on her buttocks from the callow William, Aelvina evaded his hands as she served the meal. She quit pouring the mead when Raymond grabbed her breast, and refused to enter the room again after Raymond pulled her down across his lap. She escaped by flinging the drink in his face, but the call was close enough. She retreated to her room, barring the door for the night.

When Aelvina did not reply to his bellows for service, Raymond sought her door. "I am not through with you, wench. Get yourself out here before I batter the door down."

Aelvina glanced nervously at the wooden door. It could withstand much battering, but not by an ax. She prayed he was too drunk to think of such means and said nothing to antagonize his anger. It was not only her own hide at stake in this battle. Raymond roared and struck at the door until he wandered off to quench his thirst, defeated by a woman's will for one more night.

This success could not last forever, but Aelvina clung to her courage. Raymond and William slept much of the day and indulged their lust for hunting both animals and wenches in the afternoons. In the evenings, Aelvina walked cautiously.

During the days, she swept, scoured, sewed, and began a judicious hoard of herbs. She'd found the remnants of an herb garden behind the kitchen, and had Gundulf clear it for her.

Some evenings she could not turn a corner without either Raymond or William pawing at her. It became a game to them. One would find her in the larder and pin her against the wall until she loosed his grip with a well-placed blow from an iron utensil. The other would catch her in the kitchen corridor and grind her breasts until her screams brought either Sir Alec or Gundulf.

Another night, Aelvina listened to the cries below as the men searched high and low for Gundulf. She did not understand their rage until Raymond banged at her door.

"We know you're in there, you whey-faced jackanapes! No sheep-tupping farmer is taking that piece from me! Get out of there before I take an ax to you!" A sudden ominous, crafty silence followed that last threatening cry. Aelvina held her breath as the drunken feet staggered down a stairway. He had gone for the ax, though she could not figure out what had triggered his train of thought.

As if to answer her question, a shuffling noise emanated from the strange European armoire. To Aelvina's shock, the door swung into the room of its own accord.

Gundulf's grim smile greeted her terrified gaze as he stepped from the wardrobe. "Unbar the door. Mayhap it can be saved for another night."

"Gundulf! I do not . . ." At his peremptory gesture, Aelvina unbolted the door as told.

"In here. It will not take him long to find the ax, though Girta promised to hide it." He took her arm and steered her through the wardrobe door, despite her puzzled protests. "Girta showed this to me. We dare not use it often for fear they may suspect, but once might be sufficient."

Aelvina stepped through the musty clothes into a drafty

emptiness. A torch glimmered in its holder on the long stairway at their feet.

"Gundulf, where are we? What is this?" Clad only in her thin chemise, she shivered with more than cold.

"An escape route. Girta tells me it leads beyond the castle walls, but I have not explored. It is a convenient hiding place."

Aelvina shivered and clung to Gundulf as Raymond's obscene threats broke overhead followed by a shattering crash and a surprised silence. She could easily imagine the startled look upon Raymond's face as the door fell open at his first blow.

Apparently the excitement had drawn all three knights to the door. She could hear Sir Alec admonishing the others not to touch her, while William made lewd suggestions of encouragement. All argument halted at their discovery of the room's emptiness.

A curse preceded a rush to the window, and Aelvina stifled a giggle at William's amazed comment: "They must have took to their brooms and be circling the moon by now!"

Gundulf clapped a hand over her mouth as Aelvina shook with laughter. Raymond's curses stalked the room as he searched beneath the bed and in the wardrobe, and Aelvina had a mental image of poor Sir Alec making the sign of the cross behind him.

The search was brief and the sounds of their footsteps echoing down the hallway brought nervous relief. Gundulf lowered his hand from Aelvina's mouth, but it lingered on her arm as they waited to be certain of their safety. As Aelvina stirred impatiently beneath his hold, Gundulf made one last desperate attempt to appeal to reason.

"We can take this tunnel to the other end and be gone

before they know it. Come with me, Aelvina, before violence is done," he urged.

Aelvina let his wish for peace seep through her like some soothing balm. Gundulf was a gentle man and wished a quiet life of work and harmony. Bitterly, she shook her head, dislodging all thoughts of tranquility.

"Gundulf, I love you as I believe you love me. It is a love borne of respect and gratitude, but not the love between husband and wife. If we left together, it would wreak a violence on your life that we would both regret."

Gundulf's grip tightened. "That which is between you and Sir Philippe is the kind of love you wish? Are you not forgetting he already has a wife?"

"I know Philippe holds no love for me, but he is the only man who can command my love. You make of me what I am not, Gundulf. You see me as I appear, not as I am. I have no wish for peace so long as that witch holds my son and those pigs rule my life. I long for the violence you wish to avert. Mayhap I have been spoiled, but I would do things my way without thought to you or others, and we would ever be at odds."

"And Sir Philippe knows you for what you are and treats you as you deserve, I suppose? If I smack you and throw you down on the bed, will I win your love, too?" Gundulf asked irritably, hiding his pain.

Aelvina smiled in the darkness and touched his cheek. "Sir Philippe had need to hit me only once, and he has ever regretted that time, I believe. He has never lifted a hand to me since, though you surely must admit I have deserved it. If I loosed my tongue on you, you would walk out, hurt and angry. Philippe takes my words and bends and breaks them, and he has no need to throw me into bed when he is done. I come willingly."

Gundulf had seen the truth of her words too many times

to deny them. He reached too high, much as a child wishes for the moon. He longed to hold her, but just as the moon evades a child's grasp, she would rise from his.

He opened the hidden door and stepped into the bed-chamber, making certain of its safety.

Aelvina followed him quietly, watching as he shut and bolted the door and searched the corners. When he turned to depart without a word, Aelvina stopped him.

"They think you a warlock now. How think you of this title?"

Gundulf's lips bent grimly. "I think we are both too fair to do justice to rumors. Should not witches and warlocks be dark?"

"Like Sir Philippe and Lady Ravenna?" Aelvina understood his implication without completing the statement. "The lady may be, for all I know, but though I once thought the knight was the devil himself, I have my doubts now. He can be hurt just like the rest of us mortals." She gestured at the darkened stairway. "Where do you go?"

"There is a cubicle at the foot of the steps where I have made my pallet. There is a door there into the kitchen, so I need not disturb your sleep when I rise." The tone was almost sardonic for the gentle Gundulf, but the torment had left his eyes.

"They think we are lovers now, do they not?" Aelvina asked.

"Unfortunately, but I know of no better way to protect you. I can hear all that goes on in here and can be here in an instant if there is trouble. From the kitchens, I cannot. Do you wish me to leave?"

"No, I will feel safer knowing you are there. It is just . . ." She sighed, knowing the folly of explaining Philippe's jealousy to an already angry man. She shook her head in defeat.

Sir Alec spoke to neither of them the next day. The unbolted chamber door had confirmed his suspicions of the more human likelihood of Aelvina and Gundulf's disappearance together.

Raymond and William, however, stayed out of the way for a while. Indulging in an orgy of drinking and sport, they sought safer quarry in the villages, and frequently did not return to the castle at all.

Their next visitor arrived during this respite. Under Sir Alec's orders, they kept the doors bolted. With no look out to warn of approaching travelers, no one answered any knock. All callers were turned away in the belief that the castle lay empty.

This visitor was more persistent, rattling endlessly at the door until the dogs roused and sent up great wailing howls that brought the castle's inhabitants running. Sir Alec clanked up to the battlements to discover the caller's identity before signaling the gates. Gundulf threw the bolt, and Aelvina opened the door to greet the lone slim figure standing in the sunshine.

"Alice!" Astonishment wiped all else from Aelvina's face as she rushed to embrace the disheveled girl.

They closed and sealed the doors, and bombarded the visitor with questions. Alice withstood them with a tired smile, until Aelvina took her to her chambers and brought water for bathing. Alice nervously refused Aelvina's helpfulness, but Aelvina had her own reasons for closing the door on the others. It took little persuasion to convince Alice to sink into the warm tub while Aelvina probed for answers.

"Why did you leave the camp?" she demanded, as soon as Alice had time to wash off some of the grime.

"I did not wish to rely on Sir Philippe's charity. Once he returned Thyllda to Dunstan, he had no further need of my tent. He continued to pay for its use so I did not have to"—Alice made a gesture of disgust—"sell myself again, but that could not go on forever. So I thought, while I still had a few coins to my name, I would seek work."

With a start, Aelvina again recognized that this worldly prostitute was a girl not much older than herself. She had heard Alice's life story in broken bits and pieces, knew the harsh existence that had forced her into this trade, and felt the kinship between them. There, but for the grace of God . . .

"Did Sir Philippe send you here?" Aelvina asked eagerly.

"No. He has done so much for me, and he has been so . . ." Alice hesitated, uncertain how to describe Philippe's frantic anger or the urgency with which he had thrown himself into his work. He was like a man possessed, and in great pain.

"He has been so *occupied* lately. I did not dare disturb him with so small a matter as my leaving. Whores come and go," she added with a trace of irony. "So I came to you, instead."

Embarrassed, Alice reached for a towel. She had come to serve the lord's lady and had been served instead. It was a strange experience, and not one she had learned to expect. She glanced at the luxurious bed and expensive tapestries and knew she was totally out of place. She had spent her life in the fields and had never dared cross the portals of a great castle before.

Aelvina laughed. "You have come to the prisoner of St. Aubyn to look for work? Alice, you are as mad as I. There is work here aplenty, but the wages are very uncertain, indeed. Hell might have more benefit than this place before much time has passed."

Startled, Alice rose from the bath. "I am sorry. I did not

think . . . I knew he was angry, but he seemed so worried about you when you fainted . . . I thought, surely . . .''

Aelvina rummaged through the wardrobe for a service-able kirtle. Since Alice was taller and more buxom than herself, they should fit Alice better.

The knowledge that Philippe had worried about her, though he was the one with the knife in his back, colored Aelvina's cheeks. She hid it behind the pretense of busy-ness. "Philippe knows I cannot be held against my will. This is a hell of my own creation, I fear.'' She located a wine-colored gown of homespun and pulled it from the wardrobe, holding it out for Alice's inspection. "Sir Ray-mond is here with one of his liege men, and I have only Gundulf and Sir Alec to protect me. Gundulf thinks I am mad for staying and Sir Alec thinks I am a disloyal murderess.''

"Sir Raymond?'' Alice looked past the offered gown to gaze at Aelvina in horror. "I thought him to be one of the deserters. Why is he here?''

Aelvina searched her face anxiously. "Did Philippe name him a deserter?''

Alice gave her a wry look. "I am not part of his privy council as you were. I only know rumors.'' She took the kirtle from Aelvina's hands and held it uncertainly. "It does not seem right that I take this from you. Whatever happened, you are his lordship's lady and I am but one of the doxies in his camp. . . .''

Aelvina snorted inelegantly and walked away while Alice donned the gown. "*Lady* is a fine word for mistress, and at present I am not even certain of that status. If Philippe sent Sir Raymond here on purpose, he thinks less of me than you.'' She swung around and asked the question closest to her heart, baring all to this comparative stranger.

"Alice, tell me: is he well? I did not hurt him badly, did I? Does he ever speak of me?"

Alice gazed at her in sympathy and understanding. "You may have hurt his pride, and if you are lucky, his heart, but you have not the strength to damage that one greatly otherwise. He heals and he curses and he drives himself wickedly. That is all I can tell you."

The wine-red gown went well with Alice's dark coloring. A white undertunic would have made a splendid contrast, but Alice would have refused such elegance. As it was, she looked nervously at the long gown covering her toes and the flowing sleeves falling below her fingers, and began to remove it.

Aelvina stopped her. "We will wash your gunna while you eat and decide what you wish to do."

Girta actually made the decision. While the others inundated Alice with questions, Girta sized up the newcomer's sturdiness, seized upon her willingness to work, and set her to scrubbing pots. Gundulf and Sir Alec looked worried at adding one more female to their burden, but Girta's muttered comments about ladies not being maids chased their thoughts in other directions.

Aelvina paid no heed to Girta's assertion that she had no place doing the scrubbing and cleaning. The work needed to be done, and she needed something to fill her time and uneasiness of mind.

Raymond and William's return increased the tension in the little household. Alice's appearance at the table brought roars of approval, but bellows for Aelvina soon followed. How much longer could she hold them off? She had not used her full bag of tricks yet, but how long would it take before they drove her to that point of desperation beyond which violence was the only solution?

Uncertain of Aelvina's powers, the knights chose a more

familiar adversary for the worst goading. Alice's refusal to
accommodate their lusts infuriated them to cruelty. They
cuffed and kicked her whenever she was within reach.
Accustomed to their brutality, Alice merely removed herself from their vicinity, but Gundulf took to following her
closely.

The constant tension began to tell on everyone's nerves.
Gentle Sir Alec smacked the flat of his sword across William's shoulders when he found him forcing Alice to her
knees to perform what Sir Alec called a sin upon mankind.
William smoldered sullenly and the angry mutters
increased in volume.

With Sir Alec glowering over them and Gundulf seated
within hearing distance, the mercenaries dared no direct
attack, but grew ever bolder with each meal. They grew
increasingly confident when Aelvina did not turn them
into toads or use her "witchcraft."

In this new mood of bravery and aided by a day-long
consumption of liquor, they summoned Aelvina to the
great hall with their bellows.

She straightened her shoulders and entered the hall,
where only the flickering firelight cast shadows over the
newly cleaned tapestries. Sir Alec sat at the far end of the
trestle table, looking sick and old. He had aged much in
these last weeks, Aelvina thought with a pang.

William's drooping mustache was damp with drink, and
bits of his meal clung to his beard where he had wiped
his greasy fingers. Raymond's muscular girth filled the
chair at the head of the table near the fire—Philippe's
chair, Aelvina thought bitterly. Both men still wore their
leather hauberks, though they had doffed the mail. The
leather was sufficient padding against a woman's blows,
but was evidence of their insecurity in their own demesne.

Sir Alec stood, staggering slightly as he gestured toward

a dark corner near the fire. "Ye had best see to the wench, lass. She has hit her head against the stones."

With a gasp, Aelvina flew to the limp form sprawled beside the fireplace. A large gash bled freely into Alice's thick hair, but the bone beneath seemed solid and her breathing strong.

"Call your leman, witch, and have him carry her out of here. It looks as if you will have to serve us in her place," Raymond called.

Aelvina shot him an icy look. She had seen the ripped shreds of Alice's bodice and the bruises already darkening beneath.

She called for Gundulf but as she followed him out, Raymond caught her arm. "You stay here. You have a way of disappearing once you are out of sight."

His grip bit into her arm and Aelvina's stomach churned, but she matched his stare. "I must tend to her wounds. Let me go."

Sir Alec tottered forward, grasping Aelvina by the shoulder, more to support himself than as reassurance. "Let the lass go. You have near killed one wench this night. That is enough."

William barked with laughter. "I know how to settle this." He picked up a length of rope and began wrapping it around his hands. "We'll put a leash on her, like a dog. Teach her to heel at our command."

Raymond readily agreed, and watched with satisfaction as the hemp was twisted and knotted over her girdle.

"Try to escape, and we will wrap it about your neck, instead," William snarled.

Raymond smiled unpleasantly, tipping his horn to his lips and drinking deeply. "Hang on to that rope, gapeseed," he warned. "Follow her and make sure she brings back fresh ale."

With the humiliating rope tied about her waist and held in the hand of the rake behind her, Aelvina hurried to the kitchens after Alice.

Alice was already stirring by the time Aelvina reached her. With a steely glitter in her eyes, she cleaned the wound and sought salves in the spice cabinet she had filled with her herb concoctions. She carried the salve back to Alice, carefully concealing a vial of powder in one hand.

By the time the wound was bound, Alice was conscious. With a stern warning in her eyes, Aelvina ordered Girta and Gundulf to stay with the patient. Gundulf looked rebellious, his eyes straying to the hempen halter, but Aelvina quelled him with a look and a flash of the vial she held concealed. He scowled and bent to Alice.

William leaned against the wall, drinking from a flask, watching the scene with idle curiosity. Aelvina ignored him, keeping her back to his hungry gaze as she filled a flask of wine and added a large pinch of powder. In remembrance of the large bruises on Alice's neck, she added a second, larger pinch. With luck, it would kill them, but she doubted they would be able to drink enough to reach that happy goal.

Leaving Sir Alec behind and holding the flask, she nodded coldly to William and proceeded from the kitchen. Aelvina shivered as she entered the hall alone with the two mercenaries. The shadows seemed to close around her, and evil crackled in the firelight. A sudden memory of another dark night when evil had permeated her body brought a wave of dizziness, and she fought for control. If she did not carry this out as planned, she would be destroyed this night.

William allowed her to pour the wine before tugging the rope and pulling her down in his lap. His hand swiftly lifted her skirts, but Raymond's roar of rage abruptly ended the molestation. "Throw the rope here! You will get your turn later."

Tugged rudely from William's unpleasant embrace, Aelvina fell to the floor. She scrambled quickly to her feet, praying they would drink the wine soon. She did not have the strength to fight them for long, and any unnecessary struggle might stir their blood and make the drug take longer to work.

Her rare impassivity as she poured the wine encouraged Raymond.

"Let us see what lies under these fine rags. Make sure she doth not have cloven hooves or a tail." He spoke to William as if she were but a piece of furniture, without sense or hearing.

William caught on instantly and grinned his appreciation, but Aelvina remained motionless, pretending not to understand.

"Take them off or I shalt take them off for you!" Raymond roared.

The words were too uncomfortably like others she had heard, and Aelvina's lashes moistened with tears. How could Philippe have left her to this? He had probably returned to Dunstan by now and was busily begetting a more legitimate heir while she suffered the fate he had once threatened.

Aelvina kept her gaze fastened on a place well above Raymond's head as she loosened her girdle. She must delay as long as possible, but the cruel twisting of the rope at her waist told her she could not procrastinate long. With difficulty, she slid the skirts through the rope and over her head. The tight sleeves of her undertunic prevented easy removal, and Raymond grabbed the bodice and tore it from her.

Aelvina read the threat in the evil glitter of Raymond's

eyes, the cruel twist of his lips, and the angry grip of his hand as it ripped the last thread of clothing from her body, leaving only the gold chain against her skin. A piece of her soul died and turned to ashes as she stood before this brute like the whore Philippe had made of her.

"At last, the nobleman's whore bared for all to see! I have waited long for this moment." Raymond drank again from the cup as Aelvina watched dully, all prayers flown. The drug seemed to have no effect, and disappointment curled with fear in the pit of her stomach.

She closed her eyes and clenched her fists as Raymond's large hands roamed across her body. William stood behind her, rubbing lewdly against her buttocks and fondling her breasts. Aelvina thought she would lose her grip on reality if they did not succumb soon.

Madness licked at the corners of her mind as one knight mauled her body into a state of readiness for the second one's use. Would they take turns with her or both use her at once? Her mind screamed the outrage she did not dare voice.

With a cuff of his powerful hand, Raymond finally knocked the younger knight flying across the floor, not noticing or caring that William did not rise again. Aelvina caught the slowness of his movement, the staggering step with which he approached, and studied the glaze of his eyes dispassionately. An icy calm flowed through her veins.

"My lord, I thirst. Will you not give me a sip of your wine before you have your way?"

He was slow-witted, but his natural cruelty worked in the way Aelvina hoped. Raymond reached for the horn and drank deeply, then flung it and the remaining contents across the floor. The last of the drug was gone.

Aelvina treaded slowly backward and tripped on a sleeping dog. The hound bounded to its feet and the sudden movement threw her off balance. Screaming, she fell into the rushes, and Raymond was upon her in an instant. His hands mauled her breasts, while his loins sought her sprawled legs and surged between them with obscene intent—but to no purpose.

As the knight's heavy body finally fell limp and collapsed over her, Aelvina fought her nausea. With unparalleled strength, she shoved him off. Struggling to her knees, she emptied her stomach of the day's meals. Bile scalded her throat long after her belly emptied.

Bracing herself, she grasped a chair for support, her head spinning as she stood. The whole world seemed to be collapsing around her, but she was still alive. Pulling on her kirtle, she staggered to the kitchen.

Sir Alec had passed out at the table. Girta had scrubbed an old burned-out pot to a glossy gleam. Alice sat in Gundulf's lap, her face buried against his shoulder, her fingers digging into his arms as if she dared not let go. Gundulf sat still, his arms hugging the girl on his lap with a strange ferocity. They heard Aelvina's command with expressions of shock.

"Give me a blade!"

No one moved. Aelvina approached Gundulf, holding out her hand. "The dagger! The time has come. Give it to me."

Gundulf rose, gently setting Alice aside. Instead of offering the knife, he reached for Aelvina, but she deftly avoided him. Running to Sir Alec's insensate figure, Aelvina grabbed the hilt of his sword, attempting to pull it from the scabbard. The sword would not budge, but still she struggled. She would avenge this night in the only manner available.

Gundulf grabbed her arms from behind and forcibly lifted her from the floor.

With the sword torn from her hands, Aelvina crumpled into his big hands. He lifted her into his arms, and without a word to their watchers, carried her up the stairs.

Chapter Eighteen

Aelvina lay feverish and ill for days afterward. Girta and Alice took turns tending to her in her chambers, while Gundulf and Sir Alec guarded the door outside. Her fevered screams echoed through the cavernous rooms, sending the guilty ones out into the freshness of brisk autumn morns.

By the time she recovered, Aelvina's well-guarded secret was known to all, even if her newly thin frame did not proudly display the formerly concealed bulge of her belly.

Girta clucked and fussed in protest as Aelvina came downstairs that first day of her recovery. The folds of her woolen tunic nearly hid the small protuberance where Philippe's child lay, but Girta's wise gaze went directly to it. Guilt had eaten at them all for not noticing the signs of pregnancy sooner.

"Sit ye down there and warm yourself at the fire. Ye shouldna be up and about, no less down them great stairs, and ye carrying the master's babe and all! Wicked child that ye are, not telling us 'til it was almost too late.''

The scolding continued throughout the morning, but Aelvina paid it no heed. She went about her tasks in a withdrawn daze, not speaking unless given a direct question, and then only briefly.

After the sun warmed the chill from the day, she worked in her garden. She spent hours there, breathing the names of the fragrant leaves and chanting their uses in a soothing litany. No one disturbed her here. In truth, they thought her still half-mad, but Aelvina smiled inwardly and touched the place where she felt the child's first flutters. This babe would not escape her.

Despite all protests, she continued to serve the evening meal as before. The two mercenaries watched her vacant gaze uneasily, and they too became uncomfortably aware of what had suddenly become a noticeable bulge beneath her skirts. In a few weeks' time what had been barely discernible before became an unsurpassable obstacle.

Sir Geoffrey appeared unexpectedly one late September evening, his mailed gauntlet ringing impatiently against the wooden doors. Gathered before the firelight in the great hall, the castle's occupants watched curiously as Sir Alec gave the signal to unbolt the door.

The handsome courtier entered in a patter of hail and rain, and they hastily closed the door behind him. His burnished armor caught the glitter of torchlight, and the richness of his purple mantle and surcoat lent a depth of mystery and wealth to his impressive figure. Sparkling brown eyes swept the little crowd, coming to light on Aelvina's slight figure, and surprise registered on his mobile features as she stepped forward.

"Welcome to St. Aubyn, Sir Geoffrey. The food is almost prepared if you would care to join us. If you are traveling without your squire, Gundulf will help you with your things."

"Sir Philippe is in residence, then?" Sir Geoffrey inquired, looking about expectantly.

Sir Alec scowled and intruded, understanding well the light in the newcomer's eyes. "Not at present. Come join us in a drink while the women fetch us some food." His glare swept over the others and they dispersed immediately, the women to the kitchen and the men to the table.

Aelvina had seen the surprise in the courtier's eyes at the knowledge of her presence without Philippe, but reacted to it dispassionately. The men would soon put an end to his questions and he would see her as the others did—a whore and an unsuccessful murderess. What she was not prepared for was his astonishment as she carried out the trenchers and prepared to leave them alone while she returned to the kitchens.

"Do you not join us, my lady?" Sir Geoffrey indicated the seat across from his, at the left hand of the head of the table, empty in Philippe's absence.

Aelvina flushed at this reference to what must now be considered her former position, and shook her head slowly in reply. "No, sire, it would not be seemly." Then she disappeared into the kitchen, leaving him to find out for himself.

Still, she could feel his gaze burn curiously on her as she returned at Raymond's bellows and poured more wine. When her nervousness caused some to spill, William cuffed her soundly, sending her staggering backward. Sir Geoffrey jumped to his feet in a blaze of anger, but Sir Alec held him back until Aelvina could escape.

The meal continued without further interruption, and Aelvina breathed a sigh of relief as the courtier made no further attempt to halt the mercenaries' crude behavior and obscene remarks. A brawl would solve nothing, and she was not worth anyone's life.

But Aelvina had not reckoned on Sir Geoffrey's tenacity. At Sir Alec's request, he bore as much as he could, but at meal's end, he slipped from the table and down the kitchen corridor. He caught her as she was coming out with fresh drinking horns. In the dark corridor, they could neither be seen nor heard, and he blocked her exit, catching her arm before she could turn back.

"What is the meaning of this outrage?" he whispered indignantly, feeling the frailness of her wrist between his fingers. "Why do you let them treat you so?"

In the dim light, he could not see the cynicism in Aelvina's smile. "How would you have them treat me sire? A whore is not above menial tasks."

"You are no common whore. Anyone with half an eye can see that!" He ignored the jerk of her head, continuing to hold her firmly. "Does Sir Philippe condone this treatment?"

Aelvina's lips twisted bitterly. "He sent me here with them, did he not?"

"And what did you do to deserve such a fate?" Geoffrey asked incredulously.

Aelvina shrugged indifferently. "I stabbed him in the back."

Geoffrey gasped and his grip loosened. Aelvina attempted to go around him, but he caught her by the shoulders. "You will tell me why, someday, but first we must get you out of here. Philippe does not deserve you if he treats you such."

His kiss came as a surprise, gently questing, holding Aelvina with the unexpectedness of it. He stroked the soft line of her cheek and supported her waist with his strong arm as his lips probed hers.

Aelvina reacted to this tenderness after months of harshness, welcoming the reassurance that she had not yet become totally undesirable, but he stirred nothing more in her. When his hand moved to her breast, she resisted, and Geoffrey set her down gently.

"You will not regret coming with me, my love. I will dress you as you are meant to be dressed, show you off at court proudly. No man will lay a hand to you when you are in my protection. I will take far better care of you than that oaf Philippe. He does not know a fine thing when he holds it in his hand."

Smiling indulgently at his hopeless kindness, Aelvina shook her head. "You are very generous, my lord. Do you not fear a knife in your back in return?"

"From your hands, I would welcome it!" He laughed gallantly.

"Do not be so certain of that, my lord. I fear you would soon regret your generosity. Leave me here, and be about your business as usual in the morning, sire. It would be best for all."

Sir Geoffrey shook his head emphatically, his hand smoothing her long silken plaits. "Never. You would not choose this hell over the glory of the king's court now, would you? You once expressed a desire to see it, did you not?"

Aelvina sighed and stepped away. "Do you think I would grace the royal tower in this condition, my lord?" She smoothed the folds of her gown over the growing roundness of her belly, rubbing her fingers over the child's resting place with loving lightness.

She watched as Sir Geoffrey's handsome smile fell away; then his face turned up again with a sad tilt. His dark gaze played across her face for a moment, debating, and then his hand dropped to his side.

"If I thought you would come to me willingly after the child's birth, I would find a safe place for you until it is born. But you have no intention of becoming another man's mistress, do you?"

"No, my lord, I do not," she said firmly, without any trace of feminine delicacy.

"God may condemn Philippe for this, but I cannot. I may thrash him soundly, though," he added thoughtfully, with a mischievous grin. "Would you care to come with me and watch?"

"I would love to but dare not. You may tell me about it upon your return." Aelvina gave her smile gladly this time. For the first time in weeks, she felt almost human again, and hope gladdened her heart.

Sir Geoffrey rode off in the morning, leaving behind increased tension. The king's messenger could only be on the way to Philippe's camp, and though he revealed nothing of his plans, the mercenaries grew uneasy. Aelvina often felt Raymond surreptitiously gazing at her, and she hid her growing panic.

Sir Alec, too, noted the other knights' restiveness with suspicion, and grew increasingly bolder in his protection of Aelvina. Fearful of the result of his rash actions, Aelvina began to use her pregnancy as an excuse to keep to her room.

But her caution went for naught. One morning several days after Geoffrey's departure, Aelvina heard the sound of horses and voices in the outer bailey, and she slipped from the safety of her room to investigate the source. Raymond and William had been putting their heads together in whispers lately, and she feared what new torment they might have planned.

The hall was empty, the great doors open to allow sunlight to stream in over the newly cleaned walls and fresh rushes. The air smelled inviting, but Aelvina knew better than to enter the unprotected yard. She turned her feet toward the kitchen.

It mattered little. The doors slammed closed and the bolt was thrown before she had crossed halfway. She swung around, facing Sir Raymond's mailed figure with undisguised alarm. Angry voices echoed in from outside, a dim chant against the terror pounding in her ears.

"I am leaving. Do you not wish to kiss me farewell?"

There was no joy in her heart at this news. The evil light in Raymond's eyes told her she would be lucky to live to see him gone. Her mind darted to the safety of Gundulf's hidden staircase. If she only knew where the kitchen entrance was—hut she did not. She must reach the safety of her room and bolt the door, but Raymond stood between her and the stairs.

All these thoughts flew through her mind in the instant it took for Sir Raymond to take two steps toward her. Then she was gone, fleeing as fast as she could down the familiar kitchen corridor, into the glaringly empty kitchens, and up the back stairway. No sounds echoed behind her, but she did not stop to wonder at it. There was only one place of safety, and she headed directly for it. Aelvina slammed the door of her chamber and screamed as Raymond stepped from the shadows, an evil grin across his face. He had guessed her destination and taken the shortest route! She had not thought him so clever. She turned to open the door, but he grabbed her arms and shot the bolt home.

"Now, witch, we will have that romp I promised you. Time is short, but this should not take me long. I have decided the best way to prevent your disappearing is to keep you tied down."

His fingers closed tighter over Aelvina's wrists as he jerked her toward the bed. With a rough shove, he sent her sprawling face first across the mattress. Before she had time to scramble up, he was upon her again. Aelvina rolled away, biting at his ungloved hand as it grabbed at her. In retaliation, he smacked her. Stunned, she fell limp, but unconsciousness did not come to blind her to what was happening.

With a swift stroke, he cut a length of cord from the rope he had tied to his belt, and knotted it expertly about her wrist. The other end he fastened securely around the ornate design carved in the massive bed frame.

Frantically, she searched for some means of escape, some means of halting this certain execution. She cursed in every language she knew, throwing evil spells about his ears.

"Use your witch's powers, if you must, but have you I will. Turn me into a stallion and I will mount you anyway. Do you think your screams will bring help running? It will take them too long to find their way through those walls and doors. I will be done and gone by then."

He knotted the rope tightly around her flailing ankles, spreading her legs wide.

Apparently satisfied he had prevented her escape, Raymond began unfastening his laces.

"I will leave your gown to cover the disgusting bulge you have grown lately. Mayhap I will rid you of Philippe's whelp while I am at it. Would that not be thoughtful of me?" His braies fell about his ankles as he began unlacing his chausses.

Aelvina screamed wildly as Raymond climbed upon the bed, his heavy weight sinking the soft mattress deeper. He smacked her again, though not hard enough to render her unconscious. In stony silence, Aelvina watched as his manhood grew stronger with each bruise he inflicted upon her.

Recognizing his need for violence to enhance his virility, Aelvina lay lifeless and silent beneath him.

Raymond cursed. His shaft sagged. Aelvina was not given time to contemplate relief as his fist plunged into her ribs, knocking the breath from her lungs.

In the brief silence before his next blow, she heard a noise from below. Gasping for breath, Aelvina covered the sound with her scream. Raymond chortled and struck her again, and she felt his manhood rising stronger against her skirts. Her screams reached a fevered pitch with the jangling sound of heavy armor outside the door.

An ax crashed through the oak beneath a mighty blow, and Raymond raised himself with a startled roar. The ax crashed again, decimating the great oak bar in a single blow, an impossible feat for an old man or an untrained farmer. Raymond flung himself from the bed without a second glance, jerking his clothing about his hips as the ax crashed a third time and the door swung open beneath the impact.

The tall, armored figure filling the massive doorway, battle-ax in one hand and broad sword in the other, caused an instant cessation of sound. His armor and surcoat were covered in a film of dust, but to Aelvina's eyes, they sparkled more radiantly than the sun as she breathed his name out loud.

"Philippe!"

Emerald eyes flared with wildfire as they took in Raymond's undressed state and Aelvina's spread-eagled imprisonment. Madness twisted his hawklike face into fury, and Philippe's war cry rattled the rafters as he smote the unarmed knight with the flat of his sword, sending him flying across the cold stone floor. Raymond grabbed his garments with one hand and his own sword with the other, and rose from the floor with the ponderous agility of some prehistoric creature, his eyes blistering coals of hate.

Philippe regarded his half-naked adversary with cold fury and hauteur. "You struck me from behind that last time, coward, and ran when you found I did not die. For that alone I should kill you. For what you have done here now, in this room, whether the wench be willing or no, I would gladly see you strung up and flayed until the life is gone from you."

Fear leaped to Raymond's eyes as he circled Philippe's armored figure, keeping the length of his sword between them, though Philippe had not yet raised his. Instead, Philippe seemed intent on placing himself between the bed and Raymond, leaving the battered door as exit for his ill-prepared opponent.

Aelvina was petrified and remained silent, aware of the pyramiding tension in the room at Philippe's revelation. So Philippe knew the man who had brought him down—the man who should have protected his back when John fell. Why in the name of all saints would he think she would be willing to take such a fiend to her bed? Philippe's menacing presence was as much a threat to her as to Raymond. She stifled her cries of rage as Philippe finally raised his sword.

"I will give you more chance than you gave me. I will not fight an unarmored man. You are free to take your chances with my men outside."

With that, Philippe lunged forward, driving Raymond backward through the door. Stumbling in his half-drawn chausses, Raymond tripped over the broken bar, and Philippe hastened his fall into the corridor with a nudge of his blade. A scream of rage resounded as Philippe added insult to injury with a well-placed blow from his boot.

The door slammed closed on the knight's cries and

Philippe faced the bed. He began pulling off his gauntlets, throwing them to the floor as he studied the leap of terror in silvered eyes. When he shed his sword and began tugging off his hauberk, Aelvina whispered in horror, "No, Philippe, for the love of God, do not!"

There was anguish in her gaze as well, but he ignored it, the blood pounding with red rage behind his eyes as he worked at the remainder of his clothing. "Whore! Nothing but a whore after all." Boots off, he shed his leggings and began to work on his chausses. "How many of them have you had? I have heard enough tales to fill your bed more nights than you've been gone."

Wide-eyed, Aelvina watched as the last of his garments fell away and he stood before her in all his masculine glory. Broad shoulders tapered beneath a thick mat of hair to narrow waist and hips where his manhood stood erect and ready. She could scarce tear her gaze away as he moved on long, muscular legs to the bed where she lay bound. He was coming to her in fury as he had so many times before, and she screamed her outrage at him.

"You bastard! You lying, cheating, conniving son of a many-horned whoremonger! You set those pigs on me and then hold me to blame! Cut me loose and I will kill you with my bare hands! Or are you as much a coward as that filth you threw from here? Cut me free Philippe, and I will show you. . . ."

The knife was in his hands and slicing at the ropes before Aelvina could finish her tirade, and his heavy weight was upon her before she could roll away. Philippe had no trouble breaching the aching emptiness between her legs. He pierced her swiftly, his long, hard body covering her as he plunged deep.

Aelvina screamed in fury as his hands molded her breasts and his lips suckled them into aching, sensitive peaks. She screamed as he plundered her body, driving harder as she twisted and fought him, until she knew not whether she rose to meet him or tear away.

"Kill me, Aelvina, I defy you," he muttered against her ear as her screams softened to groans. "It is the only way you will rid yourself of me, little Viking."

"I hate you!" she sobbed as his lips closed over hers, demanding—and receiving—surrender. His tongue ravaged her mouth as his arms gathered her to his chest, and his full weight struck deeply between her thighs.

Aelvina cried out with the joy and pain of this battle. Philippe was a conqueror, a man who did not know defeat, and he suffered none now. Her arms circled rippling muscles of his back and her hips arched eagerly to take his thrust. The explosion that came for both of them sent the blood pounding so fiercely in her head that she saw pinwheels of light. His lips burned against her cheek as she turned away in rage and shame

"Whore," he murmured softly. "I do not think your other lovers satisfy you as well as I. You seem hungry for a man's thrust."

"Pig! I loathe the very sight of you," Aelvina replied vehemently, but she did not have the strength to beat her fists against his hardness.

"Just as I am filled with revulsion every time I look upon you," Philippe replied evenly, rolling from her and trapping her with his leg as he grasped the bodice of her kirtle. He ripped it cleanly from neck to toe and did the same with the chemise beneath. He held her hands still as he surveyed the milk-white curves thus exposed, his gaze finally resting on the small bulge of her belly.

The scar on Philippe's cheek whitened against his dark face as he ran his large palm over her enlarged breasts down to the swelling in her middle. "Whose is it? Or do you even know?"

"You bastard!" Aelvina muttered between clenched teeth, unable to move from beneath his firm hold. "If you do not know whose it is, why should I tell you?"

"The problem is easy enough solved, I should think," he replied with that same exasperating calmness. Throwing himself from the bed, Philippe padded on silent feet to the broken door, unashamed in his muscular nakedness as he flung it wide.

Aelvina scurried to cover herself as she realized Gundulf and Sir Alec waited outside, as they probably had since the moment Philippe broke through. Were they ever doomed to have an audience to their lovemaking?

"Where's that cowardly bastard?" There was no calmness in this roar as Philippe discovered Raymond among the missing.

"He rode off before I could order the men to stop him. Several have ridden after him, but his horse is fresh and theirs are not. I fear the other got away before you arrived." Sir Alec's gaze traveled over Sir Philippe's shoulder to the room beyond, but it was much too broad to see past clearly.

"The other! There was more than one?"

"Sir William accompanied him. We thought you had ordered them as guards."

"A murrain take thee, you fool! Did you think me mad, too? I would as soon trust my chickens to the fox as to let those two near my woman. Have you taken leave of your senses?"

Behind him, Aelvina breathed a sigh of relief and sank deeply into the softness of her mattress. Whatever happened now did not matter so much as knowing that he had not released those beasts upon her on purpose. He could rage with fury, beat her, lock her up with only bread and water, but those would not break her trust and love as much as the other. Punishment for her grievous wrong she could understand, but not humiliation and degradation.

Philippe's great fist dug into the doorframe as he strained to contain his rage and pain, unable to face the slight figure he had sworn to protect and had so miserably failed. The question he had come to ask seemed negligible in the face of this greater wrong. Gundulf's angry voice forced him to look up.

"My lord!" At Philippe's hesitation, Gundulf continued. "Until this day, she has been protected from any violation. Only you can know what happened behind that door today." His tone was accusing.

Stunned into silence, Philippe absorbed this information slowly. Then, remembering other words, his eyes narrowed in suspicion. "You dare tell me this? You, who have held her in your arms in these chambers every night since your arrival! Because she came to you in love, that was not a violation?"

Aelvina could not see Philippe's face, but pain crackled in his voice as he spoke those words, and the muscles of his back knotted in rage. She could not bear the sight of his suffering, particularly when her gaze rested on the fiery scarring of the newly healed wound of his shoulder. It would serve him right to suffer as she had, but she could not bear it.

She rose, wrapping the sheet around her. Her bare feet made no noise against the stone floor, but the relieved expressions on the faces of the two men in the hall awakened Philippe to her presence. He turned and gave her room beside him.

"You came to me in anger. Was that not a violation?" she demanded. Before he could answer, she continued.

"For love, Gundulf slept at my chamber door in the secret passages you must know, though he knew his only reward would be your rage. 'Tis my own foolishness that would not allow me to take him in my arms, though I knew his love to be true. You said once you would send me back to him when I grew heavy and ugly with your seed. That time has come and I am ready to go."

Aelvina stared at them defiantly, vaguely aware of Gundulf's sorrowful smile and Sir Alec's incredulous surprise, but mostly seeing the play of emotions across Philippe's dark face. Anger and disbelief warred with admiration and some other emotion she feared to give a name.

"No, that time will never come." Philippe's voice rang firmly as he pulled her into the room and slammed the door in the faces of his startled men. He gripped the linen covering her, a defiant gleam in his eyes, and Aelvina dropped her hold on it. He flung it aside, allowing his gaze to roam over her swelling curves once more. "The child is mine, then," he stated, as if just the words would make it so.

"You have accomplished what you set out to do," she returned defiantly. "You have proved your manhood once more. Would you keep me to prove your virility for all the world to see? Let me go."

Philippe's lips twisted with a wolfish grin. "Nay, I have but plowed my seed in fertile ground and now wish to watch it grow. I will never lack for bastards if I tend you regularly."

Aelvina shrieked with rage as he lifted her from the floor and carried her carelessly to the bed, flinging her into the downy softness before falling beside her. When she would turn away, he walloped her backside and pulled her beneath him, his manhood already rising to the challenge as he straddled her.

"I have developed a sudden taste for tupping women heavy with child, though you do not look very heavy as yet," he stated crudely, his hand covering the barely rounded bulge of her once concave belly.

Aelvina had no desire to argue with him. She loved his crudity and roughness as well as she did his occasional kindness and his passionate lovemaking. She had no desire for the polished gallantry of Sir Geoffrey; no amount of flattery could win her as Philippe's honesty and ardor could. She would rather he raged than dissembled, rather he hit than ignored her. This was the man she loved, and she would take him in whatever ways she was allowed.

Philippe's big hands were gentle this time as they sought the bruises of her fair skin, and his lips burned their healing touch against them. He drank of the sweetness of her breasts and found solace for his rages in the gentleness of her touch. They kissed and caressed and discovered each other anew, and blended easily into one without pain or regret.

"If this be hate, I fear the day you find someone to love," Philippe whispered wickedly against her ear and was rewarded with a jab to the ribs.

"You are detestable and have taught me well not to trust any man," Aelvina replied to his teasing. He touched too close to her heart and she dared not let him know it. He was a married man and she a highly expendable mistress. Love had no place in their battle.

"Good. That is as it should be. I will have you turn only to me for your needs!" Philippe ignored her grimace, admiring instead the pert tilt of her breasts beneath his hands. Catching a glint of gold, he hooked his finger in the chain and lifted the heavy ring to his palm. "What is this? I do no remember your wearing it before."

" 'Tis my father's ring. Thyllda held it for me until you

sent me here. She thought, perhaps, to protect me with my father's memory."

Philippe dangled it between his fingers, more interested in the play of light across silver-blue eyes. "If this be the one I returned to her, it has improved greatly in appearance since I saw it last. Mayhap it is the difference in location." He grinned as he dangled it between her breasts, then took it in his hand to examine it more carefully. "Your father's, you say? He must have been a wealthy man to own such a piece."

"It belonged to his father. He would not part with it even when we were most in need, and neither have I. Besides my costume, it is all I have left of my family." Aelvina watched with curiosity as Philippe's brow pulled down in a puzzled frown. She drew her fingers along his furred chest, attempting to distract his dark thoughts.

"Have you never noticed the design on it?" he asked, staring down at her with a gaze that could not be read.

"Of course. It is the same as that my father carried on his shield—the Fairfax family crest. It died with him, I suppose." These were simple and unimportant things that she had taken for granted all her life. The insignia on Philippe's shield also meant nothing to her, other than the fact that it was his.

"Do you not recognize it?" he asked incredulously. He searched the innocence of her eyes for the devious plan that must be lurking there, but saw only bewilderment. He sought another tactic. "How many times have you been though the gates of Dunstan Castle?"

Aelvina wrinkled her forehead as much at the strangeness of his question as in thought to the answer. "We went through it when Thyllda and I first came there. I do not remember going out them again. I went through once more with Marta, when I was looking for you. That is all. Why?"

"And neither time you noticed the great iron insignia over the gates?" At her frown of incomprehension, Philippe sighed. She was as innocent as she looked. Thyllda more likely fit the role of guilty party. "Tell me more of your father," he asked cautiously. Then, with a sudden thought, he waved his hand as if to wipe out the words. "No, do not tell me yet. First, before you say anything, I wish to tell you something. It may be meaningless to you now, but remember it for the future."

Aelvina studied his suddenly serious dark features with astonishment. "Tell me something, my lord?" she asked incredulously. This was a Philippe she had not seen before. He told her nothing unless forced, relying on commands and occasional meaningless love words for communication. What change had come over him? "What need has a baron to tell his whore anything?"

Emerald eyes held a glint of amusement at her always defiant defensiveness, but again she saw that other emotion hovering in the background. His gaze was almost tender as he traced his hand along the line of her jaw.

"Mayhap the time will come when I will be free to tell you everything, but that time is not now, sorceress. Be lucky I do not turn you over and warm that lovely bottom as it deserves." The smile playing across thin lips made mockery of his threat.

Philippe scooped her up and gathered her against chest as he rolled to his back. "When Sir Geoffrey found me and regaled me with tales of Sir Raymond's presence here and of your retirement to your lover's arms each evening, I thought seriously of slaughtering all of you. I think, mayhap, I will only kill Sir Geoffrey." At Aelvina's angry glare, Philippe chuckled and tickled her nose with a strand of silver hair. "Then again, should I ever find Sir Raymond, I may run a blade through his rotten carcass. I owe him for more than this day." His eyes glinted dangerously.

"Is this what you wish to tell me, my lord? Brave threats and foolishness?" she asked scornfully, unable to bear his teasing after all she had suffered—and would suffer in the future—in his name. To bear and raise his bastard would be no easy task.

Philippe gave her a look of total exasperation. "If you were not such an obstinate creature who must fight me at every turn, you would see what I am telling you. I am no Sir Geoffrey. I cannot pamper you with pretty phrases, nor am I a free man to make promises I cannot keep. Now will you listen to what I have to say?"

Aelvina gaped at him in astonishment. What else could he be saying but that he thought her whore enough to take every man in the castle to her bed? She was no more than a possession to him, one he guarded selfishly, it was true; but he would do the same with a good dog or horse. Romance and love were not part of this knight's nature. He had told her so himself, in very explicit terms.

"I am listening, my lord," she replied obediently, not knowing what else to say.

Philippe frowned, thinking her mocking him, but he let her innocent expression convince him otherwise. "I was on my way to London when Geoffrey found me."

"London! Does that mean you have taken the keep? Have you been to Dunstan, then? The babe—is he safe?" she asked eagerly.

"The keep is rubble, the baron a prisoner of the king's men," Philippe interrupted. "My business requires I go directly to London before Dunstan, which is what I am trying to tell you, if you will let me. Thyllda and Chauvin are with the babe. He is safer in their care than mine for the moment. They send me word my heir crawls with great agility, if that has some meaning to you."

Philippe's features were stern as he answered her questions, but there was warmth in his gaze. Aelvina brightened from within at his image of her son scurrying across the floor. His arms tightened as she pressed a light kiss to his cheek. It was a moment he savored, storing it for those times when they must be apart.

"Now if you are ready to be silent . . ." At her nod, he continued. "I must leave for London immediately, before my lady wife hears of my intentions and takes drastic measures. I wish to pursue the possibility of an annulment, but only if my son can still be made heir to St. Aubyn."

He felt Aelvina jerk involuntarily in his arms, but he deliberately ignored her inquiring gaze. "Dunstan is not so much a matter of concern to me, though this ring you wear tells me I may need to reconsider that in the future; but I intend to bring my son to St. Aubyn as heir, not bastard. Do you understand me?"

Aelvina gazed into those emerald mists of Philippe's eyes searching for the meanings hidden there. That he loved his son enough to protect his future was one conclusion she could draw, though she found it difficult to believe of a man who had not even known the color of his child's hair. Beyond that, she was certain of nothing.

"You will bring the child here, then?" she asked tentatively, fearful to express her hopes.

"To live with you and this new one you are breeding for me," Philippe agreed gruffly. "There will be no talk of cottages or milk cows or whatever. You will stay here and raise my sons under my protection."

"And if there is no annulment? Will I ever see my first-born then?" Aelvina cried.

"He will be brought here whatever happens. These are his lands, and it is time I looked to them."

"And I? The Lady Ravenna will scarcely look kindly on a known whore raising the heir to her lands, even though that whore be the child's mother."

Philippe's lips set grimly. "The Lady Ravenna can have no concern in what is not hers and has no power over me. And you will do wisely not to anger me further by using vulgar language to describe yourself. Unless you know something I do not, you are my woman, mother of my children, and you will be treated with the respect that position deserves. You are to remain here as the lady of this household and there will be no quarrel about it. Now tell me of that ring you wear; it may give me further argument when I state my case to the king."

The sudden switch of subjects left Aelvina confused. "What is there to tell you, my lord?" She took the ring from his fingers and studied it, attempting to understand what he saw in it; but it was simply the ring her father always wore.

"The crest on this ring is the same as that on Dunstan walls, *ma chérie*. I would know how that happened. Who was your father? What name did he go by?"

"He was known as Richard the Fair-Haired, son of Aelgar. I know of no other name. He had been dispossessed of his lands before my birth and did not speak of them. It was a bitter subject and forbidden to me."

"He was a knight, then? A man of some breeding?" The name stirred some long-forgotten memory, and Philippe searched for it as he continued his questioning.

Aelvina gave him a look of disgust and attempted, unsuccessfully, to squirm from his powerful hold. "What does that matter now? He is dead and I have no dowry. I am no better than the serfs who work your land, whatever my name."

"Answer me!" Philippe roared, growing impatient with this prickly termagant he had taken under his wing.

"Yes, my lord!" Aelvina screamed back at him. "He was a knight of some fame, my lord! A mighty warrior, but one of more kindness than you would ever know."

"And your mother a harem dancer!" Philippe taunted, recalling an earlier conversation.

"The daughter of an Angevin nobleman, my lord! Her family was killed in the Holy Land, where my father found her. Holy Land!" she snorted derisively. "It is hell that place has brought me and mine. It was while my father was there with his men that he lost his lands to Stephen and the robber barons, though crusader's lands were supposed to be protected."

Memory returned with a rush and Philippe sat up suddenly, his fingers digging into her shoulders as his gaze bore holes deep into her soul. "Describe your father to me. Do you remember the phrase he used going into battle?"

Aelvina stared at him as if he had gone mad. "He was not above average height, but he towered above my mother, who was quite small. I inherited my mother's stature, but my father's hair, though they were both fair. His was much lighter than my mother's, and his eyes the same color blue as mine. The battle cry I cannot help you with much. I can repeat the phrase, but it is meaningless to me. It is in a language more ancient than the Celts."

"It means literally, 'Conquer the foes, secure the morrow.' I asked him once." Philippe's tone was almost absent as he made this amazing statement, threading his fingers through her hair. Before Aelvina could express her astonishment, he looked at her with a strange quirk and asked, "Do you remember once being in a great hall with sunlight coming through stained glass windows? You were wearing a blue gown the color of your eyes with silver trimming along the borders, and your hair fell loose down your back. You kept brushing it from your eyes as you chased a wooden ball across the floor, rolling it in some fierce game you played with yourself until an exceeding rude young man caught it and hid it behind his back?"

Aelvina's eyes widened as she stared into Philippe's dark face, seeing again his hawklike countenance, the handsome charm of his flashing smile, and the glittering amusement in emerald eyes beneath heavy, dark brows. She saw them again, without the etched lines around his eyes and lips or the jagged scar across his cheek, remembering their emerald glitter with utmost clarity.

"And I used that cry on you before I kicked you in the shins!" Her laughter bubbled up from a well she had thought long drained, remembering the younger Philippe's startled expression at such an unfeminine lack of docility. "You spanked me quite rudely, my lord! It was after that I made my father give me a knife. I swore no man would ever lay a hand on me again!"

"It was lucky, then, I left shortly after, or you would have put a hole in my back much sooner than you did. I hope your thirst for revenge is quite quenched by now, my lady?" Laughter returned the handsomeness to Philippe's face and relaxed the lines of weariness and pain for a while.

Aelvina gently touched his rough cheek, her heart swelling with gladness that so mighty a warrior could still carry such a tender memory with him. "Aye, for the moment, but I make no promises. Why do you ask me these things? They happened so long ago. What importance have they now?"

"You do not even know where you were that day, do

you? You were in the home of Maud, Countess of Anjou, King Henry's mother. Henry was not much older than yourself at the time, but I was in the count's service, and your father one of his hired mercenaries. He told me once he served only because it was at Maud's request. He wished to be in her armies when they recaptured England from Stephen."

"Yes, and you see where such gallantry brought us. We returned to England as paupers, wandering the roads from one castle to the next." Aelvina's full lips twisted into a caricature of their usual soft smile. "The men of his lands that did not die in the Holy Lands died in Maud's wars, and there were none left with which to fight the thief who usurped my father's rightful property. We had nothing on which to raise an army."

"And what lands were these that were taken? Do you know?"

"No. I was too young and had heard pieces of the tale too many times to listen carefully. I was happy as I was and did not understand our poverty until my parents died. Only then did I realize they had given me everything at cost to themselves. It is painful to not know what you have lost 'til it is gone."

Philippe held her closely, cupping her head in his palm so that Aelvina's soft cheek rested against his broad chest. He could feel the moisture of her lashes and the light brush of her breast against him with each soft breath. "Your father was working in Henry's service then. I am certain of it, just as I am certain Dunstan must be the lands he lost. Thyllda would have known the family home, would she not?"

These startling words mattered little to Aelvina. The comfort of Philippe's embrace and the strength she derived from his strong arms were matters of the greatest importance. With some stretch of the imagination she could almost think he cared for her and not the lands or name. He had Dunstan already. What mattered that it might once have belonged to her father?

"Thyllda knows everything. She has been with my father's family since she was a child. What are these matters to you, my lord? It makes little difference to what is past and done, does it?"

"It may make none to us, my love, but it may mean everything to others. Let me borrow the ring for while, Aelvina. Will you trust me with it?"

To hear softness from his deep voice, to hear him ask and not demand, were gems for which Aelvina would gladly trade all. He had used her in anger before but never betrayed a trust. She slipped the chain from her neck and held it out to him.

Their gazes met and held as he transferred the chain to his own neck. The gold scorched against his skin, but not so heatedly as Aelvina's trusting gaze. Against his will, Philippe reached to slide his hands across her slim shoulders and into the thickness of heavy ivory tresses. Though he had just satisfied himself with her passionate demands, his loins ached again for the pleasure she brought to him.

"There is much work yet to be done this day," he murmured as she reached a tentative hand to his chest.

"Yea, and there are better things to be done with this time than listening to you," she replied mockingly.

"Then do not listen to my words, sorceress, but heed my touch." There was no sense in fighting it any longer. She had made a slave of him as surely as if she had put a chain around his heart. No other touched him as this one had. Perhaps the memory of that bright-haired little girl with her fierce spirit and enchanting loveliness had held him enthralled all these years. To be certain, no other woman he had ever known presented quite the challenge this one did. Even as he pulled her into his arms and felt her come willingly he doubted he had conquered more than her woman's body. To conquer more would take a lifetime of battles, but it would be well worth the bloodshed.

Philippe's mouth closed over hers as his weight bore her down to the bed once more.

Chapter Nineteen

The flames in the great fireplace burned brightly, warding off the chill of a cool October evening as Philippe threw open the great front door and entered. Several of his men followed, their duties done and their bellies empty.

For the first time since his hasty arrival, Philippe glanced around him. The stench that had greeted him on his last arrival here was no longer noticeable, and upon closer inspection, he understood the change. The moldering areas of dampness were gone from the walls, the rushes clean and sweet-smelling, the rotted tapestries washed and mended. Torches gleamed against recently scrubbed stones, and the whole room gave the appearance of a well-tended household.

As if to compound his surprise, Aelvina appeared from the kitchens bearing flagons of wine and mead, and behind her, Girta and Alice carried trenchers of food. His men hastened to find seats around the trestle tables that had been set up across the hall, but Philippe lingered at his place, watching as Aelvina filled his tankard.

She had donned a light wool gunna of deep blue over a linen kirtle of silver gray, but had no jeweled girdle to bind the bodice as it was meant to be. He thought he recognized the gown and knew it was none he had bought for her.

Azure pools turned up to meet his stare as he remained standing. "My lord, are you displeased with something?" she asked anxiously.

Philippe understood little of the sharp fangs of guilt and desire and hope gnawing at his innards. A strange feeling unlike any other he had known before struck at his heart. He blamed it on a desire to possess her totally—as he did not, yet.

"I sent you here as prisoner, not servant. How have you wrought such changes in so short a time?" he asked sternly.

But he was unable to hide the warmth of his gaze and Aelvina relaxed. "Sorcery, my lord. A witch's broom sweeps clean, they say, and I am not accustomed to living in sties."

She turned back toward the kitchen, but Philippe's voice halted her. "Whither dost thou go? I have servants to tend the meal. Sit you down here, at my side, where you belong."

Aelvina turned an incredulous gaze to his imperious figure. Philippe stood tall and strong against the firelight's blaze, pointing to the seat at his right on the dais, and his darkened features brooked no denial.

Still, she tried to protest. "My lord, Girta is too old to fetch and carry, and Alice cannot do it all herself. My place is with them."

"Sit!" he roared, and she did.

The men at the table had watched this tableau with interest and now broke into chuckling cheers as Aelvina took her place at Philippe's side, fair cheeks flushing with color at this undue attention. From beneath lowered lashes, she gave Philippe a baleful look, but he only grinned back as Sir Alec raised a tankard in toast.

"Ye have half tamed the sprite, my lord. 'Tis more than any mortal man can do."

"It is my brat she carries. That makes her as mortal as any other now, I suspect," Philippe replied calmly, but with a gleam of pride as another cheer went up about the table at this news.

His hand covered Aelvina's as each man at the table sought to top the other in words of tribute and celebration to the occasion. Beneath the noisy roar, Philippe spoke softly, for her ears alone.

"I mean to put an end to all rumors, little Viking. You may not be my lawful, wedded wife, but you are mistress of this hall and mother of my child. It is a position that demands respect, and I intend you receive it."

"You seek to be kind, my lord, but I am your vassal and servant and no more. Mistress is a position deserving only of scorn and ridicule, whatever you would make of it," Aelvina replied dryly. "A king's mistress might command respect through power, but even she is scorned as a mother of bastards."

Philippe scowled. "You will command more power and respect as my mistress than my unfortunate wife. My men understand loyalty and courage and care little for the moral niceties. You are my lady and will be treated as such."

It was an end to the argument, and Aelvina recognized it as such. To be lady to this mighty knight was a grander position than she had ever aspired to, but it was an insecure one, nonetheless. Still, she gained some comfort from the fact that Philippe intended to recognize his bastard and not cast her aside, as so many might have done.

"Then you must find Girta help in the kitchen, my lord, if you expect your men to be fed and served."

Defiance still tinged her voice but more as a lingering habit, Philippe observed. He smiled as her gaze grew warm and confused beneath his scrutiny. For too long, she had been forced to protect herself, and surrendering this responsibility to him would not come easily. Yet she was woman enough to enjoy a man's protective concern and had learned well to appreciate his greater strength.

"Girta!" He bellowed at the old woman as she hobbled around the far end of the table. With a smile creasing her lined face, the old woman approached her new lord and master and made an awkward curtsy.

"Where are the vassals sworn to give me service in these halls?" Philippe demanded. "Are there no women in the village willing to work for their living?"

"My lord, there are those eager to seek the shelter of these halls, who dared not without word from you."

"Bring in those few you can trust. I will be leaving shortly, but I would have my lady live in comfort, not squalor. When I return and can lend my protection, we will staff these walls accordingly." He hesitated, his eyes falling once again on Aelvina's worn attire. "Was there no part of my mother's finery left behind but these moth-eaten remnants? I had not thought she took all her jewels, nor the cloths yet unmade into clothing. Is there nothing suitable to be found in the storerooms?"

"My lord, I beg you . . ." Aelvina began, embarrassment again coloring her features. To rely on this man for all her clothing and shelter was a notion to which she could not grow accustomed. "I have clothes. They may be old, but they cover me, and I would not cost you more."

Philippe waved away her protests, waiting for the reply behind Girta's beaming smile.

"When the old lord died, we buried the gold until ye came to claim it. There are trunks of fine cloths in the donjon storerooms, waiting to be made up. The lady left much behind."

"Knowing my mother's wasteful habits, I do not doubt it," Philippe replied wryly. "All colors she thought unsuitable to herself will be there. Surely one or two would make a gown that would suit my eyes better than these."

Aelvina bit her lip at the disdainful gesture indicating her mended garments. She had worn old gowns of her mother's most of her life and had thought little of reworking these garments. They were finer than most, but apparently still not suitable to a lord's mistress.

"Your mother? Does she still live in Normandy?" she diverted the topic from herself.

"Nay. She did not outlast my father by long, though she did not know it. Like King Henry, I now have lands in both Normandy and England, though mine are scarce so great," Philippe added wryly.

"Then you have no other family? Will you not have to return to Normandy to oversee those lands sometime?" These were only a few of the questions that nagged at Aelvina's thoughts now that it seemed her fate was inextricably tied to his.

Philippe grew quiet, swirling the wine in his goblet as he studied her. He remembered her as a child now, the much loved daughter of a great man bent with more than his share of sorrows. She had been gently reared, and he had used her as whore. She knew nothing of him, but gave him her trust—had given it to him from the first. Yet he had spoken nothing of himself to her.

Setting the goblet aside, he covered her hand with his, playing idly with her fingers. "I have a younger brother, *chérie,* in Normandy. He has no legal rights to my mother's lands since they were given as dowry to my father, who left them to me, his only heir. My brother is a bastard, borne of an affair after my mother returned to Normandy."

The words were quiet, and Aelvina knew they were an admission Philippe did not readily make. In them, she found some understanding for his insistence that their son not be declared bastard, too.

"You feel her lands belong more to him than you? You must love him much, my lord," she replied softly.

"It is difficult not to love someone with whom you have grown up. He is my family now. I know he will care for my lands well and fairly, but there must always be resentment that they are rightfully mine, though they have been his home all his life. No, I do not think I will be returning to Normandy soon."

The matter lay settled there. St. Aubyn was Philippe's home for the future and Aelvina was mistress of St. Aubyn. It should be all she could want, but a nagging emptiness still filled a corner of her heart.

She sat quietly by Philippe's side as the men drank and relaxed and told bragging tales of war and women. They had been long at the business of war, and welcomed the respite of hearth and home and the fairer sex. More than one eyed Alice with remembrance of earlier times, but Gundulf seemed ever present when she was about. They gradually lost interest when she showed no liking for their advances. A night of drinking with no need to rise early or be wary met their needs as well.

Philippe, as usual, drank little, but enjoyed the luxury of relaxing. He leaned back in his chair, meeting a soft look that sent his blood racing. He held out his hand for hers. "Shall we leave them to their idle boasts and start new tales of our own?"

His callused palm tenderly crushed Aelvina's offered

hand, but she lingered uncertainly. Noting her hesitation, Philippe did not rise, but waited patiently.

"My lord, do I have the right to refuse? If I say you nay, will you take me as you have in the past and did today? Am I bound to you by oath or action in any way?"

A plea played in her eyes as she watched the firelight dance across his dark visage. Philippe considered the question carefully.

He sighed and rubbed his thumb across the back of her hand. "I am not a man of fine words, Aelvina. I wish you did not have to ask, but I suppose I have given you reason enough to do so. Once, I thought you a wench free with her favors and took you as such. Since then, I have learned differently, but in anger and distrust, treated you little better. Now, knowing not only your loyalty, but that you are a maid gently reared, I must bow to what my conscience has told me all along. I will not take you against your will again, Aelvina. I give you my word."

Philippe raised her to her feet, his smile sad as he continued to hold her hand. "You know well that I desire your warmth and no other's to fill my bed, but if you should refuse, I will abide by the few promises I can give you. You bear my child. This is his home and yours, whatever you decide. Will you come with me?"

Aelvina swept from her place by the table to stand by his side, her eyes ablaze with a light so brilliant that it rivaled the moon's. She rested her hand against the deep crimson of his surcoat and murmured, "As you can see, I need little persuasion, my lord. I am a shameful wanton, I fear, and not the gentle maid you think me."

Philippe's grin spread widely across his face as he grasped her in his arms and swung her up in the air, catching her by surprise. "Gentle maid! I am no such fool. Do you not have me groveling like some simpering ass to

keep from feeling your knife in my back whenever I choose
to pleasure myself between your legs? Coward, I may be;
fool, I am not!''

Though they heard not his words, his men roared their
approval. Their laughter filled the hall as Philippe firmly
carried off his laughing, protesting lady, her small fists
beating futilely at his broad back as they ascended the
stairs.

Aelvina shivered at the sudden coldness of the bed and
woke drowsily to seek the source of heat that had warmed
her throughout the night. Her discovery that the bed was
empty brought instant alertness, but she relaxed when she
located Philippe's naked length stoking the coals in the
brazier.

As he returned to her, Aelvina studied the taut, powerful
muscles that carried him like some graceful beast of the
jungle. The bulging biceps and massive chest that made
him an expert in his chosen profession effectively disguised
the true man underneath; the man who could use his big
body to pleasure her with gentleness and whose intelligence knew her innermost thoughts before she spoke
them. She welcomed him eagerly as he joined her again
beneath the covers.

"I did not mean to wake you, *ma petite,*" Philippe murmured, taking her supple body into his arms to warm the
chill from his bones. She squirmed enticingly in his hold,
and he smiled at the eagerness with which she sought
him . . . a far cry from earlier days.

Aelvina slid her hands behind his neck and kissed his
lips tenderly. "But I mean never to sleep through any
minute you are awake and with me, my lord. These last few

months have taught me how precious our time together is. How long will you stay?"

"My Viking grows romantic. Is that an effect of motherhood?" Philippe deftly avoided her last question as his hand navigated the tempting curves pressed against him.

"Romance was not the result of my last childbearing, my lord, if you will remember. It is yourself who has taught me the pleasure of your company. Is there no room in your hard heart for mine, or do only your loins seek my presence, sire?"

Philippe sighed at this ingenuous questioning. Why did women always seek reassurances of their fantasies of love after they had been bedded properly? He had thought this one to be different, but evidently only circumstances had prevented her asking before. He had never spoken words of love to a woman; in truth, he had never felt more than lust for any woman. Why should this one be different? Yet, he knew she was, because never before had he chosen a woman to bear his children and share his home. He lay her back against the mattress and covered her with his length, letting his rising ardor speak the truth of his reply.

"I desire you as I desire no other woman, and I have made you mistress of this keep above all others. Does that not tell you something of my thoughts? If you wish chivalrous words, seek Sir Geoffrey and his ilk, for I have no faith in them."

Her fingers combed through his unruly hair. "If you are not bound to me by words of God or love, then I must accept your lust as seal of your approval, but it is a poor seal at best, my lord. What becomes of me when I grow too bulky to ease your needs? Must I accept, also, that others will share your bed when the need arises? Perhaps you will seek your lady wife to breed true heirs?" She needled him, knowing she had hit her mark when his hands ceased fondling her breasts and moved to part her legs without further ado.

"By my faith, woman, I will use you until you have no doubt as to my faithfulness, and when the time comes I cannot get between your legs for the size of your belly, I will teach you other means to satisfy my needs. Now halt your nagging or you will give me cause to regret my choice."

Aelvina arched upwards with an eager cry of joy as he entered her. She let the swift rhythm of his movements transport her to another world where all that mattered was Philippe's arms about her and the crescendoing drive of their passions. His name slipped past her lips as he fused their bodies into one.

Philippe plied her with the tender kisses he had denied her earlier. "It pleases me to hear my name from your lips, *ma chérie*. I would hear it more often," he murmured, kissing the edges of her mouth, teasing her with his tongue.

"I have been your vassal too long, I fear, to change easily. I cannot think of myself as your equal." Beneath his caresses, Aelvina radiated with the bliss of his touch.

"If what you have told me is true, you are more than my equal, sorceress." Philippe kissed the curve of her lips, the sweep of long lashes, then rolled away. There was work yet to be done and it would not be accomplished by lying abed. "You are an earl's daughter and I but a lowly baron. Do not demean your worth." Thus saying, he stood and sought his clothing.

Aelvina burrowed into the warmth where his body had just been and watched him as he pulled on his chausses, unable to hide the admiration for his masculine form that sparkled in her eyes. Philippe grinned and sat beside her as he pulled on his sherte, and tousled her hair when his hand was free.

"Come lazy lie-abed. You must show me what this keep needs to make it a palace for my countess."

"All titles died with my father. I am a trollop, not a countess." With the dignity of a ruffled princess, Aelvina swung her long legs from the bed and sat beside him.

"You are an obstinate wench who tries my patience." Philippe stood and lifted her easily to the floor, giving her a lusty wallop on the backside to send her in the direction of her clothes.

They passed the day in an easy companionship that raised eyebrows among the men who remembered Philippe's towering rages of the last months. It seemed the sorceress had struck their leader with more than a knife that day, and only she held the cure. As Philippe bent his ear to Aelvina's words while they traipsed the keep and inner bailey in intimate converse, his men exchanged knowing looks. A woman who could divert Philippe's attention from war was a woman to be reckoned with.

Admiration lingered in Philippe's eyes at day's end as they beheld Aelvina's entrancing figure garbed in an ivory silk she had converted from his mother's leavings. His esteem was as much for her cleverness in transforming the trailing gown as for the loveliness it accentuated. A gold filigree girdle he had rescued from Girta's hiding place now rested about the curve of Aelvina's hips, and the golden chaplet holding pale ivory-blond hair became a crown upon her noble head. She was every inch the lady he had declared her, and pride lit his eyes as he escorted her to the table.

Girta had been true to her word, and already new faces appeared in the hall, carrying trenchers and flagons of drink. The liquor flowed freely, but this time Philippe imposed a limit. He wanted his men ready to ride in the morning.

Aelvina heard him give this order with an inquiring look he could not ignore. With a half smile he hoped would cover his concerns, Philippe explained gently. "I have tarried too long already, *ma chérie*. We must ride to London on the morrow if I am to set my affairs aright and bring your son safely back here."

"Could I not go with you, Philippe? My heart aches every day that I am kept from my son, and it would ease me greatly to be at your side when he is returned."

Philippe frowned. "No further attempts endangered either of our lives while we were apart. Raymond was guilty of one attempt, I know now. But I cannot believe he would put an ax through my head over a woman, and he would know nothing of poisons. There is an evil about I have not yet uncovered, and I would feel better if you remained safe behind these walls."

Aelvina twisted her fingers in her lap, knowing his concern lay even deeper than that; she sensed it in the care with which he chose his words. "Philippe, if there is any chance of danger to you or the babe on this journey, I would go with you. You do not know what it is like to sit patiently and wait on others to do what you long to do yourself. I have waited long enough, Philippe. If you go without me, I will go to Dunstan myself."

Philippe's lips set in a grim line. Docile and demure as her fair form might appear, he knew it hid a will of steel. "Aelvina, you must think of the child you carry now, and the others you might bear in the future. To go to Dunstan now would sacrifice all."

To his surprise, a thin veil of tears moistened her lashes when she looked up to him. Aelvina was not one to resort to weeping, and the sight smote his heart mightily. Her words decimated all argument.

"I can only bear you bastards, my lord, and not even

that if you should be taken from me. Bastards cannot hold the lands of Dunstan and St. Aubyn. Though the claim be a false one, our firstborn is the only hope for the future of those lands. I have agreed to all you asked in his name, even to bearing the name of shame I carry, but this time I cannot yield. The child is in danger and I cannot help him by remaining here."

She was right. Matters would be greatly expedited if she could be presented to Henry immediately and the full story made known. If they moved swiftly enough, he could storm Dunstan and have his wife removed before she knew his whereabouts. If Henry would not give him permission to cast off his wife, then he could still remove the child from her vicinity. While his wife knew not what he planned, the child was safer in Dunstan than with him. The danger would come later, if he had rightly gauged the Lady Ravenna's vengefulness.

Still, he hesitated. "Though my heir means much to me, Aelvina, I would not lose you and the child you carry. I mean to leave most of my men here and to ride hard to reach London swiftly. Such a journey cannot be safe for you or the babe."

She stood and moved beside his chair, resting her hand on his shoulder as she smoothed the silk over her barely noticeable belly.

"My children will learn to ride before they are born, as I did. If my mother could carry me from the Holy Land to the shores of Normandy, I can safely make this short journey."

Philippe's arm circled about her waist as he looked up into Aelvina's loving gaze and knew he could not bear parting with her now. He would take her to the king and present her as she was meant to be.

"You are a conniving wench and I can see you cannot

be trusted out of my sight." He gestured at the farmer settled in a far corner, never too far from Alice or Aelvina. "Gundulf, come here."

Gundulf rose and stood before his lord and lady. "My lord?"

"Aelvina rides with me on the morrow. You have protected her well and I thank you, but if you will trust me with the duty now, I think I might offer her equal protection." Philippe's irony did not escape Gundulf's detection and the yeoman stiffened suspiciously. "For your service, I would like to offer a better place than that of foot soldier. Aelvina tells me you have a talent for growing things and have often raised twice the crop in your fields as any other can. Is that true?"

Gundulf transferred his suspicious glance to Aelvina, but she merely smiled at him. "My lady is overkind, but I will not deny her words," he answered carefully.

Philippe snorted and gave Aelvina a mocking look. "The lady is known for her deceitful ways, but I do not doubt her honesty. If she speaks the truth in this, I have more need of you on my lands than in my army. I wish you to return to Dunstan as overseer. If you teach my people your ways, I will profit as well as they, and your share will increase accordingly."

Catching something in the younger man's look and noting his reference to Aelvina as "my lady," Philippe realized the young farmer knew as much of her origins as he did. It made for a divided loyalty at best if Gundulf chose to serve Aelvina and not himself, but that was a small matter and easily resolved.

"When you return to Dunstan, I would have you take word to Thyllda of our plans. There might come a time when she will need to take the child from the castle, and you could protect him best until either I return as lord of

Dunstan, or Aelvina as lady. Do you understand me?" Philippe asked cautiously.

A flash of relief lit Gundulf's eyes and his whole stance altered, as if a tremendous burden had been lifted from his shoulders. "I understand, my lord, and will do all that you ask, gratefully. May I ask one boon?"

Philippe concealed his surprise and nodded.

"The maid, Alice, has asked to enter my lady's service. I would return her to Dunstan with me to await my lady's wishes, if you would."

Philippe felt the slight stiffening of Aelvina's posture beside him, and gave her a sidelong glance to judge her reaction, which he should not have doubted. She was obviously fighting to stifle a giggle, and he deliberately lifted an inquiring eyebrow, forcing her to make the reply.

Aelvina rose to the occasion. "Gundulf, you are a charlatan and a fraud. Your loyalty was out of duty and not love, and all the time you had your eye on another maid. Why did you not tell me?"

Too much had passed between them for Gundulf to take this berating as from mistress to servant, and he lifted a less than respectful gaze to his lady. "Would the lady of Dunstan have listened to a lowly farmer when she will not even listen to the lord of St. Aubyn? I surrender my duties gladly. Alice is not only pleasing to the eye, but eager and obedient."

As Philippe's chuckles threatened to turn into a roar of laughter, Aelvina jabbed him in the ribs and refused to look upon him. "Even knowing what Alice has been, will you marry her? I will not see her trifled with again."

That sobered both men. Gundulf glanced down at his feet, then up to Philippe's frowning gaze, and reluctantly returned to Aelvina. "She is a good lass and has been with no other these last months. I am not certain she will be willing, yet, nor if she will accept a poor farmer with a large family to support. These things take time, but I will not trifle with her.''

His words seemed to relax the tension created by Aelvina's mention of marriage, and Philippe gestured amiably. ''As overseer, you would do better to find a bride with a dowry.'' He grinned, undisturbed at Aelvina's irate intake of breath. ''But if you choose to play the fool and put a shackle about your neck, I will see if my overseer cannot be provided more private accommodations for his bride than in his mother's house. Will that suit?''

'' Most certainly, my lord.'' Gundulf's usual staid expression met Aelvina's gaze with joy. ''Thyllda will be pleased with your decision, and we will see no harm comes to the child. Go with God's care.''

Tears sprang to Aelvina's eyes as Gundulf was dismissed, and Philippe hastened to rise. ''It will all work out for the best, *ma chérie*—you will see.'' But he made no promises. The future still held too many uncertainties.

Chapter Twenty

The group of men and horses emerging from the castle walls in the early dawn was a silent one. In their midst rode a slight figure in a fur-lined pelisse of palest blue, the large hood hiding any sight of the silver-gold tresses beneath. The small gray palfrey she rode seemed even tinier next to the massive destriers at her side, but their pace was equal as the small party broke into a gallop on the open road.

By nightfall, exhaustion rimmed her eyes with darkness, but Aelvina moved gracefully about the fireside, preparing a more flavorful meal than the men would have readied for themselves. Philippe had surrounded her with his best warriors—men of strength and quickness on the battlefield. They were mere pups in the hands of this delicate girl, Philippe mused sardonically, watching as the youngest accepted Aelvina's offering with an almost worshipful gaze.

It did not take long for even the youngest of women to

learn the ease with which their wiles twisted men into putty.
Philippe had avoided the artful ways of females for too
long, making it plain he sought only one thing from them.
Now he was not only married to the most treacherous
bitch he had ever encountered, but had managed to bind
himself hand and foot to this forest sprite who had cast
some secret enchantment upon his senses that no logic
could dispell. The bitch he would cast off, if he could, but
the other . . .

Philippe sighed and drank deeply from his flask. A man
had to settle down sometime and he could find no finer
wench to warm his bed. It galled him that his brats be
born bastard, but with a woman like that at his side, it
would be worth it. He had never been one to believe in
romantic notions. Likewise he had never imagined
aligning himself with other nobles through a well-placed
marriage. His mother's marriage had soured him on the
state of matrimony long ago, and he had not thought
wealth or power worth a ball and chain. Yet, somehow, he
had managed to entangle himself with two women: one
not to his liking and the other unobtainable.

Philippe's eyes narrowed at this astonishing notion.
Aelvina was literally unobtainable from the vantage point
of marriage, since he was already married. At any time,
she could walk out of his life and he had no legal means
of stopping her. He had taken for granted that she would
stay with him because of the child, a rather rash assumption
on his part, knowing Aelvina's mercurial temperament.
What was it she had said? If you are not bound by words
of God or love . . . That worked both ways. He was bound
by honor to support her, but she had no ties at all. She
had him fairly shackled while she flitted freely, possessed
only in bed and only by her will, since he had agreed not

to take her by force again. Damn ... she had made a simpering ass of him, for certain.

Yet, when she came into his arms that night, he desired nothing more than the blending of their bodies. She gave herself totally, telling him without words that she would never leave, and he believed her.

While Philippe's small party raced down the road to London, a lone knight crossed the portals of Dunstan Castle. Covered by the grime of his hasty journey, he positioned his helm beneath his arm and pushed back his leather hood, contemplating his surroundings with a grim expression.

The stooped figure of an elderly crone hurried to meet him, and his expression grew grimmer. He had asked for the lady, not the servant. It had been in his mind to make a cuckold of Sir Philippe as revenge for his humiliation. Marta's presence warned of a delay in those plans.

Grudgingly, Sir Raymond followed the ancient servant to a small windowless anteroom, where the old woman turned on him in hissing anger. "Fool! What brings you here in daylight? Do you not know the place is full of Philippe's spies?"

Raymond shrugged indifferently and looked about for so much as a jug of water or hunk of bread. The ride had been a long one, but hospitality was not a byword in Dunstan Castle. He grieved at the lack of refreshment and bent a bored ear to Marta's warning before replying

"Philippe knows I am the one who attacked him. It was not a secret that could be kept once that other little witch returned him to life, you knew that. Now he rides to London on who knows what hellish business. I need fare to make my way back to Normandy. If I am caught, I will tell all,'' Raymond responded at the end of Marta's tirade.

Marta cast him a malevolent look. "London? How do you know this? I thought you were at St. Aubyn. Will you tell me also that your perverted habits have not yet destroyed the girl? You have had more than enough time to beat her into submission."

A look of annoyance crossed the knight's countenance. "Philippe walked in as I prepared to put an end to the she-devil. Apparently, he was more eager for his whore than for his wife."

Marta cursed. This incompetent fool could enter walls she could not, for all her claim to witchcraft, but he seemed incapable of carrying out a single task to her satisfaction. Even her own attempt had narrowly missed completion. Those two must live charmed lives, but if she was to retain her lady's place, she must act quickly.

"They cannot be allowed to return from London. Kill Philippe, and the girl is yours to do with as you wish. None will miss her except the bitch in the nursery, and I can rid myself of her easily. It is Philippe who can have us all hanged. You receive no reward from us until you carry out the task you were given."

She spoke firmly, and Raymond glared. "I have already risked my neck for the girl and the gold. My chances of escaping a second time are slim. Why should I try again?"

A tall, slender figure slid from the shadows, her voice a husky, sensuous promise as her long nails scratched seductively over his chest. "Shall I show you why, Sir Raymond?" she whispered sibilantly.

As her lady wrapped her talons in the knight's weak flesh, Marta slipped from the room. The Lady Ravenna's witchcraft was of a carnal nature, but just as effective as any other. There was time to prepare. By morning, Sir

Raymond would be fully eager to carry out the necessary execution.

Marta chuckled smugly as she imagined the moon child caught in that one's ugly grasp while her lover's blood flowed into the ground. Such a delicate flower would not live through the bruising Sir Raymond would give her once he drank of Marta's goodly potions. It was a pity she could not be there to see it.

Mayhap that could be arranged, also.

The ride the next day was even more arduous than the one before, but by nightfall, it brought them to the riverbank and in sight of London's outskirts. At the sight of Aelvina's drooping figure, Philippe ordered camp made there for the night. The king and his court could wait until morning.

That night, he cradled her in his lap, resting Aelvina against his shoulder. Their goal was so close now, just within reach. . . . She snuggled closer and covered her belly with his hand. At the first flutter of his child in her womb, Philippe melted, and he knew with a certainty that the shackles had closed about him—put there by his own hand and no other.

A messenger left the camp early the next morning notifying Henry of Philippe's arrival and requesting an audience. The king's reply returned with the messenger, and the little camp packed and began its sojourn into the city.

Inside the walls, Aelvina gazed about with curiosity, but having seen some of the great cities of the Continent, London left her unimpressed. Most of the houses were of wooden framework, an open invitation to fire, as many another city had learned well. Few houses were of more than one story, and these few had a peculiar tendency to lean toward each other, as their wealthy owners extended their luxurious solars over the narrow, winding streets.

The churches, on the other hand, were magnificent edifices of brick and stone with towering arches and steeples. The halls of court and government were rapidly gaining the same magnificence, thanks to Henry's penchant for stone fortresses.

As Philippe slid his hands around her waist and lifted her from the palfrey, Aelvina gazed up at White Hall with trepidation. What was she doing here? Though the clothes she wore were of rich materials, they were not hers. The man beside her did not belong to her either. She was a nobody, come to see the king. It was madness, and she shrank from entering that seat of power.

Philippe gazed at her with impatience. On this final leg of their journey, he had grown aloof, his thoughts mulling over the arguments he would present to win his cause. She understood he was eager to get this matter over and be on his way. The courts of kings held no attraction for him. He tugged Aelvina's hand, and she followed unwillingly.

It could not be said that Henry waited for them. As the king strode through the great hall arguing with a tall man of saturnine complexion, he waved a greeting and continued his pacing, his hands gesticulating vehemently while his eyes darted about, observing all who were present. He occasionally interrupted his quarrel to make comments to one or more clerks and advisors hovering near by.

The youthful King Henry II was not a tall man, but his stout body was heavily muscled and his leonine head rested on a bull neck that fit his thickset chest proportionately. Aelvina observed the royal attire with some bewilderment and felt a dash of relief at her own ill-fitting garments. Though his clothes were of the finest materials, they hung about him awkwardly, as if he had no patience with the trappings of royalty, betraying his distaste for tailors.

Eyes turned at their entrance and Philippe met greetings with offhand absentness. Aelvina was almost forgotten at his side, until Sir Geoffrey miraculously appeared to bow gallantly over her hand.

"I see the beast has finally agreed to show you the finery of court, my lovely lady. Do you not agree it has some advantages over St. Aubyn? Or have you not had the chance to see much of it?"

"Sir Geoffrey, I would be anywhere but here, this moment. Do let go my hand, for it will surely shatter with sheer nervousness if you do not. Is the king angry with that man? Why does he argue so?" Aelvina pulled her mantle more closely about her, aware of Sir Geoffrey's roving, smiling eyes and Philippe's dark frown.

"That is the chancellor, Thomas à Becket, and Henry delights in proposing absurd principles for his priestly advisor to punch holes in until Henry switches sides and à Becket finds himself defending that which he argued against earlier. It is rather like watching a whirlwind change courses, is it not, Philippe?" Laughter quirked the corners of the insolent young knight's lips as he noted Philippe's scowl and his possessive grip on his young mistress.

"They play at words like two youths just discovering their wit. Excusable in Henry, perhaps, but Thomas is old enough to provide a steadier course. A worldly priest is like a fish out of water."

Startled by this astute observation from the taciturn Philippe, Geoffrey opened his mouth for argument but found a firm hand clapped on his shoulder, moving him aside as a resonant voice boomed behind him.

"Let me through, Geoffrey, before you make off with this vision of beauty and Philippe pulls the walls down about our heads. Forgive my poor hospitality, my lady, in not greeting your arrival. Philippe?''

Though shorter and younger than Philippe, Henry carried himself with an air of majesty that was as compelling as his knight's commanding presence, and Philippe gestured in respect.

"Sire, I wish to present Aelvina, daughter of Fairfax." A warning slanted the timbre of Philippe's voice, and the message in his eyes caused both men to turn their gazes to his companion.

Aelvina made her curtsy but said nothing. Appearing on Philippe's arm without lady or maid in attendance had labeled her instantly, as soon as it was clear she was not Philippe's wife. Nothing could be said in answer to the king's frown.

Henry took her hand; as she rose he studied her. Aelvina was relieved that she had retained her pelisse and her figure remained hidden from his piercing scrutiny, for this man would immediately see all. As it was, her chin jutted under his inspection, and Henry chuckled.

"This one would do well for herself here, Philippe. Where did you find her?"

Aelvina blushed and stepped closer to Philippe's protection, knowing full well the king understood her position.

Philippe's scowl deepened. "That is what I wished to talk to you about, sire, if we could speak privately."

Henry's eyebrows raised, but Philippe was not known to be a frivolous man and sought the court's assistance all too infrequently. He gave a curt nod of agreement and turned to Geoffrey.

"Show the wench to the women's quarters. She has had a long journey and would probably appreciate a rest."

And she was thus easily dismissed, as she should be.

Aelvina offered a halfhearted smile at Geoffrey's whispered jest as he led her away.

"And the queen would dearly love to pry your romantic story from you, he means. Come, you will like Eleanor. Philippe is dismal entertainment."

The door slammed closed behind Philippe as Henry turned to face him. The wide window behind the king cast his stocky figure in silhouette, and Philippe could divine little of his expression.

"Where is your lady, Sir Philippe? Why do you bring your mistress to court when you have not yet presented your wife?"

"The story is a long one, sire, if you will bear with me."

Incapable of inactivity, Henry paced the room, placing and displacing books upon the shelves, staring out the window, hefting objects on a table, as Philippe gave a terse account of his first meeting with Aelvina and his later discovery of his heir's true parentage. The story of his forced marriage Henry knew well. At the end of this part of his tale, Philippe produced a packet from within the folds of his tunic, and presented it to his restless king.

"This is Chauvin's account of all he discovered of my wife's behavior. There are worse rumors, but none proved."

Henry took the vellum packet but made no effort to read it as he faced Philippe. "As this tale has not been proved, what makes you think the girl speaks the truth?"

Philippe gritted his teeth. He was a man of action, not words, and Henry knew it. How could he describe Aelvina's anguish, her honesty, her innocence? Henry asked the impossible.

"Sire, you must speak with her yourself if you doubt my judgment. I did not believe the tale myself until forced."

"This is the girl who sent the message when you were wounded? The words were not Sir Alec's and the messenger said your mistress was the scribe."

Philippe's lips quirked involuntarily. "I knew nothing of the message, but Sir Alec must have been greatly concerned for my well-being if he allowed Aelvina to write you. It speaks of her doing."

Henry relaxed slightly at the mocking look in emerald eyes. Philippe was no love-besotted fool, but a man who had come on a serious purpose. Remembering the ephemeral creature clinging to this tall knight's arm and the warning in Sir Philippe's introduction, Henry tried a new attack.

"Who is she, St. Aubyn? There are few wenches who can write so fair a hand."

This time it was Philippe's turn to stare out the window. He had an uneasy feeling in the pit of his stomach about revealing Aelvina's parentage, but in all fairness, it must be done. He must use every weapon in his arsenal to convince Henry that Aelvina, and not the Lady Ravenna, was the true mother of his heir. From there, he could seek the rest of his wishes.

"She is the daughter of Richard Fairfax, the late Earl of Dunstan, my lord." Philippe leaned against the window frame and watched Henry's startled reaction.

"You have proof?"

Calmly, Philippe removed the chain from about his neck and handed it to the king. "This belonged to her father. Along with several memories of your mother's court and my own knowledge of the man, I am quite convinced. The girl, herself, was scarcely aware of her heritage. The title actually died, I presume, with the passing of her grandfather while Richard was on crusade, and the lands were usurped by one of Stephen's robber barons."

There was bitterness and irony in that voice. The woman Philippe had married not only had not borne his child, but held false title to the dowry she brought him. Philippe knew well enough that Henry was free to grant those lands as he wished, but the manner in which they were stolen from their rightful owner irked his soul.

Henry looked thoughtful as he returned the ring bearing the Fairfax crest. "If what you say is true, the girl is daughter of a true servant of my court, a decent and loyal vassal. She deserves better than the lot fate has given her. I had best speak with her."

Philippe's sardonic gaze melted to one of gratitude. "There will be no doubting her story when she is done, sire. She came of noble heritage and it is reflected in everything she says and does and is." His lips twitched at a second thought. "She also inherited her father's Viking nature. Do not think to add her to your list of royal conquests. She not only carries my babe, but a silver dagger she wields well, as I have learned to my regret."

Henry gave the older man an assessing look. "Two bastards on an earl's daughter. I thought you a man of some temperance with women."

Philippe shrugged. "Other women, maybe. Not this one." He resisted the temptation to add, "This one is mine." That was a challenge too great for the fates to resist.

While Philippe conversed with the king, Aelvina was transported to the living quarters of the queen's ladies, given a room in which to bathe and rest, and a maid to aid in her service. Too tired and bewildered to protest, she gratefully soaked in the perfumed waters, and then donned the silken kirtle offered her after she dried.

As the maid carefully combed and brushed the tangles from hip-length silver-gold tresses, the door swung open, and a tall, graceful figure entered. A tight barbette hid most of her dusky curls, but the exquisite beauty of her features and magnetic brown eyes made it apparent she was a lady of royal breeding. The richness of her wine kirtle confirmed the impression. The maid's deep curtsy and murmured, "Your Grace," verified the visitor's identity.

Aelvina stood, her hair tumbling over her white gown, as she fearfully glanced at the queen before making a deep obeisance.

A small smile curved Eleanor's lips. "Rise, child. I have not come to pass judgment on you."

Not at all certain the queen had not come for just that purpose, Aelvina rose and met the lady's intelligent gaze with a nervous but defiant stare. She had heard much of this queen and knew her in no position to pass moral judgments on anyone; but she had power and more in this court.

Older than Henry by several years, Eleanor of Aquitaine was still younger than Philippe, and had a beauty and presence that had brought the most powerful rulers of Europe to her feet. Married to King Louis of France, she had grown bored with that pious noble and found a wild spirit to match her own in Henry's devilish countenance. Divorcing a king to marry a duke did not seem so foolish once the world realized the match put most of the lands of France and England within the couple's ambitious grasp.

Though there was little doubt that this spirited queen had had lovers of her own, Aelvina flushed at the woman's prolonged stare.

Eleanor sat and gestured for Aelvina to do the same. "I have heard whispers of the handsomeness and manliness of your Sir Philippe, but to my knowledge, though his name causes some of my ladies to pale with desire, none but the Lady Ravenna have succeeded in capturing his interest. Since my gossips tell me you are mistress and not wife, perhaps you would care to share your secrets in obtaining such an elusive lover. Is that his child you carry?"

She missed nothing. Aelvina resisted the urge to cover the small roundness of her belly beneath the clinging silk. "It is, my lady. It seems I have no secrets."

Eleanor's laugh chimed like tiny tinkling bells. "Not in this court. You had best tell me all, for I will learn it soon enough from less reliable sources."

Under the queen's skillful questioning, the entire story was drawn from her lips, more than she had ever related to anyone. Eleanor treated it as highly amusing entertainment, but something in her eyes spoke of understanding and determination, and Aelvina appealed to these qualities.

When the tale was told, Eleanor's smooth countenance beneath the barbette's frame revealed no expression. "You love this mighty knight, then? If he seeks Henry's aid in obtaining an annulment, does he mean to marry you?"

It was a natural assumption for one not acquainted with Philippe's unromantic nature, and Aelvina smiled gently. "I love him, yes, but no words were said of marriage. He wishes to rid himself of a dangerous alliance, but his main concern is the legitimacy of his heir. Though the Lady Ravenna be the devil himself, Philippe would remain married to her if it were the only means of protecting the child's name."

Eleanor shook her head with a slight smile. "It is the action and not the words that count, my pet. Your Philippe shows every sign of having fallen victim to Cupid's arrow, but you are right in one thing: He will never marry you as things stand now. Perhaps that is for the best, since all my experience tells me love cannot survive within the confines of marriage, but marriage has its other advantages. Would you marry him if asked?''

Aelvina allowed herself the brief pleasure of contemplating such a future: to bear the St. Aubyn name, to have Philippe at her side for the rest of her life, to bear his children and raise them as heirs to St. Aubyn instead of bastards, to be given the true title of lady to his lands and all the power and responsibility that entailed. It was an awe-inspiring thought for one raised in the back of an army cart who had never considered herself eligible for marriage to the lowliest farmer . . . an impossible dream.

With a lost sigh, Aelvina shook her head. "I would never marry him unless I knew he loved me and asked of his own free will. That would never happen, even if by some miracle of fate he should be free to do so."

Eleanor rose and Aelvina did the same. "Anything is possible if one puts one's mind to it. It's just a matter of manipulating fate to your liking. Henry will probably ask to see you shortly. You will need a wardrobe. Let me see what I can do."

And then she was gone, leaving Aelvina to stare at the door. It was all very well to speak of manipulating fates when you had the power to do so, but at the moment she was unable to even choose her surroundings. She was trapped inside the royal palace and at the command of everyone but the servants. With a weariness that had little to do with physical fatigue, Aelvina lay upon the small couch and slept.

Daylight had faded from the window when she was awakened by a brisk maid carrying an assortment of gowns over her arm. A little preliminary assessing of Aelvina's petite figure produced a kirtle of what appeared to be spun gold, so delicate was the fabric. The long, wide wrists of the sleeves revealed a fine white silk undertunic, as did the long, trailing skirt that the maid fastened into the filigree girdle Aelvina wore.

Refusing the barbette produced, Aelvina plaited her hair with ribbons of silver and gold and donned the delicate gold chaplet Philippe had given her. Again, they were borrowed clothes, but they fit more perfectly than any other, and she lovingly smoothed the elegant material.

Philippe met her at the foot of the stairs, his dark features gleaming with a delighted smile as she descended toward him. Broad shoulders clothed elegantly in a forest-green supertunic over a tawny gold kirtle, narrow waist belted with a wide, jeweled girdle, he looked more than ever the noble baron she knew him to be; but despite the warmth of his gaze, Aelvina's spirits sank lower.

"You are magnificent, *ma chérie*. I worried when Henry insisted you appear in the hall tonight. He kept me detained so I could not take you to a seamstress, yet you appear more elegantly gowned than I can imagine. How do you do it?"

Aelvina threw him a worried smile. His look of approbation told her nothing of what had happened, only that he was pleased with her now.

"The queen sent these to me, but that matters little. You have talked to the king? What did he say?"

Philippe clasped her pleading hands against his chest, gazing into her eyes with understanding. "He wishes to see you, my love. You must realize it is difficult for others to believe this tale we tell without proof. Henry will hear all sides before making any decision. Whatever happens, we will still return to Dunstan for the child. You have nothing to fear."

"You do not think the Lady Ravenna will harm him

when she learns where we have been? She means to keep Dunstan at any cost."

"She may have Dunstan. I only fear she will hold the child hostage to insure her hold. That is why I am eager to see my suit set in motion and be gone. Speak plainly to Henry; he will hear you."

It was on the tip of Philippe's tongue to warn her of the pitfalls ahead. She had little understanding yet of her great beauty and how it turned men's heads, but he trusted her loyalty to see her through.

Heads turned as they entered the great hall. They made a striking couple, but gossip turned more heads than looks. Whispers filled the air as Philippe took his place above the salt at the king's table and sat Aelvina beside him.

Aelvina did her best to listen politely to the idle flattery bestowed upon her, but her thoughts were not on her dinner companions. They rested on the bull-necked man at the head of the table. It seemed necessary that she learn all she could of this young king before he questioned her.

Henry could not tolerate sitting in one place long enough to complete his meal and rose with drumstick in hand to make his way along the long trestle tables, stopping to address a few words to any who caught his eye and to exchange banter with the men who served him well. He clapped a hand on Philippe's shoulder as he gazed down upon Aelvina with open speculation.

"I remember your father well, my lady. He once threatened to turn me over his knee if I did not listen when he spoke."

Startled eyes flashed upward. "You knew him, my lord?"

"The Earl of Dunstan was one of my most loyal vassals when he was not objecting to my impatient ways. He returned to England at my request, though I was not aware of the hardship I was invoking upon him. After we eat, perhaps you will give me the opportunity to learn more of him.''

If she were an impostor, this announcement would spear fear in her heart, but Aelvina met the news with a radiant smile and a relaxing of tension. "There is nothing I should enjoy better, sire.''

Philippe heard this sally with a sardonic grunt, and watched Henry's departure with relief. In this place he dared not put his arm around the wench and tweak her saucy nose, but he had a need to return Aelvina's thoughts to himself and not the royal personage.

"Just wait until I have you in bed later, vixen, and see if we cannot find something you enjoy better than exchanging pleasantries with the king," he murmured wickedly in her ear.

Aelvina giggled and for the first time that night felt gay. The king was no ogre but a young man who remembered her father, and Philippe's splendid company was all that she could desire. She caught his muscled arm and turned a mischievous look up. "I await my just deserts with eagerness, my lord.''

Still, when Aelvina found herself alone with the dynamic young king a short time later, she felt some trepidation. This was a man who commanded armies and ruled a large corner of the civilized world, not a man to be trifled with.

"Philippe tells me you are the true mother of his son and that I have forced him into a marriage rife with deception and intrigue. I am not a gullible man, demoiselle; convince me.''

Henry's eyes seemed suddenly dark and unfathomable as Aelvina gazed into them, and she wished desperately that she had taken to her heels and run that day of Philippe's first arrival. But the time for escape was well past and she must now face the consequences of her brash action.

While she followed the king's restless pacing, Aelvina quietly told her tale. He evidently had heard much before from Philippe or Eleanor and once convinced she added nothing new, he waved it aside and urged her on. The discovery of her father's title intrigued him most, and he drew on her memories of that long-ago past when she had been but a spoiled child playing in the halls of Maud's court while the world of political intrigue swirled about her.

At the end of her story, Henry swung around abruptly and tilted her chin up to the firelight. "I was half in love with your mother once," he admitted, smiling. "I could not have been much more than a lad of ten, but I thought her a goddess of beauty. There is no doubt you are her daughter, and if Richard claimed you, I must believe your tale."

His hand caressed her cheek and Aelvina shivered, attracted against her will by this man's compelling magnetism. She stood completely still beneath his touch, but the smile in his eyes told her he felt the current, too. He carefully lowered his hand and Aelvina breathed a sigh of relief. "Thank you, my lord," she managed to exhale.

"Of course, I cannot allow the daughter of the Earl of Dunstan to continue in this homeless state. I will have to consult my advisors about restoring your lands, but in the meantime, you will be a ward of my court."

Aelvina's eyes flew to meet his. What was this talk of lands? Had he understood nothing of what she had said? "My lord, I only wish my son . . ." she pleaded, but he waved her words away.

"I am well aware of what you want and Philippe asks. I cannot twist the law to suit the occasion. My advisors are consulting on the matter of the child's legitimacy, but it already seems their opinion that for the child to inherit St. Aubyn, he must be a product of a legitimate union. If Philippe tells the world the child is not his wife's, the child becomes a bastard. I'm sorry; that is the way it is."

There did, indeed, seem to be sorrow in his eyes as he confronted Aelvina's tormented gaze. Taking her hands in his, Henry attempted to reassure her. "I will do what I can to right the wrongs you have suffered. There is the matter of this present child. We must see what can be done to prevent it from being declared bastard, also."

At his mention of the child she carried, Aelvina's eyes grew wide with increasing panic, but Henry held her firmly.

"Perhaps it can be arranged for Dunstan lands to be returned to their rightful owner. Along with the promise of an earldom, it would be a tempting dowry, even for a childbearing bride. Philippe would not object to the loss of Dunstan if I found equally rewarding lands for him elsewhere."

Aelvina began to shake her head in violent disagreement, unable to voice the rising terror in her soul. This time, Henry did not disregard her panic, but spoke with authority.

"You are not listening to what I am offering. Philippe will still live within a day's ride of you. His son can be fostered in your home and you can raise him as your own without harming the inheritance. He will still be able to see the child you carry as often as he wishes. It is the ideal solution. Philippe can place his harlot wife in a convent if he wishes, once I remove Dunstan from her. The only problem is in finding the proper man for you to marry. An honorable man might be found to claim the babe you carry as his own in return for an earldom, but it is doubtful if one can be found who will enjoy being a cuckold. You

will have the children and the lands, but you must give up
Philippe."

The room seemed to grow dark and tilt crazily. Aelvina
felt herself sinking into that blackness she had thought
gone for good, and welcomed it. But a will stronger than
her own claimed her, shaking away the darkness she
sought.

She woke lying across the pillows of a window seat while a
broad figure sat beside her rubbing her wrists, murmuring
words of sympathy. Nonsensical words, they sounded like a
reassuring stream over her head, until her lashes flickered
open. Then Henry's passionate gaze locked with hers and
all became clear again.

"You are even more than Philippe said, my dove. A man
would gladly surrender a kingdom for a lifetime in your
arms. You have no need of a dowry."

Henry's words were an impassioned plea and not meant
to be taken seriously. Aelvina hastened to right herself,
trying to avoid the king's gaze, not fully understanding
what had come over her. "My lord, please, if I could just
be allowed to return to Sir Philippe . . ."

To her amazement, he shook his head negatively, and
terror once more seized her. "Why, my lord?" she whispered in anguish.

"A royal ward cannot be the mistress of one of my barons. Whatever you decide you cannot go back to Philippe.
He will understand that and must know it himself. You are
an earl's daughter, Aelvina, and you must conduct yourself
accordingly."

Henry's gaze was sympathetic but firm. Aelvina felt the
nightmare close in on her again, but this time it was all
too real. Philippe had brought her here, knowing this
would happen! How could he have failed to realize? He
and Henry had worked this all out together. His bastards

would have names and titles, and he would roam, unfettered once more. Rage began to burn unchecked in her soul. Lips tightly compressed, she kept silent, and Henry cast her a worried glance.

"You understand that we are doing only what is best for you. If you had a preference for a convent, that could be arranged, but I do not think that suitable. Of course, if you wished to become a royal mistress . . ." Henry's warm voice slanted temptingly as he studied her face. His hands had not lost their hold on her, and now they slid with expert persuasion over her shoulders, urging her into his arms.

Her eyes glittered dangerously. To flaunt herself as the king's mistress would serve Philippe right. Making love to Henry would not be an unpleasant ordeal; she could easily learn to enjoy it and present royal bastards who would eventually be given noble titles.

Aelvina slid from grandiose dreams of revenge back to practical reality with the flutter of the child in her womb. Depression engulfed her, but she would not let Henry see it.

"I have no wish to commit the mortal sin of self-slaughter," Aelvina commented dryly, moving from beneath Henry's hold. "Your queen would see me dead before she allowed you to betray her, and rightly so. She loves you, and I would not come between you. With Philippe, it was different. I belonged to him before the Lady Ravenna came between us."

Henry gazed at her with a thoughtful frown, but carefully refrained from touching her again.

"You say you belonged to Philippe first?" he asked casually "How so? Did you pledge yourself to him?"

Anxious to be gone from here, Aelvina gave the now aloof king a puzzled glance, but answered as truthfully as she was able. "Yes, sire, in exchange for his protection. I agreed to give myself to him and no other. To me, it was an agreement of honor by which I still feel bound, especially now. You must see why I can marry no other man."

Henry drew in his lip and his frown deepened. "And Philippe? Did he pledge himself to you at the same time?"

Aelvina gave him a wry smile. "He was a man with only one thing on his mind, my lord. He pledged his protection and, if he had been a less honest man, would have promised the moon. He has attempted to keep his word and, I think, feels equally bound."

Henry's eyes sparkled at the thought of the powerful Sir Philippe stooping to make eager promises to this enchanting filly. She was right. Philippe did not make promises lightly, and the notion struck him with an eagerness to return to his advisors.

"We had best return to the hall, then, or Philippe will soon come crashing through that door to protect your honor." Henry stood and offered his arm.

Aelvina hesitated. She had no desire to return to that hall and act as if nothing had happened when her whole world had just been shattered. She needed time to think, and Philippe's traitorous presence would not be conducive to rational thoughts.

"Please, sire, if I could just be allowed to return to my room . . ."

Her pleading gaze had its effect and Henry bowed to her wisdom. A maid was summoned, and Aelvina was escorted out the back way to the women's quarters while the king returned to his court.

When Henry returned alone, Philippe's eyes narrowed, and he lost no time in elbowing his way to the king's side.

"Where is she?"

Henry gave the taller man a wry glance. Philippe's dark face with its swiftly whitening scar warned him this was not likely to be a pleasant interlude. "She has returned to her room."

"Her room! Her place is with me!" Philippe's fists clenched.

"Not any longer. I believe her story. As an earl's daughter, her place is as a ward of the court."

"So help me, Henry, if you have seduced that girl, I will . . ."

Henry wisely led him safely out of earshot of eager listeners. "You know better than that." At Philippe's disbelieving glance, the king made a self-deprecating gesture. "I'll admit trying, as what man wouldn't when closeted with a woman of her beauty. But as you warned, she put me in my place, though I think her delicate condition has sapped some of that Viking spirit you told me of. Either that, or I did not push her quite so far as you did." Henry gave the older man a speculative look at this thought, and was rewarded with Philippe's darkening flush.

"Then I do not know what game you are playing, Henry, but I want her back. Earl's daughter or not, she bears my child, and is my responsibility."

"She mentioned you might feel that way—something about a pledge between you. What oaths have you sworn her, Philippe?"

Frustration warred within Philippe at his inability to control this situation. He should never have brought Aelvina to this place. He should have known better than to appeal to a higher authority when swift action would have worked equally as well. He must be growing old, or the wench was draining his senses with his sudden desire for peace.

Philippe replied curtly, without giving much consideration to the question.

"I swore her my protection, trusted her with my life, and gave her St. Aubyn as her home. She is mine, my lord."

There. He had said it this time. Were the fates listening, ready to make a mockery of his declaration?

"You made these oaths before you married the Lady Ravenna?" Henry prompted with interest.

"Aye, except for St. Aubyn. She was virgin, and I thought to ease her worries. She was a spirited wench, and not one likely to be content with a roll in the hay and a kiss."

Henry grinned. "Well, you have seen to her protection by bringing her to me. You may have done yourself a disservice, because I am considering returning Dunstan to the lady as a dowry, but you will be adequately recompensed, never fear."

Philippe choked and stared at Henry, aghast. "Dowry!" was the only word he could force between his teeth.

"Of course," Henry replied calmly. "We cannot have the rightful Countess of Dunstan bearing a bastard. It will take a considerable dowry to persuade anyone to give your child a name; it seems fitting you should provide it. Now, I have other things to do this night. As soon as my advisors have researched the question, they will let you know about the legitimacy of your heir. Any annulment, of course, will have to go through the church and will take a considerable time. Too long," Henry added meaningfully, before pacing off to another petitioner ready to bend his ear.

Despair and frustration and rage drove Philippe from the hall. In an instant of madness, he contemplated storming Eleanor's tower and carrying Aelvina off, but the moment passed. He remembered the times Aelvina had called herself whore, remembered her heartbreaking plea for their son and the words she had used to force him to bring her with him. She would bear the name of shame he had given her no longer. Anguish ate at Philippe's innards as he turned away from the cold tower and sought solace elsewhere.

Chapter Twenty-one

The announcement that she had a male visitor snapped Aelvina from the reverie she had wrapped herself in since the night before. Many had come to greet the Earl of Dunstan's daughter, but they had all been gossips and curiosity seekers among the tower's occupants. Men did not normally frequent the women's quarters.

She found Philippe in the solar. He still wore the tunic of the previous night, looking much as if he had slept in it, but at least it was not his hauberk. He was not yet ready to ride off and desert her. He stared out a window and sensed, more than heard, her approach. When he turned, she saw his eyes were bloodshot, as if from too much liquor, but his lips were set in firm lines.

"Did you come to bid me farewell, my lord?" Aelvina asked mockingly.

"With Eleanor's permission. The king seems to think my presence will diminish your salability," Philippe replied bitterly. She was breathtakingly lovely in the morning light, gleaming more brilliantly than the sunbeam in which she stood. His gaze roamed to the small roundness where his child grew and his lips pressed together, biting back harsher words.

"My salability?" Aelvina asked disdainfully. "Does that mean you are regretting your agreement already? Or were you under the mistaken impression that Henry would continue to allow you to enjoy my bed until the nuptials were announced?" Aelvina's voice rose in anger, but not so loud that others might hear as she vented her rage. "Perhaps you had some thought that you could marry me off to rid yourself of the problem of any future bastards you might breed on me! It was quite considerate of the king to allow you to continue living within a day's ride of me. Did you think I would fall into your bed whenever you felt the need once I was safely married? Then let me change your thinking, my lord! If you persist in this folly of marrying me off, I will consider all vows broken, and give my loyalty to my husband. No man will share my bed but the one to whom I have given my pledge. I will breed no more bastards for you, sir knight!"

Aelvina's tirade slowly drained the color from Philippe's face and his knuckles went white with strain as he clenched his fists at his side. Henry's words had not hit him with the reality of Aelvina's. He had not imagined her sharing another man's bed and bearing another man's child, until her tongue forced the picture upon him. Now he wanted to slap her face and make her take the words back, but could not.

As he watched fury color Aelvina's cheeks and set fires in her eyes, Philippe thought wryly of Henry's declaration that her Viking spirit had dimmed. He was grateful she had chosen not to wear her knife. He had determined to see her treated as she deserved, but this speech left him not at all certain Henry knew what he was about. The wench needed a good lashing more than she needed a title and lands.

"Are you quite through?" Philippe asked tiredly as her words slowed to an irate glare. Before she could reply, he held up a hand for silence. "If you think I had anything to do with Henry's decision to make you a royal ward, you are quite mistaken, but then you have not been the only one to be mistaken these past days. I never should have brought you here."

Aelvina's mouth fell open, then shut again as she moved closer to better see his face. He still stood in the window, a mighty figure outlined against stone walls, but the expression on his dark face was one of pain, and gray mists clouded emerald eyes. No laughter lit that stern visage now; only tormented concern etched lines of hurt.

"My lord, if you mean that, take me from here," she whispered, not daring to voice her hopes stronger than that.

The pain grew as Philippe reached out to touch her, then swiftly drew back his hand, devouring her with his gaze instead. "I cannot. Henry would be forced to come after us. There is not a corner of this earth I could take you without his finding us, and I would not ask you to lead such a life. Henry is right in trying to protect you from me. I can only bring you shame. He is trying to make it easy on us, though it be difficult to see."

Tears sprang to her eyes as Aelvina watched his face and sought futilely for some reassurance. If she could just know he loved her, she could withstand anything; but though she had seen his pain, his stern features hid any more, and anguish was the only result of her search.

She hid the hurt beneath brave words. "He cannot force

me to marry against my will. There is not a man in the kingdom who can hold me.

For a brief moment, emerald eyes gleamed and a smile touched the corners of Philippe's lips. "Oh, yes, there is," he murmured.

Aelvina moved temptingly beneath his heated gaze, taunting him with her closeness. "Then do it, my lord. Hold me, and never let me go. Or do you admit you give me up willingly?"

For answer, Philippe grabbed her and crushed her to his chest. Her breasts pressed painfully between them as his lips came down hard and demanding across hers. There was no gentleness in his embrace Passion, hunger, and rage tore at her as he moved to take all that he could from her in this last moment before they must part.

Hope soared in Aelvina's heart as his taking dissolved into a yearning caress and she thought she had won. But before desire could take control of his senses, Philippe set her firmly aside.

"I give you up willingly," he stated with taut control. "I will not bring further shame on you or our children or continue to dishonor your father's memory any longer. You will marry and give my child a name and take our son into your home to be taught the loyalty and duty of a lord of St. Aubyn. You will do this for me and for our children and for your own well-being."

He turned to go, but Aelvina cried out to him to wait. The devastation of his command had left her an empty shell, and shamelessly, she sought his strength.

"Philippe! Where do you go now? To Dunstan?"

The plea was there in her eyes. Did he leave her to go to his wife, to make what he could of his disastrous marriage?

Philippe yielded slightly to her shattered look. "Dunstan

may no longer be mine. I await the king's command; then I will go with my son to St. Aubyn. If the Lady Ravenna loses her lands, I will see her in a convent or one of the halls at my command. I will not have her near our son.''

Aelvina nodded, grateful for this information, and sought to keep him no longer. He had spelled out the life that must be theirs forever, and she could neither hold him back nor say him nay. He was gone from her life, and she must accept it. At least he had given her his children, and she could hold them to her when the pain grew great; but they could never, never take the place this mighty knight had in her heart. That place must be eternally empty.

Tears streamed down her cheeks as she lifted her head to find Philippe gone and Eleanor in his place. The queen held out her hand and silently led her back to her chambers.

When Aelvina was led down to dinner that evening, she was surrounded by eager well-wishers, congratulating her on her rescue from obscurity, pouring compliments on the memory of her father, making themselves agreeable while they passed judgment. Aelvina paid little heed to these sycophants. She searched for Philippe's sturdy form in a far corner and took comfort in knowing his gaze was on her alone.

Henry paid attention to these flatterers, however, taking Aelvina's arm and leading her to a place at his table befitting an earl's daughter. With a promising smile, he seated her next to a silent man of nondescript fairness

"This is Sir Robert of Leicester," Henry indicated the blond knight. "The Lady Aelvina . . .''

Aelvina scarcely heard the introductions. She was well aware the solemn knight beside her was studying her intently, but she could summon no resentment. Henry had wasted little time in setting her upon the auction block, and she could scarce blame him. If he were to see her married, it must be done before she grew great with child. An involuntary action sent her hand to cover the growing tautness of her belly, and when she looked up, she discovered Sir Robert's gaze upon her. She met it steadily, and he nodded approval.

"You do well to protect the child. There are those who would see it destroyed. You would make a good mother for a man's children, I think," Sir Robert murmured thoughtfully, for her ears alone.

Henry had wandered off, as usual, and Aelvina was left to judge for herself this man who was evidently considering her for bride. He was a widower, she had heard Henry say, with a son of his own already. She thought him some years older than Philippe, but not so old that he would have trouble bedding her and getting her with child in the years to come. He was no weak stripling, but a mild-mannered man who spoke to her with love for his lands and his home. She wondered if he would have the energy, the ambition, and the decisiveness necessary to be a good earl, and feared he would not. Still, she thought him a gentle man. He would not harm her, though she might find it difficult to respect his passivity. Henry had chosen carefully for a docile maiden, with little knowledge of Aelvina herself.

Aelvina sought Philippe, finding him seated on the opposite side of the table, his eyes still fixed solely on her and the man chosen to sit next to her. She felt a knife strike through her middle as their eyes met, and his pain was transmitted to her along with his approval. There was no harm in Sir Robert, his look seemed to say, and he would be near to protect her, whatever happened. The message would have broken her heart had it not already been shattered earlier in the day. Aelvina turned back to the knight beside her, who had not missed the exchange of glances.

"I am not a warrior, like Sir Philippe, but with an earldom at my command, I can protect my wife from another man's bed. She will belong only to me, and her children will be only mine."

The firmness of his tone was surprising, but the message not totally unexpected. Aelvina stared down at her untouched dinner. "Sir Philippe is a man of honor, and a woman's loyalty belongs only with her husband."

That should convince the most astute man of my docility, Aelvina thought grimly. *If this is the man they have chosen for me, I will become whatever he wants in order to win him, but it will not be an easy task.* Anger and rebellion already rumbled through the ashes of her soul, and it would not take much for fury to raise its ugly head.

What did this man know of her that he was willing to take her as his life's companion simply because she had lands and a title? She was young and not ugly, but that would count for naught were it not for the prospect of her dowry. What would this man do should she throw a temper tantrum or come at him with a knife? Probably think her mad and lock her in a tower, she thought glumly. Would he expect her to lie coldly in his bed and submit to his desires whenever he felt the need, as if she were no more than a convenient vessel or breeding cow? If she came to him with desires of her own, desires Philippe had taught her, would he think her a wanton hussy? The answers to these questions did not bode well for a peaceful marriage, unless this shattered shell Philippe had left behind stayed broken, and then she was better off dead.

The meal ended and Sir Robert made no objection when Aelvina left his side to drift aimlessly toward the door through which she had entered. Her path was blocked by

Geoffrey's mocking figure, and she attempted to turn aside but he caught her by the arm and led her to a quiet corner.

"If I did not know the Lady Aelvina lived, I'd think you her ghost. Are you well? Eleanor has not poisoned you for seducing her husband yet, has she?"

Aelvina gave him a slight smile. Sir Geoffrey had been the one to send Philippe to her when she most needed him. Beneath his jesting exterior lay some understanding and she could not resent his attempt at kindness. "The queen has been exceedingly kind, and I have had enough of husbands lately, thank you."

Geoffrey touched her cheek so that she looked up at him, silver eyes glittering with tears. "I would offer for you, but I would probably throttle you the first time I heard Philippe's name on your lips when we made love. Even an earldom could not pay me for the anguish I see in your eyes tonight. There is no other way, then?"

Geoffrey's gallantries had their place, and Aelvina dried her eyes, grateful that someone understood the turmoil in her breast. "No other way, I fear. Philippe has commanded it, and I obey. What other choice have I?"

"Is it not preferable to be called countess instead of whore?" he asked quizzically.

Aelvina gave him a dry smile. "There is a difference? I am being sold for the price of a title."

Geoffrey frowned, an occasion so rare Aelvina thought it might crack his face, and she anxiously held her breath. It seemed a portent of some deep thought, again a rare occurrence, and she risked a smile to distract his attention. Whether it worked or not she could not tell, for he spoke as if he did not see her.

"Since you are determined to be sold, let me be the one to buy you. I have made no secret of my desire to take you from Philippe. With time, is there not some chance you could come to me as you do Philippe?"

A soft smile stole across Aelvina's face, the first hint of healing. "I can think of no better way to die, Sir Geoffrey. Yon knight they would give me would see nothing in my sighs or tears and would gaze upon my rages in bewilderment. You would see Philippe in my every word and touch, and rightly so, methinks, and would meet my rages with the back of your hand. If we did not kill each other, Philippe would do it for us. I think I prefer your friendship."

Disappointment faded to a self-mocking smile and a hint of relief. "I am a lover, my lady, not a fighter of temperamental females. Still, there is some truth in what you say. If your arms did not welcome me, I would quickly find others, and that would be the end of a beautiful friendship. Philippe is the only man to control you, and I shall tell Henry so."

With Geoffrey gone and Philippe not in sight, Aelvina was temporarily alone and took advantage of the moment to escape the stifling confines of the smoky, populated hall. She had need of fresh air and open spaces, night skies and the crackle of coldness against her skin. Life was yet too dear to give it up, even though she felt as if it had been crushed from her with Philippe's words. There must be a life beyond this one, and she sought it feverishly as she raced down cold, dark corridors.

A movement behind the stairs leading to the tower caught her attention, and she slowed. It would not do to be seen racing from the hall; people might think she sought to escape. As she walked, Aelvina waited for the person in the shadows to show himself. Surely it was impolite to lurk in the dark without making your presence known. Her steps slowed as fear clutched at her heart. Who would linger so, here within the king's walls?

She was a fool to be out alone, even in the safety of court. Who knew what kind of people haunted these halls? She could find privacy elsewhere. She stopped and began to turn away, but the shadow moved faster than she. He grabbed her by the waist and covered her mouth with his gloved hand. Heavy mail pressed against her back as the figure squeezed her tightly to halt her struggles. Aelvina gasped for breath, and a throaty chuckle behind her seized her with greater terror. Raymond!

She kicked at his padded legs, scratched at his encompassing arms, brought her head backward sharply, trying to connect with his jaw. His arm was squeezing the life from her, and pain shot through her midsection. The babe! He would destroy the babe!

She went limp, her body falling lifeless in his grasp, and Raymond gasped with surprise at the deadweight he now supported. His grip loosened, and Aelvina tore free, screaming furiously as she raced down the corridor in the direction from which she had come.

Eleanor's long, trailing skirts were her undoing. The side fastenings slipped from her girdle. Cascading lengths of material fell between her feet, and Aelvina stumbled, catching herself on the stone wall, but not in time. Her screams echoed through long, empty corridors as Raymond once more pounced upon her, his hand gagging her cries.

"Bitch! You wilt have them all out here." Sir Raymond's powerful arm snapped her head backward to stop her screams, then swung her around to face him. Dark eyes burned with madness.

Aelvina swung at him, but he batted her hands away, then caught her against his chest again. In the darkness, she was just able to make out his malevolent grin, and horror creeped along her skin as he lowered his stinking breath to cover her face.

She tried to scream, but his tongue forced its way between her teeth, gagging the sounds in her throat. Cruel fingers twisted at her tender breast and he chuckled as she stiffened at the pain of his marauding fingers.

The clamor of running feet and clanking steel gave fair warning, but to Aelvina's astonishment, Raymond made no attempt to escape them. He pressed her hard against the stone wall, hands on either side of her head while his hips pressed lewdly against hers, and his mouth continued its plundering. The taste of his foul breath was nauseating, but the obscenity of his embrace was worse. Humiliation seared Aelvina's cheeks as voices sounded behind them and she could do naught to escape his hold. She felt the jolt of the broad blade as it smacked against Raymond's armored back, but that shock was not so great as that of Philippe's voice.

"Unhand her, you bastard!"

The words rang loud and clear in the hall, followed by the mutter of irate voices as Raymond insolently took his time at releasing his captive, adjusting his clothing suggestively as he lifted himself from her.

"Philippe!" Aelvina cried, catching sight of the knight's towering figure, menacing in its massiveness, broad sword gleaming in his ungloved hand. He wore no armor, but the guards behind him did.

"You have some objection to my idling my time with my woman, sire?" Raymond asked slyly, his hand not totally releasing Aelvina as it fondled her breast.

"Let her go so I might smite you from stem to stern like you deserve, you varlet!" Philippe thundered, his sword inching closer to Raymond's broad girth.

"If you challenge me, I gladly accept. The wench is mine, and I will prove it over your dead body."

Aelvina grew faint as Raymond drew her out for the crowd's inspection, his hand on her breast claiming possession for all the world to see. Before she could struggle free, a new voice broke the silence.

"The Lady Aelvina is my ward. Let her go." The royal command was unmistakable.

Shaken by the words he uttered as much as by the royal presence, Raymond released his prisoner, and Aelvina stumbled into Philippe's arms. Keeping the sword pointed at Raymond, Philippe encompassed her with one mighty arm.

"Sire, this is the knave who near cost me my life. I want his blood on my sword."

"He lies!" Raymond answered hurriedly. "The wench is mine, and he covets her. I demand to be allowed the satisfaction of meeting his blade, to show the world the lady belongs to me and no other."

The speech was not done well as Raymond hastened to cover his lapse and acknowledge Aelvina as lady. The king eyed him with repugnance and replied dryly.

"The Lady Aelvina is not a prize to be fought over and won like a sack of coins. She is a noblewoman and to be protected as such." Henry eyed Philippe's intimate hold on Aelvina skeptically, but continued. "If it is a tourney you desire, Sir Philippe seems eager to agree, but the prize will be your life and not the lady."

Aelvina gasped and buried her face against Philippe's broad chest. The king had just granted a duel to the death and Philippe could easily be the victim! She wanted to scream her protests but could not. Philippe's hand held her firmly, and she could feel the blood lust racing through him. He wanted this battle, needed to wreak his wrath on someone, and her protest would go ignored. Only she seemed to understand that Raymond would never have provoked this fight unless assured of winning.

A lady's maid arrived and threw a cloak over Aelvina's shoulders, urging her away. She could hear Philippe's voice demanding an immediate meeting. Aelvina knew he had neither the patience nor the vanity to wait for a grand tournament to draw crowds and set hearts pounding. He was eager for the kill now and would have taken on his armored opponent in the king's court, if Henry had not interfered. He had no thought to his own life, and spared not a thought to hers should he die and leave Raymond unleashed upon the world. Aelvina cursed and railed at his male stupidity as she was led into her room, but she knew the warrior knight would never change.

As the maids clucked and pecked over her, Aelvina flew into a rage at their smothering actions and ordered them out, flinging back the cloak and glaring at the foolish creatures with the wild-eyed fury of her ancestors. The young girls scampered fearfully from the room, making signs of the cross.

Aelvina had little time to storm the room, ripping her shredded clothes from her back as the door reopened and Eleanor entered. Grabbing up a chemise, Aelvina hastily donned it beneath the queen's amused gaze.

"Henry keeps telling me what a gentle, obedient child you are." She chuckled. "But you seem able to stir up more trouble than a nest of hornets and strike terror in the hearts of all who cross you. Why have you kept my husband in the dark?"

"Because he is the king, my lady," Aelvina replied glumly as her rage died, quenched by the utter futility of her position. "And because he does not truly listen to a woman's words."

"Hmmm." Eleanor had a goodly idea why Henry had not listened. Like many men, when lust beckoned, he heeded its call and little else. "There is somewhat of truth in your words. I have heard of the tourney. It is foolish to rage against that. You must have known Philippe meant to kill Raymond if what I have heard is true."

"Raymond put an ax in his back! He tried to rape me! Why did my mighty defender not kill the bastard then, or now?" Aelvina raged at the stupidity of males, not caring that it was to the queen of all these lands that she carried her complaint.

"Because Raymond is one of the king's men, and Philippe, despite his protests to the contrary, is an honorable man. He would not kill a vassal of his liege lord on less than a field of battle. That is why Henry agreed to let them take it to the death. He respects Philippe's loyalty under what must have been very trying conditions." This last was added with a wry twist of Eleanor's elegant lips.

"He has just assigned Philippe to his execution, then!" Aelvina swung around to face her queen, eyes flashing silver daggers.

"Nonsense!" Eleanor exclaimed, somewhat taken aback by her vehemence. "Philippe is the better man. All say so."

"Does that not tell you something? Raymond has no desire to die. Why did he challenge Philippe knowing he would lose? Raymond is a coward. By all rights he should be on his way back to Normandy by now. Instead, he comes here, and deliberately instigates a quarrel. *Deliberately*, I tell you. He was waiting for Philippe to come."

Eleanor grew thoughtful. "Perhaps he truly thinks himself the better man," she said doubtfully.

"Raymond would not even stop to consider the notion. His first instinct its always to run. Why do you think he tried to kill Philippe from behind? No, he knows something that we do not. He has been assured Philippe will die in this match. Think me a fool if you like, but the Lady Ravenna is behind this somehow—she and that evil witch of hers."

Aelvina's voice broke and she hid her tears in the drapery of the window, clutching at thick folds with desperate fingers. She must sound like a malicious, jealous woman, but she knew with a certainty that she spoke the truth. Philippe would die on the morrow and there was nothing in this world she could do.

"That makes no sense. You are distraught. Why would Philippe's wife wish him dead?"

"Raymond did not know I was ward of the court; neither will Lady Ravenna. She will not know of my claim to the land. She thinks the child certain heir and fears Philippe will set her aside. With Philippe dead, she can control the land through his heir."

Aelvina attempted to hide the sob in her voice. It was so clear to her. What did she have to do to make others see? Philippe might understand and know what to do if she could but go to him. The thought no sooner sprang into her head than it was acted upon.

"Let me go to him, my lady," Aelvina pleaded suddenly, turning to her benefactor. "Philippe would know of what I speak. He must be warned."

Eleanor's eyes narrowed shrewdly. "And if he dies upon the morrow, you would have this time with him, tonight. Am I right?"

Aelvina nodded miserably. To be torn from Philippe's arms, never to feel his touch again . . . It was too abrupt. She must have time to reconcile herself to the emptiness of her life to come, a life without Philippe, whatever the morrow brought.

"Men are such fools," Eleanor stated scornfully, rising and going to the door. "It is not as if you are a virgin bride. You cannot go alone. I will send a page to guide you."

Aelvina could have shrieked with joy and surprise. She had not dared hope the request would be granted, but anticipation flooded her veins as she hurried to make herself ready. She chose a deep blue wool with elaborate trim from among the kirtles that had appeared at her door that morning. She would go unnoticed as much as possible in the dark corridors beyond. A white silk undertunic rubbed enticingly along her skin as she pulled her plaits back from her face and secured them in a braided knot at her nape, hiding her one identifying trait. The materials of these new gowns were of the finest, and they fit as if made for her. The rich fur trimmings and extravagant braids and embroidery, however, were made for royalty. They had surely come from the queen.

When the knock came, Aelvina was ready. She slid silently out the door to join a young page, and together they hurried through the cold, dark night.

Chapter Twenty-two

Philippe growled at the knock on his door. Still garbed in tunic and surcoat from the evening meal, he lay half-propped against the wall and pallet, his broad sword on one side of him, a flask of wine on the other. He had sharpened one and sipped from the other, although what he truly wished to do was slay and guzzle. No man in his right mind would knock at the door at this time of evening before a joust. Philippe's temper was precarious at the best of times; tonight, it bordered on demented.

When the knocking continued, he roared an irritable, "What dost thou want?" but made no effort to rise from the bed. He tried to fight off images of Aelvina lying beneath him with pictures of the mutilation he was preparing for Raymond, but his imagination sorely failed him.

"My lord, someone to see you. It is urgent," the page called to the barred door.

Philippe grumbled and swung his feet to the floor, deciding it better to have someone else to curse at than himself. With caution, he hefted the sword in his hand and unbolted the door.

The shock of finding the slender figure of his dreams standing before him was so great, it took a moment to fully regain his senses, and the page was gone before he could halt him. Philippe devoured the sight of that fair face with long dark lashes sweeping over azure eyes, the faint pink of full lips and high cheekbones, but he did not move from the door to welcome her.

"What art thou doing here?" he asked gruffly. His very veins were inflamed with desire just at her proximity. He could not allow her to come closer.

"Philippe, let me in. Someone will see," Aelvina whispered, the blood rushing to her cheeks beneath the intensity of his stare.

"You are wearing one of the gowns I sent you," Philippe muttered, stubbornly refusing to budge. "It becomes you."

"You! I thought they were from the queen—they are so beautiful. It seemed strange they fit so well." Aelvina smoothed the fine wool of the dark kirtle lovingly between her fingers.

"I meant for you to be dressed regally, but they took you from me before I could do it properly. The seamstress had to take my poor words and transform them. The blue is as I hoped. You appear as some sea nymph rising from the ocean's waters." There was madness in his brain tonight, loosening his tongue and shifting his moods with the vagaries of an east wind.

Philippe longed to reach out and smoothe an escaped tendril of flaxen hair, but he knew his hand would not stop there. Pain held him in check, and he gripped the door frame so tightly his knuckles whitened.

His words supplied the strength she needed to meet his

gaze, and Aelvina turned the full force of her smile on him, every secret of her heart bared to him with that look. His phrases told her more than she had ever dared hope. The knight had stooped to fine words and gentle gifts for her, and she had reason to know he did not do these things lightly. Her smile reached out to touch him as her fingers could not.

"Then you must take me in to admire your gift properly, my love," she whispered softly. "The hall is chilly and I would not have other ears hear what I wish to say to you alone."

"Aelvina," he groaned, "you do not know what strength it takes to keep from grabbing you and carrying you off now, with just your smile to give me hope. Do not tempt me further. Let me take you back to the tower." Her words and looks fed a flame in him that must go forever unquenched. He was in agony standing here staring at that which he could no longer have, and thought strongly of slamming the door to ward off temptation. It was much like cutting off his hand to prevent his touching, or plucking out his eye to keep from seeing, and he could not do it.

Aelvina had not come thus far to be denied. She had only this one night to carry with her the rest of her life and she would not let fear or honor or loyalty interfere. With a soft sigh for his obstinacy, Aelvina lifted her hand to his face, tracing the chiseled cheekbone and the disfiguring scar with loving fingers, moving close enough for her scent to fill his nostrils and her presence to inflame his blood.

With a muttered curse, Philippe grabbed her to him, swinging her into the room and slamming the door. The seductive scent that he remembered well, that had haunted his dreams and thoughts since that first night together, now wrapped him in its folds as he clasped her close and buried his lips in her hair. He could feel her heart beating against his chest as his hands ran up and down her spine, and he knew without any further doubt that their hearts beat as one, and his would go with her wherever she went, leaving him empty.

"Philippe! Oh, Philippe," she breathed against his ear as he lifted her from her feet, his lips greedily covering her eyes, her face, her throat, everywhere but where she wanted. "If I could have but just this one night . . . There is so much I have to say."

He shuddered and clasped her closer, willing himself to stillness. "Aelvina, it will only make it harder if you stay. You must go. I do not know how you found your way here, but you must go back. You are no longer mine to claim."

Sliding her hands behind his neck, her fingers entwining in hanks of his thick hair, Aelvina raised her eyes to meet his gaze. "No. You must give me this one night. I was unprepared before; now I will know this is the only time we have, and I will make the best of it. There are so many words I have not said . . . I am yours to claim. I will always be yours. There can be no other for me. I want you to know that."

"Aelvina, you are destroying me," Philippe groaned. "If I should kiss you now, I would not be able to stop until I had you stripped and beneath me on yon bed." He clenched her waist tightly with his hands and tore her from his grasp, setting her small figure at arm's length.

Aelvina glared back at him, fists clenched. "Philippe, for once in your life you will listen to me if I have to stand on the battlements and scream it to the world! You could be killed tomorrow and you would deny me this one chance to love you? I do not know who is the greater fool: you for your unreasonable honor or me for loving such a great, hulking gapeseed!''

Amusement briefly hid his pain as he stared at the outraged butterfly in his hands. If her stature were half as large as her passion, she would match him in height.

"Is this what brings you here then? You fear that stinking oaf will take me in battle? I do not thank you much for your confidence." Philippe released his hold and stood with hands on hips, waiting.

Exasperation flared higher than anger. "Philippe, someday I will teach you I have more brains than you have brawn, if you live to see the day! Raymond does not intend to fight fairly. He has come from Marta with some devil's plan, else he would not be here at all."

"Do you wish me to default and give him the day?" Philippe asked with impatience, moving to the flask at the bedside. Foul tasting as the brew was, he needed sustenance to combat this need in him, or he would never get the king's ward back to her bed this night.

Aelvina watched him lift the flask with uneasiness, another night returning to mind. Philippe could consume large quantities of liquor; one flask would not impare the morrow's battle, but she did not like the feel of it.

"Where did that flask come from, my lord?" she asked suspiciously.

Philippe glanced at her; then, understanding immediately, looked at the flask with distaste. "I do not know. It was here at my bedside when I returned. It has too bitter a taste to be from Henry's choice cellars."

Alarm immediately etched itself across Aelvina's brow. "Bitter? How much of it have you tasted?"

"I am not dead yet, so it cannot be what you are thinking." Still, Philippe set the container down without tasting from it again.

"No, he would not want you dead. They planned for him to win me in fair battle, remember? It will be some evil potion of Marta's to make you sicken and weaken your strength. Drain that flask and you will scarce be able to lift your blade, I am certain."

"Perhaps that would be the easiest thing for all," Philippe muttered, "to die honorably in battle and not suffer the torment of the damned for the rest of my life here on earth, watching you on the arm of another man, bearing his brats, knowing I have only myself to blame."

Tears trickled down Aelvina's cheeks as she watched his broad shoulders slump and turn away. She had been right to come, whatever the consequences.

"Philippe, must it be that way? It is you I love. There can never be another for me, even if you should die. No man can command my heart as you do. Honor and titles mean nothing to me. Must I marry another?"

The room's one small candle flickered, illuminating silver-gold tresses in a halo as Philippe turned to see her. The fine woven wool of her gown fell in folds along her slender figure, losing itself in a ripple of cloth in the darkness at her feet. Azure pools flecked with silver held his gaze.

Ignoring her question, Philippe answered wonderingly, "I have waited weeks—nay, months—to hear those words, thought never to hear them after what I have done to you. I admired your loyalty, your courage, your willingness to endure anything for the sake of our son, but I thought your hatred of me too deep for affection. And now that I know I have won that treasure I most sought, I must give it up. It would have been better had you held your tongue."

Despite his words, he had drawn closer, until his hand could reach out and loose the ribbons holding her hair. Emerald eyes studied her carefully as he drew his fingers through long plaits, untangling them and spreading the silken tresses across her shoulders and breasts. Aelvina stood still beneath his caress, her gaze fixed on his, her heart beating wildly at just the lightest of his touches.

Words would never win him as actions would. She did not care if she must live in sin the rest of her days, if she could but change his mind. He had not yet said the words she wished to hear, but they were there in his actions, in the look of his eyes. A man did not act as he had done out of simple lust. He would never have proclaimed to all the world that she was of noble blood if he only wished to have her warm his bed. She understood that now, and acted accordingly.

Aelvina's hands slowly went to her girdle, unfastening it and casting it aside. Without a word, her fingers next returned to the laces of her bodice and began loosening them.

Philippe's dark fingers covered hers, halting her progress. "Let me do it, as you have done for me," he murmured.

Large hands worked deftly to free her from the confining bliaut, tunic, and chemise, pushing the delicate fabrics from her shoulders and arms and down to her waist. A dark hand cupped a youthful, uptilted breast, measuring the weight of it as his gaze raked her hungrily.

"For me, there is no woman so beautiful as you in this world, and when you are carrying my child, your beauty surpasses all measures. If I must go to my death tomorrow, I will do it as a happy man."

He kissed her then, a lingering kiss of pulsating promise. Aelvina's hands slid over his shoulders as she pulled him closer, her skin on fire with the warmth of his touch as his hands curved themselves to her shape, caressing her with love. She sensed the raging inferno behind his kiss, held in close check, yet ready to emerge at the slightest crack in his resistance. He wished to savor the pleasures of her flesh first, before consuming her entirely. This was what she needed to slake her thirsty soul, and she pressed against him eagerly, urging him on.

Philippe needed no urging. With impatient hands, he pushed her clothes off her hips and to the floor, lifting her from the puddle of material to carry her to the narrow pallet. In a few eager tugs, he had divested himself of all garments and lay beside her, his heat warming her more thoroughly than any fire.

Aelvina traced the sculpted line of his nose, the jagged white scar over high cheekbones, the obstinate jut of his jaw, memorizing them for future use. Thick dark hair fell over his brow, and she brushed it back before placing a kiss on his wiry cheek.

One kiss led to another and his mouth covered hers with urgent demands. His large hands rode over her fragile frame as they held her tightly so that they touched intimately at every point of their bodies.

He laid her against the pallet, covering her with his length as his lips traveled down her throat to the tempting hollow at its base. The ecstasy of his heated mouth drinking of her flesh brought Aelvina arching against him, and his hand slid beneath her to hold her there.

Aelvina gave a cry of impatience as her fingers dug into his hair, her body afire with the need to fully encompass him. Her legs opened eagerly to meet him, but it was his kiss Philippe planted there, and the shock sent shivers of pleasure rippling through her as his tongue plied her warmly.

Unable to restrain himself any longer, Philippe rose to cover her, sinking his flesh deep within her to the music of Aelvina's cries of joy. This was his woman, his wife, mother of his child, and he had a need for her that could never be satiated. She moved instinctively with his every thrust, enclosing him tightly in the hidden warmth of her womanhood, and he surrendered to the pleasure of her love.

The tide of love and need and desperation drove them to new heights, to new plateaus. They found ecstasy as their bodies crested and shook at their joining. Waves of after shocks held them up, making their fall a gentle one as they drifted back to the cold cell of reality.

Aelvina shivered, and Philippe drew a fur cover over them, holding her close to his warmth.

"God help me, Aelvina, for you have made a simpering ass of me, in truth. Eleanor's troubadours could not sing better of the state I am in. If it is possible for a man's heart to be ripped from his chest and still go on living, you have stolen mine. Do you hear the foolish words you have me say? Take pity on me, Valkyrie, because I cannot stand to think of the parting that must come," he whispered against her hair.

"Must it come, Philippe? Is there no other way?" she cried against his chest, her fingers wrapped in the dark curls she found there. To find his love and have it torn from her was too cruel a fate.

"No, my little sorceress, even your charms cannot solve this one. If this madness that possesses me is love, I love you, and because I love you, I must give you up. I have spent the day badgering the priests for some other solution only to discover Henry has been gentle to me. There is no other way." Philippe removed the chain from his neck and returned it to Aelvina's. "I cannot claim the Earl of Dunstan's daughter."

Aelvina pulled away and stared down at him. "Why? The title means nothing to me. Is it your own claim to Dunstan that holds you back? Does your son's claim mean more to you than mine?"

Philippe caught her arms and pulled her down to him. "I came here with the intention of setting aside my marriage, sacrificing Dunstan, and marrying you. I used your title and our son as means to prove to Henry that you are my true wife and none other. Do you remember the time I told you of my plans to journey here?" At her bewildered nod, he continued. "I had decided then to take you for wife. You had every right to hate me, but I could not get you out of my blood. My only desire was to have you and our son safely installed in St. Aubyn under my protection. When I learned of your parentage, I knew it was the key that would either bind you to me forever or lose you for all times. I gambled, and lost."

His words were firm, forcing her to understand, but she did not. "Why, Philippe? Even if it means this child be born bastard, could I not wait until your marriage is annulled and marry you then? That is what Henry wants, is it not? The earl's daughter safely married and Dunstan in proper hands? Surely a second child's heritage cannot be so important as to throw away all happiness? Or can the marriage not be annulled?" she asked at last, with horror.

Philippe laughed shortly. "That was my greatest fear, that I could not get an annulment. It was for that reason I wished to show Henry he had forced me to marry the wrong woman. My knowledge of church and legal matters is slight, but his is great, having to deal with them every day. It seems the annulment is a simple matter, after all. I have only to show I was forced to wed against my wishes. The knowledge that I never kept my wedding vows adds to the ease. Within months the Lady Ravenna will be set aside with the Pope's blessing; I have seen to that."

Aelvina felt the coldness of his hand as he idly stroked her back and she shivered. What was he trying to tell her now? "Then why, Philippe?" she whispered.

His fingers dug into her flesh as he forced himself to admit what Henry had so politely omitted telling him. "Because the church will not condone marriage between adulterers, even should the spouses be set aside or die. We can never marry, Aelvina! Because of my foolishness, we are forever forbidden to marry and there is nothing— *nothing*—I can do about it." The words were wrung from him in anguish.

"And Henry will not allow the Earl of Dunstan's daughter to live in sin and bear bastard claimants to the title," she added for him, bitterly. "I should never have come here. To be with you is all I desire and it matters not to me under what vows or sins. For the sake of a title we must both suffer."

"For the sake of the sin I committed by taking you by force. I made a whore of you and must now suffer the consequences. Henry is right. You cannot continue to live as we have done, and I will not let you. This night is our last together. Tomorrow you will go back to your women's quarters until Henry has found the right man to be your husband. Sir Robert is a good choice. He will be kind to you and the children. Henry will choose wisely. You need not fear the man chosen."

His hands had fallen away from her as if already disclaiming his possession, seeing her as another man's wife, and Aelvina's tears poured unchecked onto his chest. A choking sob fought its way from her throat as she pummeled him with her fists, negating his words, denying the life fate had assigned her.

Unable to let her wretchedness go uncomforted, Philippe gathered her into his arms and began to kiss the tears away. She seized upon his caress with a thirsty need for his love, covering his face with eager kisses, fastening her lips upon his as if she never meant to part. With convulsive joy at this reprieve, Philippe pulled her over him.

Aelvina's natural instincts took command. Her hands slipped over Philippe's hard-muscled chest as her hips slid tantalizingly near to his. Her breasts brushed lightly against him until he groaned with desire and circled her waist with his hands. She followed his direction and pressed against his fully engorged manhood, enjoying the sensation of controlling his maleness.

At his muttered, "Witch!" Aelvina chuckled and rose to mount him, a thrill of pleasure shooting through her at being given the choice of where and when and how. But when he filled her, she could only groan her pleasure and succumb to his thrusts as his hands held her firmly in place. She had no need to be told who was in control, and no desire for it to be any other way. This was one man she could accept as master, for he accepted her as equal.

The exquisite pain-pleasure of his final lunge snapped her back into that world of joyous explosions he had taught her as her insides swelled and blossomed and took him fully. It was no wonder he kept her belly filled with his seed, she sighed, sprawling across his chest with contentment. If she had not already been with child, she would surely be so now.

As if to confirm this thought, the child in her womb moved so that even Philippe felt him. He looked startled, then pleased, as he rolled her back against the pallet to examine the increasing life that was his child. His large hand covered the small swell of her belly with curiosity and pleasure.

"I had thought to watch this one grow, to be there at

his birth," he said with regret. "You would make a domestic man of me, yet."

Aelvina smiled and touched his cheek. "Did you think to spend your life at war, my lord? If all you tell me of this king is true, he wishes his lands and not the purses of hired warriors to grow rich and fruitful. He has need of men to look after his people. It is not I who will domesticate you, but Henry."

"There is truth in that. St. Aubyn must be revived if it is to provide a home for my son. Mayhap I can persuade your Gundulf to come to me if Dunstan falls in other hands, but I think he will remain loyal to his rightful lady." Philippe's hand continued to roam her curves, memorizing them for that bleak time to come.

"You will return to St. Aubyn after the morrow?" she asked wistfully.

"I must see to our son's safety first. I fear the Lady Ravenna will use him as hostage to hold Dunstan. I will keep only one of my men with me for the tourney tomorrow. The rest will leave before the joust begins and take command of Dunstan until either I or the king's men can claim the child."

The unspoken words made Aelvina blanch. If Philippe should die tomorrow, it would be the king's men who held Dunstan. She tried to imagine Philippe's face without the life and vitality that she loved, and shivered. If she could not hold him, she would hold his son. The decision was instantaneous, but she spoke not a word of it. The time had come to take matters in her own hands. She had let Philippe know of her feelings and they were not enough. Now she was free to act on her own.

No further words were left to be said. A lifetime's passion must be condensed into one night, and they bent their wills to draining every last precious moment together. When the page's knock rapped against the door, they were ready. The words had been said, the decision made, and only the pain of the future remained. There were no farewell kisses and no tears; they had been spent and wasted.

Philippe stood strong and determined as Aelvina pulled on the hood of her pelisse, watching her straight, slender figure march out the door without a second look. She was gone from his life forever, and his heart went with her.

Chapter Twenty-three

Aelvina obediently followed the page back to her room, but once in the privacy of her cubicle, she began hasty preparations. Her hand lingered lovingly on the tawny silks and rose wools of the new kirtles she now realized came from Philippe, but they were not suited to her purpose.

She donned the remade gown she had worn on that long ride here and wrapped another dark gown in an old mantle. She added several other oddments necessary to her plan and the golden girdle Philippe had given her. She might have to part with the others, but she could not bear to part with everything. Then, carefully inspecting the passage for observers, she threw on the fur-lined mantle and fled down the dark corridor to freedom.

The guards at the entrance ignored her reappearance. Ladies were known to keep odd hours when they had lovers, and this one had already arranged one assignation with the queen's permission. A second one just before dawn was scarcely surprising and of little interest. They were there to keep interlopers out, not the ladies in.

Cautiously, Aelvina made her way through the predawn darkness to the stables. Not many stirred at this unreasonable hour, and what few were up and about ignored her flitting shadow. The stable was cold and musty and filled with the noises and smells of animals, but quietly so. Even the animals knew it was a time for sleep and allowed her to pass unheralded.

Aelvina recognized Philippe's mighty destrier, and in the darkness sought the other mounts they had used, locating the small gray palfrey with ease. The horse whickered its recognition as she patted it fondly and stood silently as Aelvina made herself comfortable in the stall. There was time for a brief nap before Philippe's men arrived.

A soft jingle of metal, shuffling footsteps, and a horse's eager snicker woke Aelvina some time later, and she stood hastily, wiping the straw from her skirts before the men approached. With a pretense of having just arrived herself, she began packing her few possessions in saddlebags.

Sir Alphonse, a youngish knight of scarce a score of years, with a broad face and broader build, approached first. When he saw Aelvina in the palfrey's stall, he halted dumbly.

"I ride with you," she stated simply.

The others came up then, the eldest in command finding himself forced to question his lord's mistress. The rumors of Aelvina's nobility had reached the knight's ears, but none other. Aelvina's impending betrothal was still a matter of state secret.

"My lady, his lordship did not mention your accompanying us. And you have no lady with you. It is not proper."

"There was no time for Philippe to tell you. The decision has just been made. I must go disguised so I can take no maid. Philippe has entrusted me and his son to your care. Do not fail him now. If Sir Raymond should find me, I would be in the gravest of dangers. Let us hurry.''

They were trained to obey such short, quick commands. Authority rang in her voice, straightened her shoulders, and flashed in her eyes. It did not occur to these large knights that she was a mere wisp of a girl. She was their lord's lady, an earl's daughter, and they understood the necessity. Although they all had confidence their lord would win the coming battle, they would take no chances. Without further questions, they saddled the palfrey along with their own mounts.

The gates opened before the small party of Philippe's men and none heeded the small figure in the center. A tournament was in the making, and all eyes faced the banners rising over the field below. The haste prevented as grand a show as the court would prefer, but the rumors of this grudge match and a fight to the death were enough to stir the blood lust of the sentries at the gate. The party passed all points unimpeded.

As they rode out into the countryside, Aelvina deliberately averted her eyes from the silk awnings rising in the grandstand. Philippe's gaze would seek her there, among the king's party. She did not wish to think of what pain he might suffer at her absence. She only prayed it would add an extra keenness to his sword and lance as they brought Sir Raymond to the dust from whence he came.

By the time Philippe reached the tournament field, he knew better than to search the grandstands for Aelvina's presence, but his gaze flew there just the same. It came away again, disappointed.

Eleanor's messenger had sought him out first. His mind

on the battle ahead, Philippe had been bothered by the queen's request for his presence, but confronted with the disarray of Aelvina's room, annoyance had fled, replaced by fear and rage. His gaze quickly took in the fact that the expensive gowns he had bought for her remained, including the blue wool she had worn for him just hours before. What was missing, he could not readily tell.

Aware the queen might believe he had something to do with the disappearance of the royal ward Philippe set his jaw angrily but told her nothing. If he suspected Aelvina's whereabouts, he had no intention of revealing them.

He rode out onto the field of battle with a new determination. Whatever tricks Raymond had prepared would have to fail; Henry might suspect, but Philippe alone knew for a certainty where Aelvina had gone and what danger she faced. He had to live, if only to find that self-willed Valkyrie and shake sense into her fair head. Only too late had he seen he'd been a fool to mention the child's danger.

The enormous steed beneath him was spirited and strong, restless after days of confinement, and Philippe turned his attention back to his surroundings as he made his obeisance before the king. Sir Raymond arrived from the opposite direction, his expression concealed behind his headgear, but Philippe sensed the other man's dark gaze upon him. For a moment, he contemplated slumping in his saddle as if the knave's trickery had taken its effect, but he rejected the notion. Let the coward shake in his boots these next hours before his death, wondering when the fatal blow would fall.

Henry accepted their bows with a grim nod and signaled the heralds for the tourney to begin.

Raymond was desperate and fought with a desperate man's strength. His lance broke against Philippe's shield in the first round, but he easily maintained his seat. As they swung around and found new lances, Philippe gauged his opponent carefully. Desperate men were often inclined to foolish mistakes, and he needed such an opening to put a quick end to this duel. He must be off after Aelvina and not playing at war with this knave who could no longer even command his respect.

He revised his opinion of the other man's abilities after the second round. Raymond was heavier than he and used his advantage to throw his full weight behind his weapon. Philippe had been nearly unseated just from the power of his blow and would have to look carefully to his seat in the future.

The deafening clangor of the mighty blows stirred the beginnings of excitement in the noble onlookers, but not so much as hand-to-hand combat might. They watched anxiously for that hit that would bring a man down or draw blood, causing the battle to enter its tenser moments. Gaily colored flags fluttered over their heads in the cool October breeze, the frost-hardened ground shook from the thunder of galloping steeds, and gasps of delight filled the stands as the two knights met again with resounding impact.

This time, Philippe's lance caught the corner of his opponent's shield, tilting it and tearing past the barrier to land against Raymond's shoulder. Raymond hung on, but the thrust had been a painful one and the first dent in his confidence. Philippe was not the weakened shell Marta had promised.

It was a short matter after that to drive Raymond off his destrier, but not before Raymond's lance caught Philippe a glancing blow. Philippe shook his head to clear the roaring from his ears and dismounted to finish off his quarry.

Raymond breathed raggedly as he swung his broad sword with both hands. With his shield bent and useless, he dared

Philippe to advance. Philippe knew he had only to ward off Raymond's blows until the latter weakened, permitting a fatal opening; but that was time-consuming business, and time was of the essence.

The crowd screamed its approval as the two men went at each other with all the strength their mighty bodies could muster. The heavy metal of their swords rained punishing blows against the weak links of mail. Blood gushed from Raymond's already weakened shoulder as he caught Philippe with a sidelong crash that sent him to his knees. A throaty roar poured from the stands as Raymond closed in for the kill, only to find Philippe unprepared to die.

Philippe rose with a roar of rage, the memory of this swine's hairy body heaving above Aelvina's manacled form giving him the renewed strength of hatred. Raymond's defense was down as Philippe painfully rose and swung his sword in a death-dealing arc powered by the twin passions of hate and love. The blow connected at the neck, and a ghastly snap spoke the outcome.

The crowd's screams were uproarious, but Philippe heard only the ringing in his ears as his gaze swung to Henry, and beyond, to the empty seat that should have been Aelvina's.

Philippe's men did not push themselves as hard as Philippe did, and the journey was not so harsh as their earlier one. Even so, Aelvina was exhausted by the pace. Her worry for the man she left behind and the child who lay ahead did not aid in her comfort. She felt no guilt in leaving Philippe; she had warned him and could do no more. The child needed her now. It was this thought that gave her strength as the hours of the days dragged by and her aching muscles complained.

Warned that they would soon be arriving in Dunstan, Aelvina called a halt so that she might don the disguise necessary to pass the Lady Ravenna's notice. The men had been prepared in advance, but as the tall, stout figure swathed in veils and black appeared from the bushes, their first thought was to find Aelvina.

Her familiar laughter warned them of the exchange, and Sir Alphonse approached cautiously. Silver blue eyes merrily stared back at him through the disguising veil, but they were half a head higher than he remembered. His gaze wandered down over the thickened waist and lumpish figure beneath the loose kirtle and came back to meet her familiar eyes again. That she was with child they had all known, but this lumpish figure bore little resemblance to pregnancy or the sylphlike gracefulness they knew so well.

Aelvina answered the questions in his eyes. Lifting her skirts, she displayed a cloddish boot laced tightly above slender ankles. "The page gave them to me in exchange for a few coins. They are padded well to stay on my feet, and the padding and heel lift me higher. Am I not a more stately stature now, sir knight?"

The other men gathered around to observe this new mode in lady's footwear and guffawed loudly at the sight, but they had to admit it gave her height. The lumpish figure they had to take Aelvina's word for, since she had no intention of displaying the various clothes she wore as padding.

The veil was an outlandish accessory in this day and time, for few women covered their faces any longer. She had invented her own grisly story about her concealment and made the men swear to it. It would have to suffice until Philippe came.

They rode through Dunstan gates after nightfall. The men dismounted and entered the keep without fanfare.

Aelvina gratefully noted that Philippe had established his own men at the door. At least the keep was not entirely enemy territory yet.

Lady Ravenna had never made any pretense at greeting guests. Even Marta was absent as an ancient retainer hurried forward to offer the lord's men sustenance after their long journey. After Aelvina gave her fabricated story, a maid was summoned to guide her to the nursery.

Aelvina's heart beat rapidly as she climbed the broad stone stairs, their darkness illuminated only by the maid's flickering torch. She was in Dunstan keep again, for the first time since that fateful day she had met Philippe. Now, it was her son awaiting her in one of the rooms above, the son she had seen but once since birth, and her prayers winged their way toward heaven.

The room she was led to was dark, but the maid lit a candle within before silently departing. Aelvina could not help but notice the girl's hasty sign against the evil eye as she turned away. Even in disguise, the ignorant found her forbidding. Perhaps it was just the strange garb.

The light roused a shadow in the far corner, but Aelvina ignored it, instead turning eagerly to the cradle against the wall. With trembling hands, she pushed back the crude netting protecting the infant within, and raised the candle high to light his tender form.

Tears rolled down her cheeks as her gaze finally rested on the silver-haired son she had known only once. Cherubic cheeks had filled out and grown round and chubby as the small body, but he was the same, her firstborn. He lay hunched on his stomach, his knees up under him, and the breadth of his small shoulders already reflected his heritage. She wished she could see his eyes—his father's eyes, Chauvin had said—but she did not dare wake him.

She contented herself with stroking a damp tendril of his hair and watching him squirm in his sleep. Her son. Philippe's child. Tears burned hot against her skin and fell down to her gown, unnoticed.

The half-angry, half-glad whisper at her back returned Aelvina to the moment. She covered the child lovingly, and turned to face the intruder.

"Thyllda! You would wake him. He would be terrified at seeing such a sight as this over his bed," Aelvina said, removing the confining veil.

"And you did not think my poor heart might stop at seeing such an apparition hovering over the babe!" Thyllda scolded, before taking her errant ward in her arms and covering her with kisses.

After exchanging tearful hugs, the two women returned to Thyllda's rude pallet, where their whisperings would not disturb the sleeping infant. Aelvina gave her a quick sketch of what had passed these last days and weeks as she removed her burdensome disguise.

Philippe's danger brought a worried frown to Thyllda's lined face, but the news that Henry intended returning Dunstan to its rightful owner brought a look of hope. "I promised your father I would see you taken to Henry when he arrived, but I feared I had failed him. Thank the good lord Sir Philippe is an honorable man, though he does have a strange way of showing it." Thyllda eyed Aelvina's burgeoning belly with suspicion. "Will he marry you and make of you an honest woman now?"

Aelvina's eyes darkened, and she closed them against the pain of knowledge. "He cannot," she whispered. "The church will not marry adulterers."

She said no more, and shocked from further speech, Thyllda too grew silent.

* * *

The babe's cries brought Aelvina instantly awake. Weak sunshine filtered through the chinks in the walls, and for the first time she heard her son's cries of waking. With a smile, she rose and went to the cradle. This moment was worth every minute of danger the journey had entailed.

As she threw back the netting, the infant grew quiet, then smiled in delight, and waved his fist in an attempt to catch a flaxen curl. As Aelvina lifted him from the cradle, the child wound chubby fingers in silver tresses.

Tears of happiness streamed down Aelvina's cheeks as she cuddled the cooing infant to her breast. Brave as his father, he knew no fear of strangers; and like his father, he could not keep his hands from her hair. With a tearful grin, Aelvina met Thyllda's understanding gaze, and went about the task of disentangling her hair from playful fingers.

During the night, one of Philippe's men had stationed himself outside the nursery door. Not daring to leave mother and child alone, Thyllda asked his aid in having food brought in. The knight refused to leave his post, but agreed someone would be sent.

Hearing this exchange, Aelvina saw to whom Thyllda spoke and addressed him directly. "Sir Anthony, we cannot take chances with the food served. One of us must take from the pot all others feed from. This place is too dangerous to trust in any but ourselves."

Both Sir Anthony and Thyllda looked shocked at the import of her words, but agreed hastily, arguing over who best ought to go.

Aelvina grew impatient. "Thyllda, does the child not have a wet nurse?"

The old woman turned, gauging her charge's impatience with ease. "I have had the child weaned in preparation for your arrival. If we must make a quick escape, it would not do to have a hungry babe screaming for his nurse's milk. I had not thought of Marta's poisons, though. Surely she would not harm the child?"

Aelvina relaxed at this sign that Thyllda had not lost the wisdom so long relied on, and she smiled with gratitude. "I am sorry, *ma mere*. I did not think. Then if it is safe for you to travel below, you must fetch the food. Sir Anthony is better prepared to defend us with his sword. Your tongue is swift, but not deadly, I fear."

The door closed after Thyllda, and Aelvina was alone at last with her child. As poignant as the moment might be, there were other factors to consider, and she laid the child upon the straw pallet while she hurriedly donned the bulky garments of her disguise.

Before Thyllda returned, Sir Anthony whispered a warning of the Lady Ravenna's arrival. The confrontation she had known must come waited just beyond that wall. Aelvina's heart raced with trepidation as she checked the fastenings of her veil, but she approached the door with calmness.

The Lady Ravenna's gaze swept over her husband's newly hired nursemaid with undisguised suspicion.

"Take off the veil," she ordered, without greeting.

Aelvina clenched her fists and prayed. If she could but get by this moment she had known would come . . . "Sir Philippe said I need not. It is the only reason I agreed to come here rather than hiding my disfigurement in a convent."

"Bah. How am I to know you are not some comely wench he has smuggled in here to warm his bed? Take off the veil or I will have you thrown from the keep." Though her words never rose higher than a rustling whisper, there was no doubt of the challenge in them.

"She speaks the truth, my lady. I heard Sir Philippe make the promise and all the court knows of the lady's misfortune. Someone set fire to the hangings of the lady's bed, and she scarce escaped with her life. She was gently born, but no man will have her now, I have heard." Sir Anthony spoke up, repeating the story they had rehearsed. It seemed a fate that would appeal to the Lady Ravenna, and Aelvina had created it with much enthusiasm.

The lady's interest did seem aroused as she strode closer, attempting to peer through the veil before circling her strange visitor. The child scooting about the floor beneath their feet held no interest for her.

"There is nothing wrong with her hands," Lady Ravenna pointed out at last.

Aelvina forced herself to relax and speak calmly under this scrutiny, keeping her voice low and soft and unrecognizable. "It would have been better that I died that night, my lady, than to suffer the torments of these past years. My hands escaped serious injury and healed well. I can hold the child without harming him, but to see my face would frighten him, and I would be forced to leave. Your husband has promised me I would find a home here."

Lady Ravenna swung around to glare at Sir Anthony. "Have you seen her face? Can you bear proof of that tale?"

Before the startled knight could reply, a slight figure bearing bowls of porridge slipped into the room from behind and answered the question. "I have and I can. While she thought the child and I slept, she rose to wash the evening's journey from her face."

Thyllda calmly placed a bowl in Aelvina's hands and set the other on the floor while she caught the wriggling child.

The Lady Ravenna glared at her, waiting for the remainder of the tale.

"Well! What did you see?" she finally asked in irritation when it became apparent Thyllda was more interested in bringing the active infant to heel than in enlightening her mistress.

Thyllda gave her mistress a sour look. "What would you have me say? She has eyes to see and a mouth to speak. They are not like yours or mine, but they work. What more do you want? I am too old to keep up with this young brat. She is strong and will be of aid to me. You certainly will not lose her to any of the knaves around here."

The lady glared in defeat and strode angrily from the room.

The door closed behind the dark wraith, and Aelvina felt the full impact of Thyllda's angry glare fall upon her.

"Fool! Why did you not stay where you were safe? If she discovers who you are, she will have two hostages to hold against Sir Philippe!"

Aelvina took the struggling infant from her nurse's hands and slowly sat to feed the babe his porridge. Even though she was reunited with her child, her heart lay heavy within her. Even now, they could be preparing Philippe's body for burial, and she would not be there to speak her farewells. She had betrayed him when he most needed her, and the thought did not sit lightly on her mind.

Still, she must grow accustomed to a life without him, whether he lived or not. The pain of parting was still too great to examine closely, and she bent her thoughts to the task of caring for her son. The child was all she had to get her through these days.

"We will be gone before she knows to take hostages," Aelvina reassured the angry servant. "Is there some way to send word to Gundulf? Is Chauvin still here? We must

hide the child and ourselves until either Philippe or the
king's men arrive. With luck, they will arrive before news
of the king's decision to take Dunstan, but we cannot put
our faith in luck.''

Thyllda grunted agreement to this wisdom. "Gundulf is
in the village; we thought it best to have one of us outside
the castle walls. Chauvin comes and goes. Some of his
brethren have arrived; they are building a monastery not
far from here on land donated by Sir Philippe, much to
the lady's wrath.''

Aelvina's lips bent in a half smile. She could well imagine
the restraints such a religious structure would place on the
lady's heathen ceremonies. When she remembered the
black night that had turned her lover from man to beast,
the smile slipped away. The evil in this place had not left
with Philippe's arrival. If anything, it was more concentrated. She could feel it in the very walls around her. Let
men call her sorceress if they would, but she knew the
danger in these walls was more than that of mortal man
or woman. They must escape the castle's hold before that
evil found them.

"We cannot wait for Chauvin to arrive. Word must be
sent to Gundulf to have mounts awaiting us outside the
castle walls tonight. Where is Marta?''

"She has not been seen since Sir Raymond left. Aelvina,
you cannot expect Gundulf to have mounts ready by
tonight. It will be difficult enough to have a message reach
him before the day is out. Sir Philippe's horses are all
within the castle walls. Either they must be smuggled out
or Gundulf must find some other means. It will take time.''

Aelvina frowned. News could not be much farther
behind them, particularly if Marta was out and about. The
delay would be dangerous but might bring Philippe or the
king's men closer. She had no idea how long it took to

gather an army to lay siege to a castle, but she feared they would need just that should the Lady Ravenna receive word Dunstan was to be taken from her. There seemed little choice, then.

"I fear tomorrow night may be too late, but we cannot make the forest's cover without horses. I fear for the lives of Philippe's men once the lady discovers our betrayal."

Thyllda nodded glumly. Seeing Charles completely captivated with Aelvina's veil and in good hands, she slipped from the room to find some messenger for Gundulf.

The menacing cloud of disaster lingered over Dunstan Castle, seeping in between the chinks of mortar and crawling beneath the doors, filling the cold stone walls with gloom. Every face wore an air of nervousness that increased with the passing hours until the slightest noise brought everyone to their feet and set hearts pounding.

Aelvina prayed Philippe would set out immediately after the tournament. His arrival soon after hers would be the safest thing for all. But as the hours passed and he did not appear, she had to face the possibility he would not. He might have survived the joust but be severely wounded; she prayed that was the reason for his delay, and not the haunting thought uppermost in her mind. She might somehow endure being married to another man if she knew Philippe lived and walked this earth. But with Philippe gone . . . it would be unbearable. She preferred death to such a life. Perhaps that was the reason she had come here.

Thyllda returned with the news that Gundulf had received their message and would be ready for them on the morrow.

Aelvina refused to spend this first day with her son in worry. She joined in his play, laughed at his antics, and held him whenever he permitted it. Delighted with this

new playmate, Charles performed like a true showman,
keeping his audience royally entertained.

But when Charles slept, Aelvina's face fell into a dark
study. Even if they should escape to safety, the future har-
bored no real hope. Without Philippe, only the child in
her arms and the one in her womb could bring her joy
again, and it would be a muted joy at best.

But life must go on as long as it existed. Thyllda brought
up the evening meal with the news that there were no
tidings; no word from Marta, no visitors from the outside
world. They had survived one day in safety, but it still felt
as if the siege had already begun, only this time from within
the walls.

It seemed preferable that one of them be awake at all
times, and Aelvina made Thyllda sleep first. She knew there
would be no sleep for her that night. She stayed awake
listening for the pounding of hooves that would indicate
Philippe's arrival. Some part of her could not believe he
was dead and would not come, though there had been
more than ample time for his mighty destrier to cover the
distance.

Aelvina did not wake Thyllda but kept her lonely vigil
throughout the dark hours of the night, dozing off only
with the dawn and the knowledge that Thyllda would
waken soon. So it was that she did not hear of Marta's
appearance until the day was past its prime.

Chapter Twenty-four

The sound of a man's voice woke her. For a moment, Aelvina's heart leapt with hope, but as sleep dissipated, disappointment rose in its place. She recognized the accents of one of Philippe's men.

She rose and wrapped the veil around her before moving behind the door Thyllda had barely opened a crack. Cautiously, Thyllda would not let even Philippe's own men see her face. She scarcely had time to catch a few words before Thyllda closed the door and turned back into the room with a worried frown.

"What is it, Thyllda? I heard him mention Marta. Has she returned?"

Thyllda tugged thoughtfully at the long gray plait she had not had time to pin up. The little demon had been intent on waking his mother, and she'd had her hands full keeping him quiet while Aelvina slept. Now Thyllda looked at the dark circles beneath the girl's eyes and wondered if it had been worth it.

Her concern grew deeper as she watched Aelvina clasp at her belly and settle back on the pallet. The Lady Fairfax had lost a number of children through miscarriage, and Aelvina was as delicately built as her mother. The long, hard journeys she had undertaken these last weeks could not have done her well, and the nervous strain did not help.

"Are you well?" Thyllda asked quietly, ignoring Aelvina's earlier question.

"I am fine. The child is restless—that is all. It will probably be another boy such as this one." She scooped up her mischievous son as he crawled across the floor to her with cries of excitement. "Philippe would father many sons. Now, what is it of Marta?"

Thyllda did not have to see Aelvina's face to know the pride and love and joy reflected in silvered eyes now as she wiped the dirt from her son's cheek. This one was meant to mother Philippe's many sons; it seemed her destiny. Fate could not be so cruel as to divert it.

"She appeared sometime last night. No one knows how she enters or departs, but she is here now. While you slept, the men have been trying to find out what she knows. They, as well as you, would like to know if their lord lives."

Aelvina clenched her eyes closed, making fast and furious bargains with the lord up above in return for Philippe's well-being. In a faraway voice she asked, "What have they learned?"

"Only that Marta is in a foul mood and the Lady Ravenna is farther removed from this world than ever. Even Marta does not seem able to reach her. If you want my opinion, Sir Philippe's wife is not in her right mind."

Aelvina sent up a whispered prayer of gratitude and

opened her eyes on the world again. "That means Philippe still lives. I fear Marta must have been at White Hall, but she must have failed or she would not be in such a foul mood. And if the lady is mad, it is the loss of Dunstan that makes her so." Another thought intruded. "How full is the moon tonight, Thyllda? Do you know?"

Thyllda shot her a sharp look. "I do not put much faith in such things. How would I know?"

Aelvina could not explain the need, but it suddenly seemed important. "Ask, will you? There is certain to be someone among those heathens who will know."

"I will ask in the kitchens when I fetch your meal."

When Thyllda returned with a trencher of roast venison and a few small apples, Charles was resting in his mother's arms while Aelvina sang a song of love learned from Eleanor's troubadours.

"It did not take you long to gain the child's heart," Thyllda murmured affectionately as Aelvina took the food.

"The bond is there. It cannot be broken. He is my son and no one can take him from me, ever. We will always find each other," she answered firmly. Time and tragedy had not served to weaken her spirit but to strengthen her confidence. "What have you learned of the moon?"

"It will be full tonight," Thyllda replied.

Aelvina nodded thoughtfully, remembering that other night when she had been sacrificed to the lady's strange gods beneath a full moon. It seemed a portent of some kind, a key to the lady's strange behavior.

"It is good we are going tonight. See that the men eat or drink nothing that they did not prepare themselves. Warn them carefully. Without their help, we cannot leave the castle gates."

Aelvina stayed within the confines of the nursery as Thyllda went about her tasks. She knew it was not safe for her to walk the halls with Marta about. Marta would be aware she was no longer in London, and she knew her too well to be fooled long by a disguise. She must stay hidden until it was time to depart. A growing uneasiness built within her as the hours passed and the sounds from the keep below filtered to her ears.

Something was not right. She sensed it. Thyllda came back and reported all was well, but there seemed uncertainty in her tone. When questioned, she could not put a finger to it.

"It just does not seem normal. Marta and Lady Ravenna are closeted somewhere, but that is not unusual. There seems to be much coming and going through the gates, but they have never been ordered closed and there is a fair in the village today. There are fewer servants about than usual. All seems to be working in our favor, yet it does not seem right." Thyllda shook her head in puzzlement.

"What kind of people are coming through the gate?" Aelvina asked, excitement and fear growing in equal proportions.

Thyllda frowned, trying to picture them. Then, realizing what Aelvina was actually asking, she shook her head. "If these are knights of Philippe's or the king's, they are not the sort I would seek. Some do seem to have rich trappings, some keep their faces hid; the Lady Ravenna greets none of them, and yet they make themselves at home. It is not natural, I say."

Fear took the place of excitement. The unseen chanters came immediately to mind: mysterious creatures in hooded robes. All of them could not have been the castle's inhabitants. There were people out there who had seen her raped and done nothing, who had seen her naked, who knew her face, when she scarce knew of their existence. They were evil people with depraved needs. Evil was here again, within these walls. Would she escape it this time?

She shook off these superstitious thoughts and sought reality. Strangers within the gates might complicate their escape. If just Philippe's knights lounged in the hall below, they could walk out undisturbed. To gain that hall in the midst of strangers would be asking for trouble, but she saw no other way out. They must leave through those gates tonight, before Marta found some way to hold them here forever—if she had not already.

By nightfall, the keep had grown ominously silent. Perhaps it was only their own tension, but Aelvina and Thyllda exchanged uneasy glances as the hours went by and none of the usual scurrying of feet resounded in the corridors. Sir Anthony guarded the door, but they did not dare send him below to see what was happening. When consulted, he voiced an equal uneasiness. Even if for some reason his fellow knights should retire early, there should be servants about below, or dogs snapping and growling over bones. All remained quiet.

Unable to wait any longer, Aelvina reached a determined decision. "Sir Anthony, do you remember the old donjon where Sir Philippe was housed when first he came here?"

A telltale grin flitted across the young knight's face. "I was posted guard at the base when Sir Philippe told me the world's fairest maiden was about to seek shelter there. Do you not remember my holding the door?"

Aelvina had the grace to blush. "I remember. Then you know the way to the tower. Is it locked?"

"Barred from the inside, but there is no reason we cannot go out it." His eyes lit with approval as he realized her intention. "No one stays in that part of the keep. The walls are unsafe, but it would be better to chance loose stones than whatever lies below."

"Good. Then you lead Thyllda and the babe out that way. I must go below and see what has happened to the others."

Two voices instantly rose in objection, but Aelvina ignored them both. If Philippe or the king's men should arrive tonight, she would see that they had safe entry. She still owed her loyalty to Philippe.

These arguments scarce convinced Thyllda and Sir Anthony, but Aelvina remained silent. Something was wrong in Dunstan Castle and she would not leave until she knew what it was. The child must be removed to safety at once.

"I will go out the front portals if all is well and meet you at the gate. If I am not there, go without me, but be certain there is someone on guard we can trust and who will let me out when I am ready."

Their minds were eased that she did not intend to linger, and with a little more persuasion, Thyllda gathered up the child and a few belongings and trailed out at Sir Anthony's side. Aelvina watched them go until Thyllda's light tunic could no longer be seen in the darkness. Then, taking a deep breath, she proceeded toward the broad stairway.

The torches in the great hall guttered low, casting deep shadows over the room's interior and making it difficult to discern the figures at the table or along the walls where the men usually slept. The abnormal silence was enough warning, but Aelvina could not leave without knowing for certain. She moved farther into the cavernous room, keeping her ears tuned for any sound.

The first figure she came upon was draped across the long trestle table. He was one of Philippe's men, and from the looks of it, the rest lay in the same state. Daringly, Aelvina reached out a hand to touch a still form. He was warm. With a sigh of relief, she moved her fingers to his neck; the blood still beat in his veins.

Fools! They had done what she had told them not to. She found a mug not totally drained and sniffed its contents. They had been drugged, of course. Her gaze swept to the other forms lying about floors and walls. Even the dogs were still. Why in heaven's name had they drugged the animals? What was happening here? The sense of unease that had muffled her all day escalated closer to a feeling of panic. What evil did they plan for this night?

Almost as if in answer, Aelvina felt the ominous vibrations of the chant that would never be expunged from her mind. She felt it before she heard it. It vibrated from the walls, hummed under doors, and echoed down empty corridors. As she advanced into the room, drawn against her will, the sound reached her ears. It was low and faraway, coming from the bowels of hell.

Aelvina's fingers slipped beneath the layers of material to clutch at the handle of the knife Thyllda had returned to her. She must leave this place at once, before the gates of hell opened up and the demons escaped, but her feet continued with a will of their own, moving closer to the source of the sound.

Behind the great hall were no giant kitchens as in St. Aubyn, but a labyrinth of assorted cubicles and corridors leading to various parts of the keep. One of these led to the dark cellars beneath the old donjon, where wine was stored and prisoners once kept. Rumors of the brutal tortures carried out in those chambers during the past years of civil strife caused many of the servants to circle wide around these stairs lest haunts of yore molest them. Aelvina wondered if that same superstitious logic had not caused the disappearance of many of the servants tonight. On how many other moonlit nights had the ghastly chants emanated from those cells of torment?

Still, that thought did not deter her as she moved noiselessly through the dark, guided only by the flickering of a single candle. The chant grew stronger but had not yet reached that peak of frenetic ecstasy she remembered. What if some other innocent virgin was being sacrificed to their vile gods tonight? Did she have a means to stop them? Or could the cause of this ceremony be worse—a war chant drawing demons straight from hell to protect Dunstan lands?

Aelvina shivered as her hand touched the latch of the planked door leading to the cellars. The growing sound of many voices joined in unison vibrated the door beneath her hand, and she felt the increasing excitement in their ominous hum. It was madness to go down there, but she must. She was drawn by a stronger force than her own will, a force that beckoned her even as the chant grew louder and more frantic.

As if in a trance, Aelvina slid through the opening of the cellar door. Guided by the small sliver of light at the top and the flickering of many candles below, she crept along the stairwell, the eerie chant filling her ears, echoing off the stones, flooding the cellars with sound. She shook with the violence of it and tried to turn away but could not.

Her heart thumped faster and an icy hollowness opened in her center as the dark shapes of those hooded figures came into view in the cellar below. They were turned away from her, facing some point beyond the curve of the stairs she could not see. Were they real? Were they figures of flesh and blood beneath garments of this earth, or the ghostly conjurations of her own mind?

Aelvina's fingers were like ice as they felt along the wall, guiding her step in the darkness. She could feel the fevered pitch of the chant now as she was caught up in its grip.

As she turned the corner of the stairs, she was staggered by the odor of incense and some other heady scent she could not place, though it tugged at hidden strings in her mind. The fumes filled the air with a smoky fog, so that the flickering of candles and torches scarce cut a swathe through the surreal gloom.

Grasping the wall for support, Aelvina swayed between the combination of intoxicating odors and enthralling sound, trying to adjust her senses to decipher their message. The erotic beat stirred an answering hunger in Aelvina's breast. She felt an almost unimaginable urge for Philippe's arms, could almost feel his body pumping inside hers, and felt her own body go moist with desire.

She could not believe this. Time had been displaced and it was as if she was back in her nightmare, frozen in place while Philippe devastated her body and she responded against her will, betrayed by her senses just as they deceived her now. And then her eyes finally found the focus of this night's ceremony and horror shocked her perceptions back to reality.

At the far end of the room a raised platform had been constructed and draped in a thick black cloth. Torches burned at either end, illuminating the center of the platform and its occupants while casting all else in shadow. The sight of the occupant of that sacrificial altar widened Aelvina's eyes with horror and kept her frozen in place.

The Lady Ravenna offered herself upon that evil altar this evening. Aelvina knew not what madness possessed the lady's mind, but of a certainty, she could see what possessed the lady's body. She lay locked in an obscene embrace with some creature barely human when seen through the haze of smoke and darkness.

Even as Aelvina watched, the chant seemed to reach that pitch of demented ecstasy she remembered only too well. The torches flared brighter and the room filled with a smoky glow as the creatures on the altar exploded in frenzied cries and the onlookers roared in a lewd release of their own.

There was no virgin in distress here, no war party gathering, and Aelvina had had more than enough. The erotic spell broke with that obscene performance. If what she had seen here tonight was any evidence, Philippe had been as much a victim of drugged sensuality as she, and she could lay none of the blame of that rape on him. She turned to steal back up the stairs the way she had come when a wiry hand grasped her wrist and a hoarse voice whispered somewhere near.

"Don't leave yet, Lady Aelvina. Your turn is coming next. What do you think yon bull will do to the bastard in your belly? It is not a pleasure our members have yet enjoyed, the sight of a childbearing member of the nobility being robbed of the fruit of her womb. The excitement might be such that they will wish to sample the pleasure themselves. It has happened, but few of the objects of their lust have survived to tell of it."

The voice continued to hiss as Aelvina was jerked around again to face the altar where the bestial mating continued. Aelvina shuddered at the thought of that lewd creature impaling her body as it did Lady Ravenna's.

Of course it was Marta who held her imprisoned, who had brought her to this evil place knowing the drug's effect could not be resisted once sampled. It was Marta who signaled for another of the black-robed figures to capture Aelvina's other hand and lead her into that sweating, half-naked, fornicating mass. Marta's voice sent Aelvina's mind spinning back to the helplessness of those empty months of her pregnancy, and she no longer seemed to be part of the body being led so docilely to the sacrificial altar.

With absent curiosity, Aelvina watched as some noble lord hitched up his black robes, exposing his naked hairy legs as he fell down upon a nude maid on the floor. It had not occurred to her that some of the chanters were women, but of course they were; it was all part of the puzzle. All those eager maids of the Lady Ravenna's had their place here as well as above.

The hands on her wrists forced her forward and ripped the disguising veil from her hair. Eager hands reached out, grabbing at her clothes, stripping away the layers of fabric she had bound herself in. None of this seemed to touch that nebulous substance that was herself except the horrifying spectacle of that obscene altar. Though Aelvina tried to avoid the reality of her nightmare, her eyes kept dragging back to it. Dizzily, she watched until she could almost feel the pain of that impalement between her own thighs.

It was that sensation that destroyed Aelvina's deceptive detachment. To have been the victim of this vile rape once had almost been the end of her, and then it had been her chosen lover who had filled her. To suffer it again at this animal's hands would be a desecration to which she could not, would not, submit. Whatever she had to do might mean losing the child within her, but she would be dead before she suffered this again.

As the creatures on the altar bellowed their triumph once more and all around her moaned in the throes of their obscene lusts, Aelvina screeched the war cry of her Saxon ancestors, rending the putrid air with the clear cry of freedom as she jerked her wrist from Marta's powerless hold. In the flash of an instant, her fingers drew the dagger handle and slashed relentlessly at her other gaoler.

The screech had frozen all motion within the cellar's gloom, but the cry of agony that followed set the statues to life. Aelvina dodged a groping hand, kicked aside an impeding foot, and ignored Marta's ranting spells as she fought her way from the throngs of this melee.

Her silver figure in its skimpy chemise stood out like a candle against the gloom, and the cries behind her gained momentum. A man bearing a torch grabbed at her and the silver dagger slashed high and wide, followed by the gurgle of death. Aelvina snatched the torch from his hand and brandished it at her attackers as they closed in around her. One drew too close and his robe dissolved in a sheet of flame. The circle backed away and Aelvina edged closer to the wall, watching desperately for some exit in the dark expanse of stone.

The room erupted in a chaos of motion. Dark figures dashed up the stairway she had just descended; others continued to roll in their drug-crazed ecstasies, while flame licked from the robe she had set afire. But blood lust burned in the eyes of those around her, urged on by Marta's hysterical cries, and Aelvina knew she was trapped if she did not find some opening soon.

With another cry of rage, she swung around, waving her flaming sword and scattering those behind her. More flames leapt in the darkness and then the wall loomed behind her. With dagger in one hand and torch in the other, she edged along this mighty protection, keeping her wary attackers at bay.

The noise grew into a thunderous clamor of screams and roars as more sought to avoid the spreading fingers of flame or join the threatening band of bloodthirsty assailants. Someone broke into a keg of wine and another cry went up in a far part of the room. Another keg crashed to the floor as people fought to drink from the first. What had begun as an orgy of lust was rapidly dissipating into one of madness.

The heat of the torch burned at Aelvina's fingers and the stench of pungent smoke filled her eyes and nostrils until she could scarcely see the hooded figures surrounding her, hovering just outside the reach of torch and knife, obscured by the gloom and haze. The sheer crush of lunacy would destroy her if she did not find escape soon.

Marta's cries split the air in warning just as Aelvina's heels hit upon nothing in the wall behind her. A quick swirl and she was dashing down a dark corridor to freedom, praying it was to freedom that it led.

Thundering feet pounded the earthen floor behind her, and curses echoed against stone walls. It was no use; she could not outrun them all. Some madman rolled a keg of wine after her. She jumped aside just in time and it bounded against a wall before splitting open. The torch was guttering low, giving her away, and with a screech of triumph, Aelvina threw its remains at the cascading torrent of liquor. Screams of horror rocked the walls as the wine burst into flame, but still her pursuers kept at her heels. Denied a night of lust and urged on by Marta's inflammatory cries, the devil worshippers sought pleasure in the chase, leaping over licking flames and following the sound of Aelvina's running feet.

Her side hurt and breath came with difficulty as she tripped dangerously over the rough floor. The gap between her and the baying pack of hooded madmen began to close, and she was no closer to finding the door to freedom.

In an instant of horror, Aelvina realized the sound of running feet came from ahead as well as behind. She was trapped! God help her, but she would go down fighting

and take as many of these demons with her as she could!
Thunder rolled overhead as she collapsed with her back
against the wall and the knife in front of her. Enough
Viking lingered in her veins to know the best defensive
position. She would go for their testicles, rip them off and
put an end to their lewd occupations.

The ones behind her were closest. Like a pack of vora-
cious wolves they circled, growling threats and obscenities
while they judged their chances against a gleaming silver
blade. The Fairfax battle cry again rent the air as Aelvina
jabbed at the first darting figure and slashed at a second,
rewarded with cries of pain and the feel of ripping flesh.

An answering cry echoed from down the corridor, and
Aelvina's heart leapt with joy and excitement. Philippe!
None other could sing that cry as he! But another moment
would be too late. Although her attackers were unarmed,
they were many and stronger. One small blade was not
sufficient, and they took little heed of approaching footsteps.

Aelvina screamed as they advanced on her all at once.
Her dagger sank into a dark shoulder and was knocked
from her hands as meaty paws grabbed at her waist and
lifted her from the floor. Her unwieldy shoes had long
since been lost and her bare toes kicked ineffectively at
bulky robes.

Pandemonium broke loose in the black corridor as her
screams echoed through the darkness. Aelvina could hear
scuffling fights in the distance, but she concentrated on
her own predicament. She sank her teeth into a hand that
dared cover her mouth and yanked viciously at a hank of
hair as she squirmed and struggled to be free of her captors. Her knee shot up with remarkable accuracy, incapaci-
tating one assailant, but she was grabbed by another, passed

from hand to hand as each attempted to keep a hold on her biting, clawing, kicking struggles.

The clang of steel gave her renewed strength, but Aelvina knew it could not last. Flames leapt before her, and she wondered dizzily if they intended to roast her as she was carried closer to their heat. Cries of warning came from behind, but the hands holding her were strong and relentless, carrying her farther from the sounds of battle.

The battle surged all around and all over. Her unarmed attackers were suddenly surrounded by a small band of mailed knights, and numbers mattered little against cold steel. A tall, strong figure in gleaming steel and dusty forest-green surcoat emerged against the background of leaping flames, fighting his way through the black-robed throng. Aelvina cried out her joy, but it was a weak cry at best as Philippe's furious grasp caught her. She would gladly face his wrath over whatever fate these demented creatures had planned, and she collapsed, exhausted, against his chest.

The rest of their flight from the cellars became a blur. Philippe's curses and commands rang in her ears. She vaguely understood he was taking prisoners, but the smoky fumes were closing her lungs, and she slipped in and out of consciousness as Philippe ran with her down long, dark corridors.

A blast of fresh air revived Aelvina's senses, but the screams and curses cutting the night seemed an unreal nightmare to her whirling mind. Philippe's arms were her only reality and she clung to them with desperation as he carried her to the noisy confusion of the courtyard.

"Chauvin! Over here. Find a mantle; she's shivering," Philippe's voice called out above Aelvina's head.

She had not felt the cold while in his arms, but his words returned some awareness. The smoke-filled cellar room had been overheated and the stench still filled her nostrils, but outside she felt the frosty cold of late October. She shuddered, and hugged Philippe's neck closer.

"Little fool," he muttered hoarsely, but this time not in anger. Philippe took the proffered mantle from the stout gray-robed figure and snuggly wrapped Aelvina in it before gently disentangling himself from her grasp. "Chauvin, keep watch over her and bind her hand and foot if she should move from this spot. I must see to the others."

Once on the ground, Aelvina's docility disappeared, and she turned on Philippe with fear and anger. "You cannot go back in there. It is hell, and those that remain deserve their fate. Leave them be, Philippe."

Philippe and Chauvin exchanged looks over her head, and Aelvina felt the monk take her firmly by the hand, his grip stronger than she had imagined.

"Those who have sinned will be punished, but Philippe cannot let his wife perish without attempting to save her. You, of all people, should understand that," Chauvin stated purposefully.

Remembering where last she had seen that obscene creature, Aelvina shook her head frantically. "No! No, you do not understand! Chauvin, stop him!" she screamed as Philippe strode off in the direction of the smoke pouring from the cellars. "He will murder her if she is not already dead! Chauvin, please!"

Philippe halted to speak to one of his men and Aelvina turned her frantic gaze to Chauvin, pleading with him. Worried gray eyes also watched that proud figure, but then turned sadly back to Aelvina.

"Then pray she is already dead, my child, for there is no stopping him. His honor rests upon it."

Tears welled up in her eyes as Philippe advanced, his long stride carrying him quickly down the pathway to hell.

Chauvin was right. The only time Philippe had acted less than honorably had resulted in a disaster for all. She could not stop him now, as she could not change his mind earlier. He must do what he felt right, just as she.

A small cry escaped Aelvina as she turned away and her gaze fell on another sight. Atop the donjon's battlements a flame appeared, a moving flame trailing a dark shadow. She screamed louder, catching Philippe's attention before he could reenter the inferno of the cellars. Pointing, she gestured to the figure on the battlements. Chauvin's hand clasped more firmly around her.

Long, trailing black hair identified the shadow. Somewhere, the Lady Ravenna had donned one of the hooded robes, but its folds lay open and the hood unworn, exposing the whiteness of her skin to the cold night air as she strode majestically to the edge of the high lookout tower. Obscene curses wailed from her lips, carried away by the wind, as she looked down upon the invading army in her courtyard below.

The madness of her words and looks was not the cause of Aelvina's scream or Philippe's halting step. The trailing flame of the Lady Ravenna's long robes held all eyes to that high tower. The wind whipping about her feet sent the flames leaping higher, but the mad figure raving on the battlements took no notice of the elements.

Philippe dashed to the hidden donjon door and stairway, but this time Chauvin's warning halted him.

"Get back, Philippe! There is no time! The wall is crumbling!"

Only the monk's authority could halt that mad dash, coupled with Aelvina's scream. Philippe glanced upward, then ran to rejoin them as Aelvina's horrified gaze fixed on another point beyond the crumbling wall.

Philippe grabbed her by the waist and swept her swiftly

from the range of danger, frantically ordering his men and the prisoners to follow him to safety. They obeyed, but none unfastened their gazes from the horrifying spectacle above.

As the flames rose higher in the robes of the wildly gesticulating creature on the crumbling wall, another shadow flitted from the hatchway and dashed to the rescue. Philippe pulled Aelvina tightly against him, protecting her from the sight of those two struggling figures atop the ancient tower, now cracking beneath the stress of heat and cold. Aelvina buried her face in his tunic, not against the sight, but for comfort against the inevitable. Strong arms held her, helpless to do anything else in this instance.

Marta's bent, stout figure was easily recognizable as she grabbed her lady's robe in a futile attempt to remove the flaming cloth. A large crack opened on the face of the wall beneath their feet, but neither of them seemed to notice.

When Philippe's grip involuntarily tightened, Aelvina glanced up in time to watch the final deadly dance. The robe ripped apart, wrapping Marta in its fatal flames and sending the screaming Lady Ravenna tumbling backward over the crumbling parapet. A sheet of flame illuminated the bent figure on the roof for one brief instant, and then with a roar and thunder and an explosion of dust, the tower followed its mistress to the ground.

The yard filled with the smoke and dust of collapsing stone, but another thunderclap above warned of the nearness of the gathering storm. Within minutes, the frozen onlookers were drenched in an unnatural torrential downpour.

In years to come, many would speak of that mighty storm with awe; about the rains that poured from the heavens and froze upon the objects below. Witchcraft and deviltry met their just ends that night, and many were the new believers that made their way to mass the next day and many holy days thereafter.

Yet, in the storm's first drenching downpour, the practical prevailed. With gentleness, Philippe pulled the mantle's hood over Aelvina's fair hair. "Take her to the chapel with the others," he ordered quietly to his monkish companion. There was no need to state his intentions this time. The woman who bore his name was buried somewhere beneath that rubble, and duty demanded that the body be given this last respect.

This time, Aelvina went quietly. The night's horrors had left her shaken and bewildered and the chapel seemed the only sane place to be.

Chapter Twenty-five

The chapel had been neglected for many long years, but in the weak candlelight recent repairs were noticeable. The straw and animal dung that littered the floor had been swept clean. Aelvina remembered it only as a decaying building and gave Chauvin a startled glance as they entered this now pristine structure, but the self-satisfied gleam in the monk's eyes could have been for another reason. He nodded toward the nave, directing her attention there.

"Thyllda!" Aelvina breathed with relief, her eyes lighting with gratitude as she saw the sleeping infant in the old woman's arms. She clung to Chauvin's arm as he helped her to the far end of the chapel. All her strength was gone, and she wished only to lie down and stare at the innocent sleeping face of her son.

A large form stepped from the shadows to greet them. "What is happening? We heard the noise, but I dared not let the women out of my sight. Where is Sir Philippe?"

Gundulf advanced, eyeing Aelvina's drooping figure with concern but not daring to offer his aid without some sign from Chauvin.

"The donjon has collapsed, taking the Lady Ravenna with it. I fear my services are needed outside. The Lady Aelvina has been through a grievous experience and would benefit from a pallet, if there is one to be found."

Gundulf unceremoniously scooped Aelvina into his large arms. "I have already prepared one for the others. There is room. There is no danger?"

"None, my friend, only much work. Still, I think it best to keep the ladies here."

Aelvina felt the exchange of glances over her head, but she was too weary to worry over their meaning. She allowed herself to be carried to a fresh-smelling pallet of sweet grasses and curled up within its warmth, not wishing to think of anything but this comfort and the friends around her.

Alice appeared with warm wine and cheese. Aelvina sipped the wine, gave her friend a tired smile, and listened to Thyllda's scolding with half an ear. Her son was in her arms again. Philippe was alive and well. The night's horrors were beyond thinking. She curled up on the pallet and slept.

She woke once to the sound of Philippe's voice and stirred, looking for him, wanting to touch his face again, to be reassured by emerald eyes, but he went away. Disappointed, she slipped into the comfort of sleep once more.

Her son's stirrings disturbed her next, and when she opened her eyes, it was to the gray mist of dawn. The night weighed heavily upon her mind, but her thoughts flew first to the infant stirring in her womb, and her hand flew to cover her belly, making certain all was well. She smiled at the light kicks greeting her and reached out to capture her hungry son and hug him good morning. He chirruped with delight and banished all horror to the netherworld.

She rose to find Thyllda and Alice cooking over a fire in the chapel aisle. It seemed a curious place to prepare a meal, but she had no desire to return to Dunstan keep. This was pleasant, and she settled into this small circle of friends with a feeling of homecoming. The Lady Aelvina was more accustomed to campfires than keeps, she thought wryly to herself.

After Charles was fed and she wandered to the chapel door, the fleeting moment of well-being fled. A strange knight greeted her at the door and insisted on accompanying her as she stepped out into the courtyard.

Aelvina looked up at him with ill-concealed amazement. "Am I to have a guard when I bathe, also? Is there some danger of which I should be aware?"

The knight remained unperturbed. "His majesty's orders, my lady. You are to be safely escorted back to White Hall as soon as possible. We have been ordered not to let you out of our sight."

The lump returned to Aelvina's throat, and she gazed up with dismay at the gray clouds overhead. Somehow, she had managed to forget all else with the sound of Philippe's voice last night. He had returned for her, and she thought all had changed. But it was not so. That was why he had not joined her last night. Dark clouds hid the sun, and the icy grass beneath her feet crackled with cold. She turned to reenter the chapel. Chauvin arrived and took her aside, questioning her health before getting to his real purpose.

"I am well. How does Philippe fare?" Aelvina asked, but no emotion tinged her tone.

"He has been up all night seeing the rubble cleared and the prisoners taken to the monastery. He has not rested in days but will not stop."

Aelvina nodded. "He is angry and needs work to vent it. He will stop in time. I wish I could send my condolences for the death of his wife, but I cannot. Her soul is in hell where it belongs. Is that a sin I should confess among my others?"

"That is one of the reasons I wished to consult with you, my child—one among many. Are you strong enough to tell me what happened last night? There has been a heinous crime committed against the church, and you are our only witness. Your testimony is needed if we are to judge those of the sinners apprehended last night."

Aelvina sank to a low stool and closed her eyes, wanting to blot out all memory of last night. "The evil was in Lady Ravenna and Marta and they are dead. The others are corrupt, decadent, but victims of evil as much as I. Must I?"

"You must leave it to the church to pass judgment, Lady Aelvina. There have been rumors of debauchery in these parts for years: young girls disappearing and never heard from again, infants slain and mutilated, crimes I would shudder to admit. A darkness has lain upon this land too long; your word could put an end to it."

Aelvina hugged her arms beneath her breasts and tried to speak as objectively as possible, to fight off the images his words evoked, to pretend what had happened to her was no more than rumor. She had escaped those evil ceremonies relatively unscathed if Chauvin spoke the truth. She must prevent their repetition. In a low monotone, she tried to tell all she had witnessed, but much the monk would have to understand for himself. When she finished, she looked up to sympathetic gray eyes and anxiously inquired, "Will Philippe have to be told? About Lady Ravenna?"

Chauvin took her hand. "He knows; he could not help

but know. She was his wife in name only and that, wrongfully. What she did to herself cannot affect him except as it would affect his name. Do not concern yourself on that matter."

"The evil," Aelvina stated hesitantly, "the evil that lives in this place, can it ever be expelled? They say this is my father's home, but I fear to enter it. In time, will it ever be safe? I would not have my son inherit evil."

The monk nodded compassionately. "Philippe has already thought of that. He is making Dunstan ready for you, ridding it of all unhappy memories. If his wife's soul abides there still, it will be exorcised this day. No evil will linger once it has been cleansed by the Lord."

Chauvin spoke quietly and earnestly. "My lady, will you answer some questions of a more private nature? I would not ask them but that they are of immense importance to you and to others."

What could there be that all did not know? Aelvina nodded for him to proceed and stared at the floor.

"I have been told that Philippe once swore an oath to you, on that day you first met. Can you tell me if that oath was said in the name of God?"

A faint smile crossed Aelvina's lips at the monk's earnestness. That day was so long ago, and so seemingly innocent in light of what had passed since. Yet she remembered well her nervousness at committing what had seemed so terrible a sin. She nodded again and turned a small smile to the monk's worried face. The question did not seem strange, for the memory warmed her heart.

"Philippe knew my nervousness. He swore on the handle of my father's dagger and in the name of the Lord that he would protect me, and in return, I pledged him my faithfulness. To me, it was as close to a wedding ceremony as I would ever know, and I have kept my vows as well as any wife. Yet I am accused of adultery. It is strange how life works, is it not?"

The monk relaxed and returned her smile with an astonishingly beatific gaze. "The Lord moves in mysterious ways, they say. Do not ever despair of His judgment. A time will come for all." He rose and, taking both her hands in his, asked gently, "You love him very much, do you not?"

There was no question of whom he spoke, and Aelvina replied easily, "Aye, Father, more than life itself, I fear. Another sin, I suppose."

"No, not so long as you use the sense you have shown in the past. Rest, now, and make yourself strong."

He departed, and Aelvina watched him go with a mild bewilderment. He had said much and so little, and she sighed, turning away. The stout monk's smooth visage, innocent of lines of age or worry, disguised a keen insight and infinite patience; but neither would be of help to her now. Church and king were in agreement in her case: Philippe would never be hers. She must begin preparing herself for a life without him and be content that he lived.

Stripped of his heavy mail, Philippe sank down upon the bed he had made his own in his infrequent visits to his wife's home. He had left no part of himself in this cold cell and no memories clung to its bare walls. It was a bed in a dry shelter out of the driving rain. His eyes closed, but he did not sleep.

Memories of Aelvina's terrified face haunted him. Obstinate fiend that she was, she still needed him, just as he needed her—a piercing need that gnawed inside of him and spread deadly thorns that could not be plucked out. He groaned with the anguish of knowing she was just beyond that wall and he could not go to her; not now, not ever. The ache spread deeper and wider.

A knock on the door jarred cruelly against his shattered thoughts and Philippe swore, hoping whoever it was would have sense enough to depart. Sociability had never been one of his strong points and he wished to lick his wounds in private. The knock rapped again, louder and more insistent.

"Go to hell!" he roared in irritation, not stirring from his bed.

"Not unless you lead me," the voice behind the door replied with equanimity.

Philippe grimaced. Only Chauvin had the temerity to speak to him in such a manner, and the tenaciousness not to be denied. Still, he tried. "You ordered me to rest—let me rest!"

"I have messages here from both the king and the archbishop and they cannot be answered without your aid. Your rest will have to wait."

Philippe closed his eyes and prayed for patience. Never would he set foot inside a court again for so long as he should live, if he could but disentangle himself this time. Had the archbishop agreed to an annulment no longer necessary? Maybe the king had ordered his arrest for the kidnapping of Lady Aelvina or the murder of Lady Ravenna. Henry had been suspicious enough to do both. Cursing, Philippe stood and adjusted his tunic before unbolting the door.

"Well, what is it you cannot answer without me?" Wearily, Philippe sat down upon the bed and ran his hand through already disheveled hair as he waited for the monk to speak.

"The king's message relies on your response to the archbishop's. Evidently, Henry has conferred with him on your behalf. Do not answer them lightly, for they hold your fate and many other's."

Philippe frowned. "I am in no mood for riddles. What do they wish to know?"

Chauvin sighed. In this mood, Philippe was capable of anything, and obtaining the answer he sought would not be easy. If they could only be satisfied with Aelvina's words, all would be well; but with no witness, that was impossible. He must have the acknowledgment of both participants. Frowning fiercely, he strove to impress the importance of this matter upon his recalcitrant friend.

"You told Henry that you and the girl exchanged vows that day you met. That seems a strange thing for a king's knight to do with a wench he had just met."

Philippe stared at the monk as if he had taken leave of his senses, then shrugged laconically. "You saw her that day. She was all silver and gold and young and terrified. She totally bewitched me. I wanted to ravish her and protect her at the same time. What does this have to do with the archbishop's message?"

Chauvin smiled grimly. "You will know soon enough. What oath did you swear to her?"

Growing impatient with this nonsensical interrogation, Philippe rose to stride restlessly about the Spartan cell. "How can I remember such things? If you wish it word for word, I cannot give it to you. I know I swore her protection in return for her affections and loyalty. It seemed little enough at the time and I meant to see she had more." His voice broke in anguish over the memory. "She came to me as a virgin bride to her husband's bed and has been as faithful as any wife, yet I have brought her nothing but shame. What matters it that I have wanted no other woman but her since that day? She is my true wife, but another has stolen my name."

The monk watched Philippe's furious pacing with growing sympathy and rising excitement. "The oath you swore before taking her to your bed, was it in God's name?"

Philippe swung around and gazed at him in incredulity. He respected Chauvin's intelligence, but this questioning seemed pointless—or was it? A small light gleamed in his eyes as Philippe contemplated the question and watched the monk's face.

"I meant to keep my pledge and wished the girl to know it. Yes, I swore it in God's name."

Chauvin gave a deep breath of relief and smiled beatifically. "Congratulations, my lord. For the price of a toss in bed you have committed yourself for life."

Philippe stared unblinkingly, all comprehension beyond the reach of immediate probability. "What are you saying?" he asked, enunciating each word as if his life depended on it, as indeed it might.

"I am saying an oath of protection and faithfulness, made in the sight of God between two consenting people who are of age and with no consanguineous relationship, though made with no witnesses, is acceptable to the church as an exchange of marriage vows. Such sloppy ceremony creates no end of havoc—other cases have not been so simple as this—but so long as you both agree you are bound, and I can testify to that fact, the archbishop is willing to declare you married in the eyes of the church. And the king is willing to recognize the church's decision in this matter, though he wishes the ceremony repeated for the sake of your heirs. He commands your return to London as soon as possible so he might be a witness this time."

As these words were spoken, Philippe sank to the bed, not certain he was hearing properly. When Chauvin stopped and waited for his reaction, Philippe sat dazed for a half minute before replying. "You are saying Aelvina is my wife, has been my wife, and that the Lady Ravenna was never mine? Charles is not a bastard?"

"Precisely, my lord."

Chauvin grinned as Philippe flew from the bed's edge, grabbing a mantle to throw over his disheveled tunic as he raced for the door. As he flung open the door, he turned and called over his shoulder, "Does Aelvina know?"

"Not yet." And Chauvin laughed out loud as the towering dark knight disappeared down the hall at the mad pace of an excited schoolboy.

The occupants of the chapel were playing a nonsensical sing-song game with the laughing infant when Philippe's voice thundered in the courtyard outside. Everyone stopped and glanced up with surprise. The king's guard was obviously objecting to this unexpected visit, but a clash of steel warned Philippe's impatience would brook no interference. Aelvina handed the gurgling infant to Alice, rose quickly, and hurried to the chapel entrance.

Both men had drawn swords, but the guard looked nervous and uncertain about attacking a baron on his own land. Aelvina's arrival eased his predicament to some extent, but Philippe's menacing stance remained unchanged.

"I wish to see my wife and I wish to see her alone. If you have any questions, find that damned monk and the king's messenger, but remove thyself from my path before you find yourself skewered to the door."

Her gaze flew to Philippe's dark face with a startled look, but Aelvina kept her tone calm and placating as she spoke to the bewildered guard. "You have my word, sir knight, that I will return with you to London upon the king's command. My son is in this chapel and I go nowhere without him. Guard him well and I am at your command."

Faced with Philippe's flashing emerald gaze and raised sword, the young knight fell before her offer. He stepped out of the way, allowing Philippe to pass.

But a quiet chat in a private place was not on Philippe's mind. As the last remaining barrier between them fell, a jubilant grin cracked his hawklike face from ear to ear, and in a few short strides he had Aelvina in his arms and was carrying her across the courtyard.

Aelvina's protests went unheeded as strong arms closed determinedly about her, and after a while she no longer protested. She was where she wanted to be, whatever the cause, and contentedly she threw her arms around Philippe's neck and relaxed against his chest. Emerald eyes flashed mockingly as he gazed down upon her, and with loving care, Philippe carried her over the portals of Dunstan keep and up the broad stairs.

Aelvina looked around her with dismay and then increasing interest. A bevy of servants applied themselves to cleaning and sweeping and scrubbing, and monkly figures could be seen flitting from place to place, lighting candles against the darkness, relieving the gloom and mustiness. The room Philippe brought her to was small but clean, and a roaring fire danced in the tiny fireplace. A bed and a chest were the only furniture, but all that was necessary for Philippe's purpose. He lay her against the furred cover of the pallet and stood back, staring down at her with exuberant triumph.

"Philippe, have you had too much to drink?" Aelvina asked tentatively. She had smelled no liquor on him and had never seen him drink to excess, but she could find no other explanation for his strange behavior. It had been so long since she had seen him smile like this. The hard lines around his mouth practically disappeared and the little crinkles around his eyes returned as he watched her with an almost wild joy. He seemed ready to burst with some great emotion, and Aelvina could find no source for such manic idiocy.

"I am drunk with joy, my love, my wife. You had best prepare yourself for a lifetime of ravishment, beginning with these next few moments." Philippe flung aside his sword and sat down on the chest to remove his muddy footgear.

Aelvina sat up hastily, her hand going to the front of her tunic as if to protect it from assault. "That is the second time you have called me that. I think you have gone quite mad. Why do you not rest while I fix you something soothing to drink?" Anxiously, she studied Philippe's effortless undressing.

"Totally, utterly mad, I agree." With a grin, he caught his hand in the old tunic Thyllda had found for her. With a flick of his wrist, he tore it from top to bottom and repeated the maneuver with the chemise beneath. "My wife need not wear rags. Wearing nothing will be fine for now, but gowns of the finest cloth will fill your wardrobe soon. I have not had time enough to enjoy you in your finery."

Aelvina clutched the torn fragments of material around her, staring at Philippe uncertainly, but he seemed quite sane in his determination. The last of his clothing fell to the floor and he rose before her, hands on hips as he gazed down at her, a bronzed god in all his masculine virility. Quietly, Aelvina cast aside the rags and tugged the ribbons from her plaits, allowing a thick cascade of waving silver-gold to fall forward across her breasts.

Philippe's gaze raked warmly over her bare curves. They were all his, to have and to hold, till death do they part. He smiled and held out his hand.

"You are perfect, for all your sorcery. The elves still look out for their own, it seems." At Aelvina's questioning gaze, he relented. "We are man and wife, my love, since that day you enchanted me in the stables and twisted that pledge of protection from me while plighting your troth. Chauvin says it is the will of God that married us that day, but he will never convince me that there was not some wicked elf hidden among the straw, tempting me with your loveliness. By church law, I took you as my wife, and with my lord's approval, I am your husband. Did you know, then, that I would never tire of you?"

Aelvina could scarcely breathe as Philippe's hands traced her silhouette, and his words held her spellbound. This could not be happening. She would wake and find she was dreaming. Mayhap she was in heaven and did not know it. But she did not think angels did what Philippe was doing now, and a fierce joy flamed through her as Philippe gathered her up in his arms.

"It is madness, Philippe, but let me die mad." She turned her lips to his kiss and the flames leapt to ecstatic heights as Philippe's mouth once more crushed against hers.

As man and wife, they fell between the covers of the bed, and with reverence Philippe reclaimed his possession, not leaving any point uncovered as his kisses burned their brand into her skin. Enraptured by the loving gentleness he displayed, Aelvina responded with all the love and passion and desire she possessed.

The past disappeared beneath Philippe's pressure. All sensation centered in the joining of their bodies, and Aelvina welcomed his fullness with a cry of ecstasy. To have him within her again was all the world she needed, a healing potion better than any she had discovered, a completeness that made whole all the shattered torments of the past. Their explosive release blended them together again as one.

Not wishing to release her yet, Philippe propped himself on his arms to ease his weight from her. Aelvina smiled back at him, and he kissed her lightly, savoring the knowledge that he was free to do so at any time.

"Have you decided you might keep me a while longer, my lord?" Aelvina murmured wickedly, tracing the hard angles of his jaw with love.

"Until the end of time, sorceress. It seems fitting punishment for your wicked ways." Philippe grinned. "You will have to content yourself with the dull, uncourtly life of a lowly baron from now on, and endure the laborious duties of sharing my bed and growing big with my sons whenever it pleases me. Are you not sorry you made me swear such a nonsensical oath that day?"

"You only swore to protect me. You said naught of love. How does that make us married?" Aelvina moved her hips closer to his, not really caring what laws men made for themselves so long as they did not interfere with her.

"I vowed to protect you until you no longer have need of me, or I of you, which will be never, and you swore faithfulness until that time. It is a better vow than many, my love, but we shall say it properly next time. I will not have the church changing its mind later." Philippe cupped her breast with his big hand and grinned. "Will you marry me?"

"If that is what it takes to keep you, I suppose I must, my lord. 'Tis a tedious thing you ask of me, but better the evil one knows . . ." She shrugged lightly, azure eyes dancing.

"Wench," Philippe growled, but the rest of his words were lost in the giggling as they rolled upon the bed.

* * *

The official ceremony was held in a small chapel in London with only friends and close acquaintances in attendance, including the king and queen. The young bride was radiant in her kirtle of fur-trimmed ivory silk, fastened by the gold filigree girdle, her silver-gold hair nearly hidden by the extravagant lace that was a gift from the queen. The large, dark man at her side stood resplendent in tawny gold surcoat and forest green tunic, emerald eyes gleaming as they gazed down upon the moonstruck figure at his side. Only after the vows were said and the couple turned to walk back down the aisle did the soft swelling beneath the bride's ivory silk become noticeable, but the groom's pride and joy as he accepted congratulations from all made it apparent this was no accidental match.

The queen beamed benevolently at Aelvina's effusive gratitude for her part in seeing this love match made, but it was Henry who held the reins. He took them in hand now, grasping Aelvina's fingers and confronting Philippe.

"I have given her to you for a purpose, St. Aubyn," Henry scowled solemnly.

Philippe raised a half-mocking eyebrow, well aware the king would never have known of Aelvina's existence without his efforts. Henry's laughing eyes told him to keep his silence and not disturb the solemnity of the occasion, and Philippe bowed his head in recognition.

"The lands of Dunstan and St. Aubyn border each other, forming a larger fief than most. It will take a strong hand to guide those lands under the laws I wish upheld. Since the Earl of Dunstan left no male heir to his title, it is my duty to bestow it where I will, and I can find no better place than on the man who holds title to those lands and to the earl's daughter. The Lady Aelvina deserves the title of countess.''

Aelvina made a low curtsy in acknowledgment of this honor, but the tilt of silver-blue eyes as they glanced back up to her husband warned Philippe to speak before she. Irreverent brat that she was, the title meant as little to her as the official wedding ceremony. With time, she might come to respect the legalities, but for the moment, he would need keep close watch on her exuberant nature . . . and keep her far from court.

''I am honored by your trust, sire,'' Philippe intoned with all seriousness. His gaze roamed over the small audience to this scene: Sir Alec; John, the squire; Sir Geoffrey, whose laughing eyes did not dance quite so merrily as they rested on the bride for a moment; Thyllda, carrying their son; Gundulf; and Alice, carrying the new, glowing weight of a babe in the making. They were all free, independent people, bound to him by their love of the land they held, dependent on him for their protection. It was an awesome responsibility, and it was time he accepted it.

Taking Aelvina gently by the waist, Philippe added, ''Thank you, my lord,'' but his gaze left Henry to rest proudly on the slender figure at his side.

Azure eyes swept upward, instantly assessing his thoughts, and without further consideration of surroundings or royal presences, Aelvina lifted her arms about his neck and pulled her husband's head down so that their lips could bind the promise of their eyes.

Queen Eleanor gave her kingly husband a laughing look of triumph and they departed quietly, without further ceremony. Nature would have its way.